An Tir Gallósek: The Mighty Land
Book One

Pippa Agrippa in Britannia Prima

by Maria Kay Anthony

I0619473

An Tir Gallósek: The Mighty Land
Book One

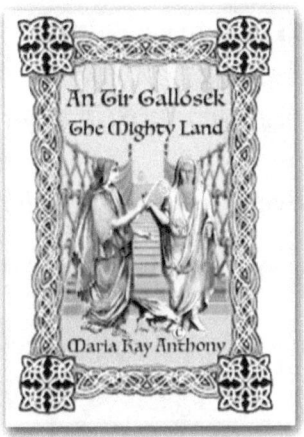

Pippa Agrippa in Britannia Prima

For More Information and a Gallery of Illustrations

Go Borlowan Books at Facebook.com

**An Tir Gallósek
The Three Volumes:**

Pippa Agrippa in Britannia Prima

Marcus Constantinides in Albion Sub Terra

Treya Meynack in the   *Western Air*

ISBN: 979-8-9920376-0-9
borlowanbooks@gmail.com
Borlowan Books/POB 1554/Lawrence/Ks/66044/USA

INTRODUCTION

These stories arose from some questions that I had been considering:

How can we tell whether something is done by magic, or by some complex science that we don't understand?
What is the difference between a god and a person with highly advanced technical powers and tremendous longevity?
What is needed for hope to conquer despair?
And, what might have happened when the Romans left Britannia?

Now and then, new scientific evidence shows up that changes the human story. It seems that technically advanced cultures have been on earth much longer than previously supposed. For people who are threatened by shifting paradigms, it's a problem. For many of us, though, it's a relief to be reminded that we don't know the whole story, we never did, and chances are we never will. Fire, water, earth and air have seen to that by repeatedly rearranging our world.

Much of the history of the known ancient world is well documented, and we have an idea of what was happening, and when. Then there are places and times where we just have to speculate. One of those is Britannia in the late 300s and early 400s. Many details have been discovered, but the overall picture is still dark.

It was a time when the Romans had finally retreated from the wild western isles that were never really theirs. They left behind a scattered population that included Brythonic, Celtic, Roman, Greek, Iberian, Frisian, and Germanic people. After Rome departed, the land and its inhabitants were vulnerable, and invasions and wars were inevitable. But for a brief time in history, the period in which these adventures occur, the British Isles were still fairly peaceful and prosperous. New trade routes were established to fill the void left by the Empire, soldiers took civilian jobs, and life went on.

The early 'dark ages' weren't really as dark as people used to imagine. It was a time of refined cultures, with stories of great heroes and epic adventures. The myths and legends were passed down in the oral tradition. By the time that the stories were written in English, centuries later, they had been fractured and redacted by the culture-blind single-mindedness of institutional religion. But they are still there, manifested in the land and in the people, resonating throughout the mysterious western islands of Great Britain and Ireland.

These books are inspired by the old tales. They are really one story, told across the three volumes, each with a different person's point of view. The stories present the archetypal hero's quest, which involves overcoming obstacles, finding one's place in the world, and connecting with others. These tales are about duty, tolerance, inclusion, kindness, redemption, restoration, accountability, bravery, and self-awareness.

We begin on the ground in book one. In book two we go deep down to get to the bottom of things. We transcend in book three, up into the atmosphere.

The Mighty Land features weaponry, clothing, footwear, jewelry, gemstones, ships, boats, rafts, maps, rivers, seas, hot tubs, cold pools, gardens, orchards, forests, fortresses, farms, castles, libraries, ice caves, crystal caverns, glowing rocks, an impossibly high tower, and a great deal of food. Also, there are festivals, betrothals, weddings, babies, fashion shows, good songs, bad jokes, spectral resonance, music, augery, and geomancy. There are animals too: cats, dogs, sheep, goats, mules, oxen, bears, dolphins, porpoises, and many birds. Also some creatures not encountered before; some are friendly, others are threatening.

These stories include some non-English words and phrases. Latin, of course, was the language of the soldiers of Rome. Spread over the vast empire, the usages varied, and there were regional dialects.

Brythonic was the common tongue. It includes Cymraeg, Welsh, which once was used throughout what is now England as well as Wales.

Kernowek is also Brythonic. It is the venerable language of the Cornish peninsula. It's related to Welsh, and to Breton, spoken in present day Brittany.

Gaelic and other Celtic languages were spoken in Eire and Scotia, and by many of the tribes throughout Britain.

These languages influenced one another, and became part of common speech, along with words and terms from all the other peoples who had moved to Britain. I have tried to represent this complex and shifting situation by introducing these words in context.

I hope that the reader will find it as rewarding as I did to realize the inherent connections in the various languages.

Hail and fare well,
Maria Anthony 2024

Here are my answers to the questions:
We can't.
Nothing obvious.
Love.
Read on...

ACKNOWLEDGEMENTS

These stories came from me. Not artificial intelligence.

When I have used quotes and verses by other authors, I have credited them in the text or annotations, except for 'Conditions for Feasting', and 'In Complaint of Women', which are by King Cormac of Ireland. I also used part of Fionn Mac Cumhail's poem 'A Joyous Peace is Summer' as the refrain for a new song, and I've included an old nursery rhyme about a mill. Otherwise, the textual content is original to me, including the songs.

I relied upon Google translate throughout this project. For the Kernowek language, I used OnlineCornishDictionary.org. They both have audio options to demonstrate pronunciations.

I create my own images using Adobe Photoshop, and its many layers of possibilities. When I've used historical images, such as the Roman paintings and mosaics, they are in the public domain. So are some of the background details. I repurpose bits and pieces, and I draw, paint, and photograph images that I then process digitally.

I use, appreciate, and support Wikipedia and Wikipedia Commons.

My thanks to the ARX Mercatura workshop and online store, for allowing me to use a photo of their beautifully carved lituus in my publishing logo.

I have been influenced by the things I've seen and heard in my lifetime. Stories, songs, books, films, and scenes of far-away places. And apparently, the fashion competition show 'Project Runway' left a lasting impression on me.

I am eternally grateful to my husband Monty Schneck for his continued love, support, and enlightened conversation. Special thanks to Megan Hurt for the encouragement and literary feedback. I also appreciate everyone who wrote the books and created the images that have provided me with information and inspiration for all these years.

Maria Anthony, November, 2024

Contents

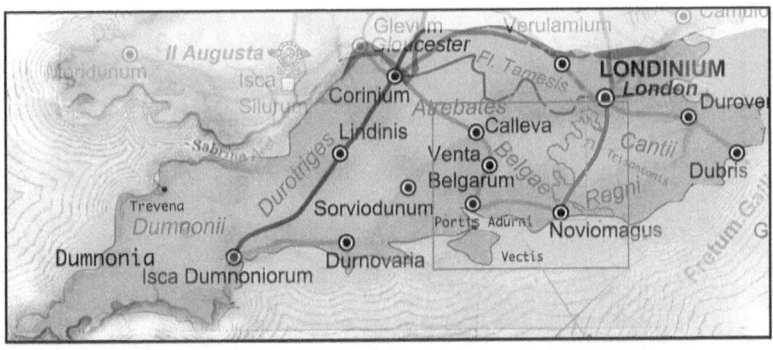

Chapter One - Apple Cake

Philippa Agrippa was walking. Technically, she was marching; commanding the march in fact, although after nine days of cold rain, her pace had devolved into a numbing trudge, with no attempt to impose a cadence on the men. The weather had finally begun to improve today, but she was still cold and dispirited. The year she had spent in training had not prepared her for the lack of supplies and equipment, or for being so overwhelmed by the elements.

At the Ares Mons training camp, food and shelter had never been an issue; there was a reliable and well-established supply chain. However, the food was often disagreeable, much of the equipment had seen better days, and some everyday items were getting hard to come by. It had been an effort to find enough gear and supplies to outfit the new recruits.

When the word came for her group of twenty to finally be assigned, things had happened quickly. Three short days after receiving marching orders, they were trundled onto the road, pointed towards the Vindavia Nova camp, a journey of ten to fifteen days, and they were on their way before they knew it. All of their trunks and tents, and all of the armor, spears and shields except for those of the front and rear guard were on the supply wagon. It was drawn by two stoic oxen, Dar and Murti. The provision wagon, loaded high, was drawn by an even more stoic donkey called Malus. The troops seemed to have been well-provided for. Making camp that first night the truth sunk in. The tent canvases they'd been issued were moldy and torn, the frame wood was old and splintery, and the fabric was threadbare.

Of course, Philippa thought, *the other four Decani and their men had taken the best of the equipment, and this is what was left.* Worst of all, there was only enough food for a few days. The main bulk of the provision wagon consisted of hay for the beasts. The funds had never arrived for travel money. Or for anything, in fact. They were supposed to get their salary every four months. None of them had ever been paid since the first coin of their recruitment; they were promised repeatedly that they would be paid in full at their new posting. She really hoped that would be true. Whenever there was a chance to buy food on the journey, she had spent her own money. The lads might have starved, or turned to theft, except for that old box of coins.

"Decanus Agrippa."
She was startled out of her reverie as the two scouts quietly fell into step beside her. Bruno and Brutus Marianis were identical twins, with chiseled features

and shaggy brown hair. They were easy to tell apart, since Bruno had a long scar from his right eye to his jaw. The brothers were excellent scouts, long legged and silent; they were also tireless and uncomplaining, unlike many of the other lads.

"Report," she said.
"In three miles the road curves to run parallel with the river. There's a sandy shoal that would make a decent camp," said Brutus. Whenever possible, they made camp beside a body of water, so as to minimize the need for guards at the perimeter. Philippa squinted at the westering sun, which had shone today for the first time in well over a week.
"Good, thank you."
The twins exchanged a glance.
"Is there anything else?" she inquired.
"Apples!" they replied in unison. Smiling, they each produced an apple to show her. The fruit was dried and shriveled; this being early spring, they were last year's apples, but they would be a delight to the hungry soldiers.

Many of her men still seemed like boys, despite the fact that she was younger than some of them were. (She was actually sixteen, but having lied when she joined, her current 'army age' was eighteen.) For the past six months, she had led the young men through some fairly rigorous training. Now they were miletes; the new soldiers of Rome. But it was the year 392, and it was getting pretty hard to ignore the fact that the great Roman Empire was slowly grinding to a halt. The British provinces, at the very edge of it all, were among the first to get overlooked.

"The Emperors have forgotten us," she had complained recently to her mentor, Centurion Aries Erasmus, when it became clear that no payroll was forthcoming.

"No, no, the Emperors love us!" he had said. "It breaks their hearts that they can not always support us. But how fortunate we are to still be able to serve with honor at this time. We are part of a noble history, part of the greatest civilization the world has ever known, greater at its decline than others in their glory days; what matter is money?" Erasmus was a grizzled old soldier, but he was blessed by Mercury with the skills of a persuasive orator.
"And you!" he had continued. "How fortunate we are to have a genuine Virgin Warrior to lead the men, as in ancient times. Think how proud your mother would be, and her Romano-Etruscan forebears. You are a part of a long and auspicious legacy; why do you think I chose you?"
"Because you're desperate," she replied flatly.

Erasmus laughed, but didn't contradict her. The enlisted ranks had shrunk in numbers the past few years, and the tight standards for new recruits had been loosened considerably. There had been no other candidates for group leader, so Philippa had been given twice the men that a Decanus should have. And ordinarily, they would have gotten two servants for every eight soldiers, but there was no coin for that either.

"Even so, Agrippa," he had told her, "you are destined to do great deeds. To walk with giants. Ask the augur if you don't believe me. The birds don't lie." He winked knowingly. She was surprised. She had been here for a year. She didn't know the camp had an augur: one who makes predictions and interpretations based on the behavior of birds.

That conversation with Aries Erasmus had happened just a fortnight ago, but it seemed like much longer. As they traveled the last few miles to the river, the sun came out, and the air grew so sweet and warm, it made the events of the past week seem unreal. Philippa recalled the journey. The first few days of travel had been mostly uneventful. On the third day, just as their food supplies ran out, they came to a large farm. She purchased a big sack of ground barley, a basket of eggs, a jar of oil, and a bag of last years apples, like the ones found today.

But the following night the rains came, and soaked everyone and everything. The tents leaked, and eventually collapsed into the mud. Then the temperature dropped, and it kept on raining. They had to go on; there was no other option. They were well past any settlements or shelters. When it wasn't raining, there was a fog thick enough to seize the lungs.
On the sixth day, Erastus Minor, a dour lad with pale hair and freckles, suddenly collapsed. Fortunately, the scouts located a small cave, and they all crammed into it, even the beasts. Everyone was miserable and exhausted, and Philippa was worried about Erastus, who was shivering uncontrollably and hot with fever.

The boys got a fire going, while Philippa and Terranes Julius, her aide, searched the meadow for the little yellow flowers which, when brewed, can help cure ailments. They'd found an abundance of them, still clinging to the plants from last summer. The tiny flowers had dried, but now they were squishy with the rain. She and the men all shared the helmet-pot full of tea with honey. The soothing steam of chamomile filled the cave. Huddling together for warmth, they slept for a long time. When Erastus awoke the next day he appeared to be better. The rain let up, and the air became a bit warmer, although the sky was still grey and thick with clouds as they got back on the road.

The next week had passed by in a fog, literally and figuratively. One day was like the next. Conversation ceased, except for the occasional curse aimed at the Britannic weather. Sights and sounds were swallowed by the mist. The trees and the fields and the sky disappeared. There was only the long road, stretching endlessly behind and before them.

Until finally, this afternoon, the skies had cleared and they were at last greeted by the sun. The dusky breezes blew gently, warm and slightly fragrant from the south. As they marched, the lads seemed to find some energy. Malus and the oxen pulled with renewed vigor, and Philippa, remembering who they were, sang out a cadence that joined with the birdsong and hum of the bees on a beautiful spring afternoon in Albion. They were moving together again, and it was invigorating. And now there was a good campsite to head towards, as well as apples for dinner. She could feel some of the tension in her shoulder muscles dissipating.

There's something about marching, Philippa thought, *that allows for reflection. Not when it's miserable out, or there's danger, but when it's nice out and I'm not worried, and not thinking too hard.* So now, when things were going easier, she felt that it might be a good time to examine her life so far. She had studied the philosophy of Socrates, who had said that the unexamined life is not worth living. Up until now, she'd been too busy to have much time for introspection. But now, she was ready to give it a try.

I suppose that means trying to think back as far as I can, she mused. That meant remembering her mother, which made her both proud and sad. She recalled the facts-- *Mother's family were from far-away Etruria; she was living in Gaul when she met Father. He was an army engineer, getting ready to return to Britannia after serving across the channel. She came home with him, but when she was pregnant with me he was recalled. She stayed here. He was killed in a bridge accident in Gaul before I was born. Mother told me about him. On his father's side, he was descended from Romans who came all the way from the Eternal City, and on his mother's side, from the Belgic and Catuvellauni Celtic tribes of Britain.*

Philippa breathed deep, listening to the rhythmic footsteps of the men on the road and the whiny creaking of the wagon wheels. Staring ahead into the lengthening shadows, she continued her recollections-- *Mother was Tuscan;*

she was brought up to be a priestess, a very old-fashioned vocation. She was exotic. Her dark hair hung in snaky coils and her eyes were lined with black kohl. Mother kept a brazier and an altar, and she always smelled like spices and smoke. She had a little collection of Greek scrolls. She was good at growing plants. She cut my hair short and dressed me like a boy. I'm not sure why, but I think she was trying to protect me.

We lived in a small round-house, an outbuilding of a large country villa. The villa belonged to what had once been a big prestigious family, but now was just an elderly couple and their servant. The gentleman had some kind of chronic illness. Mother tended the villa's herbs and flowers. She made tinctures for the old man, and did the washing for the old woman. In return, they let us live in their garden.

Mother taught me things; about the Gods, the sky, history, medicine, plants, art, music, and warfare. But not for very long; I was only six when she died. One morning she just wouldn't wake up. She had been fine the night before. I went up to the big house and told them, "Mother won't wake up." The old lady came to the hut to see. She said that Mother wasn't going to wake up, that she was with the Gods now.

There was a small funeral, and then I was bundled off to meet the Sisters of Charity, who made a regular circuit of the area, collecting alms and gathering up children who had nowhere to go. I joined a little group of orphans who were being taken to a nearby town to be put up for adoption. They were heading for a boat dock on an inlet of the river Trisantonis, to meet the barge that would carry them to Bognor Villa. There was once a variety of places for visitors to stay in the area, but they had all gone out of business years ago. So the group stopped overnight at Mount Temple, which was a bit out of the way, but was safe and clean and offered free lodging to those in need. From the main road, it was four miles up the old switchbacked drive, then four miles back down. It was another three miles on the main road to reach the river.

Mount Temple in its prime, during the glory days of Roman Britain, was a popular destination for pilgrims and holiday-makers alike, as well as monks, mendicants, medical patients, and anyone who wished to be suppliant to the Gods. For a small fee, a token offering could be purchased which would help your wish reach the appropriate divine ears. But no curses allowed. For that you could go supplicate Minerva Sulis in Bath.

Once, there were many of these sites in the southeast of Britain. The Temple complex back then was like a combination of a sanctuary, hostel, health resort and parkland. Mount Temple was located upon a hillside bluff overlooking the River Trisantonis, in a place of great scenic beauty. It had its own little windmill, with a bakery and a popina, a small restaurant. There were many fine buildings, connected by broad lanes which were paved with pearly white stone. There were flowers and trees and birds; domestic ones, and also species from the far east, somehow suited to this part of Britannia.

There were four small but elegant two-story wooden temples, dedicated to Mercury, Ceres, Mars and Venus, and one large one, made of concrete and stone in the grand traditional style, and dedicated to Jupiter. There were stalls and souvenir shops throughout the complex, and commemorative columns and altars to local deities. The smell of juniper incense and baked confections filled the air. The place prospered, and the Gods seemed content to dwell there and bestow many blessings upon the visitors.

But that was a long time ago; about one hundred years before Philippa arrived with the other orphans. Temple culture had begun to wane by the mid-300s, but it was a force of nature that put an end to the popularity of Mount Temple. There came a time of great storms, and the Trisantonis, prone to flooding, swelled with tremendous force. It eroded the bluff, causing a landslide that sent much of the complex into the river below. It was the off-season, and amazingly no one was hurt, but it was a disaster. The temples themselves were left standing, although the four smaller ones had been irrevocably damaged. Only the temple of Jupiter remained intact. The statues of the other Gods were moved in to share the Jovian divine space. The graceful and intricate temple portico survived, but the only dwelling left standing was one of the adjacent guest-houses.

Mount Temple was never deserted; it would have seemed inauspicious after all that, but it was left with a minimum of caretakers. Where once there were many priests, now there was only one, assisted by a young acolyte. They lived in the guest-house on the first floor, which also included the kitchen and the guest bedrooms. The upper floor was the dormitory, an open space furnished with a neat row of cots. The Sisters would temporarily house orphans there when they were passing through.

When the coach had arrived with two of the Sisters, Philippa, and six other recently orphaned children, it was night. They had been traveling for many hours. The children were given some soup and put straight to bed on the upper floor, in the dormitory. For most of them, the shock of losing their parents had given way to exhausted numbness. Some were crying themselves to sleep. Philippa was exhausted too, but she was also angry. The Sisters had informed them that they would be taken to one of the towns, to find new families. She did not want to go to a town, and she did not want a new family, who might make her be someone else. It was clear to her that she wasn't like these other children, especially not the other girls. They all seemed soft, and vulnerable, and they didn't know or care about the things that she considered important. She wanted to continue being herself, but she believed that she was being threatened. Lying on her cot, Philippa wept silent tears of frustration in the darkness until she finally surrendered to sleep.

The light was so bright it stung her eyes. For a moment she didn't remember where she was, and she didn't understand what she was seeing. Her little cot was on the end of the row, in front of a window. The full moon had risen, piercing the cool night air, and she had been awakened by its light. She rose and looked out. The temple shimmered and sparkled in the moonlight, and the portico shone brightly.

Still barefoot and in her nightclothes, Philippa slipped quietly into the stairwell and exited the dormitory. She padded across the courtyard, wincing a little from the gravel on her bare feet. She was fascinated by the temple, and she wanted to go inside. She came to the front steps. There was a door, which was shut. She couldn't see a way to open it. There were no handles or hinges. It wasn't a regular door, more like a hard curtain made out of some sort of woven fibrous material. It was stiff, but not completely; as she pressed on the bottom, it flexed a tiny bit, just enough for her to slip into the gap. After nearly getting stuck halfway, she managed to pop through, and she found herself on the inside of the Jupiter temple.

She was in a long darkened room. The only light was a brazier at the far end. She walked cautiously past the statues of Ceres and Mars on the left and Venus and Mercury on the right, bowing respectfully as she passed. The firelight made the shadows of the Gods jump across the room in flickering bursts, and the floor seemed to crawl with strange images. By the time she reached the brazier, the floor had grown warm. It felt good on her chilled bare feet. She found herself looking up at the glossy pale marble statue of Jupiter, slightly larger than life, handsome and hirsute, seated in a relaxed pose, with curly hair falling down over his shoulders. He was holding a staff, and a watchful eagle perched on the back of his chair.

A voice somewhere cried, "Papa!" Suddenly weeping, she realized that it was her own voice. She climbed up into the lap of the statue. It was also warm from the fire, and she was suddenly very sleepy.

She awoke shivering. The pre-dawn light was spreading through the temple. The brazier had burned low, and now she was chilly. She climbed down from the statue, and headed to the door. She marveled at the floor, which the early light had revealed as an intricate mosaic depicting fabulous plants and animals. The floor was rather damaged, but still glorious. She walked past lions and crocodiles, lush vines and palm trees, dolphins and fish. At the door, she turned to wave goodbye to the Gods; then she quickly slipped through the small flexible opening. It was easy this time. Within moments, she was back in the dormitory and in her cot. She'd barely had time to warm her feet before the Sisters came in to rouse the children and get them prepared for their journey.

After a quick breakfast of porridge and honey, they assembled under the portico in front of the temple. The priest, assisted by his acolyte, was preparing to give them a blessing before they departed. Father Florian was old, with wispy bits of what was once bright red hair. He was bent by time and walked slowly, using his miter as a cane. His assistant Tomasen seemed sweet and simple.
It was very quiet. Philippa suddenly said, rather loudly, "If you please, I don't want to go to the town, and I don't want a new family. I wish to stay here." The other children laughed. One of the Sisters said, "Don't be ridiculous. You can't stay here." The other shook her head disapprovingly and said, "You're coming with us, child. Don't be ungrateful."
Philippa was suddenly seized with anguish, and overcome by a feeling of being crushed. Then, remembering how she had felt inside the temple, she stood up straight, drew a deep breath, and announced very loudly, "No! I'm staying with my father."
"Your father is dead!" said the oldest of the boys.
"NO!" she screamed. "HE'S HERE!" Everyone was staring in shock at this unexpected outburst. Philippa suddenly bolted to the door of the temple and slipped through the secret opening like quicksilver, disappearing from sight.
She heard one of the Sisters exclaim, "How did she go through that closed door?"
"She's a ghost!" cried a little girl. The priest hurried to the temple, sliding open the door with a scratching, bumping sound. He went in, followed by his acolyte. The Sisters led the children away, but the oldest boy slipped right back to the temple. He hovered in the doorway, too curious to leave. One of the Sisters came after him. Across the room they saw that Philippa was in the lap of Jupiter, fiercely holding on to the statue. The priest stood nearby.

The elderly man looked very surprised. The acolyte smiled.

Philippa shouted defiantly, "I'm staying with my father!"

From the doorway the boy called, "Jupiter's not your father, stupid!"

Philippa hollered back, "I'm not stupid. Jupiter's everyone's father!"

To her amazement, the priest laughed. He said, "She's right about that!"

To Philippa, he said, squinting at the androgynous-looking child, "Look at me girl... you are a girl, is that correct?" She nodded, and he continued.

"I am Father Florian, the priest of this temple." Philippa bowed her head respectfully to the elderly gentleman, but did not let go of Jupiter.

"So tell me, child," he said, "are you as clever as you seem?"

"Yes, sir," she said without hesitation. The boy at the door snorted.

The priest continued, "What skills do you have?"

Philippa responded, "I can read and scribe, I can listen and remember; I can draw and sing and cook and clean. And if I have to, I can fight!" This last was directed to the boy still hanging around the door, who shook his fist at her. The Sister, having had enough, pulled him away by his ear.

Philippa, the priest and the acolyte emerged from the temple. Father Florian announced, "Young Philippa will be staying to assist my acolyte. Tomasen here has the world's kindest heart, but he is not gifted with intellectual skills." Tomasen continued to smile benignly. One of the Sisters complained, "But she's a girl-"

Philippa interrupted loudly- "I swear to Hestia and Hygieia, and to Jupiter and all the Gods that I choose a life of service, and that while I serve, no man may have me!"

To that Father Florian added, "So be it. The child will stay here." Tomasen clapped his hands in delight. The Sisters took the other orphans away. So began Philippa's life at Mount Temple.

"We're here," said Bruno.

Philippa called, "Company, halt. Fall out and make camp."

Brutus and Bruno slung bags over their shoulders and went to get the apples. Another lad, a red-haired Hibernian named Tyronius Danu, went hunting in the river with his bow and returned after a while with three trout. While the rest of the group set up camp, Philippa went with Terranes and Erastus to forage along the river bank, gathering young ferns, still coiled and tender, as well as some bitter greens and wild onions. She was tempted by some mushrooms but she didn't recognize them, so it was not worth the risk. Terranes, following her too closely as usual, was watching her every move with big blue eyes.

"Decanus Agrippa?"

"What is it?" she asked, although she already knew.

"May I call you Philippa?"

"You know that's not appropriate."

"But... I love you."

"Again, not appropriate. And back up!" She gently shoved him away from her, adding, "Give me some space."

"But I want to marry you."

"Enough! Do you understand what is meant by Virgin Warrior? You're not allowed to address me that way. You need to stop, soldier. You're not just annoying me; you're committing a punishable infraction."

"What's the punishment?" Erastus asked with sly interest.

"Well, according to the old scrolls," she replied, "it's castration."

Terranes, who had apparently not grown up on a farm, asked innocently, "What's castration?"

Before she could respond, Erastus chimed in, "It's when they cut your penis off!"

"Is that true? They cut the penis off?" asked Terranes with alarm.

"No, of course not," she replied. "How would you go pee? They just cut the testicles off."

"Ohhh, well I guess that's bad too." Terranes seemed to be weighing the options, while Erastus snickered.

"Erastus, there's a nice patch of ferns right behind you; will you pick them please?" He slunk off. Alone for moment with Terranes, she said, "Look, soldier, you are fooling yourself. You don't love me."

"But you're the most beautiful woman I have ever known."

It's true, she was no longer androgynous. She had her mother's big shiny brown eyes, full lips and creamy tan skin. From her father, she had light brown hair that turned to gold in the summer, and a little spray of freckles covering her nose and cheeks. She had grown tall. She had also grown curvy, which, along with strong muscles, made for an impressive physique. The camp armorer had made a special cuirass that enclosed her full bosom and tapered down to her small waist.

"And how many women have you actually known, Terranes Julius?"

Silence.

"That's what I thought," she said. "Just be patient. You'll meet someone you are really suited for, and you'll realize that you only have affection for me as a comrade."

"I want to be married," said Terranes.

"Yes, I get that," Philippa said patiently.

Erastus was back with the ferns. "I thought that only officers could marry."
"That used to be the case, but these days any soldier can marry. At least here in Britannia Prima Sud Est." Erastus looked dubious.
"It's true. I checked. Someone kept asking me about it," she rolled her eyes at Terranes, "so I checked with Centurion Aries."
"But," sighed Terranes, "when I do find a woman... will she love me in that way too?"
"Not if I get to her first!" teased Erastus.
"Enough!" Philippa exclaimed, throwing an onion at him. He guffawed. She was encouraged by this shift in attention away from herself. She gushed at Terranes.
"Of course! With your lovely blond hair and blue eyes, she'll be enchanted. And as a man with a job, you'll be a good catch." *Provided we ever get paid,* she thought, and she could feel the muscles in her shoulders tensing up again.

The camp had been made and the fire was ready. The herbs and vegetables were delivered to Tyronius, who was preparing fish stew in the battered and retired helmet that had become their cooking pot. Hector Magnus, the other archer, had shot a rabbit, and it was already roasting on a spit. The scouts had returned with two bags full of apples, and were processing them with their matching belt knives.

The barley flour had been a good purchase. It had gotten soggy, but that only seemed to make it better somehow. They had eaten it every day, in porridge and stews and fritters, but there was still plenty left for baking. It was brought out, along with the remaining eggs, and their most precious supplies: a jar of honey and a box of salt, which were used for both food and medicine. The men looked at her expectantly, and she nodded. Thus began the ritual. Two lads went to the provision wagon, returning ceremoniously with a cooking pan nearly the size of one of its wheels. There was also a beat-up old lid for the pan, a very large and chipped ceramic bowl, a huge wooden spoon, and a battered bronze spatula. The iron pan was ancient; the original metal was covered with thick layers of char. The top rim was chipping and flaking away, and if you weren't careful the occasional bit of charred metal would get into the food, which was why the cooks at Ares Mons had let her take it.

This pan was actually the secret to her success as a leader. The twenty men assigned to her command were not happy about being led by a female. Not on the first day, anyway; they had been sulky and slow to follow orders. Plus, she hadn't received any rosters yet, and she was having trouble learning who they were, and telling them apart. Some of the men had easy names, and features that stood out, but the rest were a blur. Philippa realized that meeting and remembering a large group of people was something she had never done. It didn't help that four of the lads were named Marcus. For some reason, all four were young and fair, painfully shy, and didn't speak much Latin. They were apparently Greek, although they didn't resemble any of the dark-haired Greeks she'd previously encountered. There were also three named Julius. Two of the Juliuses resembled the four Marcuses. All six had long Greek second names, all different. It was confusing. Usually people who all resembled each other had the same last name, not first. The other Julius was tall, with dark skin and a loud voice. His name was Julius Phaedonis, but he was called Big Julius.

That evening of the first day with her new recruits, back at their tents in Apollo Row, after a mediocre army dinner, the men discovered that their Decanus was also a baker. As the scent of something sweet filled the air, they had gathered around their fire, watching the steam rise around the edges of the black iron pan.
"What is it?" Big Julius asked with interest.
"Apple cake," she replied.
"Is it... for us?" He asked tentatively.
"Yes."

They continued to watch intently. After checking under the lid a few times, Philippa finally heaved the great pan out of the fire and onto a stone, and removed the cover. Aromatic steam issued forth in a great cloud. After a few minutes of cooling, she sliced the giant cake and began coaxing the first pieces out. As she did, one of the men started to chant- "Apple cake, apple cake, apple cake." Soon they all joined in, and continued to chant until their mouths were full. They ate in silence. Then one of them had said, "Thank you, Decanus Agrippa." They all repeated it.

"You're welcome," she had replied. "The pan gets scrubbed with sand and wiped clean. The other items get washed. Put them near the fire until they dry. Goodnight, soldiers."

They'd followed her instructions. In the morning she had found everything cleaned and stored. Thus began the nightly ritual of apple cake. From that time onward, the lads followed her orders without any problems. She was able to bake on most evenings; when she did so, the chant would start up and continue until mouths were full. When there were no apples, other fruits were used, such as pears, quince, bramble, and plum, and in the fall there had been hazel and chestnuts. When no fruits or nuts could be found, other substitutions were made such as celery, cabbage, and carrots. When nothing civilized could be located, there were nettles, sorrel and herbs.

The last one she had managed to cook in the damp fog was composed mostly of young dandelion greens. She thought it was disgusting, but nothing deterred the men from enthusiastically eating her apple cake. They always chanted, "apple cake, apple cake", even though, as she pointed out, there was often a complete lack of apples in it. The men had created a comforting ritual, and the apple cake had created a group of loyal men.

Chapter Two - Mount Temple

The next day dawned as bright and sweet as a spring morning should. Most of the young men were Britannic natives, and appreciative of four seasons; for them the past week's misery was now entirely forgotten. However, some of the other lads were from, or had lived in, more tropical regions. They looked up at the sky suspiciously, as if they were resentful at the impertinence of the local climate to act now as though the past week's torturous weather hadn't even happened. They weren't quite ready to forgive and forget. But after a hearty breakfast of salted barley porridge, they were all marching in the sunshine, next to the river. The banks were vivid with moss, and curly ferns bobbed in the gentle breeze. Any leftover grouchiness disappeared.

After establishing the cadence, Philippa had fallen silent. Some of the lads were in a playful mood, making up their own silly marching songs. She didn't care today, as long as they kept moving. When this had happened previously, she had given them a lecture about being defensively ready for danger at all times. But in truth, this mostly empty area of the southeast had not seen conflict for so long that it was thought to be safe. The tribes who regularly came to harass the island did so mostly in the north. That's also where clashes between old and new factions of the Romano/British establishment occurred.

If the Empire had been fully functional, the men might have been posted somewhere that actually needed defending. But without being able to pay the soldiers, it was tricky enough to even man a peaceful garrison in Britannia Prima. So far there had been no open rebellions from troops, just grumbling, but desertion was on the rise, and recruitment was very low.

She called out to Big Julius and put him in charge of the march. He had a loud resonant voice. He was also the one making up most of the silly songs. They were really silly. Now he sang,
"Right, left. Right, left. Don't let a bird poop on your head." The men loved it, repeating it back to him. *So, we're letting our guard down a bit*, she thought, but for once she was too relaxed to care very much, and the silly songs seemed good for morale. And it gave her a chance to think some more about her life, and the events that had brought her here.

She had been a happy child at Mount Temple. She'd quickly made herself useful and kept busy. The Sisters soon found a place to lodge orphans closer to the river, so it was just the three of them, with the very occasional visitor or pilgrim. The Sisters would sometimes send them wine, fruit, honey, and bags of grain. Father Florian had no coin to speak of, and they were isolated, so they needed to be as self-sufficient as possible.

Philippa took over. She cleaned the living areas, tidied the white gravel paths, and removed the cobwebs and grime from behind the statues of the Gods. Father Florian had managed to keep their fronts clean, but the harder to reach places were filthy. She fought the weeds, pruned the hedges and restored the herb garden. Tomasen would show up when he wasn't busy with Father Florian or the cats, saying, "Pippa, I'll help! I want to help, Pippa!" She wasn't sure if Pippa was a nickname, or if he couldn't say Philippa, but she liked it.

She had learned to cook simple dishes, and she taught herself to bake. She made friends with Mount Temple's pair of she-goats, and after some trial and error, figured out how to milk them. She found a little cask, tucked away on a hidden shelf in the kitchen. It was filled with cinnamon, a rare and marvelous spice good for cooking and medicine.

The temple was nearly out of candles. In the middens, she found a huge pile of burnt down stubs, and used the wax to make new candles. She unraveled an old curtain to get material for wicks. She spent two entire days making candles, standing over an outdoor fire, stirring hot wax in an old cooking pot. She had little scars on her hands from getting splashed.

She explored everywhere. In a shed behind the temple, she found some large sections of the material that the temple door was made of, and some stacks of lumber. With Tomasen's help, she built a snug little dorm room for herself, right up against her window. She studied the construction of the temple's sliding door, and installed a similar one in her room.

The temple floor mosaic was in rough shape, with cracks and empty patches. On the furthest wall, behind Jupiter, she discovered a small cabinet, built into a recess in the wall. It contained some tools, including several sizes of trowels, and a dust-caked stone mortar and pestle. There were also some bags of colored glass fragments, so she concluded that this gear was left over from the original laying of the floor. She worked on the floor whenever she could, on her hands and knees, repairing the pictures, and replacing the tiny missing tesserae. Sometimes she could find the lost puzzle pieces, but more often than not she had to improvise with little chips of stone or bits of broken crockery. There was no new mortar, so she ground down loose chunks of old mortar and reconstituted it. She worked on the restoration when she could. She realized that she could work on this her whole life and it still wouldn't be complete, but she felt it to be a duty, and she enjoyed spending time in the temple.

When she wasn't doing cleaning and maintenance, she was occupied in reading the scrolls, the texts that the priest kept collected in a large wooden crate. The crate was very old, but sturdy. Inside was a wooden grid. The scrolls were neatly organized into the slots. It was a treasure trove of information about history, medicine, religion, astronomy, divination, earth magic, anatomy, animal husbandry, and agriculture. There were many texts on philosophy, including some that Father Florian himself had written. She read all the scrolls, several times. She added to her knowledge of healing herbs, and she made fortifying teas for Father Florian. He taught her songs, prayers and chants. She sang them back to him in a clear tuneful voice as Tomasen clapped in perfect time. As she worked in the temple, she spoke to the Gods, recounting their stories, praising their deeds. She studied the heavens. She would gaze into the darkness at the celestial divinities. Mars was fiery red and could often be seen in the same night sky as Venus, who would still be glowing diffusely in the morning. Saturn shimmered with soft light, and was often elusive. Jupiter was bright and sparkling in the pre-dawn of winter and spring. On autumn nights, his evanescence was bright enough to obscure the stars.

The library was the only thing at Mount Temple that was neatly organized. It wasn't Father Florian's fault, she had soon realized; he had been priest here for twenty years, but he'd been a crippled elderly man before he arrived, and most of the decay dated back much further. *Back to the time just after the disaster,* she supposed, *when there wouldn't have been much interest in restoration.*

It had taken even less time to understand that the acolyte Tomasen, who was meant to do the brunt of the work, was a sweet simpleton who was utterly incapable. Even though the priest's daily rituals never changed, Tomasen had to be instructed every time on what to bring, what to hand him, and when. He could only accomplish the most basic task. If she asked him to clean a statue, he would rub it once with the rag and be done. If she told him- that was good, the foot was clean, now do the leg- he would. But then he'd be done again. So it was easier to do the work herself instead of trying to micro-manage his tasks. On the positive side, he was useful for lifting and carrying, which is what they really needed help with. Left on his own, Tomasen could be found playing with the many cats and kittens that lived in the complex. He used to play with frogs too, but one day he accidentally squashed one to death. Devastated, he never chased frogs again, and would start to sniffle loudly at the mere mention of the creature. He really was sweet and kind. She wondered how he was doing, and if Father Florian was still alive.

"Bees! Bees!" yelled Davines West. He was a pale boy from somewhere in the west. Too poor for a proper last name, she had heard it said, but soldiers were supposed to have two appellations, so his direction of origin became his surname. He had a sixth sense for finding honeycomb, which the group had benefitted from on several occasions. Sure enough, he had spotted a honey tree, deep inside the forest by the river.

Philippa cried, "Company halt. Go get it!"

There weren't many things that would stop their march, but the chance to get more honey was always welcome. Bruno quickly unpacked a flint-stone and steel, and in moments had lit some tinder and then some kindling. Davines had located a dried-up shrub and yanked it hurriedly out of the soft ground, spraying dirt in a great arc. He stuck it into the lit kindling and it began to smolder. Holding it aloft, he ran to the tree at top speed, heedless of the briars, the branch billowing with thick yellow-grey smoke. He managed to scurry up the tree, still holding the burning branch, and started smoking out the bees. Tyronius ran after him with a bucket. Most of the others ran too, filled with excitement. Philippa stayed with the front and rear guard on the road and watched the action. For a moment the bees were loud enough to hear, then they were quiet. There was a thud, and then some rustling. The men all ran back, shouting with excitement. Davines returned triumphantly with the comb, and only a few stings. The other lads followed cheerfully, except for poor Tyronius, who had unfortunately received the most stings. He ran ahead howling, and jumped into the cold shallows; the other fellows laughed and fished him out, plucking the stingers from his flesh and wrapping a dry cloak around him.

The honeycomb bucket was hurriedly stashed. The bees could be heard once more, so Philippa hollered, "Quicktime march!", without even calling the soldiers to attention.

They scurried down the road, the boys still laughing, finally collapsing out of breath at a safe distance. The bees were no longer following. The honeycomb would be processed later when they had made camp. Even though it was stuck with leaves, and still contained some bees, it had become a tradition that the thieves got a sample of the stolen goods. The lads who had been on the hunt stuck their hands in, pulling off globs of honey and pieces of comb, laughing and spitting out the occasional bee. They quickly washed up at the edge of the water. The bucket was secured, and they fell back in at attention without even being told.

Philippa ordered, "Forward march." As they moved, the lads continued to talk about food; the extra honey was enough to sweeten several days worth of apple cake, and maybe even the breakfast porridge, and still have plenty left over in case of illness or injury, as honey was known for its curative qualities.

She smiled. These fellows loved talking about food. Almost as much as they enjoyed talking about girls. It was pure speculation; most of them had never even met a girl that wasn't a relative. As the population had dwindled, the chances of meeting a suitable mate had gotten much slimmer. Philippa had heard their conversations and realized that they knew even less than she did about procreation. The poor things really hadn't a clue. She didn't actually know any more than they did about the ways of love, but she still felt slightly smug; she knew how things worked from a biological standpoint. She had read the scrolls about anatomy and animal husbandry with both interest and revulsion. It was disconcerting information, but it explained a great deal. She remembered thinking ---
So that's why there are so many kittens around here!

They maintained a leisurely pace. Philippa let Bruno and Brutus call cadence. They did it in unison; it was charming. She dawdled a bit, and seemed to be in a day-dream as she marched, but she was actually using this time to continue the examination of her life so far.

The years had gone by quickly at the temple, filled with quiet steady activity. Father Florian gradually became more bent over and slow. Except for growing some straggly facial hair, Tomasen didn't seem to change at all. The seasons came and went. The Sisters sent supplies when they could afford it. The temple would receive a visitor every now and then; a pilgrim, curiosity seeker, or just someone in need of lodging.

When she was thirteen she had begun her moon-cycle; inconvenient and uncomfortable, but at least not a complete mystery, thanks again to the scrolls. She fashioned underclothes and a tunic for herself out of more of the old curtains. Father Florian and Tomasen took care of the daily prayers and the temple fire; she did virtually everything else. She spent most of her time outdoors. She collected seeds from vegetables, trees and flowers. She planted half of them. She made a little fabric envelope, full of neatly labeled pockets, for the rest. She kept the precious package on the shelf with the cinnamon. She experimented with herbs and tinctures. She made goat cheese. She came up with a special chicken food that doubled egg production from their little flock of speckled hens. Much of the once proud orchards of fruit and nut trees had been lost. She did her best to cultivate what was left. She dug holes and planted new rows of apple, quince, pear, plum, hazel, and chestnut trees.

She explored the grounds. There were some surprising things buried in the dirt. She pulled out stacks of old broken bottles, jars and lamps. She rinsed them in the rain barrel, and created a sparkling array upon the garden wall. It looked pretty, and she hoped it would keep down the number of squirrels who thought the garden was their own. She discovered and unearthed a fountain. It didn't have water anymore, so she grew flowers in it.

She became fascinated with the furthest part of the estate, where the land had fallen into the sea. It was a treacherous area. After the landslide, someone had built a timber fence out of the wood from the damaged temple buildings, along the edge, to keep curious visitors from plummeting to their deaths. She found some rope, and one day she used it to tie herself to the fence, so she could go beyond it, just a little, and look out over the undercut earth. From this dizzying height, she could see the remains of the devastation: a colossal heap of mud, filled with trees and stone blocks and what looked like bits of old furniture. She gazed down at the river below, peaceful and calm these days, and wondered at it all.

She would have stayed contentedly on at Mount Temple, but that was not to be her fate. The Gods had other plans for Philippa Agrippa! She was just fourteen when the old priest's health finally failed; one day he simply couldn't get out of bed. He was conscious, and still had his wits, but he could no longer walk or stand or even sit up without help. She had been doing her best to take care of him for nearly a week, when a tradesman arrived for a night's lodging. Philippa gave him a message to take to the nearest settlement. Several days later, a carriage arrived, bringing some men she had never seen- a local official, a guard, a priest named Father Maximus, and his acolyte, Jenisec. The official announced that Father Florian, along with Tomasen, would be going away. Father Florian would be retiring to a religious hospice. Father Maximus was to be the new priest.

Philippa was distraught; she wept and pleaded for Father Florian to stay, or to take her with him, but the official said no. Father Florian said that he would have preferred to stay, but he was resigned to leaving.

He tried to calm her. "You've been the blessing of my old age. You have learned everything I know and more. It's all yours now. Go out and share it with the world. Now kiss me child, for the time has come." As she bent down to kiss him, he whispered intently in her ear, "I know this priest. You can't stay here. The Gods will guide you."

Philippa was beside herself with grief and anguish. Tomasen was weeping as he carried the frail old man to the carriage.
"Goodbye Pippa! Pippa! I love you."
She bawled, "I love you too, Tomasen. May the Gods be with you."

The carriage took them away, along with the official and the guard. Father Maximus did not even acknowledge her existence, but went in to inspect his new quarters. Jenisec stood, leering at her. It was un-nerving. She fled into the temple. It had always been her place of sanctuary. Jenisec followed her in. She stopped in the middle of the room when he entered.
"Hey, girl, you can't be in here. No girls allowed."
He sidled up to her, uncomfortably close, adding, "I can make an exception, though, if the price is right." His breath stank of wine. He put his hands on her. She bolted and ran out of the temple and up into the dormitory. She considered going to the priest for aid, but then she thought of Father Florian's warning. She ran to her little room. There was no way to lock the door.

She paced in agitation, breathing deeply, trying not to panic. She would have to leave Mount Temple. But how? She was many miles away from any settlement. *And what if she somehow made it to one? Would there be more bad men?* She prayed to the Gods to help her find a way out. She stood by her window. She watched Jenisec leave the temple and come into the guesthouse. She went to the dresser and took out her carving knife and her hammer, the closest things to weapons she had. She sat on her cot, determined to stay up all night if need be, and she prayed to Jupiter to grant her an auspicious escape.

She awoke to a pounding on her door. It was morning. She was slumped over on the cot, still holding the knife and hammer. "Get up, lazy girl, we're hungry."
She heard Jenisec go back down the stairs. *I suppose they assume that I'm the cook here,* she thought. She tied up her hair, put on her most shapeless smock, and went downstairs to make breakfast.

She had worked for Father Maximus, as a housemaid and cook, for five grim days. The priest never looked up or spoke to her, except to occasionally grunt some orders. The orders usually consisted of- "More wine, girl." His name suited him. He was gross, gluttonous, and drunk all the time. At least he slept a lot. Jenisec also seemed to be a drunk, but he was intent on trying to get her alone. She fabricated a bolt for her door and kept it locked at night. Avoiding him became a full time endeavor. Fortunately, she could see and hear much of what was going on from upstairs. If she heard him come up one stairwell, she went down the other. If she saw him leave the house, she would go downstairs to do her chores. Once she caught him trying to spy on her in the privy!

After that first day, she monitored the men's movements from her window. She never saw either of them go into the temple. That would mean that no one was honoring the Gods, or tending the holy fire. After three days had passed, she decided to go in herself. She fed the men a heavy lunch, with lots of wine. When she thought that they might be sleeping, she slipped away and into the temple.

The old sliding door of the temple had long since crumbled, and there was now just a heavy curtain. She pushed it aside. It was dark and cold. The creepy acolyte had let the brazier burn down! That proved that the lazy priest hadn't been doing his job. She was so livid, she began to walk past the Gods without greeting them. Then she remembered, and turned back to do so.

When she reached the brazier, she opened the ornate brass cover to poke around inside. There was a tiny ember. She got a handful of fuel and fed it slowly to the glowing coal. It burst into a little flame. She fed it some more. She wanted to stay, but she was too afraid of Jenisec finding her in there, so she filled the brazier the rest of the way, then quickly departed.

On the sixth morning a carriage arrived. She heard it coming up the hill. As she went to greet it, the priest called out, "If that's a guest, make sure they can pay." It was an uncharitable and shocking thing to say! No matter how poor the temple had become, they would never turn someone away because of a lack of coin. She tried to regain her composure; after all, it wasn't the guest's fault that the priest and acolyte were lazy, greedy, drunken degenerates. She was embarrassed by their shameful behavior.

There was a young man driving the carriage. It stopped, and a Roman soldier got out. He wore a white bronze breastplate, and a red cloak with silver embosses. He carried his helmet, which had a transverse crest. He was middle-aged, stout but still fit, with blue eyes and short grey hair. His weathered face looked kind but tired.

"Welcome to Mount Temple, good sirs," she said.
"My thanks." The soldier bowed. "I am Justinian Justinius. I need lodging for the night. This is my servant, Atticus," he said, indicating the driver.
"I am Philippa Agrippa." She bowed in return. "I am honored to greet you, Justinian Justinius." She turned and bowed again. "Welcome Atticus. This way, please."

Philippa led them to one of the guest rooms, which were located on the ground floor. It had a canopy bed for the guest and a cot for the servant. It wasn't the best room, but it was furthest from the priest's chambers, and she thought that would be preferable. (Father Maximus had taken over the nicest room. It was next to Father Florian's little cell, in which Jenisec now slept.)

On the way, she recited a brief history of Mount Temple, from its glory days to now, praising the Jupiter temple and the statues of the Gods.
"I'm impressed, Philippa Agrippa," said Justinian. "You certainly know your history."
"I was fortunate. From the age of six until... just recently, I learned from the great scholar and philosopher Father Florian, who shared his whole library with me."
"So you read also?" he asked. She nodded.
"And scribe too?" She nodded again.
"And what subjects did you study?" he asked.
"History, geography, languages, art, music, the Gods, biology, philosophy and agriculture. And military campaigns," she added, wanting to include something he might be interested in.
"Fascinating. Are all the girls around here as interesting as you?"
"There are no girls around here," she said matter of factly.
There was a slightly awkward silence, broken by Justinian-
"Well, Philippa Agrippa, I'd like to hear more, but for now I have to go to meet some people. They are at a villa north and east of here, Danova Rhea, do you know it?"
She shook her head. "Sorry."
"That's alright, we'll find it. I'd like dinner tonight when I return."
"Yes, sir. It will be my honor to serve a soldier of Rome." The visitors to Mount Temple were usually pilgrims; they only cared about the Gods, which

was fine, but this was an interesting change. She liked Justinian Justinius, and she was determined to make him a good meal, despite her current predicament.

She spent the entire day in the kitchen, grinding grain, baking bread, cooking beans, prepping vegetables, boiling eggs, and preparing her specialty, apple cake- made not only with honey, but also some of the rare cinnamon. No one bothered her all day. She got the impression that the drunken duo, as she had come to think of them, did not want anything to do with the guests.

When all was finished, she prepared a tray with a portion of stew and bread. She brought it to Maximus's chamber, set it down, knocked on the door and quickly left before anyone could appear. They didn't get any side dishes or apple cake, just a big jug of cheap wine.
That should keep them busy, she thought, *so they won't disturb Justinian Justinius during dinner.*

The carriage returned in the late afternoon. Philippa had gone to her room to change clothes. She watched from the window as Justinian Justinius came into the guesthouse. He looked unhappy. Atticus stabled the horses and came in after him, carrying a book and a banner.

Philippa went down to the kitchen. She got a small bottle. It was a restorative cordial she had made from rosemary leaves, honey and lemon. She poured some into two small glasses, put them on a tray, and carried the tray to their guest room. She knocked on the door. Atticus opened it partway. She held out the tray. "Here's a drink for Justinian Justinius, and one for you, Atticus. It soothes the throat after traveling on the dusty road."

She returned to the kitchen to make some final preparations, then she set the table in the dining room and fetched a jug of wine from the cellar, a much finer vintage than she had served the duo. She poured two cups of the deep red wine, put them on the tray, and set it on a table in the reception area. A moment later, Justinian and Atticus appeared.

"Greetings gentlemen. Would you care for a cup of wine before dinner?"
"Yes, please," replied Justinian. He and Atticus each took a cup. "And by the way," he continued, "thank you for the restorative. I'm afraid it would take more than that to entirely lift our spirits, but it was helpful."
"Did your meeting at Danova Rhea not go the way you had hoped?" she asked.
"It did not. The Gods were not on our side this time." Justinian mused, "Perhaps I was amiss in not paying my respects first. I should have visited the temple before we left, and asked their blessings, but I was distracted."

Philippa said, "There's no way of knowing if that was the reason, but if that's how you feel, perhaps you should visit them now, while they are on your mind. Whatever your endeavor, it may not be too late for an auspicious new turn of events."

Justinian looked almost annoyed at the suggestion, but he set down his cup, which was still full, and responded, "That's a good idea; I will go and greet the Gods, admit my faults, and ask for their blessing. Come, Atticus. Let us go and make amends." Atticus also put his cup back on the tray, but not before gulping down the contents. Philippa smiled.

When they returned fifteen minutes later, she had finished laying out the meal, and was waiting for them in the courtyard. As they approached, she could see right away that Justinian was in a far better mood. *That's the Jovian effect,* she thought. *Jupiter makes good people happy.*

"What a temple!" he exclaimed. "I was not expecting such excellent likenesses of the Gods, especially of the Deuspater. It was refreshing. I've been too long away from temple life. It's a relief to be reunited with the Deities."
Atticus chimed in, "The brazier was almost out! I fed it."

"Thank you, Atticus," she said gratefully.

Justinian went on, "And the floor mosaics! Fantastic. Thank you for the suggestion, Philippa Agrippa. One should always remember the Gods before beginning... " He trailed off as they entered the dining room. "Is all this... for us?" He and Atticus both stared in amazement.

There was fresh bread, bean stew, greens with boiled eggs and mustard sauce, a toasted hazelnut loaf, plum compote, and in the center of it all, a perfectly baked apple cake, stuffed with walnuts and topped with cinnamon crumbles.
"Of course," she said smiling. It was an impressive spread, she had to admit to herself, even if there was no meat. She said a short blessing over the food, then conversation ceased as mouths and bellies were filled.

When they had eaten, she began to get up and clear the table, but Justinian said, "Atticus will take care of all that. It's what he does at home, and I'm sure he must miss it." Atticus rolled his eyes, smiling. He cleared the table, then he went into the kitchen. Philippa could hear him storing the leftovers and rinsing the dishes. She had some time to relax, which was good, because she wanted to talk to Justinian.

"My father was in the Army," she said. "He was an immune, a bridge engineer. What sort of soldier are you?"

"Well, I'm a recruiter. I am an old centurion, but for the past twenty-two years I've been locating new soldiers for the Army."

"That would explain the book," reasoned Philippa.

Justinian looked sad, and he sighed. "Yes, well, I'm afraid my career is over. I haven't met my quota this season. It's because I am an honest conscribit." There was bitterness in his voice. "I won't resort to intimidation or bribes. Soldiers enlisted under those conditions are a liability to Rome and a danger to their comrades. Danova Rhea was my last hope. There was a prominent family with twelve sons, three of which seemed like a certainty."

"What happened?" asked Philippa. Justinian was silent, eyes downcast. It was Atticus, returning from the kitchen, who said,

"They were gone. Moved back to Rome a month ago."

"Oh," said Philippa. "How many recruits do you need to keep your job?"

"The bar has been set so low," said Justinian, "and still I have failed. The command at Ares Mons ordered me to return by tomorrow with at least two regular soldiers, or one with leadership potential. I will be discharged. That's what happened to the other recruiters."

Philippa stood up, her heart pounding. "Take me! I am learned in many subjects and I'm sure that I have leadership potential!" Her face was flushed and she was suddenly very warm. "I have already taken an oath of chastity. I will not marry. I will be a Virgin Warrior, like my forbears in Etruria who fought for Rome in the old times."

"You mean like the Amazons?" asked Atticus.

"No, not at all!" said Philippa. "Virgin Warriors were citizens, sworn to the Gods, and loyal to the Republic."

Justinian chuckled. "Beware, Atticus, a little knowledge is a dangerous thing. And that's what you have, a little knowledge."

Philippa laughed nervously, and poured both men another glass of wine, her hands trembling a little. Justinian continued, "But my dear, I'm afraid the idea is unprecedented."

"No," she said, "it is documented in the scrolls... " Suddenly the events of the past week came rushing into her mind. She set down the bottle abruptly. "Please, you must take me with you; the new priest is a drunkard who scorns the Gods, and his acolyte won't stop trying to molest me!"

"By Jove, that's scandalous!" Justinian exclaimed. "Of course we will take you to safety if you are in danger. You are under no obligation to this priest?" She shook her head, revolted by the thought. "Then," he said, "we can transport you to a safe place in one of the settlements-"

"No!" she cried. "I want to be a soldier. It's my destiny to be a soldier! By Jupiter, Mars and Mercury, I swear it is!" She hardly knew what she was saying. She began to speak rapidly. "The scrolls. The history of old Etruria. Father Florian left his library box here for me. It's still in his room. The new priest cares nothing for the scrolls. There is now a big crate of wine sitting on top of them. He doesn't use the room, only Jenisec. We could get the scrolls while he's away. We could trade out the library box for another case of wine; I'm sure they wouldn't notice the difference." She stopped. The two men were looking at her in confused astonishment. "And then, you see, I can show you the historical texts that describe the Virgin Warrior. Then it won't be unprecedented."

"Well, Philippa Agrippa," said Justinian, "I can see that you are quite capable of strategy; you do display the potential for leadership. But I am afraid that when we show up at camp they will laugh at you."
"They will not dare to laugh at me!" she said with fierce determination.
"Well... they may laugh at me," said Justinian grimly.
"What does it matter, if you get to keep your job, sir?" exclaimed Atticus. "And besides, what have you got to lose? Aside from your villa and lands." He added dejectedly, "And your loyal servant."

Justinian asked, "How do we get to the scrolls without alerting the priest?"
"You don't have to worry about him too much," she said. "He almost never comes out of his chambers. It's Jenisec who is always prowling around, watching me and following me."
Justinian said, "Perhaps we can use that fact to our advantage."
Philippa understood. "I can be a decoy!"

She had put on her tightest tunic and loosened her hair. From her window, she could see Jenisec. He was in the yard outside the priest's room. He was urinating on the white gravel path.
What a disgusting pig! she thought, not for the first time.

Philippa scampered down the stairwell, picked up a basket, and walked to the garden. Jenisec saw her and began to stalk her, right on cue. She moved casually along the path. When she disappeared behind a bit of wall, she ran, and when she was visible again, she slowed back down. She thus managed to stay ahead of him for a while, but she eventually came to a wide open point on the path where she was completely exposed. He came hurrying through the flower beds intending to cut her off, but just before he stepped onto the path-

"Good evening, Centurion," she said loudly. "How are you enjoying the garden?"
Justinian had suddenly appeared on the path, coming from the other direction. "It's very nice, thank you."

Jenisec took one look at the burly soldier and melted back into the landscape. Philippa and the soldier walked together chatting pleasantly. When they were sure they were quite alone, Justinian said quietly,
"The box is secured. Replaced with a crate of wine, as you suggested. It's with my luggage, covered by a blanket. Atticus is guarding the room. We'll leave at first light. You must prepare yourself for departure; quietly so as to not attract attention." She nodded, trembling.

The soldier bowed, and in a louder voice said, "Then I will say goodnight."

She went to her room and stood at the window, heart pounding. Then she remembered that she needed to gather her belongings. Hands shaking, she took her hammer, knife, a small bronze statue of Jupiter she'd found on the grounds, and some feathers and little stones. She put them together with a few personal items, and wrapped them with her clothing into a small bundle. That was it. Then she remembered the cinnamon and her seed collection. Should she go back down to the kitchen? No. She didn't want to encounter the drunken duo, or wake them, and risk any confrontation or complication.

She put on tomorrow's clothes, the brown tunic and leggings she had recently made from one of Father Florian's old robes, and slipped on her sandals. Then she sat on the edge of her cot, clutching her possessions. The night grew dark around her; she hadn't lit a candle. Still she sat. This had been her room, her bed, her life, but now it was ending. The trembling spread through her body. She couldn't stop shaking! Why couldn't she stop shaking?

She went to the window again to look at the temple. The way she always did. Suddenly decisive, she set her bundle upon her cot, and returned to the window. She had only been in the temple that once since the drunken duo arrived. She did not dare to go in there when Jenisec was awake, for fear of getting trapped. She had to keep the door to her room bolted at night so he wouldn't come into her room while she slept, as he had tried to on several occasions. And since her door bolted on the inside, she had only one option. She sat on the sill, and swung one leg through the open window. Philippa stopped. She had a brief moment of doubt; was this too much of a risk, when she was so close to escaping?

No. If she didn't go to thank the Gods and bid them farewell, she would never feel right about it. She swung the other leg over. Clinging to the brickwork, she walked slowly and carefully. The window ledge gave way to a much skinnier ledge, and then it widened into a window ledge again. She quickly went through. She was in her familiar stairwell. Slipping silently down the stairs, she headed to the temple. She was careful to stick to the edges of the building, where there was no gravel to make a crunchy sound that might give her away. It was the new moon and all was dark. She felt for the curtain at the front of the temple, and pushing it aside, she went in.

The brazier was burning, thanks to Atticus. She walked by, saluting Ceres, Venus, Mercury and Mars. *For the last time here,* she thought. *But I will meet them elsewhere; in other forms*, she reassured herself.

When she reached Jupiter, she went to the statue and embraced the stone figure, weeping a little. She said aloud, "I'm sorry, but I have to leave. Thank you for everything. Please don't forget me."

The brazier sizzled, and the pictures on the floor danced in the light. *The mosaic,* she thought. *It's as finished as it's going to be. I should clean up my mess.* She slipped behind Jupiter. There, she gathered up the supplies. She scooped the loose pieces back into the bags and placed them in the mortar and pestle, returning them to the small cabinet. She collected the trowels, and set them alongside. Sighing, she closed the door of the cabinet. It popped back open. She pushed it shut. It popped open again. She felt around inside. *That's odd*, she thought, *I put everything back the way I found it. It ought to shut.*

She took all the gear back out, and shut the door. It popped back open. She got on her knees and tried to look inside but it was too dark. She began to methodically run her hands up and down the inside of the cabinet. Suddenly something shifted into her hand. It was heavy and rectangular. *Oh no*, she thought, *a stone has come loose.* But it felt more like metal. And it was much heavier than a stone. She carried it around to the front of the statue. In the light of the brazier, she could see that she was holding an old bronze box. It made a slight chinking sound when she moved it.

She set it in Jupiter's lap, located the latch and opened it. She gasped. It was filled to the very top with coins. They were mostly silver denarii, but there were also coins of copper, and many of gold! They gleamed in the firelight.

Her mind reeled. She closed and latched the box. Leaving it with Jupiter, she went behind the statue, placed the tools back in the cabinet, and shut it. It stayed shut. Returning to the front, she embraced the statue once again. This time she wasn't crying.

Philippa took the box and left the temple. She entered the stairwell and cautiously traversed the ledges back to her window, holding the heavy box close to the wall. She entered her room, picked up her bundle, repacked it with the treasure tucked deep inside, and waited.

It was getting close to sunrise. Atticus carefully opened the door, and began to set their gear in the hallway.

"Good morning!" she whispered. Atticus jumped, but quickly realized that it was Philippa.
"By the Gods, you scared me!" he whispered back. She had been waiting in the dark hall in front of their room. Justinian appeared, bleary-eyed but brisk. Atticus grabbed their luggage, and Justinian hefted the library box. Philippa was left to carry the banner and book, and her small heavy bundle. As they neared the door, Justinian stopped, put the box down, and opened his purse. He pulled out two copper coins. He left the payment on the table next to the door, picked up the scrolls, and they went out.

They hurried quietly to the stable. She was relieved to discover that Atticus had already harnessed the horses. They shoved everything into the carriage, and Justinian and Philippa got in. Atticus climbed up, made a soft clicking sound, and the wagon began rolling, crunching softly on the white gravel. They were moving!

Philippa turned her head and watched Mount Temple recede into the distance. Then they went around a curve, and it was gone.

Chapter Three - Precedence!

The sun was high in the morning sky when they stopped. They had been heading east the whole time. After Mount Temple had vanished from sight, Justinian Justinius had looked at her and smiled, patting her hand in a comforting way. Moments later he was snoring. *The two men had not gotten much sleep last night either,* she supposed. Up in front, Atticus was asleep with the reigns in his hands. Fortunately, after the long Mount Temple driveway, it was a straight road; besides they were heading to camp, and the horses knew it. Philippa was looking out the window, enjoying the rapid pace of the carriage ride. Eventually her head had nodded and she too drifted off. The three of them slept for several hours.

They stopped at a place beside the road, next to a slowly moving river. It looked like a once popular rest area; overgrown but still welcoming. There were stone picnic tables and benches, and a shrine to the river goddess, carved with nymphs and acanthus leaves, and sunken partway into the earth. Larks were singing, and blackbirds were swooping through the rushes and reeds. There was a grove of crabapple trees, just coming into flower and filled with bees and butterflies. Some very old and gnarled rowan trees created a low canopy overheard.

Philippa got out of the carriage, stretched, and went off behind some bushes to take care of her personal business. When she returned, Justinian was sitting on a bench, studying a weathered map which he had laid upon the table. Atticus was repacking the carriage, strapping the luggage on top to make more space in the cabin. Philippa went directly to the library box and opened it. Justinian came over to peer inside.

"That's an impressive collection," he said. "I've never seen so many texts before."

Philippa scanned the collection, and pulled out a particularly ancient looking scroll. "This is it!"
She studied the text for a moment, and then declared, "Here it is. Precedence!"
She handed it to Justinian, who sat down again to read it. After a while he began shaking his head, but it was in amazement, not negation.

"Extraordinary!" he exclaimed. He handed her the scroll, and she put it back in the box.

Atticus came over with the banner and stuck it into the earth. He went back to the carriage and returned with the book.

"So?" he inquired, "are you enlisting her?"

Justinian shrugged. "I can't think of a reason not to."

Smiling, Atticus set the old book on the table. On its spine were the faded letters SPQR, representing the senate and the people of Rome. On the battered cover was the Aquila, the eagle, a symbol of virtue, a sign of Jupiter and the standard of the Emperor. He opened up the book. It contained a ledger, some documents, and a clever little quill and ink set, designed for traveling.

"What happens now?" asked Philippa. She could feel her heartbeat increase a little.

"You recite the Sacramentum. It's the oath of service." He handed her the text. She clutched it nervously. "Just read it out loud," Justinian said reassuringly.

Clearing her throat, she carefully spoke the words that were written on the paper.

"I do swear that I shall faithfully execute all that the Emperor decrees, as commanded by his Generals, that I shall never desert the Army, and that I shall not seek to avoid death while in the service of Rome."

"Well done. Now we fill in the details. Philippa Agrippa. Roman citizen. Child of Roman citizens. Father- what was your father's name?"

"Phillip Agrippa," she replied.

"Naturally," smiled Justinian. "And he was an immune, Army engineer, correct?" He continued writing. "British Roman. Deceased. Killed during active duty. And your mother's name?"

"Altheia Ilithia."

It seemed strange to say those words after all this time. Justinian asked, "How do you spell the first name?"

"A-l-t-h-e-i-a."

Justinian continued, "Etrurian Roman. Deceased. And your age?" She didn't respond.

"What's your age, Philippa?"

"Um... what's it supposed to be?"

"Well, at least sixteen."

"I'm sixteen," she quickly replied. *Bless me Mercury, for I am lying,* she prayed earnestly. Justinian and Atticus exchanged a glance.

"Sign here," Justinian said, handing her the quill. As she carefully wrote her name, Atticus produced a gold coin, worth about 25 Denarii, and slipped it into a coin purse. He handed it to Justinian, who gave it to her, announcing loudly, "By the command of the Emperors Flavius and Honorius, by the grace of Jupiter, Mars and Minerva, Philippa Agrippa is now a candidate soldier of Rome. Congratulations!"

Just like that, it was done.
"This calls for a celebration," said Atticus, pulling a basket from the carriage. As he unpacked it, Philippa said in surprise, "The leftovers! You brought them!"

They feasted happily on the last night's leavings, which seemed to taste even better today. As Atticus cleared up, Justinian went to a trunk which was attached to the back of the carriage and began rummaging around.

He returned with an armload of equipment. Some items seemed fairly new, but some looked (and smelled) positively ancient. There was a battered cuirass breastplate, the soldier's skirt called the pteruges, a pair of greaves for the shins, some arm guards, and a red neck-scarf called the focale. There was a plume-less helmet that looked like it had seen some action. It had a dented ridge running along the top from front to back, and places to attach a chin strap, which was missing. There was also a sword-belt with a sword.

"You can get better fitting gear in camp, but this will be a start," said Justinian. He stopped for a moment and asked, "Do you have some coin?"
She nodded. *She most certainly had some coin!* She had forgotten about that until just now.
Justinian continued, "Good. You may need to purchase whatever I can't provide you with. Be sure to get sandals that fit well." Looking at her feet, he continued, "You might have to special order them."

He inspected Philippa's gear. The cuirass was way oversized, but he cinched it down as well as he could, and fastened the skirt, which was a bit too long. He strapped the greaves onto her shins, and the guards onto her upper arms. He girded her with the sword belt, and placed the helmet on her head. It all felt heavy and strange, but not in a bad way. The soldier's skirt swung rhythmically as she walked. She drew the gladius from the scabbard. The blade was in better shape than she had expected. It was a real sword!

Justinian was talking. "Ares Mons training camp has been around for a long time. It hasn't always been in the same spot; military camps are subject to move, but it has been in its current location for over twenty-five years. As the population diminishes and Rome withdraws support, army camps in this remote part of Britannia Prima tend to stay where they were last put."

Justinian told her that it was around twelve miles, traveling east then north, from the entrance of Mount Temple to Ares Mons. He showed her on the map. She tried to act as if she understood. She hadn't left Mount Temple since she had arrived as a child. They'd had no horses, and no neighbors. There was no way to go anywhere even if she had wanted to leave.

Father Florian had once asked her where she had lived with her mother. She couldn't tell him, even looking at a map. She realized that, for all her book-learning, she had very little understanding of distance and direction, and she hoped that her training would include some basic navigation. She longed to be more worldly.

Justinian taught her to salute. Then he instructed her to take the uniform back off for now. He went to rummage for a bag to store her gear in. Atticus was clearing up the lunch. Philippa went to the carriage, grabbed her bundle, and disappeared behind the bushes again. She thought she had better get some of the coins out of the box, and put them in her new coin purse. She got the box out and opened it. She sifted through and grabbed a handful of silver and copper coins. Enough to seem solvent but not enough to look suspicious. She went to put them in her purse, but first she took out her enlistment coin. She put it in a little pocket that she had sewn into her brown tunic. Then she re-tied her bundle, and returned to the carriage.

They reached Ares Mons in the mid-afternoon. The road ended at a gate. Tall wooden palisades and stone walls stretched out in both directions. They stopped at the gate and Justinian got out of the carriage and spoke to the guards. He got back in and they continued.

Philippa tried to take it all in. There were groups of tents and huts at regular intervals. Most were plain, but then they passed some that were more ornate, with timbered structures, crenelated awnings, and brightly colored banners.

She saw soldiers. Some were marching in formation. Others were sparring and working on tactical skills. They passed an obstacle course, some archery targets, fire-pits, a poultry yard, horses in a pasture, a stable, and a vegetable garden. Then there was a saw mill and lumber yard, with piles of felled trees and dozens of neatly stacked palisade timbers.

They stopped by a large building and got out. On one side of it there was a long awning. Below it was a stable of carts, wheelbarrows and wagons. She saw two men by the wagons. One was talking and pointing and the other was making notes. There were neatly stacked piles of shovels, rakes and saws.

Justinian, Atticus and Philippa approached the entrance. There were fire barrels here and there along the way, some blazing, others just smoldering. Goats were wandering around, baa-ing loudly. She could hear the clash of weapons and the loud voices of men. It was all very different from Mount Temple!

"Wait here a moment." Justinian took her bag and went in. After several minutes he came back and motioned for her to follow. She entered a large room, full of shelves and trunks and stacks of gear. Philippa sniffed the air. She remembered one of the guests at Mount Temple, who had brought a hunting dog. After it had rained, the dog had carried a particular scent. This big room smelled a bit like the wet dog.

There was a large man, pale and bald, behind a counter. Justinian said, "Agrippa, this is the Quartermaster, Anselenus Markus. This is Tiro Philippa Agrippa." She saluted with fist over her heart, as Justinian had shown her. The quartermaster looked skeptical, nodding slightly in her direction.
"Here's some more gear," Justinian told her. "We've replaced the pteruges with a shorter one. There are some sandals that may fit. We've also got another cuirass for you to try, but you may end up having to special order one of them too. And look, they got a new shipment of red tunics and leggings. I think that these will fit you. Try them on."

She stepped behind a stack of shields, took off her brown clothes, and put on the red ones. The wool had that wet dog smell too, but it was soft. She re-appeared, and Justinian nodded in approval. He helped her put on all the uniform pieces. The new skirt fit perfectly. The cuirass fit only slightly better than the other one. The sandals too, were a little large. She cinched them down as tight as she could. The battered helmet's chinstrap and plume had been replaced.

When she was dressed, Justinian went to the wall of shields, chose one, and handed it to her. Meanwhile, Anselenus Markus had brought out a trunk. It already contained a bedroll, extra blankets, empty sacks, a soft white tunic, a towel, assorted toiletries, a flint and steel set, a copper pot, a parcel of salt, a ceramic cup, and a small shovel. She put her brown clothes in there too.

"You have some coin?" asked Justinian.
She reached under her belt, pulled out the coin purse, and showed him the contents. He picked out three silver coins and four copper ones. He handed them to the Quartermaster, who looked quite pleased. Anselenus Markus said to her, "Come by tomorrow and we'll take some measurements for the sandals. If you're still here, that is."

Atticus came in and helped to carry her gear. They returned to the carriage, stowed her trunk, and continued on the track, which made a circular loop around the camp. On the way, they passed the engineers and blacksmiths. There were siege engines, forges, anvils, and rows of iron tools. She saw barricades, bits of scaffolding, tent canvases, and other things that she didn't recognize. Justinian was talking.

"We'll go to meet the centurions. One of them will have to choose you. You may not work directly for him, but you'll be under his banner. There's no proper cohort here, there's not enough manpower; it's more of a reformed collection from several different centuries."

"What do you mean, a centurion has to choose me?" That statement was making her nervous.
"These days the centurions take turns picking the new recruits," he replied.
"But there's only me."
"So, they will have to fight over you!" He spoke lightly, but she thought that he was putting on a brave face, and that deep down he was afraid that no one would want her. He continued,

"Since the workers and builders need assistance and soldiers need skills, you will apprentice to work for one of them. On top of your regular training and studies of course. Your father was an engineer, so perhaps you'd be interested in that-"
Philippa cut him off, saying, "He was killed by one of his bridges, no thanks. Besides I'm not so good with math. I'm good at growing food. But I'd like to work with metal too. I'm interested in how things are made."

They arrived at the camp of the officers. It was the area with the elaborate tents she had noticed the first time around. They got out. Atticus removed the library and her trunk from the carriage. Justinian handed her the shield, and picked up the box of scrolls.

"They should be ready for you," he said. "I sent notification when we entered the gate."

A soldier appeared from one of the tents, saluted Justinian, did an about-face, and marched back into the tent. They followed. Justinian went first, one hand carrying the scroll box by its strap, the other on one end of the trunk, which now contained her bundle too. Then came Atticus, who was holding the other trunk handle. The recruiting book was perched on top, and in his other hand he carried the conscribit staff. Philippa followed them. They went right through the tent and came out the other end. They were in a sort of courtyard, surrounded by the officers' tents. Justinian and Atticus set down the trunk. Atticus stuck the staff into a holder, and Justinian picked up the book.

Four centurions were seated at a table, beneath the standard of a bull. They stood. Silver bosses held their red capes in place. They approached, and then they stared.

Philippa saluted. She tried to look calm and capable, but she kind of felt like an imposter, a little girl in dress-up soldier clothing. The oversized cuirass and shoes weren't helping. The centurions acted amused.
"Justinian Justinius, what on earth have you brought us?" one of them asked. "Is recruitment so difficult these days that you have to bring us a girl to play soldier?"
"She's not an ordinary girl," Justinian replied, "and she can do more than just play. I'm submitting her for decanus training."
"That's a laugh," said a short fellow with a closely cropped red beard. "I don't want her."
"Well, I certainly don't!" said another one. He was tall, and wore an eyepatch.

Philippa could feel her face getting hot. Before the other two could comment, another centurion appeared from one of the tents. He was rather handsome, if grizzled, with dark skin and grey hair. His face was deeply lined, and there was a blotchy scar on his left cheek. He was accompanied by a tall pale soldier.

"Sorry I'm late. Greetings, Justinian Justinius." Then seeing Philippa he stopped, looking very surprised. Before the others could say something derogatory, Justinian announced, in his best orator's voice,
"I present to you, Philippa Agrippa, citizen of Rome, daughter of Philip Agrippa, engineer immune, deceased in the service of the Empire."

The four centurions were making rude noises. Justinian raised his voice and continued, "I officially submit her as candidate for soldier and decanus. She has studied since childhood with the famous scholar Father Florian-"

The new arrival interrupted, addressing Philippa directly-
"You studied with Father Florian? Florian the Red? The follower of the teachings of Zino of Citium?"
"Yes, sir," she replied, "but I believe that his later ideas on Stoicism were more aligned with those of Marcus Aurelias than Zino of Citium's."
The centurion looked impressed.

"Father Florian is well-known for his philosophical writings," he said, "even in Rome." The others fell silent. Justinian quickly added,
"And she comes equipped with Father Florian's entire library, which he left in her possession." Justinian motioned to Atticus, who opened the scroll box to reveal the contents.

"And, in this scroll here," Justinian said, pulling it from its slot, "is precedence for the role of the Virgin Warrior, dating back to the fourth century BC, when female Roman citizens of Etrurian descent fought for the Republic against the Samnites at the Battle of Mount Gaurus."
He opened the old text and unrolled it on top of the book that he held. He showed it to the centurion, who read the relevant passage. Justinian continued, "Tiro Agrippa has long since taken vows of chastity to Hygieia and Hestia, as well as vows of service to Jupiter and Mars."

There was a moment of silence, broken by the grey-haired centurion.
"She has said the oath and received the coin?"
"She has," said Justinian.
"Then I'll take her."

There was an outcry of derision from the other centurions. The learned man addressed Philippa formally, "Welcome, Tiro Agrippa, to our training cohort, composed in part by the newly reformed Tungrian of Britannia Prima, comitatenses of the Sixth Legion, Victorious, Sud Est. All honor to the Empire. All honor to Emperors Flavius Theodosius and Augustus Honorius."
He smiled at her, and continued, "I am Centurion Aries Erasmus. You'll be under my command, as long as you pass the physical, which you should, you look healthy."
The other centurions walked away muttering. Justinian gave Philippa's documents to Aries Erasmus with visible relief. Aries Erasmus motioned to his aide, who had been standing nearby. "This is Septimius Gallus. He will tell you what to do next. You don't mind if I keep these scrolls safe for you?"
"No, sir."
"And it's alright if I study them?"
"Yes, Centurion Erasmus, I'm sure that Father Florian would be honored."
"Then I will see you on the training grounds." She saluted him, and he returned the salute. Septimius Gallus picked up the library, saying, "I'll be right back," and he and the centurion disappeared into his tent.

Justinian was happy. "That's a relief. We did it. You did it, Tiro Agrippa!" He patted her back. "I'm sure you'll do fine. When I return, you'll be soldier."

"Justinian, are you leaving?" she asked with concern.

"Oh yes, I must keep moving. I'm going home for the planting season, but then we're off on a tour of the region to find more recruits. I'm not out of trouble yet, but thanks to you I have another chance. If all goes well, I will see you in six months."

"How many new recruits will you need to find?"

"At least ten."

"In that case," she said, "I will pray for you to find twenty!"

Justinian laughed delightedly. Then he said, "We must be on our way."

"Goodbye, Philippa Agrippa," said Atticus.

"Goodbye, Atticus. May the Gods be with you." She turned to Justinian and saluted. He saluted back, and then they were gone.

Septimius Gallus returned with two other soldiers. Philippa saluted. Septimius said, "You don't need to salute us. We're not officers. In the ranks we do this-" He extended his hand and gripped her forearm. She clasped his in return. The two soldiers picked up her trunk. They all walked back through the tent and out the way they came in. Septimius turned to the soldiers and said, "Wait here." They set down the trunk and stood by it.

Philippa followed him to a large white tent nearby. The banner in front displayed the staff and serpent of Aesculapius. "Just a moment," he said, and went inside. A few minutes later, he reappeared and motioned her in. He had clearly briefed the doctor about the unusual recruit. The physician acted unsurprised that she was a female. He listened to her breathe, felt her pulse, and had her run in place. The oversized sandals made it awkward, but she managed. He looked in her mouth and ears. He had her read some letters and numbers that were posted on the far wall, felt her head, and pronounced her healthy. They returned to join the soldiers, who picked up the trunk.

Then they turned on a path which led into the center of the camp. It went through a close grouping of tents, and then into a slightly more open area, with the tents more spread out. They turned up a lane. A sign read: Apollo Row I-IX, and it showed a picture of the sun. They passed eight tents which looked unoccupied. At the end of the section, they stopped and went in to number IX.

It was a snug little pavilion, smaller than the other tents. It had a cot, and a little table and chair. On the table there was a ceramic jug, a wash basin, and a mug, and there was a broom with a dustpan by the door. Against the wall across from the door was a small empty altar.

"These are your quarters," said Septimius. "You don't have a servant?" She shook her head. "Then you'll have just enough space. There's storage under the bed. Here's the stove." He pointed to a grey metal box on legs. It had a tube coming out of the back and going through an opening in the tent. "Firewood is out back. You know how to make a fire?" She nodded. Septimius continued, "Make sure the chimney doesn't get blocked. Fire safety is crucial. Do you understand?" She nodded, and asked,
"Where is the nearest water?"
"There's a cistern in between each row of tents. You've got several nearby." Pulling back a divider curtain, he continued. "Here's a bucket. Look, you've even got your own little tub. And you've got your own latrine, just out back. You'll see, it's very private. This tent was set up for a female visitor. It was used by the thin-striped tribune's niece when she was here. That was a couple of years ago."

He closed the curtain. "You can unpack later. Leave your helmet, sword and shield here. Let's go find your command chain. And some dinner." She took off her helmet. Her head felt like it was floating. She set the helmet with her sword and shield on the cot and they exited.

They made their way to the dining hall, past rows of supply tents. There was a scaffolded A-frame with game meat curing on it, and an open area under an awning, stacked with water barrels, amphorae, and wine casks. As they approached the large dining hall, it was growing dark. Torches and lamps were being lit all over the camp. It was enchanting to see. As they entered the dining hall, Philippa saw some altars, lit with burning lamps. On one side, there was a large altar with icons of Jupiter, Mars and Minerva. On the other side were two smaller altars, one decorated with the bull of Mithras, and one with the anchor of the Christ.

The room was filled with long tables and benches. Men were beginning to file in. Servers were busy setting out large trenchers of food. Septimius pointed to a far table where two soldiers were seated, one tall and thin with shaggy blond hair, the other stocky and muscular with short dark hair. The men were looking at some documents.

"There they are," Septimius said. He and Philippa approached them.
"Salvete, gentlemen," he said. The men rose.

"Salve, Septimius Gallus." The soldiers exchanged arm clasps. Septimius introduced the men to Philippa. She exchanged arm clasps with the tall one. She saw that the other was some kind of officer, but before she could salute, he too exchanged arm clasps with her.

"This is Senovara Domini, and Marshall Tristanus Albia. They will be in charge of you and your training." He handed Senovara, the tall one, a document, then motioned for them all to sit. Senovara added the document to the others and then tucked them all into a messenger bag.

"Welcome, Philippa Agrippa," he said. "I'll be in charge of turning you into a soldier. With a little help from Tristanus here." Tristanus nodded at her and smiled. No one was making a big deal about her being a female. *So far so good,* she thought. Senovara continued,
"We'll begin with marching. Drill formations and movement strategy. You'll like it. Then physical strength and agility training. Maybe not as fun as marching, but you'll be stronger when we're done."

Tristanus said, "Then it's my turn. I'm your weapons trainer. You have a sword?" She nodded. "Make sure it's clean and rust free, and put it in your trunk for now," he continued. "We'll work with wooden gear first."
Senovara said, "You'll need a vocation to assist with. Is there something you're already good at? Or something you want to learn?"
"I'm good at growing food." She was good at cooking it too, but she wasn't going to mention it. She had no desire to work in the kitchen. "And I'd like to learn metalsmithing."

Septimius said, "Good, it sounds like a plan. Sorry to be so abrupt, but I smell fish stew, and I would like to get some before it's just broth." They all four rose and got in the food line. Several soldiers stared and whispered as she went by, but for the most part everyone was polite. They reached the servers. She got a small cup of the stew, a chunk of cheese, some hazelnuts, a pile of curly green cress, and a piece of bread with bramble jam. To drink, there was weak red wine and water.

Returning to their spot, they ate quickly, as soldiers tend to do. They cleared the table and Septimius said, "I had better get back to my centurion." To Philippa he said, "Do you think you can find the way to your tent?"
"Ummm... I think so."
"We'll walk you there," said Tristanus. "Where are you?"
"Apollo IX," she said. At least she remembered that. She thanked Septimius, and he bid them goodnight.

On the way out, Senovara grabbed a lit candle in a holder. They walked in easy silence. She was relieved, and a little surprised, that no one had asked her any personal questions. She had heard that for the most part, the regular Roman soldiers were serious about honor and integrity. It seemed to be true, so far anyway.

They reached Apollo IX and went in. "It's a little dusty," said Tristanus. "And chilly."
Senovara set the candle on the table and asked, "Is that your trunk?"
"Yes."
Very quickly, the two men had opened up the tent, swept it out, dusted the surfaces, unpacked her trunk, made her bed, filled her water containers, and lit a fire. Tristanus inspected her sword, then put it into the trunk and closed it. She was impressed by their thoughtfulness and efficiency.

"Thank you," she said. "That was very kind. I really appreciate it."
"Well," said Tristanus with a grin, "in a couple of weeks, when we are torturing you, remember how kind we seemed at first." She laughed weakly.
"Breakfast at eight, training at nine," said Senovara.
"Goodnight soldier," said Tristanus.
"Goodnight," she replied.

She was suddenly so tired she could barely stand. She sat on her cot. The white tunic was laid out, so she figured that was the nightgown. She slipped out of the uncomfortable oversized sandals without even unbuckling them. She unclasped and removed her armor. She took off the red clothing, and put on the nightgown. Then she went out back to her privy. She came in and washed her hands and face, brushed her hair and cleaned her teeth. She set her gear carefully under the bed, except the helmet, which didn't fit so she put it under the table. She opened the trunk, rummaged in her clothes bundle, and found a hand cloth.

Wrapped up inside it was the bronze sculpture of Jupiter, no taller than her palm, that she had found in the temple garden. She had tried to clean it; it was green and blotchy in places, and indistinct with age, but it was clearly an image of Jove, and it still stood on its own. She set it upon the little altar, and added her collection of feathers and stones. She whispered,
"Thank you, Papa."

The bed was more comfortable than she had expected, or maybe she was just that tired. As she drifted off, she thought, *I did it. I'm going to be a Roman soldier. I am living my destiny.*

Chapter Four - Ares Mons

This was all a terrible mistake, thought Philippa. *I should never have tried to be a soldier.* The current situation was causing her to doubt her chosen path. What did she know about destiny? She was just an orphan girl, after all. She was even wondering if was too late for the Sisters of Charity to find her a family in a town. If only she hadn't made such a big deal about being a soldier! If only she hadn't fought so hard for this opportunity. It would be too humiliating to quit. She thought of all those who had gone out of their way to help her. The idea of letting them down made her feel terribly guilty. And what would become of Justinian if she washed out? He might be dismissed after all. Atticus would be without a job too.

It was the sixth week of training. There had been some bumps at the beginning, and some unique challenges, but this was the only thing that had actually defeated her: she couldn't do a pull-up! She had to do five in a row and she couldn't even do one. She had tried and tried.

She had managed to pass all the other parts of the obstacle course. They would have been much easier without full armor, but she understood why that was a requirement. Her legs were strong, and she could easily run up the wooden slope and jump to the next platform. She wasn't too intimidated by heights, so she conquered the challenges that took place on the wooden training tower. And she didn't mind getting wet and crawling through the mud, so she did alright on the tests that required her to navigate through the swamp.

Senovara had given her a pair of small weights the first week to build up her arm strength. She used them frequently, and she could tell the difference. Things that once seemed heavy were easier to lift. She was able to hold the sword and shield up for much longer. Not her own sword and shield, she hadn't reached that point yet. It was the sword and shield from the camp's old collection of wooden gear, which for training purposes were nearly twice as heavy as the real things. She could barely lift them at first, now she could use them for an entire five minutes without her arms and back feeling like they were on fire.

Aside from the pull-up bar, the horizontal ladder test had been her greatest challenge. Placed eight feet above the ground, trainees were required to make it across the entire twenty rungs without dropping. Senovara had demonstrated. She'd watched him swing easily from end to end, chatting with her the entire time. "You don't have to grab each rung; you can skip every other one."

He showed her what that looked like. "The trick is to get a rhythm going." He'd finished the demonstration with a graceful swooping jump, not even winded.

The first time she had tried, she barely made it from one rung to the next. It had taken three weeks for her to finally complete the test from one end to the other. It must have been excruciating for Senovara to watch, but he was patient. When she finally passed, she skipped no rungs. She had no rhythm. She had slowly and awkwardly pulled herself from one end to the next.

"You did it!" called Senovara. As she dropped to the ground, he had added, "Good thing there's no time limit!"

But now the pull-up bar seemed to have defeated her.
"Take a break," Senovara said now. "Have a rest, do some stretching, and we'll try again in a little while." He disappeared. She sat on a bench and sipped water from her canteen. Dejectedly, she stared at her feet. *My feet,* she mused. *They had been the first problem.*

The morning after she arrived, she had been awakened at dawn by pain. Because her sandals didn't fit, her feet were covered in fierce raw blisters, some of which were stuck to the bedclothes. Extracting her feet from the bedding with a muffled cry of pain, she had surveyed the damage. She wasn't sure what to do, but she knew that she wouldn't be able to put those sandals back on any time soon. She had dressed in her small clothes and her red tunic and trousers, but there didn't seem to be much point in adding anything else when she couldn't even walk.

When she didn't show up for breakfast, Senovara had come to her tent to find out why. He called to her through the closed tent flap. "Tiro Agrippa?"
"Yes."
"It's Senovara Domini. May I come in?"
"Yes, sir."

She was sitting on the chair, and her feet were in the washbasin, which she had set on the floor in front of her.
She began to say, "I'm sorry-" but he cut her off impatiently. He had obviously seen this situation before.
"It isn't your fault, it's the Quartermaster's. Anselenus Markus has got one new trainee to fit, and he couldn't even get that right."
"He knew the sandals didn't fit, but they were the smallest pair he could find. He told me to come back and get measured for new ones today." She added dispiritedly, "If I was still here."

"Show me," said Senovara. She lifted her feet from the basin and he inspected them. "It isn't so bad," he said encouragingly. "We'll get you fixed up in no time. Is that salt water?" She nodded. "Good," he continued. "Go ahead and let your feet dry." He whisked back out of the tent.

When he returned, she was lying on the cot, feet propped up on her folded towel. Another man came in before him. He moved very quickly. She saw by his white clothes and the insignia of serpent and staff on his satchel that he was a healer.

The man set his bag down, and pulled out some thin gauze strips and a candle. He handed the candle to Senovara, who went to the stove to find an ember that he could coax into a flame. Then the healer deftly wrapped her injuries, securing each piece of gauze with a drop of candle wax.

He said, "Now don't you worry, soldier. Once these wounds are wrapped, you just keep them clean. I'll leave you extra bandages. You can keep the candle too." He extinguished the flame, continuing, "I understand that you need to get measured for custom sandals. Be sure to get that done today. By the time they're ready, your feet will be too. Where are your civilian shoes?"

She pointed to the pair of soft tan sandals that she had left by the door. "Right, you can put those on if you need to step outside. But don't try to go anywhere for a couple of days. Give yourself a chance to heal."
With that, he scooped up his bag and was gone before she could even thank him. Senovara said, "I'll be back," and he too left the tent.

She lay on the cot. Her feet felt somewhat better already, and she was relieved that she wouldn't have to put those sandals back on. She was wondering how she would get any food today, when Senovara returned. He had brought her a breakfast tray! A boiled egg, a dish of salted porridge, bread with butter and honey, and a cup of milk. He set them on the table as she moved to the chair. He also set some documents on the table.

"You might as well study while you're laid up. You'll be getting a visit from Jacamus Sands this morning. He's the supply clerk. He'll take your shoe measurements. I'll check on you later."

"Thank you, Senovara Domini," she'd replied. With that he was gone again. She ate her breakfast, looking at the documents. One was a list of rules.

The Roman Soldier

The Roman Army depends upon each and every Soldier to do his duty:

The Roman Soldier is always prepared.
The Roman Soldier understands the chain of command.
The Roman Soldier knows that communication is essential to victory.
The Roman Soldier gains as many advantages as possible before battle.
The Roman Soldier gathers intelligence from multiple sources.
The Roman Soldier misinforms and misdirects the enemy.
The Roman Soldier never lets the enemy know his true goal.
The Roman Soldier never deserts his post.
The Roman Soldier never steals from the Army.
The Roman Soldier never abandons his weapons.
The Roman Soldier never flees from battle.

She liked that. There was also a list of apportionments:

Contubernium. A squad of eight men, led by a decanus.
Century. A group of 8-10 contuberni, led by a centurion.
Cohort. A group of six century, roughly 480 men.
Legion. A legion of 10 cohorts, roughly 5,000 men.
Horse Legion. The cavalry unit of a legion consisting of 120 men.

Looking at the long numerals made her sleepy. She focused on learning the rules for now. She had just gotten them memorized, when there was a voice at the door.
"Philippa Agrippa? It's Jacamus Sands, come to measure your feet."
"Yes, come in please."

Jacamus Sands was short, with red hair and freckles. He greeted Philippa with an arm clasp. "Sorry to hear about your badly fitting sandals. We'll get you some new ones that fit perfectly, I promise." While he spoke, he had wrapped various colored ropes around her feet and legs, simulating sandal straps. He marked the interstices with chalk.

"Now I'll have to ask you to stand." He set a piece of vellum on the floor and motioned for her to step onto it. He took the chalk and made some swift outlines of her feet, made a few more measurements, and wrote them on a pad. While she was still standing he got down on the floor and peered at her arches. He motioned for her to sit back down, then he wrapped the ropes up with the vellum and chalk and put them in his tunic.

"Now, what else do you need?" he asked. He held the pad and graphite stick.
"Well, I would like to get another set or two of red tops and bottoms. And some whites ones, if you have them." He nodded, making notes as she spoke. "And I don't have a cloak yet."
"Red or brown?" he asked.
"Brown, I suppose. And maybe an extra scarf or two? And a second nightgown?" He nodded.

"How much will that cost?" She was prepared with her coin purse.
He asked, "How much coin did Anselenus Markus get from you already?" She told him. He looked a bit cross, and said, "I think that should cover it." She drew a silver coin and tried to hand it to Jacamus Sands.
"Well, this is for you then. Thank you for coming here to help me."
"That won't be necessary." She didn't lower her hand.
"Please take it. It will make me feel better." He laughed and accepted the coin.
"I'll get these measurements to the cobbler right away. Goodbye for now, Philippa Agrippa."
"Goodbye, Jacamus Sands. Thank you."

Her new sandals had arrived five days later.
She had spent the first two days studying, and exercising her upper body. On the afternoon of the second day, Jacamus Sands showed up with her signaculum, her identification tag. Inscribed on it was 'Philippa Agrippa, of the Temple Mount'. It was carried in a soft leather pouch, and hung on a thin cord.

On the third day, she had put on her red clothes and her civilian shoes, and accompanied Senovara to the agricultural department. She spent the morning planting carrots and celery, distributing the tiny seeds evenly across the long neat furrows, gently covering them with earth as she went. The garden supervisors praised her quick work. Right as she finished, the rain began, so they didn't have to water the new seeds. The garden supervisors then decided that her presence was auspicious, and invited her back anytime. She ran through the rain to the mess hall, and ate lunch alone, self-conscious in her damp clothes and non-regulation shoes. As she was leaving, Senovara appeared.

"Well done in the gardens today. Sorry I missed you. They loved your work. Are you up for more walking?" She nodded; her feet had mostly healed. "Then let's get your cuirass and go to see the armorer."

It had stopped raining. They swung by her tent and she grabbed her cuirass, and her coin purse, in case this would cost money. She couldn't quite figure out exactly what required coin and what did not, but she remembered rule one, 'The Roman Soldier is always prepared'.

They walked for some time. It was the opposite way from the dining tent and gardens. She'd only seen this side of the post from the carriage on that first day. They passed the place where the catapults, battering rams, and other siege weapons were stored. Then they approached the industrial workshops. Under a huge awning she saw carts full of hardware, barrels of coal and ore, and stacked iron ingots. There were large crucibles, mounds of sand, and a forest of cranes and towers, connected by diagonally running troughs.
They reached a metal shed, surrounded by a corroded but still solid iron fence. The yard was full of sheet-metal awnings covering concrete molds, and barrels of sand, oil, and water. There were forges of various sizes. Some were being used by smiths.

The air smelled hot and sharp. Philippa liked the acrid odor. There was a guard at the entrance to the shed. He stood aside as they went in. They first came to a counter in front of a metal wall, behind which nothing could be seen. An attendant at the counter wrote down their names and their business. Motioning them in, he pulled a cable, and part of the wall slid sideways with a great screeching sound. They stepped inside, and the door shut noisily behind them.

They were in a large and well-lit hall. The walls were twice as tall as a man. The red-tiled roof was much higher still, held up by six concrete columns, and overhanging the walls, so that there was light all around, but the rain stayed out. The air was hot and smelled like burning coal, wax and pitch. She saw more forges, powered hammers, grinding and polishing wheels, and other crank-driven machines. There were dozens of racks, covered with hammers, tongs, pliers, and other tools, as well as a huge array of anvils, all attached to sturdy tree stumps. Some were traditional anvil shapes, while others seemed to bloom like a forest of metal mushrooms. One corner of the room was crammed with smaller workbenches, and covered with more diminutive tools. Behind a tall folding screen there were kilns, and trays of colorful ground glass for enameling.

Philippa's attention was drawn to the gallery of weapons that seemed to cover every inch of one of the long walls. There were swords, knives, hatchets, and spears, displayed in a wide variety of styles and sizes. On the opposite wall, in equal numbers, were helmets, cuirasses, chain mail, and various types of segmented armor called lorica.
"Impressive, isn't it?" said Senovara. She nodded, smiling.

By the closest concrete post, there was a great drafting table, piled with sketches, measuring tools, renderings, charcoal, chalk, pens, calipers, bundles of wax, and sheets of burlap. A large muscular fellow greeted them.
"Philippa Agrippa," said Senovara, "this is Hestius Attacroni, Master Smith."

Hestius took the cuirass she was holding, and looked her over, saying,
"It's been many years since I made a breastplate for a woman." He put the cuirass aside.
"Never mind this; we'll be starting from scratch. I'll need to get a mold."

He motioned to an assistant, who carried a huge ladle of hot wax to the table and set it down. The assistant dropped a large sheet of burlap into the wax and swished it around with two pairs of tongs. He then fished it out and draped it over a wooden bar to cool. The warm wax dripped off, making little conical towers beneath. Meanwhile, Hestius took a sheet of thick fabric, already heavily impregnated with wax, and began flexing it over some coals in a nearby forge.

"This will be warm," he said, "but it won't burn you, I promise. Forgive me, but I have to get up close and personal."
Then he took the fabric and without further ado, slapped it onto her chest, squeezing and smoothing it until it followed her form. It was bit of a shock, but she managed to stay calm. "Right, now, deep breath!" he said. Philippa inhaled, and the assistant brought the waxed burlap, slapped that on top of the fabric, and both men commenced to squeezing, pulling, and smoothing the layers.

"You can exhale now. Breathe normally, but stand still."

She let out her breath, feeling a bit lightheaded. Her entire torso was hot, but not unbearably. The assistant waved a large wooden fan at her, cooling the wax. Then he and Hestius grabbed the waxed sheets and lifted them away carefully, so as to not distort the form.

"There you are," said Hestius, holding up the mold of her torso. He lay it down on a pile of sawdust to cool the rest of the way. "We'll forge it in white bronze. Give us a week or two to make it. I'll let you know when it's time for a fitting."

Senovara said, "Actually, trainee Agrippa would like to learn to assist here in the forge. May I leave her with you this afternoon?"

Hestius looked at her and said, "Sure. She looks like she could make some nails."

Thus began Philippa's time as a nail-smith. The assistant showed her how to make a tapered four-sided nail with a head. The length of iron bar had to be heated until it was glowing red, but not so hot that it burnt up. Then it was held with tongs while being hammered upon, quickly before it cooled, turning it occasionally. The bar was four-sided; each plane needed to be drawn to a taper. Then the piece was cut off with a different hammer, a sharp one, at just the right length, and stuck into a metal cube with a hole in it. The bit sticking out of the top was then hammered into a nailhead.

It took over an hour and a dozen or so failures before she managed to turn out an acceptable nail. She showed it happily to the shop assistant, who said, "Good. Now make fifty of them."
She managed to make eight before she had to stop. Her right arm felt like it was going to fall off, and her ears were ringing. She found Hestius, and showed him the nails.
"That's a fine start," he said. "Come back whenever you want. We can never have too many nails."

Her sandals arrived right on time. They were a bit stiff at first, but she could tell that they fit well. Jacamus Sands brought them to her, along with the other gear she had ordered. Dressed in everything but her breastplate, she had begun to march in the early mornings with a group of four decani who had eight men apiece. The decani took turns calling the cadence. Even though she was still a trainee, she was scheduled for leadership, so she was also put in the rotation. She quickly picked up the routine. Calling out orders came naturally to her, perhaps from telling Tomasen what to do every day for so many years. The others liked her voice and her marching songs. She drilled with them each morning.

Afterwards, if there were no classes to attend, she would go to work in the gardens until lunch. After lunch, there was physical training, and then she would go to the forge to make nails, and to watch her cuirass take shape. She would gaze in fascination as Master Hestius alternately heated and hammered a piece of bronze, comparing it frequently to the wax mold, until it gradually took the shape of her torso.

One day it was finished; heat treated and polished, she took it to the leather-men to get it fitted with rings and straps. The next day, finally in complete uniform, she had modeled it for Hestius. "Excellent. Now, be sure not to gain any weight!" The big man had winked at her.

Gear fighting had been added to her morning schedule, right after drilling. In full uniform, hoisting the heavy wooden sword and shield was difficult. She couldn't do it for very long, but she liked to think that she was slowly but surely getting stronger. Tristanus was in charge; she wouldn't have blamed him if he was frustrated with her, but he was always patient and encouraging. So it had gone for five weeks, until afternoon physical training had moved from the field-work to the obstacle course, and her vexation began.

After all my hard work, she thought, *will I be defeated by a pull-up bar?*

Senovara returned. He had brought Tristanus with him. She groaned inwardly. Tristanus Albia was a Master of weapons. He was the First Marshall of the entire camp, and an expert strategist. And he had been summoned because a trainee couldn't do a pull-up. She was mortified.

Senovara left them alone. Tristanus approached. She stood and greeted him,
"Hail, Tristanus Albia."
"Hail, Philippa Agrippa." They clasped forearms.
"Let's sit down for a bit," he said, motioning to the wooden bench. They both sat. "I understand you are having trouble with the pull-up." Seeing that she looked chagrined, he continued.
"It's nothing to be ashamed of. Many men can't do it either, at first. I think that it's probably an especially difficult move for a female." He turned and looked at her directly.
"I believe that you have the physical strength. I think it's something else that's lacking. Something like an intensity of desire."

"But I really want to do it!" she exclaimed.
"And why is that?" he asked gently.
"So I can pass my physical tests. So I can be a soldier."
"And why do you want to be a soldier?"
"Well... so I can devote myself to service."
"Admirable. And... who or what do you serve?"
"Rome."
"What does that mean to you?"
She thought for a moment. "It means working for a right and just cause. Serving the good, and protecting the innocent."
"Protecting them from what?"
"Well... enemies. Bad people. Predators and evil-doers."

There was silence for a moment. Then Tristanus said,
"I don't pretend to know your life. But I can see that you are an independent

woman trying to find her way in a man's world. Have predators and evil-doers ever come after you personally? I don't need to know, I just want you to think about it. Think about it, and if something makes you angry or agitated, bring that energy to the pull-up bar. You are pulling yourself up. The predators and evil-doers want to keep you down, but you are coming out on top."

As he spoke, he had taken her hand and led her to the bars. The lowest bar was just out of her reach. She usually used a step. Tristanus didn't bother with the step; he lifted her in the air himself. She put her hands on the bar, and he said,

"For the innocent. To defeat predators and evil-doers." She was thinking about Jenisec. She had been so afraid of him. She thought of his groping hands, his stinking breath. He dared to accost her in the temple. Her temple! She suddenly let out a groan, and with a great convulsion, she pulled her body up until her chin was over the bar.

"Yes!" cried Tristanus, "keep going!" She repeated it, with a great effort. Then, twisting and grunting loudly, she pulled herself up one more time. Then she dropped, hanging by her arms. She couldn't go on.

Tristanus called, "That's it! Two more. The predators and evil-doers aren't getting away with it!" She wriggled and squirmed, and with what felt like the last bit of her strength, managed one more. She hung from the bar, shaking and crying, drenched with sweat.

"One more!" he cried. "For the innocents. Because you're a Roman soldier, working for a right and just cause." She roared so loudly that some men on the other end of the obstacle course turned to stare, as she thrust herself into the air one last time. Then sobbing, she dropped to the ground. Tristanus caught her.

"Congratulations, Philippa Agrippa," he said. "You're a Roman soldier."

Chapter Five - Apollo Row

The weeks passed by. Philippa had a semi-regular schedule. She gradually grew in strength and confidence. She learned everything she was supposed to. She tried archery, and discovered that she was a natural. She practiced everyday with her bow.

She was promoted to decanus, although she had no men of her own yet. She had quite a bit of free time. Her tiny tent had become a home. She had built a campfire near the path, and put large flat stones around it. The gardeners gave her fruit and vegetables, honey and eggs. She had gone to the kitchen and begged for a big old skillet with a lid. Behind the dining hall, she bought a big mixing bowl, plus a spoon and spatula, from one of the cooks. She made cakes and shared them with the gardeners, the cooks, the metalsmiths, and her trainers.

She fed grain to the birds and learned their songs. She found new pretty rocks and feathers to keep Jupiter company on the little altar. The garden crew had also given her some flowers and vegetable starts, which she had planted on Apollo Row. The other Apollo tents had remained vacant. Her neighborhood was peaceful and quiet. She knew nearly everyone who lived in the sparsely populated training camp. They all seemed polite and earnest. She had heard that there could be corruption and backstabbing in the Roman Army, but thankfully there didn't seem to be any here.

She had finally moved past the wooden gear, and was now training with real, but dull-edged, metal blades. She used her own gladius for solo drilling on her own time. She sharpened and polished it the way that the metalsmiths had shown her. One day, while repacking her trunk, she remembered the coin in the pocket of her brown tunic. Her enlistment coin. She tucked it into the pouch with her signaculum.

On a morning in late September, she was in the orchard gathering chestnuts, when she heard someone calling her name. It was Justinian! He and Atticus had returned, and had come to find her. She hugged them both.

She said to Justinian, "You must have found some recruits!".
"Guess how many?" he asked. Before she could reply, Atticus exclaimed,
"Twenty! Twenty recruits! Because you prayed for us, Philippa!"
"Well, I don't know if that's why," she said happily, "but congratulations!"

"It was an auspicious prediction, my dear!" said Justinian.

"And they are all here for you!" said Atticus.

"What do you mean, for me?"

"They are going to be your men!" said Justinian. "They are moving into Apollo Row as we speak."

So began the winter training cycle. In the wet and freezing weather, it was much tougher than the spring training regiment. In less uncertain times it would have been put off until the next year, but these days there was a feeling of urgency, brought on by a sense of doubt about the future, and waiting didn't seem like an option. The other decani and their new miletes had already gotten their marching orders. Their four centurions had gone with them. They were sent further west along the southern coast, much to their disappointment. The centurions had hoped to be sent east, to Londinium, Dubris or Durovernum, closer to civilization, closer to the ships that would eventually take them back to the continent. Instead, they were being deployed to try and rebuild the ranks of Durnovia, in defense against the Hibernian tribes, who were coming from the western waters and attacking Roman settlements. They had all left in early October, after the harvest was finished.

So it was just Decanus Agrippa and her twenty young recruits, marching and training through the wet and cold winter. When they weren't training, the men worked in the kitchen and stables. The camp had never seemed crowded to her, but now it felt really empty.

We might be the last ones, ever, she had mused. The sense of uncertainty about the future had grown into more of a feeling of finality, as Roman supplies and payroll to Ares Mons seemed to have abruptly ended. She thought of the gardens, the orchards, and the workshops, the soldiers who had created them, and the earnest locals who supported them. It made her want to cry to think that it would all soon be abandoned. It really did look as if the Great Roman Empire was coming to an end.

She comforted herself with the fact that, if she had lived during its heyday, she would never have gotten to be a soldier. Or even a temple acolyte. That brought Tomasen to mind, and remembering that perpetual boy had made her think of her trainees. They were a real mix. There were farmers, shepherds, spoiled second sons, impoverished city dwellers, and lost souls.

None had any sort of military background. Aside from the farm boys, they were completely undisciplined. They were gullible and childish. She was astonished at their inability to engage in critical thinking. They weren't actually stupid, just thoughtless, not thoughtless in an inconsiderate sort of way; but actually devoid of thought. Like Tomasen, most of them had to be taught every basic skill. Unlike Tomasen, thankfully, most of them seemed capable of learning, and developing those skills.

Apollo Row had been noisy and messy when they first moved in. It was aggravating. Even though they were her own age or older, she thought of them as children. Whenever they started to really get on her nerves, she would find herself thinking about Jenisec.

Children only learn what they are taught, she understood that. *Who knows*, she thought, *Jenisec might have been alright, except for the tutelage of evil-doers.* Why, she herself might have turned out evil in the wrong hands!

She felt responsible for the moral development of these young soldiers. Her superiors knew she took that seriously; that's why they gave her these men, to help mold their characters. Gradually, discipline began to take hold, and camaraderie had grown. The row of numbered tents looked sharp now, and the young men took pride in keeping things squared away.

She had hardly seen Centurion Aries Erasmus while she was in basic training. He would show up every once in a while on the training ground to say hello, or to mention something he'd read in the scrolls, but that was it. Now she spent a great deal of time with him, in his rather luxurious quarters, looking at big maps, and moving toy troops around on his war-room table. And eating grapes, which he seemed to always have on hand, no matter the scarcity or season.

The centurion was determined to fill the gaps in Philippa's military knowledge, which mostly had to do with directions and measurements. She tried her best to listen. She came away with a very basic understanding of navigation and military strategy. Also a love for grapes, which might not be easy to fulfill once Aries Erasmus wasn't part of her life anymore, for unlike the other centurions, he would not be accompanying his decanus. He had officially released her, and given her the command of her soldiers. He reluctantly handed Father Florian's library back to her. He would be staying at Ares Mons until the very end.

In the early spring, the new soldiers graduated from training. Awaiting orders, Philippa spent much of her free time in the comfortable atmosphere of Aries' large tent, conversing with him, Septimius Gallus, Senovara Domini and Tristanus Albia. They knew a great deal, and were happy to advise her about what she was getting into.

Then the orders came, from the General of Vindavia Nova, which, they told her, was a small semi-permanent garrison, northwest of Ares Mons. It was located in a remote river valley, along a broad tributary of the Trisantonis. They had never been there, and it had been many years since Ares Mons last sent them any new troops. They didn't know much else about the post.

"It's apple country," said Senovara, knowing her love for orchards.

"Thank you," said Philippa. "You've all been so kind. When I first came here, I had heard that relations within the Roman Army could be treacherous, even dangerous. Bitter rivalry and backstabbing, that sort of drama. But everyone here has been really nice, and hardworking, and helpful. I really appreciate it."

Tristanus pointed out, "Training camps tend to be fairly stable. We don't get deployed so there's not much chance to win glory. And we're clearly not in it for the glory, so there's no need for drama."

"Except when the payroll doesn't come," Septimius chimed in.
Aries laughed, and added, "You may have noticed, we don't have a legatus, a general. Most high ranking officers aren't interested in running a dwindling training camp on the edge of nowhere. We had a thin-striped tribune some years ago, but even he didn't stick around for long."

"Above all, generals set the tone for their command," said Aries. "If they are serious and honest, the troops will tend to follow. If they are lacking in moral character, the troops may be too. But even the best of generals seem to come with a sort of cult of personality, and followers who compete for proximity to them. Not as much these days as before, but still, there may be some drama."

"Who will you be serving under, Philippa?" asked Tristanus.
"I'm to report to General Cassius Ambrosius," she replied.
Tristanus shook his head, not recognizing him, but Aries exclaimed,
"I haven't heard that name in years! I didn't know he was still on active duty."
Senovara said, "I've never heard of him."

Aries explained.
"Cassius Ambrosius was a great hero and commander. He was originally from Londinium. When he was a young man, he won several big victories on the continent. He was then promoted, re-posted to Britannia, and given the newly created position 'Warden of the Weald'. His cohort was re-formed, like ours was, only theirs also had auxiliary troops. Not the Gaulish ones he'd had before, these were new ones, brought over from Germania."

"Things were pretty quiet in the region at the time. The Weald Cohort was mostly meant to maintain a presence. But the leader of the auxiliary had gone into the pay of the Saxons, and the auxiliary-men betrayed the rest of the cohort. They took their own sworn comrades completely off guard, and slaughtered half of them before they even knew what hit them. That was, let's see, around fifteen years ago."

Aries added, "I never heard what happened to Ambrosius after that grim episode. It's good to know that he's still a General. Your new General," he said, shifting the attention back to Philippa.
"Does his attachment have a name?" Tristanus asked.

Philippa had memorized the text. "The orders say Vindavia Nova, Fortress of the Quattro Ventis Potens, late of the reformed Tungrian of Britannia Prima, comitatenses of the Sixth Legion, Victorious, Sud Est. Like us, right?"

Tristanus explained, "The few remaining troops in Britannia Prima are all loosely considered reformed Tungrians. Vindavia's standard should incorporate the Tungrian symbol of the Bull. From the Legio Sexta Victrix. And the boar from the western Legio XX Valeria Victrix. And possibly the Bear, Signifier, also from the west. Anyway, we're all attached to the Sixth Legion Victorius, even if they don't know we exist. I've never heard of this Quattro Ventis Potens attachment. Sounds interesting."

The night before they departed, there was a feast. It was not a huge crowd, even though everyone came. The smiths, the gardeners, the medical and supply staff, and even some of the local farmers came to see them off. Aries sat among Philippa's men, chatting pleasantly, and doing his best to boost morale. Philippa was busy, saying her farewells, as well as taking care of some last minute logistics. Terranes, whom she had appointed to be her aide, carried a list and followed her closely wherever she went.

After some hearty toasts, many cheers and a few tears, the goodbyes had been said, and Philippa and her men went back to Apollo Row. It seemed strange in her little room. Her cases were packed, and ready to move in the morning. She was sad but excited, and more than a bit nervous. She had already put her little Jupiter statue in her trunk, but she addressed him anyway.

"Thank you for helping me get this far. I hope that you like it, where we're going. I hope I do too."

"Vindavia Nova! We're here!" one of the front guard suddenly hollered. Philippa was surprised out of this last series of recollections. They had been climbing on a gentle incline for the last half-mile. Now the trees opened up to reveal the view.

"There's the fort! We made it!" cried Terranes. They could see Vindavia Nova below. Wooden palisades, stone walls, army tents, cabins and huts all shone in the mid-day sun.
Philippa called, "Company, halt!" They stopped abruptly.

"Thank you, Mercury, God of travel," she cried. "Thank you, Jupiter, God of strength. Thanks to the river, the trees, the sun and moon, and all those along the way who helped us. Thanks to the beasts, for bearing our burdens. Thank you, my soldiers! All honor to the Empire. All honor to Emperors Flavius Theodosius and Augustus Honorius! All honor to General Cassius Ambrosius. Forward march!" The men cheered loudly, and set off again at a brisk pace.

They began to descend a gentle ridge line. The river had snaked past them and spilled down into a green valley, falling dramatically through rocky bluffs before it settled down and ran next to the road again. They approached the fort, passing some burial grounds. The guard house was a sturdy combination of stone and timber. The palisades stretched out along each side. More guard towers could be seen down the line.

They reached the gate.
"Company, halt," she said loudly.
"Identify yourself," said one of the guards. The bosses holding his cape displayed a round quadrant symbol, decorated with a boar, bull and bear.

Philippa was ready. She had the orders in her hand. She'd kept them wrapped in wax cloth in her tunic these past two weeks. They were somewhat rumpled, but clean. She handed them to the guard, saying, as she had rehearsed, "Decanus Agrippa, and twenty miletes, trained of late at Ares Mons, of the newly reformed Tungrian of Britannia Prima, comitatenses of the Sixth Legion, Victorious, Sud Est, reporting for duty."
The guard handed the orders back to her. "Through the gate and turn left. Stay in the left lane. Follow the ring road. Welcome to Vindavia Nova."
The other guard pulled back the large armored gate.
"Thank you," she said. "Company, forward march!"

Their helmets and armor gleamed in the sunshine as they entered their new home.

Chapter Six - Quattro Ventis Potens

They were traveling the ring road, a broad white two-lane path with a central red dividing line. It ran between the tall outer gate and a lower defensive wall. There was a narrow green space on either side of the road, artfully landscaped with flowers, ferns, and succulents. Several sheep were grazing on the greenery. There were monuments and shrines scattered throughout. They marched by several dozen numbered rows of tents and huts. Then a green space with exercise equipment, and a bath house and cistern. Then more tents and huts, another green space, more baths and cisterns, and still more tents and huts.

They were not alone on the road. Several other platoons were marching and drilling. Their uniforms and standards displayed the quadrant symbol and the three creatures. Two civilians leading a donkey train passed them, going the other way. Philippa and her men marched by several more guard towers on the outer wall. They passed still more tents and buildings, but these at least now had some variety to their size and shape.

The road widened into a circle, with numerous offshoots, and the green space ended. There was a signpost. There were many plaques attached to it, pointing in several directions, but there was one large one that said 'Intake and Reception' in red and gold letters on a white background. That sign pointed to the right. They stayed in their lane, guided by the red line on the road.

No one had paid them any mind up until now, but there were more people here, and some were interested in watching them march. It wasn't just soldiers; there were civilian workers, women, and even some children and dogs. It was a lot for Philippa to take in.
This must be what a city is like, she thought.

They were heading into the center of camp. The road widened and ended. Carts and wagons were parked diagonally beside a row of stables and a large green pasture. Donkeys, oxen, kine, goats, sheep and ponies wandered around, grazing. Some stable attendants came forward and took the reins of the carts. Hay and grain were provided, and the three quadrupeds stood and munched as the soldiers continued.

They were on a large oval course, crisscrossed with broad footpaths. Philippa hadn't called cadence since they arrived. She was feeling self conscious with all these strange people staring at her. None of them seemed surprised to see her.

She expected that. The General and his staff had been thoroughly briefed by messenger from Ares Mons, and it was unlikely that news of the impending arrival of a female decanus would have remained secret for long.

She was busily scanning the area for the intake office, being careful not to trip. She saw what must be the dining hall, with some long tents behind it. She spotted the office, beside a large water tower that had something written on it. As they got closer, they saw that the water tower doubled as a lookout, and that written on it was Vindavia Nova, Quattro Ventis Potens. She realized that the quadrant symbol was a depiction of the four mighty winds, Aquilo, Favonius, Auster, and Eurus. North, south, west and east.

The dining hall, tower and office were enclosed by a large square with another low wall, and a strip of grass and shrubs. Goats and sheep wandered around here too, contentedly grazing.
They reached the office. She called, "Company, halt!"
A thin, pale elderly man emerged briskly from the reception building. Two braids of white hair hung down from under his helmet. He held a roster.

"Greetings Decanus Agrippa. Welcome soldiers," he said formally. "I am Paulinus Valinus, Beneficiari." That meant he was a veteran enlisted man, now serving as a clerk. She clasped wrists with him. Another man, dark skinned and slightly younger, came out of the office, carrying an eagle standard, which he set into a holder on the ground. He was a thin-striped Tribune, a bureaucrat, not to be confused with a broad-belted Tribune. The broad-belted type usually commanded auxiliaries. She recalled the story of the Saxon betrayal; it was unlikely that there would be any auxiliaries welcome here, ever.

Paulinus Valinus continued, "This is Tribune Augustus Ionias." She saluted him, and he returned it. "Welcome," Ionias proclaimed loudly, "to Vindavia Nova, Fortress of the Quattro Ventis Potens, late of the reformed Tungrian of Britannia Prima, comitatenses of the Sixth Legion, Victorious, Sud Est. All honor to the Empire. All honor to Emperors Flavius Theodosius and Augustus Honorius. All honor to General Cassius Ambrosius."

Philippa handed him her roster, and he checked it against his own. She had finally received a list of her soldiers' names before leaving Ares Mons. It helped her to fill in the blanks, although the long list of unpronounceable Greek second names was baffling to her. About half of the men she still didn't know very well, due to their shyness and the language barriers. But they were all dedicated soldiers, and she was happy with them. Paulinus Valinus then called the roll from his roster, and Philippa and her men responded.

Philippa Agrippa
Brutus Marianis
Bruno Marianis
Erastus Minor
Terranes Julius
Hector Magnus
Davines West
Tyronius Danu
Julius Phaedonis
Caelias Caelinus
Hadrianus Lupus
Otho Petronius
Enemno Antonius
Kunolindo Lucius
Smerto Aelianus
Marcus Constantinides
Marcus Anagnostopoulos
Marcus Diamantopoulos
Marcus Kefalogiannis
Julius Papastathopoulos
Julius Grammatikopoulos

Paulinus turned to Ionias and said, "All present and accounted for, sir." The Tribune took the roster and disappeared down one of the lanes.

Paulinas said, "The General will be here to inspect you shortly. You've got time for a quick break. Have some water, check your uniforms." He looked at the soldiers. "Get your helmets on straight. Then form a single row, facing the standard, and centered on it. Decanus, you'll be last in the row."

Philippa called, "At ease." They all had a drink and straightened up their uniforms, then she called them back to attention.
"Second column, left-face, forward-march. Right, left, right, left. Column halt. Second column, right-face. One step, forward-march. First column, right-face. Cover down left." They now formed one long evenly-spaced line.
Philippa eyed the line for straightness, then she took her place at the end. By now a small crowd had gathered around. There was a sense of anticipation. The afternoon sun was shining directly on them. Philippa was flushed from the heat; or was it nerves? She breathed deeply. Her new commander, General Ambrosius, was a great and mighty warrior. She pictured someone resembling Aries Erasmus, only much fiercer and more grim. Would he consider her worthy? And did he actually want her, or just her men?

There was an excited murmur, and the crowd parted. A group of well-dressed officers passed by, consisting of centurions with their optios and other aides. They were accompanied by four guards with long pikes. They all traveled in a closely packed, wedge-shaped group. She could see an ornate General's helmet within the group, but that's all. She continued to look straight ahead. To her left, she could tell that the General had stepped out of the little crowd, and was beginning his inspection at the other end. She longed to turn her head and see, but she didn't dare break attention.

The Tribune announced in a loud clear voice,

"Hail, the great and mighty General Cassius Ambrosius! Valiant Warrior of Rome! Victor of the Battle of Tameris Bridge! Victor of the Battle of the Red Mere! Victor of the Battle of the Gaulish Sevens! Warden of the Weald! Magisterial Protector! Gate of the Four Winds! Chosen one of the Gods! All hail!"

"HAIL!" responded the crowd.

Then, accompanied by Tribune Ionias, the General slowly made his way down the ranks, greeting each man as the Tribune identified them by name from his roster. She couldn't tell what was being said, but occasionally the General's entourage would laugh.

As they drew closer, she could hear better. The Tribune was calling out names.

Then the General was saying something to each soldier but she couldn't make out what until they got closer.

"Hector Magnus, Archer."

"An illustrious name," said Ambrosius. "May you bring honor to it."

"Tyronius Danu, Archer."

"Ah, one of the Romanized Hibernians," the General said. "I hear that your distant cousins are up to no good."

"If they are enemies of Rome," Tyronius replied, "I will shoot them all!"

"Good man!" said the General. Addressing his followers, he quipped, "Glad he's on our side." There was laughter from the group. Philippa was surprised. He sounded... jovial.

"Erastus Minor."

"Yes he is. Let's put some meat on those bones." More laughter. She could see from the corner of her eye that the entourage followed him very closely, absurdly close, like a herd of cats following a milk jug.

"Davines West." Philippa braced herself. She couldn't bear it if he picked on Davines. Like Jacamus Sands, he had no lineage or proper second name. It was through no fault of their own, but it was still a stigma. The General said,

"West is good. It's the home of Auster, the mighty west wind, and you appear to have the makings of a mighty soldier." Philippa's heart filled with pride for the young man.

"Terranes Julius, Camp Aide." The General sighed, and said to his followers, "They get younger every year, don't they?" Some of what he said was funny, but the group laughed even when he was merely witty. Some of the laughter sounded a bit forced. She wondered if this wedge of followers was the "cult of personality" she had been told about.

"Brutus Marianis, Scout."
"Well done. The Army is only as good as its Scouts."

"Bruno Marianis, Scout."
"What, am I seeing double? No, wait, this one has a crack in it. That's convenient!"

This time everyone laughed, especially the twins. Philippa laughed too, although she was still standing stiffly at attention and staring straight ahead.

"Philippa Agrippa, Decanus"
Suddenly the General was in front of her. He was shorter than she'd thought, and they were nearly eye to eye. He was not what she had been expecting! He had a broad face, clean shaven, weathered but still boyish, creased equally with worry's deep lines and laughter's crow feet. He had round ruddy cheeks with a dimple on one side. But mostly it was... his hair! She had seen many different men's hairstyles. There was an Army standard, but it wasn't enforced in the provinces; nobody cared as long as the hair was kept clean. And some religions dictated certain ways of wearing it. But she hadn't seen hair like this since...

"Jupiter," she heard herself whisper. The General took a small quick step back, and his eyebrows shot up, disappearing under the mass of dark wavy curls that framed his face beneath his helmet and tumbled down to his broad shoulders.

Philippa turned red with embarrassment, but the General immediately regained his composure, stepped forward again, and said,
"Philippa Agrippa. Or may I say Pippa Agrippa?" His entourage laughed obediently.
He continued, "Pippa. That's a nice name. Has anyone ever called you that?"

She was completely caught off guard, and reminded of Tomasen.
"A... dear companion once called me that."

"Well," he said, putting his face even closer to hers, "now your dear General calls you that! And let's see, you're a Decanus." He looked down the row of soldiers.

"But you have twenty men. Wouldn't that make you a Vigintus?"

She laughed with surprised delight. She had made up the same joke and shared it with Senovara, who just told her she was silly. *Well, then, who else was silly? The great and mighty General, Cassius Ambrosius.*

The General and Tribune Ionias went and stood at the standard. For once, the followers didn't follow, just the four guards. Philippa gazed in wonder at the General's armor and attire; it was like a dazzling mosaic of purple, red, silver, bronze, and gold, with white plumage and jeweled buckles. A richly enameled quadrant of the four winds, surrounded by images of a boar, a bull and a bear, decorated his silver cape bosses. His long red cloak was lined with grey silk and had gold trim. It hung perfectly, rippling gently in the breeze.

"Welcome to Vindavia Nova," said the General. "I can't promise to make you rich, but I promise that you will be treated fairly. We respect everyone here. As long as you do too, you'll fit in just fine. We take our work seriously, but we also like to have fun. No fighting, no gambling for money, and no unauthorized visitors." Then he paused, and proclaimed dramatically,

"You lucky people. There's no other place like this, in the Army or out of it. Let's enjoy it while it lasts."

His voice had been loud, but still conversational. Now suddenly he roared with so much volume that Philippa jumped-

"VINDAVIA NOVA!"

"VINDAVIA NOVA!" The voice of a very large crowd roared back. Philippa and her men forgot their stance. They looked behind them and saw that they were surrounded by people, soldiers and civilians, who were responding to the General.

He roared a second time-

"QUATTRO VENTIS POTENS!"

She and her men were ready this time, and they joined in loudly on the crowd's response.

"QUATTRO VENTIS POTENS!"

Some of the men in the crowd began to beat their chests, chanting, "Cassius! Cassius! Cassius! Cassius!" The General saluted, and with a flamboyant swish of the cape, he disappeared back into his wedge of followers. The crowd dispersed.

Philippa re-assembled her men. Now that the excitement was over, they were all dead on their feet. It had been a long two weeks. They were directed to the dining hall, where they ate a light meal. As they were clearing their table, a large bald man with dark skin, tattooed cheeks, and a short grizzled beard came towards them. His uniform was elegant. More subdued than the General, but just as fine. He wore a sash with the Four Winds insignia and a shining array of medals.

"Welcome, soldiers, welcome to Vindavia Nova. I'm Philemones Calla, adiuncto to the General, Cassius Ambrosius, honored be his name. If there's anything you need while you're settling in, I can try to point you in the right direction."

Philemones Calla accompanied them on the footpaths, talking to Philippa as they walked. He told her that Vindavia Nova was set up differently, compared to other Army posts. There were more bureaucrats than there were field officers. To make up for that, the regular soldiers were well trained in strategy and logistics, so she mustn't think that it left them unprepared. Even though there had been no combative conflicts for many years, they still worked diligently at both defensive and offensive training. There were no broad tribunes or auxiliaries here, as she had suspected. In fact, there was no active or field rank above centurion. That was the General's policy. Those who held other offices, Calla explained, were administrators, veterans and specialists.

Back on the road, he said, "I will bid you goodnight here. Tomorrow afternoon you'll get physicals and finish being processed. Get some rest. Sleep late if you like."

He turned back onto the footpath. Philippa and her men returned to their carts. Two soldiers from the stables were there to guide them to their tent. It was long and narrow, with a stout timber frame. The soldiers helped them unload, then took the carts back to the stables. The animals had earned a long rest too.

The row of cots reminded Philippa of the dormitory at Mount Temple. At the end, there was a curtain, and behind the curtain was a slightly bigger space for her. It had the same minimal items as her last room, minus the stove and the washtub, but she did have her own privy. She unpacked, made her bed, changed, washed up, and put things away.

There was a little altar, just like at Ares Mons. She unwrapped Jupiter and set him down. She had brought some of his flowers and feathers, slightly squashed now, but she set them around the little statue.

She lay down, numb with exhaustion, and mumbled,

"Thanks for getting us here. We're in the real Army now. Or maybe it's some kind of cult. A cult of personality."

She laughed, remembering the joke- *Vigintus. Keeper of twenty.*
Then she slept.

Chapter Seven - Payday

"They said *what?*"

It was their second afternoon at Vindavia Nova. Philippa and Terranes were in the office of the Quaestor, the paymaster, who had become indignant. The big red-faced man was wearing a tunic with a wide purple border, and his lavishly plumed helmet was perched on a stand, next to his candle and wax stamp. Just like the Quaestor at Ares Mons. Before they left the training camp, Philippa had reported to him and received an invoice for all of their salaries, to give to the paymaster at their new posting.

"They said that you would cover our salaries retroactively when we arrived. It's all there in the documents." Her heart sank as she spoke. She'd been afraid this would happen.

"I am sorry, but that is most irregular," the Quaestor said huffily. "And we simply don't have the funds." He could see that she was getting very upset, so he switched to a cajoling tone, "Besides, you'll be provided for here. You don't need money."

"NO!" she shouted. "That's unacceptable. My men deserve to get paid!"
After all they had been through! She began to cry in frustration. Terranes suddenly spoke up.
"Quaestor, sir, you say you don't have the funds. But you know who really doesn't have the funds? Ares Mons Training Camp. If it's any consolation, they won't be bothering you anymore. They are all but gone. We are the last of the trainees."

The Quaestor looked surprised to hear this. "That's a real shame," he said. Terranes continued,
"I can see that you are honorable sir; we implore you to honor Rome's commitment to us, and pay us at least this once for our service. It's not that much coin, surely, especially after taxes and deductions."
The paymaster stared at him. "What's your name, soldier?"
"Terranes Julius, sir."
The big man nodded slowly. He rang a bell, and a junior officer came in. The Quaestor took the candle, dribbled wax on the invoice, waited a few seconds, then applied his stamp. To the junior officer he said, "In full," and handed him the approved document. The officer left the room. The two of them waited in

silence. The Quaestor was perusing the other documents on his desk. After a while, the officer came back in and handed a leather satchel to Philippa. She gave it to Terranes.

"Sign the invoice, here," said the officer. She wrote Decanus Philippa Agrippa. She and Terranes saluted the paymaster, who saluted back and said,
"Terranes Julius. You have the makings of an administrator."
Philippa supposed that was a compliment. Terranes seemed pleased enough.

They returned to the barracks, and she told the ones who were there that Terranes had saved the day, and to go find the rest of the men. It took a half hour to retrieve them all, but she wanted everyone to be present. As she sat waiting in the common area, she was relieved. She had considered using the temple coin to pay her soldiers, but it would have been difficult to explain. Also, she thought that the temple money might be special, and she was reluctant to use it. She had only spent a tiny bit of it, on necessities. The box stayed rolled up tight in a bundle of her spare civilian clothes at the bottom of her trunk. She had taken some wool and stuffed it inside so it wouldn't make any sound.

The lads were all there. The word had quickly spread that Terranes was a hero of sorts. Everyone was jubilant. Terranes had laid a cloth on the table. He ceremoniously unpacked the satchel. There were three bags of coin, as well as the receipts. He set the documents out with decorum, then he sat down, emptied the first bag of silver coins into a neat pile, and read the first name.

Each soldier came up and signed the ledger. Terranes recited, "Three silver denarii," before handing them the money. When the first bag was gone, Terranes opened the next. On it went, until Terranes signed his own name and collected his three coins. That left ten coins. Philippa signed her name. Terranes said, "Ten silver denarii, covering backpay and promotion." The mood was joyous.
Philippa said, "Remember, no gambling for money. Keep your coins put away until you need them."

Their long tent, designated Vulcan XII, was surrounded by a strip of landscaping. It had its own little fire pit and outdoor recreation area, as well as a small exercise yard and a cistern. The other long tents were set up the same way. The other tents each housed a decanus, eight miletes, and two servants. The tent areas were separated by shallow ditches which were lined with stones. Everything they needed was within close walking distance; training fields, dining hall, supply warehouse, cisterns and bath houses. Even though they had no servants, the soldiers from Ares Mons were used to doing their own housework, and number XII was squared away.

There was a morning formation up by the standard, six days a week. Anyone who wasn't on duty or otherwise excused was expected to attend. There was also an evening formation. When the other troops went to formation, her group fell in with them. When formation ended, they all marched away again. There was no opportunity to ask any questions. Philippa wasn't sure who, if anyone, she should report to, or when. No one had approached her in the dining hall. So she just carried on. On the third day, she had established a daily practice of marching, training, inspections, classes, and recreation activities. By the fifth day, it was already routine.

When evening came to the neighborhood of Vulcan V through XII, the soldiers would gather outside their own tents. Occasionally, they visited others nearby. Some had come over to greet them. She used the coin from her salary to get more baking supplies. She had figured out that a likely place in a camp for procuring food items was the area behind the kitchens; there was always someone willing to barter or trade. The dried apples here were plump and smelled sweet.

She made apple cakes in the evenings. The lads had built her a little tent, and improvised a metal cover on stilts for the fire, so she could bake even when it was raining. A few of the soldiers from other tents had occasionally wandered over, drawn by the baking smells. They got apple cake too. She had hopes to eventually see more of the camp, but so far the routine was therapeutic after the long journey.

Philippa hadn't seen the General, or his entourage, or any other officer, except from a distance, during morning and evening formation. On the morning of the fifth day, just as they had returned to the barracks after breakfast, the General showed up at their tent. The only one with him was Philemones Calla.
The two officers walked in, and the General said, "Hello, soldiers!"
Tyronius Danu was about to go out the same door, and practically running into them, squeaked out, "Attention! Officers on the floor!" There was a bit of a scramble.

"At ease!" boomed the General. He and Officer Calla were wearing regular training clothes. It was odd to see them dressed that way. Philippa came forward and saluted. The officers saluted back. The General said, "I've come by to see how you're settling in. Good? Good!"

Looking around, he said, "I like what you've done with the place. Very cozy. Have you practiced any fire safety drills? No?" He looked at Philemones, who handed them a small document, and said, "Here are the instructions. Stick this by the front door. Practice the steps."

"You've done very well so far," the General said. "I realize you haven't received much direction, but that hasn't stopped you. It shows initiative. And discipline. I've heard good things from my observers about your daily routine."

He turned to Terranes and said, "And I understand you got the Quaestor to pay you what you're owed? I'd ask you to work your magic for the rest of us, but I don't believe that lightning strikes twice in the same place."
He put his head closer to Terranes, saying, "Watch out. He thinks you'd make a good Quaestor. I think it must be a dreary job, but someone has to do it."

The General turned to go. "Alright, mustn't keep the guards waiting." The General was required to have at least four guards to go everywhere with him. They were posted outside the tent. The officers departed, giving them much to think about.

Philippa said, "What did he mean? Do you suppose nobody here has gotten paid in a long time either? Now I feel bad for taking the money."
"Nonsense," said Erastus. "But I wonder, who is observing us?"
"What does it matter," said Terranes, "unless you have something to hide?"
Davines teased, "Erastus wants to hide his archery scores!" They all laughed, Erastus too. He had tried archery, reluctantly. They were all expected to try. He never even hit the target. He shot so wide that his comrades confronted him about his eyesight, and he admitted that he had cheated on the eye test by looking at it up close real quick while the doctor was out of the room.
They pardoned him, and from then on he was exempt from archery.

At the end of formation the next evening, the General declared, "And now, a special announcement." Paulinas Valinus had appeared with a scroll and a banner. He said,
"Decanus Agrippa, please bring up your men." Philippa was completely surprised.
She marched them to stand before the General.

"Well," said Cassius Ambrosius, "we had to think of something to call you. You're not a training unit any more. So this is what we came up with. It honors the legacy of Ares Mons, and binds you to us."
Paulinas undid the scroll and read it out in a ringing tone.

"Declared this holy year of 392, we name you Ares Mons Quattro Ventis Potens, of the reformed Tungrian of Britannia Prima, comitatenses of the Sixth Legion, Victorious, Sud Est. All honor to the Empire. All honor to Emperors Flavius Theodosius and Augustus Honorius. All honor to General Cassius Ambrosius."

The crowd cheered and applauded. Paulinas handed the banner to Hector Magnus. It showed the quadrant of the four winds over a mountain. It also depicted Mars, both the God and the planet. To honor the Tungrian, there was a bull, a boar and a bear.

The newly formed Ares Mons Quattro Ventis Potens marched happily back to their tent. Hector Magnus, their new Standard Bearer, proudly stuck the banner in the holder outside the front door. They had arrived!

Later that evening, Philippa was by the fire. The days were getting longer, and warmer. They hadn't lit the fire until well after dark. So the cake got made later than usual. That didn't stop an enthusiastic crowd from devouring most of it. There was a celebratory mood, and men had stopped by from the other tents to say congratulations, and to get a piece of cake. The next day was Saturn's Day, and there were no formations. Everyone was relaxed, up past their usual bed-times. There were even some jugs of wine for the soldiers to enjoy. Philippa had been handing out cake slices and pouring wine for some time. There were just two pieces of cake left, along with some crumbly pieces, and a quarter of a jug of wine.
It was a humid spring night. The fire was almost too warm. Everyone had drifted off elsewhere, even Terranes. She was glad that he seemed to be finding himself. He had shown great fortitude in dealing with the Quaestor. She scooped the leftover pieces of the cake and the crumbly bits onto a clean cloth. She was absent-mindedly scraping the pan, when she heard a voice say, "Salve, Pippa."

Startled, she didn't see anyone at first, then she realized that Cassius Ambrosius was standing nearby, just out of the firelight. He came forward quickly, finger on his lips to keep her from hailing him. He was wearing a simple dark hooded cloak. He was alone.
"Sir?" she said quietly when he was near. He didn't reply, but he eyed the apple cake wistfully.
"Do you want some cake?"
"If everyone has already had theirs."

She was so surprised. He was not like the glib and confident General she had met. He seemed tentative, almost shy.

"Let's go where it's cooler," she suggested. She picked up the cloth and a cup, and motioned for him to bring the jug. They moved to the far end of the main table. No-one was near. She placed the cloth before him, uncovered the cake, and poured some wine into the cup. They sat in the semi-darkness.

"Here you go," she said. "Hope you like it."
He picked up a piece, tried a bite, then proceeded to devour it. He said, "That's so good! I'd heard about your cake. But words can't describe it!"
"Have the other piece," she offered. "I cut them really small tonight. We had a lot of guests."
"But surely that one is yours."
"No, go ahead. I'll eat the crumbly bits."

They sat in silence. He ate the second slice more slowly. She nibbled at the little pieces. Soon it was all gone. They shared the cup, then she poured the remainder of the wine into it. She had been scanning the darkness since he arrived, trying to spot the General's guard.
"Sir," she asked, "are you alone?"
"Yes."
She said, "A Commanding Legatus walking around late at night, alone, unarmored, isn't that... irregular?"
He chuckled. "Irregular. You sound like a Quaestor."
She giggled, then said in a deep serious voice, "I'm going to require a receipt for that statement."
He laughed, too loudly at first, then hushed himself, still chuckling.

He saw that, despite their levity, she was still waiting for an answer.
"Well, I didn't want to have to bother the guard just so that I could maybe get a piece of cake."
"So you snuck past them?" she asked. "What about someone to fetch the cake for you? It isn't that I'm not pleased to see you. It's... a matter of security, isn't it? Where's your personal aide? Who's your personal aide, for that matter?" She had never seen him with one.
"Ahh, that was Andreas. He got very old, and moved on."
"Oh, I'm sorry," she replied.
"Eh?" He laughed. "No, not like that. He retired to a villa in Iberia. Andreas was an old centurion when he first came to me, and he'd been with me for thirteen years. He was so ancient that his nose hairs were growing to join his ear hairs."

She giggled at the image. "When did he leave?"
He thought. "A month ago, maybe more."
"That's a long time! Why haven't you got a new aide?"

He took a drink of the wine. Then he said, "It's not easy finding someone who really fits the job. It needs to be a dedicated soldier who doesn't have their own agenda or political goals; someone who is energetic but unobtrusive, naturally intuitive, content in service... and for me personally, it has to be someone with a sense of humor. Most of all, it needs to be someone I can trust."

"You just described me," she said. Philippa felt her cheeks get warm. She wasn't used to drinking wine. Perhaps that's why she was being so forward.
"Oh, you wouldn't want the job," Cassius said. "It's exhausting, and thankless."
"I have a great deal of energy," she insisted. "And I don't do well with too much praise."
He peered at her in the semi-darkness. "You would still need to oversee your men."
"That's no problem. They're quite disciplined, whether I'm around or not."

There was a silence. Then the General said, "I'll consider it." He stood, bowed, and said, "Decanus Agrippa, I am honored by your hospitality."

"Goodnight sir." He disappeared.

She left everything where it was and went inside. It was late, and all was quiet. She got ready for bed. She stretched out, then sat back up. She went over to the altar and quietly sang her nightly prayer,
"Utinam habeum quod nunc habeo, et etiem paulo plus. Ita, me amabit Iupitter."
(May I keep what I have, and maybe receive a little more. Thus, will Jupiter love me.)

She lay back down on her cot. It caused her a twinge of concern to think of the post commander walking around alone in the dark night. *That's why,* she thought, *that concern, that's the very reason I am probably getting the job. Because I care.*
"Oh Papa," she said to the little statue, "what have I gotten myself into?"

She slept late. Coming out of her drowsy morning sleep, it took a moment to remember the events of the night before. As she did, she was suddenly wide awake, her heart pounding a little faster. *Did that really happen?* Was she possibly going to be the General's personal assistant? It seemed like a dream.

She got dressed and went outside to clean up. There was the empty cloth and wine jug. So it wasn't a dream. But that didn't mean she would get the job. He may have just been being polite when he said he'd consider it. By the early afternoon, she decided that she had to put it out of her mind. She grabbed her quiver and bow and was heading to the range.
A soldier appeared outside the tent. He was a messenger. His cloak displayed the symbol of Hermes/Mercury, a caduceus, a staff with two entwined snakes.

"Decanus Philippa Agrippa?"
"Yes."
"Orders." He handed her a piece of vellum from his messenger bag. In a scribe's neat handwriting, it read-
'Decanus Philippa Agrippa- You are hereby ordered to report to General Cassius Ambrosius to assume the position of personal aide, effective immediately. A cart will arrive in approximately two hours to bring you and your gear to the General's quarters. This transfer comes with a raise in pay grade.' Below that, in what must have been the General's own hand, was written-
'Appoint one of your men the new Decanus.'

"Holy cats!" exclaimed Philippa. It was really happening. The thought of telling her men made her very anxious. Her mind was racing. The messenger turned to go.
"Wait!" she cried. "If you please, sir, where is the General's tent? How far away?"
He reached into his bag again, saying, "I'll show you on the map."
He pulled out a stiff rectangle of high quality vellum. On it was a concise map of the entire camp and the area around it. She was intrigued.
"It's a fifteen minute walk, or a five minute cart ride from here." He pointed to the route. "You go up this road, turn right. The road widens and curves left, and you come to an inner ring road. Turn left, stay left. The General's tent is halfway around the ring. You can't miss it."
"Thank you very much. That's a really helpful map. Is there somewhere I can get one?"
"You can keep this one."
"But that one's yours."
"Actually it belongs to the Army, so you have just as much right to it as I do. I can easily get another." She took the map. The messenger said, "Farewell," and went away.

She went back inside. She was still holding the bow and quiver with her left hand. She set them down. Her right hand, holding the map, was trembling.

Bruno and Brutus had been watching her. Simultaneously, they asked, "What was that all about?"
She just stared for a moment, overwhelmed.

Then she said, "I need to speak to everyone. Can you gather them?"
The twins went off to do so. Terranes had come in and caught the tale end of the exchange. "What's going on?" he asked, looking at her with those big blue innocent eyes.

Philippa sighed. "Terranes, we need to talk."

Chapter Eight - A Late Afternoon Bath

She was relieved to have had a chance for a private discussion with Terranes before the twins came back with the rest of the men. They gathered in the common room, and she told them the news: she had been ordered to report to the General to be his personal assistant. She'd be leaving in approximately two hours. It had come as a shock. To everyone but Erastus, apparently, who exclaimed, "I saw this coming! She was always too good for us."

The men were muttering and complaining. Two of the Marcuses had collapsed upon one another, in tears.

"Please," said Philippa. The moaning continued.
"PLEASE!" she hollered. "First of all, I will still be overseeing you. Secondly, I am not going very far away." She held up the map, and recited, "It's a fifteen minute walk, or a five minute cart ride. Up this road, and it's on the far end of this circle. Here's a map." She put the map into Bruno's outstretched hand. He and Brutus held it together, and said,
"Thank you, Decanus." Tears were sliding down their faces.
Her new map! They meant to keep it. *Oh well,* she thought, *it would be a small price to pay. And maps mean a great deal to Scouts. Besides, she was going to live in the Command tent; there would be plenty of maps!*

"Oh, of course, I want you to know where I'll be," she said. "And now you can study the area." The sniffling had diminished, and the two Marcuses were on their feet again.

She continued, "I'll see you every day at formations. And I'll look for you in the dining hall. And I should still have time to drill with you and have classes."
Will I? she wondered.
"But who will be our Decanus?" asked Big Julius with concern. "Who will lead us?"

Philippa and Terranes exchanged a glance. She smiled. "You will, Julius Phaedonis. You are to be promoted to Decanus. Terranes will be your able advisor."
"What, me, are you sure? I make up silly songs."
"Yes," she said. "You're a natural born leader." He was also big, handsome, likable, and amazingly strong. He could flip the heavy baking pan like a coin. The men of Ares Mons would be well represented.

"But," said Bruno, looking at his brother, who chimed in, "what about apple cake?"

This caused a new ripple of dismay. She raised her hand to speak, thinking quickly. She didn't have the heart to tell them that she would probably be baking for the General now, not them.

She said, "You will make it yourselves. It's not my apple cake, after all, it's yours. You're the ones who made up the annoying chant." There was a tiny bit of laughter. She continued. "There's nothing keeping you from making it. At first you just helped me prepare it, but now you actually do all the work, in case you hadn't noticed. Try baking it yourselves. You could make a contest out of it. Whoever makes the best cake becomes... Master of the Pan."

"You'll leave us the pan?" asked Terranes. He knew that she loved that battered old thing.

"Yes. And I'll make sure you have ingredients. Be generous when others come around. You are Ares Mons, and so is the cooking pan, the bowl, the spoon and the spatula. Keep them together proudly."

She was starting to tear up. She tried to hide it, saying, "I must begin packing."

Tyronius Danu took an orator's stance and said,
"Gain is loss and loss is gain. People come and go. That's the Army, that's life. Like the Big Man said, let's enjoy it while it lasts."

When her ride appeared, she was ready. The men had neatly stacked her trunk, library, and gear bag by the path. Everyone had gotten hugs, several times. The men of Ares Mons had marched in formation to see her off. Hector held the Standard. Julius was in command, with Terranes one step behind him.

Her things were quickly loaded onto the cart. She saluted the men of the Ares Mons. Then she got in, and the cart took off.

As they passed the familiar landscape of tents and fields, her heart was still heavy. The cart driver wanted to chat. She was glad of the distraction. He was a local civilian.

"Where did you come from, miss?" he asked.

She replied, "Ares Mons."

"I've never heard of that. But then again, I've never left Vindavia Nova. How do you like it here so far?"

"Very much, thank you. Do you have a family here?"

They chatted. Yes, he had a family. A wife and young son, and an almost grown and very attractive daughter.

"My daughter seems intent on marrying a soldier," he said. "Can't blame her. Me and the wife are simple folk, but she wants a proper second name. It's tough times for soldiers, though; some of them are getting transferred or even discharged. So the wife says it's alright as long as she finds someone who has a good chance for advancement here, and won't get recalled, or sacked. I don't suppose you know a likely candidate? Sorry to go on about it, but I told the wife that I would ask all my passengers."

"As it happens," she replied, "I think I do know a likely candidate. Blue eyes, fair hair- a temperate and scholarly young soldier; very thoughtful, on the track for promotion."

The man laughed with excitement. "That sounds perfect. I'm Dimocletus, by the way. You can usually find me at the cart pool."

"I'm Philippa. I'll look for you there, once I've gotten settled in."

The cart had gone through the parade ground, passing the standard. Then it went down one of the roads she hadn't explored yet, the one on which the officers came and went. *We go up this road, and turn right,* she recalled. They did so. She fell silent now, gazing at the changing landscape. They were going up a gradual incline. There were more tents and huts, bath-houses, and a small temple complex.

The road widened and curved left. There was a large parade ground, another bath house, and then, something she'd heard about but never seen: a commissary. This post had a shop! A place to buy supplies! It was in a big warehouse building. People were coming and going. There was a long table outside, laden with jugs of wine and baskets of bread. Chickens and coneys were cooking on spits over open fires.

They approached the inner ring road. It was surrounded by a tall berm, covered with spikes. The entrance was guarded. The two guards parted and let them through, waving at Dimocletus, who waved back. This ring road was for one-way traffic. *Turn left, stay left,* she recalled.

They were clearly in the officers' section. The quarters were nicer than any she had seen at Ares Mons. There were shiny white tents with silver and red trim, crenellated tarpaulins, and brightly colored banners. The tents were reinforced with stone and timber. The masonry and woodwork were beautiful. Some of the walls were plastered, others were waxed canvas. There were trees and gardens, fountains and shrines. The curbs on the road were bright yellow. A quarter way around the ring-road, she noticed that the color of the curb had changed from yellow to black. The ring road also displayed the wind quadrants, by color: white-north, red-east, south-yellow, and black-west.

The officers' houses were close together. Then the General's quarters appeared, higher up and on its own, flanked by several small guard huts. It wasn't any fancier than the others, just a little bigger. On each side, standards appeared with images of the Four Winds, the Bear, the Boar, the Bull, Mars, Mercury, Jupiter, Ceres, the River God Trisantonis, the Sun, and the Moon.

They stopped. Philippa got out. Two servants appeared. Dimocletus handed her luggage to them, said farewell, and drove away. She followed the servants up a shiny black gravel path and across the yard. There were two guards positioned at the door. They nodded politely.

She went in. The servants followed, setting her things down by the door. One of them helped her to remove her sword belt, hanging it on a hook. The other took her helmet and set it on a shelf. Then they stood on either side of the entrance. Philippa could hear some sounds coming from a room off to the right of the front door. The servant standing closest to it called, "Sir!"

There was a bit of a clatter, and the General emerged. "Pippa! There you are." He greeted her with a hearty hug. He was wearing a brown leather cuirass and matching segmented pteruges, over a white tunic. It was nice combination. "I'm afraid your room isn't quite ready. I hadn't realized how cluttered things had got in there since Andreas left. I've been using some of the space for storage."
He turned to the servants and said, "I would be grateful if you would prepare the room for my new assistant." They nodded.

"Pippa," he said, "this is Artemis and Beni. They will be around to serve you. Except on their days off." Artemis and Beni bowed to her. Beni was a short man with a little bushy beard. She couldn't tell if Artemis was a man or woman. The servants went into the long narrow room.

Cassius motioned broadly to the interior of the quarters and said, "I'll give you the tour. That will be your room." They went to the door of the long skinny room and looked in.
"It's a bit awkward, but no matter, you'll be spending most of your time in here with me."

The main space of the tent was partitioned with some screens and curtains. Going sun-wise, he pointed out the features.

"This is the Strategy Room. Once we called it a War Room, but these days survival is all about strategy. The strategy of not starving."

There was large screen displaying detailed maps. There was also a big table covered with maps and toy men, like at Ares Mons, but this one also had other things: bits of plants, little piles of grain, wool, and feathers.

Seeing that she was staring at those items, he said, "I've been marking where the flocks and herds are, and where crops seem to do best. We haven't seen any combat for a long time, thank the Gods, so we've mostly concentrated on not going hungry. The supply chain seems to have broken, and we must fend for ourselves. But we're not ready. Pray that Rome sends us a payroll, and soon!"

Next, there was a seating area with a couch, chairs, a small stove, and a writing desk. On the desk were many bottles of ink, graphite sticks, wax seals, and piles of documents. There was plenty of light throughout the quarters, Philippa noticed, coming from a series of clever skylights. There were no windows.

"This is my office. Your office too! You can scribe?"

"Yes, sir." They continued their turn.

"The heat stove." It was large and ornate.

"The dining area." Behind a little screen was a small table with two chairs. "Big enough for two."

"And my bed. My favorite place." The bed was twice as wide as any cot, and much higher. It was covered with plush fabric, and bolstered on the back. Philippa gaped in amazement.

"It's also big enough for two." She looked at him with sudden concern.

He exclaimed, "To sit on, that's all!" He hopped up onto the bed, legs crossed jauntily, his back up against the bolster.

He patted the spot next to him saying, "Check it out. It's good for reading, eating, working... sleeping, of course." She sat beside him, her back against the bolster.

"See how comfortable it is?" He grinned at her.

She had never felt anything so luxurious. She smiled back.

He continued, "So, feel free to use it. There are some tray tables." He motioned to a stack of folding trays. "I like to work here. And don't worry, I know that you're a... "

He struck a dramatic pose and then whispered loudly, "Virgin Warrior." She laughed.

He suddenly sighed, and said, "I'm chaste myself these days. I haven't taken vows or anything. It's for... health reasons. Anyway, on with the tour. There's much more to see." He hopped off the bed and she followed. Near to the bed was a small room bordered by framed curtains. Inside was a big wooden bathtub on a bed of white gravel. There was a tall trellised screen on one side. Flowering hibiscus vines, originating from several ceramic pots, were growing all over it. There was a large brazier. The room smelled like wood, flowers, beeswax and sage.

"The bathtub," said the General. "The servants will fill it for you. And empty it afterwards. They give the used water to the plants. While we're here, step this way."

They left the tub room and entered a short corridor, made of plastered timber. He stopped at a small alcove.
"In there's the privy," he said.
They continued, emerging from a door onto a partially roofed patio that contained a fire pit with a grate and a brick oven. *A real oven!* The fire was burning and there were large kettles of water heating on the grate. Two guards were patrolling the back area. The ground was gently terraced. They walked down several broad mossy steps, into a small grotto. There was a flower garden, a pond, and a shrine with a small stone statue of Jupiter. It was like a little version of the one at Mount Temple. She ran to it in recognition and reverently saluted, then planted a kiss on the statue's head.

Cassius Ambrosius smiled at her earnest yet whimsical devotion. He went back inside and she followed. "That's my wardrobe," he said, pointing to a tall wooden cabinet with closed doors that took up nearly a quarter of the room. On top of it were boots, sandals, and shiny ornate helmets.

"And armory." There was a rack on either side of the wardrobe, holding swords, shields, and spears.
"There are more weapons under the bed," he added. "And by the door. And under the big table. There might be some in your room, too."

On the other side of the wardrobe was a large red silk curtain that hung nearly all the way to the door.

"Moving on, my pride and joy: The library!" He pulled the curtain aside to reveal a cosy room, completely lined with shelves. The shelves were stacked with scrolls, documents, drawings and more maps. There was a large white sheepskin on the floor, with some cushions, and two low tables.

"Do feel free to use it," he said proudly. "There are some interesting topics in there."

Philippa suddenly laughed with delight. "Speaking of interesting topics, I have something I'm sure you will like."

She went back to the entryway and retrieved the scroll box. It was easier to carry now than it once was; she really had gotten stronger. She brought it to Cassius and said,

"Have you ever heard of Father Florian the Red, the scholar and philosopher?"

"Of course," he replied.

"He was my teacher, from when I was six, until I joined the Army."

He smiled, saying, "That explains a great deal about you! How fortunate you were to have such an education."

"Yes, I was. I'm very grateful. Anyway, this is his library. It's yours now, if you want it. I've read everything in it, and it's already done the job of getting me in the Army." So saying, she opened the box, took out that one special scroll, unrolled it to the relevant passage and showed it to him. He read it in silence and handed it back to her. She carefully replaced it.

"By the Gods," Cassius said slowly, examining the scrolls. "I am amazed. Humbled and amazed. This is an unexpected treasure." Visibly moved, he wiped away a tear. "I can hardly wait to dive in." He shut the library box.

"Meanwhile," he said, "the tour ends in the pantry."

They stepped out, and he pulled the curtain shut. Between the library and the door was a narrow closed cabinet. He opened the door. There was a selection of food and drink. Philippa said, "Grapes!"

"Yes," said Cassius, "grab a bunch, will you? And some cheese." He set up one of the bed-tables and poured some wine into a cup. He took the grapes and cheese from her, and put them on the tray, along with the cup. "Alright, climb up." She settled herself in, sitting crosslegged against the bolster. It was like sitting on a cloud. He set the tray onto the bed in front of her and carefully sat down next to her. He pulled a knife from his belt and sliced the cheese.

They ate in silence for a while. Then he asked, "Did your men take it pretty hard?"

"Yes. I had to let them keep the cooking pan."

"Aww. You can get another one. Did you appoint a new leader?"

"Yes, sir. Julius Phaedonis."

"The big gorgeous black man?" She nodded.

"Well done," said Cassius. "We'll promote him at the next evening formation."

He was thoughtful for a moment. Then he said, "See that map, the colorful one with the torn corner? Grab it, will you?" Beside the bed were two small tables, piled with documents. He pointed to the one on her side.

She handed him the map. He examined it, saying, "It's a real shame about Ares Mons. I never went there, but the troops who came from there are excellent soldiers. Present company included." He smiled at her.

He went on. "It became the engineering and industrial center of Sud Est. I've heard that it was really impressive."
"Very impressive," she confirmed, "and so full of interesting things. I learned to forge nails there!"
"That's a useful skill," he said. "Here it is."

He showed her the map, pointing to little red letters that read 'Ares Mons - Field Training Unit '. His finger traveled north and slightly west. "And here we are," pointing to the caption 'Vindavia Nova - Roman Fort'. "And where did you live with Father Florian?"
"At Mount Temple."
"One of the old temples?" he asked. "Really? Where is it?"

She looked hard at the map. She found the wide bend of the Trisantonis, just west of the road that led to Ares Mons. "It's right around here," she said, pointing to a spot around fifty miles south of Vindavia Nova. "But I've never found it on any map."
"Well, we'll have to keep looking," he said.

Artemis came in and said, "The room is ready. Would you like us to unpack your trunk, miss?"
"No, thank you," she said, "I'll do it."
"Very good. Will you be having your bath, sir?"
Cassius said to Philippa, "I usually take a late afternoon bath. But I am more interested in perusing Father Florian's library right now. Perhaps you would like the bath?"
"I'm not going to say no to that," she replied.
"Go get things in your room sorted out. By then they'll have the tub filled."

She climbed down from the bed and went to her room. Her luggage was in there. Most of the stored items had been shoved into the back half of the long narrow room. A curtain had been hung, and a folded screen had been placed, to make her a private space. She opened her trunk. She didn't need her bedroll. The cot was already made up with soft clean bedding and a fluffy pillow. She got out her towel, a set of underclothes, her civilian shoes, a red tunic, and trousers.

She went back to the trunk, dug around and pulled out the little altar bundle. There was no altar in the room, but there was a small table. She made a space for Jupiter and set him down. She still had some flowers and feathers from Mount Temple, as well as more feathers and some seeds and stones from Ares Mons. Also, a dozen nails that she had made herself. She laid everything out in a nice pattern. Then she stripped off her armor and clothing and set them on the trunk.

She slipped on the red clothes and her shoes, wrapped her underclothes in her towel, put her brown cloak back on, and went to take a late afternoon bath.

Chapter Nine - A Bit of Drama

Cassius Ambrosius and Philippa Agrippa were on their way to morning formation. As they walked past the officers' tents, the centurions, optios, and lesser officers appeared, and joined the General's group. They did not follow him quite as closely today. They seemed a bit put off by Philippa's presence. She looked radiant in the morning sun. Her polished armor gleamed, her skin glowed, and her hair shone.

The bath had been extraordinary. She had never actually been submerged in warm water. The Army had pools and tubs, but the bath houses were only for men. Her private tub at Ares Mons was really a large wash bucket. She would crouch in it and shower herself with water from a pitcher. At Mount Temple, they'd also had personal wash buckets, which were even smaller.

As she had eased herself into the big wooden tub filled with warm water, the sensation was immediately overwhelming. She had never been so relaxed. She felt as if she would never be able to move again. Or want to. She lay perfectly still, breathing deeply. The brazier was warm, and the steamy air smelled good. She lay very still for a long time.

"Agrippa," came the General's voice through the screen. "Alright in there?"
"Mmm. Yessir." Even her speech had relaxed.
"Alright. Don't fall asleep and drown."
"Mmm hmm," she replied. She would have to move in order to drown, and that wasn't happening. After a long time, she realized that the precious warm water was starting to cool, so with great effort, she sat up. There was a dish of bath soap, a white powdery substance that smelled like cedar wood. She took a handful and washed, starting with her hair. She lay back and rinsed. The little bubbles ran off of her and into the water, popping as they went. Her hair floated in swirls all around her. She sat back up, and slowly, she pulled up and heaved herself out of the tub. She dried off, put on her clothes, and left the bath room. The slanting rays of the late afternoon sun were coming through the skylight. Somehow she had expected it to be night time.

Cassius was on the bed, reading. He had said,
"That was a long bath! Did you like it?" She nodded. She wanted to tell him how much she appreciated it, but talking seemed like too much effort. Her muscles felt like jelly. He'd asked her, "Have you ever had a real hot bath before?" She shook her head.
He motioned to her. "Come sit down for a moment. Drink this." She sat on the

edge of the bed and drank the beverage, water with lemon. It was so good!

"I think you must be very tired," he said. She had nodded. "Do you want some dinner, or would you like to go to bed?"
"Mmm. Bed."
"I thought so. Alright, off you go. Beni put a warmer in your cot. Don't burn your feet on it. Have a nice rest. Formation in the morning."
"Thank you. G'night sir," she had mumbled.
"Good night, Agrippa," he had said. "Sleep well."

Most of the columns had arrived. As they awaited the call to attention, the General was talking to his officers. She slipped away and found the Ares Mons unit. They were delighted to see her.

"Decanus Agrippa!" cried Davines. "We brought you some apple cake."
He handed her a small piece of cloth with something wrapped up inside.
"We want you to judge too, to see who becomes Master of the Pan. I made this one."
"With a little help," added the twins.
"It's good," said Tyronius. "Not as good as the original of course."
She tucked the cake into her satchel, saying, "I can't wait to try it. Thank you. I'd better go now."

After formation, she and the General walked back home with just the guards. The other officers were still on the parade ground, huddled in a tight group, talking in low voices.
The General said, "I've ordered Julius Phaedonis's promotion for this evening." That reminded Philippa of the cake. She took it from her bag and unwrapped it. The General asked, "Is that apple cake?" She told him briefly of the men's dismay that she wouldn't be baking for them anymore, and how she had challenged them to make their own cakes until they voted on a 'Master of the Pan'.
Cassius laughed. "Brilliant strategy, soldier."
"Thank you, sir. Anyway, they want my opinion too, so I expect I will be getting more samples."
"That seems like a big responsibility. Perhaps you'll need some help with that," he said, eyeing the cake.
She laughed, and broke the cake into two pieces. They ate as they walked. "Not bad," he said. "Not bad at all for a first try. You must have taught them well."

They were nearing their tent. The standards rippled in the breeze. The General said to her, suddenly serious, "I have to take a private meeting here at mid-morning. It might be better if you weren't around. Do you have any errands to attend to?"
"Yes sir. I'd like to do some shopping." She was thinking of the commissary.
"Good. Ask the guards if you need help with anything. Get a cart to take you if you like; that's what they're for."
That made her remember another important errand!

They went inside. Cassius said, "I've got some paperwork to catch up on now." He was fiddling with the attachments on his cuirass.
"Uhh!" he grunted. "Help me get this thing unbuckled will you? My right arm doesn't always work so well." She undid the buckles and helped him to slip off the heavy armor.
"It goes on the side of the wardrobe. There's a hook." She hung up the armor. He was already seated at his desk, scowling at a stack of papers.
"Light my stamp candle." She took the candle, lit it from a hanging sconce, and returned it to its holder on the desk. She hovered for a moment.
He didn't look up. He just said, "Dismissed."

She went into her room and opened her trunk. She took out the folded empty sacks that she had been issued the first day at Ares Mons. They had remained empty, but now she was hoping to fill them. She checked her coin purse. It was still full of coins, mostly from her salary, although there were still a few temple coins left over too.

She went out to the patio. Some cooking items were stored on a shelf. There were roasting pans and loaf pans but nothing like a cake pan. She inspected the fire grate, then looked at the oven, measuring it with her hand. She went back inside the tent.
"Sir. I'll be going now. Is there a small map that I could take with me?"
"Here," he said, reaching across his desk. He handed her a copy of the same street map she had gotten from the messenger. He was already back to his paperwork. He seemed tense. His shoulders looked stiff.
"Thank you." She patted him gently on his broad back. "See you later."

She left the tent and asked the first guard she saw, "Please, can you direct me to the cart pool?" She held out the map. "It's right here," the soldier said, pointing to a big circle on the map. "It's a long walk, but you can get the cart-driver to take you. He's parked at the entrance to the officers' tents. If he's not there, wait a bit, another one will show up."
She walked until she found the cart. She said, "Good morning," and got in.

"Where to, miss?" asked the driver.

"Well, I eventually want to go to the commissary. But first, I'm looking for a driver named Dimocletus. He said I might find him at the cart pool."

"That's a fair bet, miss. I'll take you there."

They set off at a brisk pace. The fine Roman carriages at Vindavia Nova were suspended by straps which were attached to ornamental holders. The ride was smooth and comfortable. She sat back and relaxed as the landscape slipped by and her hair blew in the breeze. *I could get used to this way of traveling,* she thought. *But then I'd probably get out of shape.*

The way to the cart pool was dotted with tents, buildings and trailers. It was at the end of a broad road. There were dozens of carts and carriages, lined up in diagonal rows. Behind the parked carts there was a large workshop.

"There he is," said her driver. She saw Dimocletus standing with some other men. She hopped out of the cart and hailed him.

"Philippa! How wonderful to see you!"

He inquired politely how she was getting along. Then, right down to business, he asked,

"So, do you have a young man for my Julia?"

"I believe so," she replied.

"Thank the Gods. I told the wife what you said, and I haven't had a moment's peace since. Will you bring him to our humble home? Perhaps two days hence? Come for the evening meal." Philippa got out her map. Dimocletus showed her the location.

"Send me a message if you can," he said, "and let me know if that works."

That business being taken care of, she returned to her driver.

"Now to the commissary, miss?" he asked.

"Yes," she replied. Then she paused. "Or no, not yet." She calculated the time and figured that the Ares Mons would be in the training field.

"First take me here. To this training area." She pointed to the spot on the map. They made a wide turn and headed back up the road.

The post seems much smaller from a cart, she thought. They were already approaching the field. She saw a group of men; was that them? Yes, they had their standard with them. The cart pulled up next to the green. She got out and started walking towards the men. They noticed her and rushed over.

"Have you come to train with us?" asked Davines.

"No, friends, I've come to tell Terranes that there's a lovely young lady who wants to meet him."

"Meet me?" Terranes gasped.

"Woo-hoo," cried Erastus. "His dream come true."

"Yes," she said, "I will come in the evening two days from now, and escort you to her parents house to join them for the evening meal."
"What's her name," asked Terranes anxiously.
"Julia," she said.
"Julia," he said. He repeated it in a whisper, "Julia."

"Alright," Philippa said briskly, "don't get nervous. It's going to be just fine." She patted him on the shoulder.
"You can all get back to training. Don't let Terranes worry too much. See you soon."
She started to leave, then turned and added,
"Oh, that was good apple cake, by the way. And it's not just me taste-testing. The General's helping too." She got back into the cart and waved goodbye.

Now they drove to the commissary. She was so excited! She'd never been in a real shop. She gathered her sacks and got out of the cart. The driver said, "I'll be waiting."

She thanked him and went inside. It was glorious. Supplies were neatly organized and sorted by categories. There were fruits, vegetables and grains on one side of the shop, and dry goods on the other. A black cat slept in the patch of sun that came through the open door.

A man in an apron approached her. "Hello, miss. You must be that female soldier everyone's been talking about. Why, you don't look any older than my Justina."

"Justina!" he called, and a girl appeared. She was about Philippa's age; her real age. Her father said, "Do you want to join the Army, daughter?"
Justina said, "Who would do all your work for you if I did?" The man laughed heartily and said,
"How can I help you, soldier?"

Philippa had made a list. She handed it to the man, who read it out loud. Justina began fetching items.
"Apples, quinces, pears, cherries, lemons, oil, oats, butter, eggs, barley meal, spelt flour, salt, honey, walnuts, hazelnuts, dried grapes, rosemary, cinnamon. My dear, we haven't had cinnamon in years. We've got nutmeg, would you like that instead?

"All right." She wished, not for the first time, she had snuck into the Mount Temple kitchen and grabbed her stash of cinnamon the night before she left.

"This is a special request, please." She handed the man her sacks. "I would like two orders, of all these same items, packed separately. I'll be taking one order with me. The other needs to go to Vulcan XII. Do you deliver?"
The man nodded. "There's a small fee."
"Of course. I also want to get some cookware."
"Why don't you look around while we are getting these things ready?"

She wandered through the well-stocked shelves, past lamps, sconces, braziers, candleholders, and a variety of candles. After the soup-pots and cauldrons, she found the cake pans. There were two sizes. One was large and shallow, like what she'd been used to. The other was taller, but would fit in the oven.

"By the Gods," she said under her breath, "I'm going to get them both!" As if to approve her decision, the cat got up, stretched, and then came over to be petted. She hadn't seen a cat since Mount Temple. It was so nice. She rubbed its chin as she continued to scan the shelves.

By the time her grocery order was ready, she had gathered up the pans, a bowl, and a matching spoon and spatula. She also got a scrubber, a stack of clean cloths, six kitchen towels, a green checkered apron, a hot glove, some tongs, and a vellum card with several cake recipes written on it. She'd never seen a recipe before. This was new territory.

As the proprietor tallied up her kitchen supplies, she kept shopping. She returned to the counter with a stack of blank vellum, a quill and ink set, a set of drawing templates and some thin brushes. If she was to scribe for the General she ought to have some equipment.

She saw a pile of maps in the corner. They looked dusty and old. She wandered over to them, asking, "Tell me, does the General ever come in here?" The man laughed.

"The Honorable Cassius Ambrosius do his own shopping! No. Not likely to happen." She looked at the maps one by one. They were mostly touring maps from far-away lands. Only a few were local, and they were the same one that she already had. She thought she had reached the bottom of the stack, but there was one more map, wrinkled and dog-eared, larger than the others, face down on the table. She turned it over. It was stained and faded, and it had the year 356 on it. She scanned the map until she found her bearings. At the top of the Trisantonis she saw 'Vindavia Nova'. She traced the winding river down towards the coast, and there it was, in tiny letters that followed the curve of the bluff, 'Mount Temple'!

She brought the map to the counter, smiling. The General would be surprised. The shopkeeper carefully rolled up the map and tied it.

As she waited, she looked at the shelf behind the counter, where some small decorative items were displayed. There was a little tray, the size of her hand. It looked like silver but the shine was softer and more muted.
"What kind of metal is that?"
"Oh," said the man, "That's tin. From the far west."
"From Hibernia?"
"No, not that far west. From Dumnonioram. Britannia Occidens. The Tin People have a wealthy kingdom by the sea. They mostly trade with the continent. It's rare to find it here."
"I'd like that too. If I've brought enough coin." She had certainly gone on a spree!
"If you haven't, we can start an account for you." That was a new concept.
"Here you go." He showed her the tally. "I didn't charge you for the map. It's out of date, you know."
"Thank you." She looked at the total. It was a shocking sum, and it did take most of her coin.
"Do you have a cart?" asked the shopkeeper.

"Yes... " She had forgotten about the driver. She felt as though she'd been in here for ages. She slipped the map and tray into her satchel. The man loaded her goods into the cart, and said,
"I'll get those other supplies delivered to Vulcan XII by this evening."
"Thank you for all your help," said Philippa.

She relaxed on the ride back, thinking about her shopping trip. She was excited about all the cake ingredients, although she wasn't sure about the nutmeg. She hoped that the General would be in a better mood now. She was looking forward to showing him the new old map. The cart dropped her off. She gave the driver the rest of her coin.
He said, "But that's too generous."
She said, "You've been very helpful. I'm Philippa, by the way."
"I'm Bruno," the man said. *Another Bruno!*
"Bruno, I have one more thing to ask. Will you give Dimocletus a message?"
"Of course," said Bruno.
"Just tell him that we will be there, two days hence, at the dinner hour."

The servants appeared, picked up her parcels, and carried them inside. She bade farewell to Bruno and followed them. They quietly set the things down in her room, then returned to their posts.

She entered the main room and said, "Oh, I'm sorry to interrupt!"

Cassius Ambrosius was still in the meeting. There was a man sitting across the desk from him. He was one of the centurions; she recognized him from the entourage. The General said,
"Decanus Agrippa, this is Centurion Marcus Augustus."

She saluted. The man brushed his forehead with his hand rather dismissively.
Cassius continued, "Marcus Augustus Major, that is. His son is his optio, Marcus Augustus Minor. There's another one, a grand-son now too, right? Congratulations. That would be Marcus Augustus Mini?"
Marcus Augustus Major laughed. It was an unconvincing sound.

Philippa said, "I shall leave you to your meeting, sir."
"No, Agrippa," the General replied, "this concerns you." She was caught off guard, and suddenly nervous.
He went on, "Centurion Augustus Major has brought it to my attention that a personal aide to me should be of a higher rank. The position is customarily held by a centurion."

Philippa's mouth had gone dry. She could feel her face growing hot. Her new life seemed to be ending before it had really begun.
"Therefore, I'm afraid I have no choice." He paused. She steeled herself. She was determined not to cry in front of this Augustus Major, who was watching her with a self-satisfied smirk. The General continued,
"I shall have to promote you to centurion."

What? She had not seen that coming. Her anxiety gave way to amazed relief. Cassius continued, "You only need to demonstrate that you can command the troops on the parade ground. I've seen you march your men; I'm sure you can manage."
Her mind was reeling, but she said, "Yes sir."

The Centurion's smirk had turned to a barely concealed scowl. Apparently he hadn't seen this coming either. The General continued, "Agrippa, you should thank Augustus Major. Because of his diligence, you are being promoted."

She suddenly realized that Cassius was rather enjoying this. She bowed to the Centurion, and in her sweetest voice, said, "My thanks to you, Marcus Augustus Major." The man got up, looking very unhappy, saluted the General and left without waiting for a response.

Suddenly light-headed, she sank down into the empty chair. Her heart was pounding. Cassius got up and stood behind her, placing his hands on her shoulders.
"Forgive me. I just can't resist a bit of drama. I couldn't help letting that sanctimonious sycophant think that he had won for a moment."
"Won what?" she asked. "Why was he so intent on getting rid of me?"
"He wanted the position filled by his son, Sanctimonious Sycophant the Second. As if I'd ever go along with that." Cassius laughed. "The look on his face. He hates me now. Not that he ever actually liked me before."
"But... does that mean he's... a danger?" she asked nervously.

Cassius replied, "That's a fair point. Under normal circumstances, yes. But you see, he's leaving. I have the orders, I'm going to give them this evening. After your promotion. And the promotion of your Decanus. It's going to be a long formation."

"He's going away?" she asked in surprise.
"Yes, they all are. The whole lot of bloodsuckers. And that should warm their cold little hearts, because they're getting what they want, passage back to Rome. To live out their days in a failing and corrupt city constantly ravaged by invaders and plague. More power to them. I can make my own centurions."

She was speechless.

"So," he asked, "how were the shops? Did you get anything good?"

The General was delighted with the map. He clipped it up on the screen by the big table. Artemis and Beni stashed her new cooking gear on the patio. There was nowhere to put the big bag of food yet, so she set in on her trunk. She showed her tray to the General.

"From Dumnonioram," she said. "In Britannia Occidens. There's a wealthy kingdom by the sea. Shining with tin. I'd love to see that." They looked at the map. It was very far away and there were no roads.
Cassius said, "Maybe we can take a boat there someday." She smiled at the thought.

He added, "You know, tin is sacred to Jupiter."
She didn't know that. That made her smile too. She went into her room and set the tray under her little Jupiter statue. She said quietly, "You ought to like this, Lord, it's tin!"

They ate a late lunch. Philippa went for a walk, and the General rested. Then it was time to go to evening formation. After the regular announcements, the General proclaimed, "I have exciting news. A promotion."

He went over to the Ares Mons, and said, "Julius Phaedonis. Front and center." Julius turned briskly and marched up to the General, who proclaimed,
"The phaedon is a bright light, shining in the darkness, illuminating places that were once hidden. Be that light, soldier. Julius Phaedonis is promoted to the rank of Decanus." He shook the young man's hand.
Then he cried, "QUATTRO VENTIS POTENS!"
The crowd roared it back. The men cheered. Julius saluted and the General returned it. Julius did a smart about-face and returned to his position.

"And now, another promotion!" cried the General. "Decanus Philippa Agrippa, front and center." She stood before him.
"Decanus Agrippa has shown great fortitude, and resourcefulness in the face of hardship. She is a proven leader. Philippa Agrippa, soldier of Rome, you are promoted to Centurion."

The crowd cheered. Terranes approached. Apparently, he was in on this too.
Cassius continued, "The Centurion displays silver."
Terranes removed her brown cape, and replaced it with a red one, decorated with a wide silver stripe. The cape was held on by two fine silver bosses, depicting a bull, a boar, a bear, and the wind quadrants, all in colored enamels. A stylized eagle was at the top of each one, wings curving around to become the bezels.

Terranes removed her helmet and took off the simple plume. He replaced it with a silver mounted transverse crest, and set it back on her head. He shifted her sword belt around so that the sword was on the left, which is where Centurions wore them. It felt strange. The General presented her with a silver handled dagger, which Terranes attached to the right side of the belt.

Terranes retreated, and the General said, "Centurion, take command." She faced the large group of columns. The men had been standing at ease. She called,

"Company... attention. Right... face. Forward... march. Right-left, right-left, right-left, right-left. Company halt." It was not a big parade ground. She didn't want to risk a pile-up!
"About... face. Forward... march. Right-left, right-left, right-left, right-left. Company... halt. Right... face. At ease."

The General stepped up and shook her hand. The men shouted their approval. The General roared, "QUATTRO VENTIS POTENS!"
The crowd roared it back. Philippa saluted, the General returned it, and she stepped back. Her heart was pounding.

Then he said, "And now, monumental news. Marcus Augustus Major, Marcus Augustus Minor, Justinian Dion Major, Justinian Dion Minor, Phyllanus Potens, Tristanus Potens, Daccus Aurelius and Marcus Treva. You have all been recalled to Rome! Pack tonight, because you are leaving tomorrow!"

This got a big reaction, especially from the nearby group of wives, who were clearly delighted. "It's the moment so many of us have hoped for," Cassius continued, with a charming smile. "You will report to Londinium to secure your passage. Vindavia Nova thanks you for your service. The Eternal City awaits you! Company dismissed."

Afterwards, Cassius and Philippa returned to the General's quarters, chatting happily. They entered. It was dark. She went and peered out the back door.
"The braziers aren't lit. Or the fire. Where are Beni and Artemis?" *Oh, dear,* she thought, *I'm already getting used to having servants.*
"They were at the formation," the General said. "I gave them the evening off. People are in a celebratory mood. We'll have to light the fire ourselves. Hopefully they built it for us. If you want to go out and check, I'll get a torch going and be right behind you."

She was anxious to examine the new cookware, and she was thinking about the bag of food, and where best to store it. She went out the patio door. Formation had been very long. It was dark already. There was no moon. She could barely see the sentries on patrol. As she made her way cautiously to the fire-pit, she suddenly froze. Her stomach felt like ice. There was the clear form of a man, right in front of her, standing in the darkness. He seemed to have come from nowhere.

Chapter Ten - Yes or No Questions

Philippa cried in a small squeaky voice, "Who are you?"
Then she recalled her training, and immediately said in a deeper voice,
"Who goes there?"

"If you don't know, why should I tell you?" said the dark shape.
"Because... I need to know for security reasons." She wished the General would
hurry up. *Unless this fellow wanted to hurt him! Cassius had infuriated a
powerful man this morning. Could this be him?*
"Security is a shifting illusion," said the shadow.
She was confused. *Was that a threat?*

"Sir, about your name?"
He replied, "What can *you* tell me about my name?"
What? she thought. *Maybe he's simple. Like Tomasen. Alright, I'll play along.*

"Well," she said in her most patient teacher voice, "you sound like a Roman
gentleman, so you'll have at least two names, most likely ending in -us, or -es,
or -um, with maybe an -ex to say where you come from."
"Very well," the voice replied, "I am Nulles ex Nusquam." (I am Nothing from
Nowhere.) Philippa laughed out loud despite herself. This was no simpleton.
Then she thought about Cassius. *It was her job to protect him.* She drew her
sword and said, "That's very clever, but I'm afraid that I must insist that you
identify yourse-"

"AGRIPPA! Put that away at once." The General had finally appeared with the
torch. "This is Brian Magnus. My... oldest friend." He held the torch aloft. The
light revealed the dark figure. He wasn't dark at all. He was tall and handsome,
in a boyish way, with smooth clear skin, silky golden hair, and almond-shaped,
amber-colored eyes.

The General said, "Brian, this is my personal aide, Centurion Agrippa."
"Really!" said Brian Magnus. "That is not what I was expecting."
"It's no excuse for being rude." He turned to Philippa, "Speaking of rude..."
"I'm very sorry, sir," she said to Brian Magnus. "I didn't know. I was only
thinking of the General's safety."
"Aww," said Cassius, "it's alright." To Brian Magnus, he said, "Don't ruin her
big night. She just got promoted."
"Congratulations," Brian Magnus said, without much enthusiasm.

Philippa said stiffly, "General, now that I know that... all is well, I think I'll retire. It's been a long day. Goodnight, Sirs."

"Oh, really? Well, alright. Goodnight, Pippa," said Cassius. As she walked back inside, she heard him say to Brian Magnus-

"You startled her!"

"She's the one who drew a sword on *me*," he replied.

"She was only protecting me. That's the whole idea, isn't it?"

Philippa went inside. She had been feeling so happy. Now she was shaken and confused. That was such a strange encounter.

It really did seem like he came from nowhere. Nothing from Nowhere.

Cassius had lit a lamp in the main quarters. She went into her room. She undressed in the semi-darkness, trying to find a safe place to put her new cape.

The food was still on her trunk. She could smell the sweet tang of the dried fruit. She put her cape over it. She took off her armor and couldn't find a place for it either, so she laid it on the trunk too. Then she remembered that her nightgown was in the trunk. She didn't want to deal with it. She climbed into bed, still in her tunic and leggings. She lay there uncomfortably. She felt grimy. Her clothes were stiff with dried perspiration. She couldn't relax.

After a while, she heard someone approach. Cassius called, "Pippa? May I come in?"

"Yes sir," she answered. "Watch out for all the stuff."

"Right." He threaded his way to her cot carefully, but he still banged his shin on her gear trunk, letting out a muffled curse. He crouched by her bunk.

She sat up. He patted her hand. "My dear, we've got the fire going--"

"I'm not up to cooking tonight."

"No, no, that's not what I'm getting at. We're heating the water. I thought you might like a bath."

"But the servants are gone."

"I'm perfectly capable of filling a bath. Besides, Brian said he'd help. He really is sorry. He had a... long journey. You know how that is."

"Yes," she complained, "but he wouldn't identify himself. And he said the strangest things. But mostly he... he came out of nowhere. I was looking at empty space and he just... appeared."

"Now, Pippa," said Cassius, "you know it was very dark--"

"What is he?" she suddenly asked.

He seemed taken aback. "Whatever do you mean?"

She asked, "Is he an officer? Or maybe an immune? He isn't wearing a regular uniform."

"Oh," said Cassius. "He does intelligence gathering."

"Like a Scout?"

He lowered his voice. "More like a Spy. He is a secret agent."

"Ohhh," she said, thinking, *that would help to explain his behavior.*

"And," she asked, "he assists you?"

"Very much," Cassius replied. "For a very long time. His knowledge is vast. He's been everywhere."

"I'm sorry that I threatened him."

"Don't be. You earned your rank tonight. You were quite courageous."

"I was terrified," she admitted.

"No matter, you did your duty. I'm really proud of you. Now, how about a bath, Centurion?"

"Yes, please."

"Good!" He looked at her more closely. "Are you still in your tunic? Where's your nightgown?"

"It's in the trunk. But the trunk is piled up with stuff."

He peered at the precarious tower of items, and said, "I'll loan you one of mine. I'm sorry this room is such a hazard. It's not safe. We'll get it fixed up better tomorrow. You should sleep in my bed tonight. I'll sleep on the couch. Or on the bed with you if you don't snore."

"I don't think I snore. What about Brian Magnus?"

"That was a bad jest. I'm the one who snores. And Brian Magnus billets elsewhere."

He was still crouching. He shifted his weight to stand, and carefully rose. "So, we'll go fill the tub. I'll knock on your door when it's ready. No one will bother you. I may come in for more wine, but otherwise we'll stay outside. I'll leave the nightgown in the bathroom."

He found his way to the door and exited. She heard them filling the tub. Then there was a knock on her door. Her comb and toothbrush were on the little table. She grabbed them; then she went to get her brown cape, and realized that Terranes must still have it. She picked up her new Centurion cape, draped it over her shoulders, said goodnight to Jupiter, and made her way to the door.

The bath water did its trick. She felt better about everything, including Brian Magnus. His job must be incredibly stressful. Tense, and highly uncertain. Poor fellow. After she dried off, she put on the General's nightgown. It was soft and worn, oversized and comfortable, and covered more than her own did. *I hope he has another one,* she thought, *because I'm keeping this one. Bless me, dear*

Mercury, for I am a thief. She smiled. She climbed into the large bed, carefully tucking herself to one side, and went to sleep.

When she awoke, it was late in the morning. She sat up in a panic. She was missing formation! She got out of bed, and slipped her Centurion robe over the long nightgown. She didn't see Cassius. There were blankets piled up on the couch. He must have slept there. She went to the privy, washed up, and went out the back door. She was surprised to find that Brian Magnus was still there. The fire was burning. He was sitting next to it, feeding it with documents from a messenger satchel.

"Good morning, Centurion Agrippa." He rose respectfully.
"Good morning, Officer Magnus. I think the General went to formation without me."
"You've been given the day off."
"Oh!" That was nice, except she felt bad about not seeing the men from Ares Mons.
"Here's some breakfast." He pointed to a tray of grapes, cheese, boiled eggs, beetroot, bread, and lemon water.
"Thank you." He seemed quite thoughtful. And he was so bright and fair; it was difficult to equate him with last night's dark mysterious figure.

Apparently he was thinking about the previous evening too.
"Sorry about last night," he said.
"Me too," she replied.
"I hope we can be friends," he added.
"Yes, friends." She put out her hand. He took it. His hand was... tingly. Or maybe she imagined it. She ate in silence. The sun was warm. It felt good to be wearing comfortable clothes.

Brian Magnus stood to tend the fire. Philippa said, "So, you've known Cassius Ambrosius for a very long time?"
"Yes," he replied.
"I was wondering," she said, "do you think he's alright? He seems to have sudden changes of mood. Maybe it comes from all the responsibility? And what's the matter with his arm? Is he in pain?" She sighed. "I want to help, if I can. I just don't know much about him. He doesn't seem to want to talk about himself. Will you tell me more about him?"

Brian Magnus replied, "Cassius Ambrosius was a raging beast of Mars in his twenties. You might not have liked him back then. He had the power of Jupiter, only very little of the joy. But in his thirties, he beheld the light of Venus. He learned how to make friends, and to make peace. He became jovial. But then, on the Weald, peace was murdered. He lost fifty-three men. And almost lost his arm. We retreated to the nearest post on the map. It was in a very remote area. The once flourishing outpost of Vindavia Nova. We've been here for sixteen years."

"There's a story here. Two years before we arrived, thirty-seven soldiers went out one day, along with their centurion and optio, and all their field gear, on an overnight training drill. They never returned. It was said by the local shepherds that the Earth opened up and swallowed them. The area was searched, for days. They found two helmets. That's all. Vindavia Nova was left depleted and demoralized. And nervous. Some still swear that on nights when the wind is still, the lost men can be heard marching deep underground."
Philippa laughed. "Is that funny?" he asked in surprise.
"Sorry," she said. "It's just that, if I were trapped underground with my men, I don't think that marching would be the priority. Is it true that the earth swallowed them?"

"It seems so. There was a nearby earthquake reported that day. Anyway, when we showed up, the base was depleted and in need of new leadership. We all needed a rest. Cassius needed a place to recover. And a reason to recover. The Gods of the Four Winds visited him in his dreams, and showed him that he had work to do still."
Brian Magnus put down the fire-shovel and sat down next to her.

"He's come a very long way. But in truth, he hasn't been right since the betrayal of the Auxiliaries. He was so badly injured. Physically and spiritually. He was in the infirmary for four months. His body began to heal, and he gradually grew in strength. He took charge of the post and started to make improvements. Mostly in an attempt to create a farm settlement in this all but forgotten place. He was worried about famine, and the desertion and crime that accompanies starvation in the ranks. Rome had stopped making deliveries here some time ago. The local farmers had been helping to support the small group of soldiers who remained. Cassius did his best to reestablish a connection with the Quaestor. He posted many letters. Rome finally responded, and began sending the occasional payroll."

Philippa sat, quietly overwhelmed by all this information. *What an orator Brian Magnus was!* He continued.

"But even though Cassius was working again, his spirit was in torment. He blamed himself for the loss of his men. As the General and the Intelligence Officer, we both deserved blame. Especially me; I should have seen it coming. It overwhelmed Cassius. He was lost. He started drinking with some of the younger men, and visiting the brothel tents with them. He gradually went down the path of excess. But when poor Timonius Justus died of the camp-follower's pox, it sobered him up. That was seven years ago."

The look of horror and confusion on her face was enough stop him.
"Oh," he said. "How old are you?"
He looked at her closely. His eyes were the color of honey.
"I'm eight--- I'm sixteen." She couldn't lie to him.
"So, you've never known a man?"
"No! I'm a Virgin Warrior."
"Oh, right, right. But you know... how things work."
"I know the basics. I've read medical texts. I'm also aware that some men allow the reproductive urge to rule their behavior."
"That's a polite way of putting it," he noted, smiling. "So, do you know what camp-follower's pox is?"
"No. A pox is a plague, right?"
"Yes, but this is different. The regular plague wipes out entire communities. That's how Cassius lost most of his family, you know. When he was ten. They got the pox. He had it too, but of course he survived. That's why his face has all those faint little scars. But the other kind of pox only travels between people who... you know." He made a rude little motion with his hands. "It starts down there." He pointed to his crotch. "Then it spreads."

He sighed deeply. "Timonius was a good friend to the General. He helped him in many ways. He was brave and energetic. But he had his weaknesses. He... allowed his reproductive urges to rule his behavior. The end result was horrific. The treatments were almost worse than the disease. He lingered for many months before his death. It was enough to make Cassius change his lifestyle. He banned those particular camp followers from coming around anymore. He actually paid them to stay away. They are not allowed within the gates."

Philippa felt as though she might vomit up her breakfast. She must have looked that way too, because Brian Magnus said, "I'm sorry, dear; that was perhaps more than you wanted to know. But that's what you get for asking!" he said cheerfully. He brought her some more lemon water, saying, "Maybe we should change the subject. But if there's anything else you are curious about, let's stick to yes or no questions, lest I say too much. I will answer honestly."

She drank her water and sat quietly for a moment. Then she said,
"Alright, this has nothing to do with any of that. Complete change of subject. Cassius said you've been everywhere. Have you been to the Sea Kingdom of the Tin Men on the far end of Dumnonioram, Britannia Occidens?"

He looked directly at her as she spoke. His gaze made her feel sleepy. She blinked her eyes.
"Yes," he said.
"What," she giggled, "did you just visit there real quick while I was blinking?"
He laughed and said, "Yes."
What a silly man! she thought. "Well, anyway, I'd like to know more about it."
"Yes or no questions, please."

"Oh, right. Let's see. Is there a mighty kingdom in farthest Dumnonioram overlooking the Hibernian Sea?"
"Yes."
"Is there a large harbor?"
"Yes."
"Can you see the castle from the sea?"
"Yes."
"Is it clad with shiny tin?"
"No."
"Oh." She was slightly disappointed. "But there is tin? I mean, are there tin items throughout the castle?"
"Yes."
"Is the castle full of nice things? Rugs and murals and tapestries and... sparkly bits?"
He laughed again. "Yes"
"Do they have gardens?"
"Yes. Very beautiful terraced gardens, vineyards, orchards and flowers." She was glad for that small detail.
"I'd like to go there someday," she said dreamily. "On a boat. Will I?"

Just then, the General came striding through the back door, carrying a messenger bag.
"There you are," he said to Philippa. She rose to greet him.
"Centurion cloak over a nightdress," he noticed. "You look like a goddess." He kissed her cheek. "Here's your cape," he said, removing it from the satchel and handing it to her. Then he set a parcel on the table. She recognized the shape.
"Apple cake?"
"Apple cake. A big piece. Ready to try?"
"Shouldn't we offer some to Brian Magnus?"

"No, he doesn't care for it." Cassius broke it in half. They chewed in silence.
"Not quite as good as yesterday's is it? Not bad though." He drank some of her water.
"I suppose we had better start a tally," he said, "or we won't remember which ones we liked."

The servants had come out to meet him. "Pippa, this afternoon Beni and Artemis are going to clear the things out of your room. It's a big job, but they are not going to stop until they've finished." She smiled at them in gratitude. The servants departed.

"The post has arrived at last." Cassius said to Brian Magnus, motioning to his satchel. "I'm going to go read it. Pray for good news."
"Here's hoping," said Brian. The General went inside. Brian Magnus turned to Philippa and said, "Yes. So, what's got you interested in the Tin Kingdom of the west?" She started to tell him about the little tray she had bought from the commissary.

Suddenly there was a great roar coming from within the tent, followed by a crash. Brian ran quickly inside. She followed. The General was standing by his desk. The crash had been his chair, now lying sideways on the floor. His face was very red. He brought his fist down, hard, on the desk. The floorboards reverberated.

Brian Magnus said, "I take it that was not good news after all. I'm sorry."
"After all their promises!" cried the General. "They are liars! Cheaters!"
Philippa picked up the fallen chair.

"They are nearly bankrupt," said Brian Magnus, putting his arm around Cassius, "and with the little they have, they are choosing to pay their own poor useless relatives."
"But we are worth supporting!" Cassius cried. "We still have a working economy, with shops, and supply chains, and a civilian work force. We have an actual chance at transitioning from an Army post to a real town."
"Will somebody please tell me what's going on?" Philippa asked anxiously.
"Oh Pippa, I'm so sorry." The General went over to his bed and lay down with his face away from them. She looked at Brian Magnus in bewilderment.
He said, "It seems that the Quaestor of Rome and his minions aren't able to pay us anymore. We thought there might still be a chance. We may soon be to the point where we could survive on our own, but not just yet. And we have to pay the troops. We really must."

"But, under the circumstances, can't you ask them to wait?"
"They have been waiting. For over a year." She was shocked to hear it.

She thought about the loyal Vindavia Nova soldiers who hadn't been paid for over a year.
Then she suddenly cried, "WAIT! THAT MUST BE WHAT IT'S FOR!"

Cassius turned over and sat up, sitting cross-legged, looking angry and confused. She ran into her room, took the items that were on the trunk, and tossed them on the bed. She opened the trunk and dug around until she found the bundle. She undid it, and took out the metal box. She set it on the table, opened it, and took out the insulating fluff. She stared at the coins. It seemed like it should be enough for a payroll, maybe even several. She looked at her little Jupiter, sitting on the tin tray. She took out a copper, a silver and a gold coin and set them on the tray, saying,
"Thank you, Sir."

She closed the box and carried it out into the main room. She sat down by the General on the bed, and put the box in front of him.
"This is for you, from Mount Temple... a gift from the Gods, to be used for something worthy. I think it would cover the payroll."

Cassius open the lid. He gasped. "I don't believe it! That is so much money!"
Brian Magnus picked up a coin and examined it. "Constans. That was thirteen Emperors ago! They're old. Old temple coins. The tithes of the faithful. How lovely." He put his face close to the box and inhaled deeply. "They even smell like a temple."
The General was trying to keep his composure. "Philippa, do you realize that this is a fortune? Why, you could buy a small villa with this much."
She thought for a moment, then said, "I don't think that even a small villa will fit in my room."

There was a second of silence and then both men roared with laughter. Philippa smiled and said, "This coin is Jupiter's blessing. I want Vindavia Nova to succeed. I want all the men to get paid. And I couldn't bear it if the commissary closed."

"Oh, Pippa." The General had tears in his eyes. "If you are sure. The men will be so grateful to you."
"No, not to me. I gave the box to you. And it should be widely known that you have decided to use your own savings to pay the men. It would inspire loyalty and gratitude."

"She's right, you know," said Brian.

Cassius seemed to have accepted the situation.
"Have you counted it?" he asked.
"No, I've taken some coins off the top, that's all."
"Really? I can't tell. It's so full!" He got up and set the box on his desk. "Well.
I'm going to count it." He went to the front door and told one of the guards, "No
visitors." He got a ledger, a pen and several wooden trays. He sat down and
began sorting the coins.

"This could take some time," said Brian Magnus to Philippa. "Let's go for a
walk. They're opening up the side gate today."
She looked at Cassius, who seemed quite happy making his little tally marks.
"Alright." She went to her room and quickly changed into her civilian clothes.
After all, it was her day off. She came back out to put on her sandals. While she
did, Brian Magnus explained that when the side gates opened in the spring, it
was a short walk to the river, and to several good swimming and sunbathing
spots.
She said to the General, "See you in a while, sir."
He looked up and smiled. "Have a nice walk."

The moment they were out of earshot, Brian Magnus suddenly said,
"Tell me about the box. Did you steal it? It's alright if you did."
She explained while they walked. She told him about her background, and
about her life at Mount Temple. How wonderful it had been, and then how
suddenly terrible. She gave a thorough account of the events that led up to her
last night there, and the morning's secret departure. He wanted to know
everything. He seemed to thrive on detailed information. *Maybe that comes with
being an Intelligence Officer,* she thought. She told him every single thing, right
down to the cinnamon she had left behind.

They had walked along a path that ran behind the tents. It led to the palisade.
The open gate beckoned. They went through. The guards saluted Brian Magnus.
There were other people, mostly men but also some women and children. The
women were carrying washing, and the children had buckets. Most of the men
were carrying towels.

They walked a little further. There was a stone bench overlooking a small sandy
beach. Philippa and Brian Magnus sat.
"You did a good thing today," he said. "You honor both God and Man."
"Thank you. I feel relieved."

They sat in silence for a while. Then they got up and walked back to the General's quarters.

"Terranes!" Philippa exclaimed in surprise as they entered the room. "What are you doing here?"
Terranes was sitting at the General's desk, writing in a ledger.
Cassius said, "I'd like to present my accountant, Terranes... what's your second name again?"
"Julius, sir."
"Terranes Julius, financial advisor to the General and Quaestor of his personal treasury."

"Oh, Agrippa!" gushed Terranes. "Isn't this wonderfully magnanimous of General Ambrosius? Using his own retirement savings to pay the troops. It's so noble!"
Cassius looked slightly embarrassed.
"It is marvelous thing to do," she replied. "And, Terranes, your new promotion comes just in time."
"In time for what?" asked Cassius.
"Tomorrow evening, I am escorting Terranes Julius to meet a beautiful young woman who is hoping to marry an up and coming soldier!"
"What?" exclaimed the General to Philippa. "You're a match-maker too?"
He turned to the young man, "The girl will be lucky to have you." Cassius kissed him on the forehead. "May your union be blessed."

Philippa decided to attend evening formation as an observer, in her civilian clothes.
Brian Magnus and the Marianis brothers met her and the General in front of their tent. The brothers were wearing some new insignia bosses. The design was the four winds quadrant, with a black circle in the center. Their cloaks were new too; a muted grey color.
"What's this?" she asked as they walked.
"We've been promoted," said Bruno.
"But it's a secret," said Brutus, grinning.
Together they said, "Secret service."
"I hope you don't mind," Brian Magnus said. "They're still attached to you, but they also work for me now."
"That's excellent, they deserve promotion," she said. "Are they officers?"
"Yes. And no. They're Securitores. Like me."
"Well... my heartiest secret congratulations to you both," she said to them.

They had reached the parade ground. The men joined the ranks. She found a place to sit on the lawn. After some brief announcements, Terranes marched up to stand beside the General.

"Soldiers! Friends! Men of Vindavia Nova. Hear me! I am Terranes Julius, personal Quaestor of General Cassius Ambrosius, honored be his name."
"I have some bad news and some good news. The bad news is, Rome has once again failed to deliver the payroll, and they've let us know that they are not even going to try to honor their commitment to us."
There was a great outcry of complaint from the men. Curses were uttered.
"Tell us the good news, quick," somebody hollered.
"I said good news," Terranes continued, raising his voice. "But it's not even good news. It is great news! Your honored General Cassius Ambrosius has taken his own retirement fund, and he is going to pay every one of your salaries! Including backpay."
There was a moment of complete silence. Then the evening exploded with sound as the men cheered and howled with joy. Some of them were crying. The chant started up.
"Cassius, Cassius, Cassius..." It went on and showed no signs of stopping. The General put up his hand. The men fell silent.

"I want to thank all of you for your loyalty and commitment," he said. "It's a scandal that you haven't been paid for so long. I hope this will begin to make up for it. There should be enough for several paydays to come. By then, perhaps we can achieve self-sufficiency."

While he was speaking, some servants brought a table and a chair. Six guards approached. Two of them carried a wooden box which now held the sorted treasury. They set it down on the table. Terranes produced a ledger, and held up his hand. The crowd grew silent. Terranes said,
"If you wish to be paid this evening, please form an orderly line. Be sure you have your identification tag. We'll also be doing payout in the dining tent tomorrow morning. Thank you. You are dismissed."

The moment he finished speaking, the line immediately formed, snaking around and around the parade ground. Men were talking and jesting and calling to one another. Some were still chanting the General's name.

Cassius spotted Brian and Philippa. He came over and sat down with them. The westering sun illuminated everything with golden light and long shadows. Cassius was smiling and looking at the men. Philippa watched him. She could

see the little marks on his face, leftover from the pox. They were on his arms, too. She thought about what Brian Magnus had told her. So much suffering.
She reached out and gently took his hand. He kept his eyes on the men, but he gave her hand a squeeze.

It was nearly dark when it ended. Cassius thanked Terranes, and he, Brian Magnus and Philippa bade him goodnight. They walked with their guards back to the General's quarters and went inside.

"And now I will say goodnight," said Brian Magnus. They said their farewells, and he went out the back door. Cassius sat down on his bed, undoing and kicking off his sandals. She sat down too, loosened his cuirass, helped him remove it, and hung it on the wardrobe.

"Well, Centurion," he said to Philippa, "I believe that you've earned another bath."

After the bath she and Cassius ate a light meal, and she went to sleep in her own room. As she dozed off, it occurred to her that Brian Magnus had actually answered "Yes" to her question about traveling by boat to the west. She reached over and lightly touched the tin tray. Then she slept.

Chapter Eleven - Pushing and Pulling

They had just returned from formation the following morning. Having sampled another apple cake, they gave it their marks on the tally sheet Philippa had made. She still hadn't had a chance to cook with the new supplies.

At least everything had been put away. Many of the items that had been stored in her room were gone, and the rest had been arranged in a way that made more sense. There was a new rack, displaying the fine collection of vintage blades and armor which had been cluttering up the back of the room. There was a place for her own armor and weapons too, a small wardrobe for her clothing, and a second small table that held a jug and basin. A narrow pantry had been installed near the door to hold the victuals, which had been unpacked and neatly stored on the shelves. Her room was still skinny and awkward, but at least it was navigable.

"Ready for a swim?" The General had taken off most of his gear, and was holding out his arm for her to loosen his cuirass.
"I don't know how to swim," she said, while putting away his armor. "I've never been in water deeper than the bathtub."
"What? I thought Mount Temple was near the Trisantonis."
"Yes, but for some reason it never occurred to me to walk for seven miles and throw myself in the river."
Cassius laughed. "Well, you need to know how. For your own safety. Also, it's great exercise. And, it's how the real Roman soldiers bathe."
She looked doubtful. "Don't they get naked first?"
He replied, "You can swim in your tunic and trousers."
"And you?"
He laughed. "I keep my trousers on. There are too many fish that like to nibble on exposed body parts."
"What?" *This was sounding worse by the moment.*
He just said, "Wear your cloak over your tunic. And don't forget your towel."

They walked down the path and out the gate.
"It may be possible," he said, "that there will be other men bathing, and without their trousers."
He glanced sidelong at her. "Have you ever seen a naked man?"
"You mean besides the naked men in the barracks," she replied, "and outside the bathhouses, and the naked statues, and all the naked men on vases, amphorae and murals? Don't worry, I won't be shocked. I have nothing but sympathy."
"Sympathy?"

"Yes, all those dangly parts hanging out, destined to be fish food. It must be challenging."
She was being a bit of a snark, but it was mostly to hide the fact that she was very intimidated by the idea of getting into the deep chilly water that was filled with hungry creatures.

Cassius led her to a secluded spot. The four guards took their positions around the perimeter. The two of them removed their shoes and cloaks. The General took off his tunic. His chest was massive and furry. She could see the scar from the attack that almost took his arm. It went up and around his right shoulder.

They walked to the shore. They carefully traversed some big stones, then stepped onto the creamy colored sand. It gave way underfoot a little. She stared at her own feet, then her eyes followed the sweep of the strand. There were muted little sparkles here and there, like stars in a pale sky. She looked up. The General had already waded into waist-high water. He had turned around and was watching her.

"Don't be afraid, just step right in."
She walked to where the sand met the river. It was like looking at two different worlds. She took a few steps into the water and squealed, "It's cold!"
"No," he said, "it's merely cool. Keep going."
She took a few more steps. The water slithered up to her torso. She gasped with shock.

"Just keep moving," he said. "That's the real secret to staying warm. And to not drowning. Move your arms back and forth. You can push and pull the water. Or, it can push and pull you. Stay in control. Push the water down and you go up. Push the water back and you go forward. Push it equally back and forth and you stay in one spot. That's treading. It's the first thing to learn. There you go."

She had been practicing the arm movements as they waded. The water was up to their shoulders. It was getting very close to their faces.

Then he suddenly moved behind her, picked her up by the waist, and propelled her into deeper water. There was nothing under her feet! She was really not prepared for this.
"Now tread with your feet." She began kicking wildly. Her foot collided with his leg.
"Ow, no!" he exclaimed. "Smaller movements. Pushing and pulling."
She was making little whining noises as she thrashed about.
"Don't worry, Pippa. I'll hold on to you. You figure out the water."

She felt like she was at the pull-up bar all over again. She tried to calm down. Cassius reminded her, "Pushing and pulling. Direct the water. Make small adjustments to stay in control. That's it. A little more force now. Good."

He let her go. She was sinking. She pushed and pulled wildly, thrashing and kicking. It was working! No, she was sinking again. She thrashed and kicked again and regained her position.

"Good! Very good." Cassius had grabbed her by the waist again. "Relax." It took her a moment to stop pushing and pulling. She hung there as before, with no ground underneath.

"Now, Pippa, stretch down with your right foot." She did so tentatively. "A little further. Almost there." To her amazement, she felt the sandy river bed. "You can stand here." He released her. She felt a moment of vertigo, then she was standing in the river, in water up to her chin.
"Barely," she replied, trying to keep her face out of the water.

He turned around. "Hold on to my shoulders. Kick with your legs. Keep your face up. Or to the side." He was moving. She held on to him and kicked. They began to pick up speed. It was exhilarating, until she forgot to keep her face out of the way and some of the river went down her throat. She coughed and sputtered. Cassius stopped and helped her stand upright. The water was waist-deep again. She hacked and spit. Her eyes burned and her throat felt raw.

"Well, now, that was fun for a moment," he said. "Wasn't it?"
She nodded. It was a relief to be standing again.
He moved to face her, saying, "Alright, now spread your legs apart, horse stance."
She did so. "A little further apart. Good. Stand firm, soldier!"

He suddenly went upside down and disappeared. He passed under her legs. There were little bubbles all around. Then she heard him come up behind her. She turned around.
"We call that game 'Pillars of Hercules'," he said. "Want to try?"
"No thanks."
"You still need to put your head underwater. It's part of the training." He put his hands on her shoulders. "We're ducking under the water. Take a deep breath, go under, and let it out slowly. Open your eyes. I'll be right in front of you."

She took a deep breath. He pulled her gently under. The water pressed on her ears. She felt a tapping on her forehead. She had forgotten to open her eyes.

She did so tentatively. The water burned. But she could see. The General was directly in front of her. He waved, grinning. He was covered with little bubbles and his hair was floating like a Gorgon's.

They bobbed back up to the surface.
"Good!" he exclaimed. "Now, on to swimming."
What? she thought. *They hadn't even started yet?*

"Sir," she said, "I've never even seen real swimming, just in pictures. Perhaps you could give me a demonstration?" *And feel free to tire yourself out*, she added in her mind. She was ready to get out of the water. Her skin felt soggy, her eyes burned, and the wet clothes were heavy and uncomfortable.

"Alright, watch me now." He lunged across the water. He swam quickly on his side. Then he swam on his back. Then he swam on his belly. Then he repeated the moves several times. He returned to her and stood up. He was heaving like a bellows.

Philippa said, "That was really impressive!"
Panting, he said, "That's enough for today." They walked towards the shore. She smiled and said, "Thank you for the lesson. I think I will like swimming. Eventually."

They returned to their quarters. "I'm so hungry!" she said.
He replied, "That's from being in the water." The servants had made lunch, a frittata, from the eggs Philippa had bought. They ate, then sat back on the bed to do some reading. Cassius was snoring within minutes. *I suppose that's also from being in the water,* she thought.

After evening formation, the General dismissed her. She went and joined the Ares Mons. They all chatted for a while. She learned that Tyronius had missed Malus, Dar and Murti, so he had taken a job in the stables. Davines had gotten an assignment in the kitchens. They thanked her for all the supplies. Then they marched away. Philippa and Terranes headed down the officers' lane. They got in a cart, and she showed the driver their destination on the map.

They traveled down the road that went to the cart pool, but turned right before the end of the road. There was a lane flanked with little houses and large evergreen trees. The lane and curbs were made of grey stone. A sign read Ceres I- XII. It showed a sheaf of grain. The row of small stone houses was neat and attractive. They made their way to number III and knocked on the door.

Dimocletus and his family were happy to meet Terranes. The match was encouraged. They burned incense at the family shrine in honor of the occasion. They declared that Julia Julius would be an auspicious name.

The daughter was very attractive; with light brown hair and a long slender frame. Her tunic gown was elegant but simple, and she was coifed and styled in the traditional Roman way. Her etiquette was impeccable. She and Terranes seemed well suited. Dinner was an elaborate five-course meal, with many items that Philippa was not inclined to try. She left after they ate. Terranes was invited to stay.

The days grew longer and the Ram appeared in the night sky. Agrippa and Ambrosius both had a fairly regular daily routine. Formation, breakfast, rest, training, swimming, lunch, rest, reading, scribing, meetings, errands, evening formation, dinner and cake time.

She used both of the cake pans. They created very different textures. She tried various combinations of ingredients. She read the recipes, and adapted a couple of them to fit her own supplies. She concluded that she didn't really care for nutmeg.

Occasionally, she would go to train, or have a class with the Ares Mons. Master of the Pan had become a rotation, as no one apple cake had truly outdone the rest. The date was set for the wedding of Terranes and Julia: on the final day of Maia; the eve of the Kalends of Juno. Dimocletus had employed an augur to watch the birds in order to choose an auspicious time. *For a Britannic family with no second name,* Philippa thought, *they are more Roman than any of us.*

Aside from formations, the General mostly stayed at home. Philemones Calla, Paulinus Valinus and Augustus Ionias visited fairly often, to discuss business or deliver messages. Brian Magnus came and went. She liked it when he was around. Sometimes they played Yes or No. But mostly he just spoke, telling her stories about Cassius, and their time together. She began to take notes, scribing on her blank sheets. He really liked to talk, which was lovely, because he was so interesting, but she couldn't help wondering how effective a secret agent he actually was.

She had learned to swim; not very well, or for very far, but Cassius seemed satisfied. She had also learned to have fun in the water. Cassius let her ride on his shoulders. Then he would throw her into the deep water. He would float on his back with his arms behind his head and she would pull him around in the shallows.

One hot sunny day, they went past their usual secluded spot. They came to a place where the river narrowed. They crossed a small stone bridge and continued on the other side. She could see that the Trisantonis had divided, and joined with a couple of other streams that were spilling down a small gorge. *And there's the mill,* she realized. She had heard about it; the mill was where all their flour and grain-meal came from. It had a water wheel, and a windmill.

They continued. The path went downhill rather steeply, then leveled out at a series of rock pools, which were being fed by a rushing waterfall. The guards posted themselves. There was a family in one of the pools. The man was standing naked in the pounding spray of water, while the woman and children played in and around the pool. The man saw Cassius, and saluted through the downpour. Cassius saluted the drenched soldier in return.

The General grabbed her hand, saying, "Careful. Slippery wet rocks."
They moved cautiously towards the pool. They put down their towels, took off their cloaks and sandals, and sat on the stone edge, near to the falling water. It was the loudest thing Philippa had ever heard. Louder even than Cassius Ambrosius. He slid off the edge and swam into the pool. She followed him.
She gasped. "That's COLD!"
"Yes," he called out to her, "this water is actually cold!" He was so smug. She flipped, and splashed him with her feet, a trick he had taught her. They splashed for a while, then hauled themselves out of the pool and onto a natural stone bench, warmed by the sun. The bench felt so good, it was almost worth getting that cold. She lay on her back and stared up at the deep blue sky, framed with trees, rocks and water. Birds were circling way up high. Ferns and mosses abounded. There were bluebells and buttercups. This was a special place.

On the way home they were silent. She felt light and tingly. She dreamed of her mother that night for the first time, ever. In the dream, they were singing a song to the Old Gods. Philippa tried to recall the song when she woke, but couldn't.

Over the next few days, she noticed a change in the General's demeanor. He hadn't been moody for a very long time, but now he was getting cross and irritated again. He didn't want to swim all of a sudden. He said his arm hurt too much. And no, he didn't want her to try and do anything about it.

When Brian Magnus appeared later that evening, she asked him why Cassius was being so gloomy and dark.

"This happens every year," he said. "Tomorrow is the twentieth day in the month of Apru. That's when his sister died, years ago."

"In the plague?"

"No, before then. He was eight when she drowned. She was six. She took one of his toy swords. He yelled at her to leave his things alone, and then she ran off crying. They found her in the river Temesis soon afterward. He's blamed himself his whole life."

"Gods protect us!" she cried. "That's tragic. Poor Cassius. So much suffering."

"I know that he can be difficult," Brian confided. "Try to be patient. He'll come around."

The next day, Philippa and Cassius walked to formation in silence, and then walked back in silence. Brian Magnus was sitting at the desk, looking through the General's correspondence. Beni and Artemis had the day off. It was very quiet. Cassius sat down on the edge of his bed, looking despondent. Philippa hesitated, then went and sat beside him. He ignored her.

She said, "Sir... I know you still feel the loss of your sister very deeply. It hurts me to see you this way. If it's any comfort, I would be a sister to you, because you mean that much to me."

The General said indignantly, "You would be my sister? How do you dare? My family traces itself back to the Gods themselves. What are you, that you could replace my sister? Perhaps I brought you up the ranks too quickly. Or do you think you have purchased that privilege?"

She was deeply shocked. She felt as though she'd been struck. Tears stung her eyes. She ran out through the front door. She could hear Brian Magnus angrily shouting at Cassius, "What in the name of Hades is wrong with you?"

She ran past the guards, wiping her eyes and trying to appear normal. She didn't plan a route, she was just used to walking to the side gate every day, and that's what she did now. Her breathing was ragged. She had a pain in her chest. She passed through the gate and kept walking. She went onto the little bridge, but she stopped halfway over. She stood there for a long time. Then numbly, she turned and walked back home. She had thought to slip into her room unnoticed, but when she entered the quarters, no-one was even there.

She went into her room, dressed in her nightgown, climbed into her bed and went to sleep.

She awoke to the sound of voices. It was late; the light was fading. Evening formation would be done by now. She realized that Cassius and Brian Magnus had returned. They were arguing. Cassius was saying,
"Just this once. Find her. It will take you less than the blink of an eye."
"No, I will not. And we should not even be speaking of these things. I will help you to search again on foot, but I will not break my covenant."
"You must love to see me suffer!" Cassius said loudly.
"Father, I am just abiding by the rules that you created."
"Yes, well, apparently I created everything. But what is the point of being all powerful, when I am clearly powerless?"

Brian's voice replied calmly,
"You command yourself, as every man does. That is the point. You commanded your tongue to say the words that pushed her away. Which reminds me. I went back and checked. She is the one who is descended from the Old Gods, not you. Not you in this form I mean. Your human family is quite ordinary."
"So," Cassius exclaimed with annoyance, "you can go back in time to look at family histories, but you won't look for her right now? Please, son, what if... what if she doesn't come back?"

"Then you are in trouble," said Brian Magnus. "If you don't put things right, this could-- Philippa!"

She had emerged from her room. Their loud and bizarre conversation was hurting her ears. Brian Magnus was facing her, a very surprised look on his face. Cassius had his back turned. He spun around, crying,
"Pippa! Have you been here the whole time?"
"What do you mean? What whole time?" She felt disoriented. "What's going on?"

Cassius seemed to be dumbfounded. Brian Magnus finally said,
"We've been searching for you. We heard that you were seen leaving the post. The General was afraid that you had run away because he had insulted you."

She said tersely, "Well, that's *really* insulting. I went for a walk. I didn't run away." She felt hot, and little dizzy. There was a cup of water on the table. She went over and drank it.
When she turned back around, Cassius stood before her.

He was weeping. "Please forgive me. I would be honored to have you as my sister. You mean that much to me too." She stretched out her arms and smiled at him. He pulled her to him.

"It's alright, sir," she said soothingly. "I would never leave you." She patted his back, but she was gazing directly into the far-seeing amber eyes of Brian Magnus.

She was dreaming. No, it was really a vision and not a dream, some part of her brain was telling her, because she was seeing it, but she wasn't actually in it. There was no sense of sound, touch or smell. She tried to look down to see if she had a body, but she could not. She could only look skyward.

First she was staring at a vast empty blue space. Then there was a soundless crackle of light, and a figure suddenly appeared; a very thin man with a misshapen head. He was suspended in the air. His pale naked body was nearly skeletal. Spines protruded from his bony shoulders. A translucent material stretched between the spines. He moved, and she could see that he had wings. They were vast and complicated structures. They seemed to stretch into infinity, way out of proportion to the figure; she could see distant stars through them. The wings were tattered and scorched, and in several places they seemed to be on fire.

The man's head was shaped like a sideways flame, or a teardrop. It was pointed at the back, fleshy and hairless. His face was flat and wide and curved, like a helmet. His eyes were round and oversized. There were no eyelids, lashes or eyebrows. Instead of normal ears and nose, there were two pairs of small dark holes, like on a bird. Also like a bird, his thin-lipped mouth went nearly from ear to ear. His head was capped by an impossibly fine net, sparkling with thousands of tiny jewels at the intersections. His skin was scorched and peeling. Below the wounds, there was an eerie dark red light.
There were thousands of thin lines, like hairs, or tree branches, almost imperceptible. They were emanating from him, gathering all around him, and shooting off into an unseen distance. Whenever he moved, waves of these tiny lines shifted around him, grouping and regrouping over and over at a dizzying rate. The lines grew beneath him like roots of a great tree, branching out time and again in endless iteration.

Now he began to flicker in and out. The wings expanded and contracted with a myriad of little movements. A smoky darkness was filling the space. There were little explosions of light. The darkness grew, and soon she could no longer see the man and his shifting filaments. He was gone.

The little explosions turned into massive bursts. She looked up. She could see nothing but clouds and flame; long bands of thick sulphur-colored smoke, and whirling clouds of purple and white gasses. She could see through the spaces between the clouds. There was a backdrop of endless royal blue behind it all.

Great swirling pillars of dark smoke began to form. They morphed into giant volcanoes, spewing forth oceans of boiling red magma, which heaved up, turned black, and violently exploded. A tsunami of gaseous tidal waves flung massive glowing rocks into distant space. She slowly realized that the air was filled with the same faint filaments that she'd seen around the figure. They were twisted together like giant ropes. Great bolts of electricity shot through them, as they grouped and regrouped at lightning speed.

Her perspective was changing. Her view was being pulled farther and farther out from the chaos. The scene should have diminished, but it just got bigger. And bigger. And impossibly bigger. Her point of view continued to expand, but it was all too vast to take in. Yellow, purple, white and green clouds were twisting and thrashing, winding and unwinding themselves in endless patterns of swirling colors. Then a mighty wind seem to pass by and blow it all asunder. A great cloud of sparkling white dust covered the scene.

The dust slowly dissipated. Overhead, the sky was banded in black and green. Occasional bolts of lightning appeared like bright rivers in the sky. She kept moving away, away, and further away. Now she could see some colorful swirls at the edges of the darkness. She continued to move away. The black and green cloud appeared to be a vast vaporous oval shape in the midst of the cyclonic cloudscape.

With a geyser-like burst, the gaseous cloud split lengthways, the top part rose up and the bottom half went down. They revealed a bright red cloud directly overhead. The red cloud was round like the sun. There was a large dark spot in the very center.

Lightning spread like veins across the darkness. The black and green clouds closed together again, vapors streaming, lightning flashing, then parted once more, and the red cloud with the dark spot turned in her direction. Then she understood- it was an eye; a giant, blood-red, blinking eye!

Chapter Twelve - A Friend or Two

The next day was Saturn's Day, the end of the seven-day week. There was no formation. Philippa lay on her cot. She had been awake since dawn. She had heard the servants come in and quietly begin their day. She heard the General speaking to them as he prepared for his breakfast. Later, she could hear him getting dressed, and then he left the tent. She hadn't heard Brian Magnus, so maybe he was gone too. She felt a little guilty for avoiding them, but she didn't want to talk to anyone yet.

In her first moments of waking, she had recalled last night's overheard conversation and her dream-vision. She felt sure that there was something... supernatural going on, and that she was somehow caught up in it. As the light of day grew, however, she reasoned that she was probably just confused. Cassius and Brian Magnus had been arguing about something complicated. They were men of the world; she couldn't be expected to understand what was being said. It was their concern, not hers. And the dream... *that was just the result of an overactive imagination, after a particularly stressful day.*

Her stomach growled loudly. She got up. She slipped on her brown robe and went to the privy. Then she washed up and went out to the patio. The servants were outside, preparing the soil in the little garden patch below the grotto. She wondered if there was any breakfast left over. It was another bright warm day. She shaded her eyes. Someone had left a covered tray on the table. She sat in the chair facing their quarters, and uncovered the tray. A boiled egg, a golden saffron griddle cake, curly cress, nasturtiums, candied walnuts, cold stewed apricots with honey, and a pitcher of water with mint. Someone had gone to the trouble to make her favorite things. She ate. The food was so good! She finished every bit of it, then drank some of the water. Philippa relaxed. The sun was warm on her back. She stared blankly at the back of the house. Then she realized that she wasn't alone. Brian Magnus was sitting on the ground with his back against the wall in the cool shadow. In the same spot where she had first encountered him. *Nulles Ex Nusquam.*

"Good morning," he said. "I didn't want to startle you. So I said nothing. Not easy for me, you know." He grinned. "Forgive me, but I'm staying over here. The sun's a bit bright for me right now."

She got up, went over and joined him. They sat in silence. Then he said, "The General's gone to see the Ares Mons. A social visit. He wants to be sure that your men are taken care of. He is planning for Terranes and his new bride to occupy one of the empty officer tents. He's got a few other ideas too. And, he's never given them the official welcome talk. His speech about how the times are changing and the future is up to them, and everyone needs to learn a vocation for when the soldiering is done. And how blessed he is to get to work with such fine men as themselves."

Brian Magnus sounded less robust than usual. He was trying to make conversation. She enjoyed conversing with him, but this morning she couldn't think of anything to say. She turned to look at him. She felt a twinge of sympathy. *Like she had towards the figure in the vision--*
She shook her head quickly, as if to shake the thought from her mind. She looked away again. He said,
"Is there something you'd like to ask me?" She sat silently.
"Are you not talking to me, Pippa?" He sounded almost sad.

"Did you send visions to me in my sleep?" *Argh! She was asking irrational questions despite herself.*
"Of course not," said Brian Magnus. "You came and collected them."
"WHAT? What kind of thing is that to say! Why do you tell me... impossible things?"
"Because... no, you're right. I forget myself."

He scooted around to face her. "Ask me yes or no? I'll say the truth."
She didn't hesitate now. "Are you Mercury? The God Mercury?"
Brian said, "Oooh, right out of the gate! Yes."
"Are you in many places at once?"
"No."
That made her think. *Maybe not even the gods can be in two places at once.*
"Are you just so fast that it seems like it?"
"Yes."
"That's why you seemed to come out of nowhere?"
"Yes."
"Why are you here? I mean, are you here now for a particular reason?"
"Yes."
"Is it to help Cassius?"
"Yes."
"You called him Father. Is he really your father?"
"Mmmm... yes."
"Is he... is he... Jupiter?"
"Yes."
"But he is a mortal?"
"Yes. For now."

She leaned back. The cool wall felt grounding and reassuring.

"You know you sound like a lunatic, don't you?" she asked.

He responded, "You're the one asking strange questions! There's nothing loony about saying yes or no." He smiled at her.

She closed her eyes. "This is nonsense. But I'll play along. You're a God, an immortal. What we see on earth isn't your true form." She thought of the vision, but this time she didn't shake it away. Very soberly, she asked,

"Is it true that you don't ever eat or drink or sleep?"

"Yes."

"I'm sorry. I hate to think that you might be suffering. Does it take a lot of energy to do physical tasks while you're... appearing?"

"Yes."

"And you're here to help Cassius. Did you know, I called him 'Jupiter' when I first saw him? When we came face to face during inspection. It was the hair."

"What did he do?"

"He seemed surprised for a moment, that's all. But then, anyone would be."

There was silence. Beni and Artemis had gone home to their nearby billet for their morning break.

She went on, talking as much to her self as to Brian Magnus.

"So... Jupiter used to come to earth frequently, according to the stories. But he wouldn't stop being almighty God just to do that. I mean he'd have to maintain some sort of connection with his divine form while he was on earth." She thought about the giant red eye, searching for contact. "But that was a long time ago. He stopped coming to earth as himself. Why? Because things on earth had changed so much? Reality might have been... looser when the earth was younger. It may have grown denser over the aeons."

I sound like one of the scrolls! thought Philippa. She continued her musings.

"The Gods in their true forms don't really have any way of experiencing what it's like to be a human on the earth. Jupiter is the father of us all, but he's so monumental that he can't really even see us, we're so insignificant. And he has kept growing all these millennia. He's too vast to come to earth anymore. The divine connection must be limited. So he must send a portion, a part of himself. An excarnation... a sort of offspring. He has to do this, to truly understand humanity. To understand love. Because it's all about love. And he has to suffer, too, for those same reasons. But he's still a mortal. Up to certain point. If he can make it up to that point, then he can somehow leave this human world and this incarnation without having the usual mortal death. Then he can take all that he's learned back to the whole, and be reunited. But if he doesn't live long enough, or well enough, he might just die a mortal death and all the effort would be in vain. That's why you are here, to guide and protect him." She thought for a moment.

"I guess that's why I'm here too, to help anyway I can. I suppose if Gods come to earth, even they need a friend or two."

Brian Magnus looked into her eyes and said, "Yes. The General told me that you were perceptive. He doesn't realize how perceptive."

"Oh, maybe it's because I'm descended from the Gods!" she chided him good-naturedly.

"Maybe it is," he said. Now that they were actually discussing these strange topics, she felt a little better. *Talking to a God is very therapeutic, it seems.*

"So, what do you mean, I collected those visions?" she asked. "Did my unconscious mind travel somewhere? To some invisible cosmic library or something like that?"

"Yes. You accessed the Record."

"That sounds very bureaucratic." She giggled. "I hope I kept my dream receipt. I might have incurred some expenses."

He laughed with delight at her playfulness. "Yes, if ever there was one who could spend coin in another realm, it's you." She laughed too. Then she said, "So... Cassius has no divine knowledge, right? He knows about all this... from you?"

"Yes. I was a friend of the family. When the fates took them, I was his mentor and guardian. I revealed to him his true nature when he was fourteen. I had to do a few tricks, to prove my point. It took some time for him to accept it. He still has some doubts. The fact that I don't age has helped my case."

"You don't age?" she asked. "In this form?"

"No, not really. Some days I'm... fuller than others, depending on how much energy I've had to expend. Which reminds me."

He reached behind him, and handed her a box. It was the metal box that the coins had been in.

"Oh, it's the temple box," she said. "Thanks for returning it."

"Aren't you going to open it?" he asked. It felt light, but she had only held it when it was full of coin, so she couldn't really judge. She lifted the latch.

She stared in amazed shock. It was her parcel of cinnamon. And her seed packets. She touched them. They were real. She could smell the cinnamon.

It smelled so good! Like a long lost friend.
"You went there and... carried these back?" *No wonder he seemed worn out.*

"I wanted to have a look around," he said. "Things have improved since you left. I thought you might want to know. Maximus is dead. From a stroke, it seems. He'd been dead for some time when he was finally discovered by a visitor. Really stunk up the place. There was no sign of that dirty acolyte. The visitor went to the local official and told him about it. Some workers came and cleaned it all up. Made it really nice. They found another priest, a good one this time, with a capable acolyte. They've got the place up and running again. They get a regular trickle of visitors. That is a lovely temple, by the way. You did an excellent job restoring the mosaics."

She was so thankful, she started to weep.
"Now, now, don't do that," he said. "Please." She sniffled and stopped crying.
"I'm so grateful," she said. "For the cinnamon, and seeds, and the information. And for you."

She went to the table and drank some water before returning to the shade. She said,
"I'm afraid that I will feel bad now about eating and drinking and sleeping when you're around."
He said, "I was not courting your pity."
"It's not pity. It's sympathy. It's love. When something hurts you, it hurts me too."
"That's why you are a friend to the Gods, Philippa," he said. "Do you know the story of Zeus Pater coming to earth to lie with a mortal woman?"
She laughed, "Which one?"

He smiled. "The one where the woman insists that the God show her his true form."

"Yes," she replied, "he didn't want to, but she wouldn't let up. Or she tricked him, because Hera tricked her. Anyway, she went mad and died, right? Or she died from being burnt by his thunderbolts. And she was possibly the mother of Dionysius. What was her name?"

"Semele. She had the same vision of him that you did. But she had to be given it. She didn't know how to seek it, as you did. That's the difference."
"Oh. But did she... feel any heat?"
"No. She saw what you saw, in the exact same way. So why did she not survive it?"

Philippa considered. "Well, why was she so insistent in the first place? Was she trying to elevate her own status or position? Was she motivated by love, or suspicion? Was she mad? Or was she just madly curious?"

"She died from fear," he said. "Fear is a sort of madness. Were you afraid?"

"No. My only real fear is of losing people I care about. I was... surprised. It was certainly awe-inspiring and overwhelming. I felt a little queasy during part of it. But mostly I felt... love. Love, and sympathy, for a force so vast that it can't discover its own boundless source of love without some assistance. A great eye in the sky, just looking for a friend." She touched him gently on the arm. "And love for a force that is so... busy, he doesn't have time to enjoy earthly delights, even when he's corporeal."

It was mid-day. Beni and Artemis had come back from their break and resumed their project in the garden. Brian said, "Cassius will return soon. I told him that I had found a source of cinnamon. And that I was going to put it in the temple box and surprise you. It was subterfuge. He doesn't need to know that I've been spying on your life again. In fact, he doesn't need to know we've had this conversation. He doesn't realize the depth of your understanding. It hasn't occurred to him that you have actually pieced the whole story together from the little bit you overheard."

"What about the seeds?"

"Plant them." Brian Magnus was looking at the garden, where the servants were making new furrowed rows.

"Oh," she said. "Good idea."

They rose. The sun had passed, and the patio table was now in the shade. Brian Magnus sat down in a chair. She took the box and went inside. She set it in the pantry, opened it, and took out the seeds. Then she closed it and went back outside. She brought the seeds over to Beni and Artemis.

"I have some seeds from... where I used to live. I was wondering if you'd like to plant any of them."

They took the seeds, looked at them with interest, and went back to hoeing the rows. Philippa went to the table and cleared away her breakfast tray.

Cassius returned in a jolly mood. If the events of the previous day had affected him, he didn't show it. He was full of news about her men.

"Terranes will be our neighbor. He and Julia will move into the empty quarters on that side." He pointed one way. Then the opposite way. "And on the other side, the Marianis brothers." He smiled at Philippa. "Remarkable lads. I thought you'd appreciate having them around."

She smiled broadly. "That's wonderful news."

"Oh, speaking of wonderful news, Davines West is engaged to be married! Last night, he proposed to one of the kitchen girls, and she said yes."
"What?" She was delighted. "That's amazing. Good for him."

Cassius said thoughtfully,
"Some young men feel the need to marry. Others don't. A good leader makes it work to everyone's advantage. That was part of my goal today, to get an idea of how many of the lads are looking for wives. Big Julius has his eye on the daughter of an engineer. That looks to be a good match."
He suddenly chuckled. "Erastus Minor. What a character. When I said to the men, 'Is there anyone else who wants to get married?' he replied, 'I'm flattered sir, but you're not my type'." They laughed.

She said, "He's a dour funny fellow."

"Yes," said Cassius. "I've also arranged for he and Tyronius to be our neighbors. The pastureland between us and the gate could be better used. Tyronius will be in charge of livestock. Erastus can assist. Mostly, I just want them around. Erastus is amusing and irreverent, and Tyronius has that lovely musical Hibernian way of speaking. They and the twins are going to make up my new entourage." He took her hand. "Not that I haven't enjoyed our time alone together, but it's only fitting for a General to have a support group. And I like and trust the Ares Mons. I hope you approve."

"I'm delighted," she said. "I think you've made excellent choices. I'll be so happy to have them around." She squeezed his hand. She felt lighter. She'd been feeling bad about her men. She didn't want to lose them, but she could feel them slipping away. She stood, and in her best orator stance recited,

"Gain is loss and loss is gain. People come and go. That's the Army, that's life. Like the Big Man said, let's enjoy it while it lasts. Tyronius Danu, 392."

Chapter Thirteen - The Realm of the Gods

Time slipped quietly by. The wedding of Terranes and Julia was a glorious event, celebrated by the entire post. The family of Dimocletus spent a small fortune on the feasting and entertainment. And they had brought in a real old-time priest from somewhere in Gaul to perform the elaborate ceremony. Philippa had never been to a wedding. She wondered if it was usual to have jugglers and acrobats at the reception.

A month later, Davines West wed the curvaceous Keli. The General married them himself, in the grotto, in an intimate and moving ceremony. As much as she had appreciated the big spectacular wedding, Philippa preferred this one.

In the late fall, Julius Phaedonis married the fair Marcella Dinas, daughter of a high ranking immune. They moved into a fine new home, in a recently built neighborhood near the commissary. The Ares Mons were moved to a much nicer and more permanent barracks in the same area. The lads were thrilled. They raised their standard proudly in front of their new home.

Even Malus had found someone. In the early spring, Tyronius and Erastus had moved some of the livestock into the newly restored pasture, and Malus had fallen instantly in love, according to Tyronius, with a girl donkey named Jenni.

In the late spring Terranes and Julia had a son. They named him Phillip Ambrosius. Even as a toddler, he was a well behaved little man. Davines and Keli had twin boys. They were called Bruno and Brutus West. The Scouts were delighted.

The garden bloomed in summer, lush with flowers and vegetables. Philippa had taken over much of its care. The servants had a lot to do, and she liked the work. They went swimming most days. The General's entourage followed him where he went, but more like a group of comrades than a herd of sheep. He seemed to thrive in their company. Brian Magnus came and went. He still liked to talk. She took lots of notes.

The following spring, Terranes and Julia had a girl, Juno. She grew quickly. She was bossy and contradictory, and brought a refreshing bit of chaos to this otherwise sedately perfect family. Philippa's notes about Cassius were being organized into a book. When he asked what she was so busy writing about, she just told him that it was a military history of a famous Roman general.

The seasons turned, and the skies with them. The months became years. There were more children, more animals, and more crops. The soldiers of Vindavia Nova still held formations, did drills and maintained their fighting gear, but the emphasis had indeed shifted to the country life: planting in spring, swimming in summer, harvesting in fall, and resting in winter.

The commissary building had been renovated, with twice the capacity. The shelves were always full. Everyone profited from the abundance of grain and produce, and from the local trade which developed from it. A community market-hall was being constructed, a large white forum building, one big room with a covered porch.

There were even some new trade partners. One day in early autumn, nearly five years after the fall wedding of Julius Phaedonis and Marcella Dinas, the General's group were all summoned to the gate. A small tribe of Celts had gathered, a combination of western Belgic and northern Catuvellauni. They had grown accustomed to getting grain from the Romans, but their previous supplier had gone away. They had heard of the prosperous Vindavia Nova, and had come to barter. There was a translator, a priest of Mithras, who was wearing a combination of Roman and native garb. Would the honorable General approve of a trade deal?

A hospitality area had been set up just outside the gate. Philippa approached with the others. The guards parted, and they went through. There were tables of food and drink, and places to rest. There were flowers in pots and some small shrines dedicated to the local Gods. Someone had done a nice job setting it up.

The Celts were unlike anything she had ever witnessed. She had never seen such ornamentation. Gold and silver knot-work, intricate enamels, jeweled buckles. And bold fashions! Fur and feathers and shells, long checkered trousers, chopped-up hairdos, tattoos, body paint and piercings. She was delighted. Things had seemed rather routine lately. This was an interesting change.

There was a table covered with strange weapons and helms. The General motioned, and his people added their own arms to the pile, as well as their helmets. The Celts stood in a cluster, quietly watching as the little formation approached them. They stopped. Philippa stood waiting beside the General. He was about to speak, but before he could, a man approached from the crowd. He was tall, and made even taller by a high top-knot of hair. He had long brightly-colored feathers in his beaded headband. His face was covered with spiral tattoos, and his ears were pierced with metal discs. He had on a saffron colored tunic, and wore a breastplate that at first appeared to be made out of human bones, but upon closer inspection turned out to be cleverly carved out of white driftwood.

To their surprise he knelt before Philippa and said, "Tha mi a'Vela."
The Romans all looked at the translator.
"What's he saying?" asked Philippa.
"He says, 'I am Vela'," replied the priest. "He is the leader of this group."
Philippa said, "Salve, a'Vela, welcome to Vindavia Nova." She put her hand out and encouraged him to rise. He did so reverently, saying, "Rega."

"Commander Vela thinks that she's your queen," said the translator to the Romans.

Cassius laughed. "I can see why you would think that. She *is* rather splendid," he said to Vela, "but we don't have a queen. Or a king. We just have a chain of command."
The priest translated what the General had said, and then pointed to Cassius and announced,
"General Cassius Ambrosius. Vela the Wise." Introductions were made all around. Vela apologized for his mistake via the translator.

"Why don't we have some refreshment?" said Cassius. Bruno and Brutus began pouring and serving. The Romans started in, demonstrating that they were not out to poison their guests. Soon all were feasting and quaffing. Then the tables were cleared, and the goods were brought out. Philippa was agog. The Celts had brought many items: brooches, hair clips, cloak fasteners, woven fabrics, combs, trousers, boots, buckles, and even some polished bronze mirrors. Everything was adorned with stylized animals, artistic swirls and maze-like patterns.

"It's all so beautiful!" Philippa exclaimed.
"Yes, but it's not practical," said Terranes. "I mean they're not really practical items."
"If we trade our excess grain for them, and then trade them for coin, does that make them more practical?" asked Cassius.
Terranes said, "Oh, I see. We can resell them. For a profit."
The Romans and Celts mingled, looking at the fine wares. Philippa stopped near a young man who was unpacking a display of torques. The neck collars were made of twisted silver and gold, terminating in two spirals.

Some of the spirals had jeweled or enameled ends. She gazed in wonder. The young man picked up an elegant slender torque. The spirals were adorned with two amethyst cabochons. He gently squeezed it open, and helped her to set it around her neck, with the opening in front. It sat right above her cuirass. He held up a mirror. The gold and silver gleamed against the red of her neck scarf. The lad motioned for her to keep it, saying, "Rega. Rega."

"Watch out, I think they want to worship you." Cassius was by her side. Philippa extended her hand to thank the young man. He smiled and shook her hand. She noticed that he had a spray of freckles across his nose and cheeks. Just like hers. She said to Cassius, "Do you think it's alright if I speak to Vela through the translator?"
He said, smiling, "I believe, as queen, you are entitled to that."
They went over to where the translator was speaking to Terranes. Vela was watching them. When he saw Cassius and Philippa, he bowed.

"Vela, hello. Fáilte." She knew that was Gaelic for welcome. She hoped that it would be close enough. She spoke to the translator.
"I want to let our friends know, my father's forebears were Catuvellauni. My mother told me that's where I get these." She pointed to the bridge of her nose. "Celtic freckles, she called them. So, I welcome you as a soldier of Rome, but also as a cousin. Fáilte."

It took the priest some time to get this translated. When he was done, a murmur went through the Celts. Some of them came up to greet her, stare at her freckles, and shake her hand. That was when she realized that some of these warriors were actually women. They were attired and coifed just like the men.

The General signaled to the farmers who were standing nearby. The farmers wheeled over three hand carts, containing sacks of freshly milled barley flour, spelt flour, flax meal, and oats. There were also six large amphorae of olive oil and three wheels of cheese, tucked in alongside the flour bags.
The Celts were clearly impressed and excited about the supplies.
Poor skinny things, thought Philippa, *they look like they can really use this food.*
The goods were exchanged, hands were shaken and further glad promises
of goodwill were made. The Celts took the hand carts, then they departed.

One day a letter came from across the sea. There was once again a solo Emperor, back in Rome. Old Flavius had died. Now it was, "All honor to Emperor Augustus Honorius".

It seemed so very far away. Until the following month, when they received a missive from Rome, the first in five years, that held unexpected news. The new solo Emperor wanted to re-establish connections in the far west provinces. He had heard of the tenacity of Vindavia Nova, and was going to start paying the troops again. Rome was reaching out to Vindavia Nova. Vindavia Nova was highly suspicious.

"Clearly, he wants something from us," said Cassius cynically.

The Emperor's letter spoke of traditional Roman values. Philippa was surprised by the contents. It was mostly about clothing and hair styles! With all the things going wrong in the Empire, to fixate on such superficial topics seemed ludicrous.

The Emperor had abolished long hair, torques, boots, and checkered trousers in the Roman capital. He warned of the moral and cultural dangers of adopted Germanic and Celtic barbarian styles of clothing.
Too late! thought Philippa.

By the spring of 398, the citizens of Vindavia Nova had wholly embraced the barbarian styles, despite the Emperor's warnings. Especially the civilians. It seemed that boots and trousers were actually quite comfortable, and practical. Philippa had gotten some of her own, and so had Cassius. Even in uniform, most of the soldiers had some sort of adornment, except for Terranes, who would not add, or subtract, from the standard uniform. Cassius wore a slender gold torque above his cuirass. The spirals were set with stones of jet black. The Celts had made several trading journeys, and two more tribal partners had been added. There was now a separate shop in the expanded commissary complex called the Emporium, which sold Celtic goods and accessories.

That summer had been extremely hot. Fortunately there had been copious rain, so the crops were thriving. The General's group went swimming nearly every day. Philippa had realized after that first time that a tunic was not good for swimming. She only needed to cover her breasts, not her shoulders or torso. So she just wore a set of her small clothes- a halter with short trousers. It made swimming much easier, and she didn't get chafed. The men tended to keep their trousers on, either through respect for her, or fear of nibbling fish.

They swam in the secluded area, and also at a broad beach that lay beyond the bridge. But mostly they swam at the Realm of the Gods, which was the name of the falls with the pools. Even though there wasn't much room for proper swimming, and even though it got tiresome, not being able to talk over the noise of the falls, and even though the water was freezing, the rocks were treacherous, and everybody had fallen or scraped their shins at least once, it was still the best spot. It was just so glorious.

It was a fine mid-morning in late August. The flowers around the falls were yellow and purple. Bees and butterflies were everywhere. Hummingbirds and kingfishers zoomed through the air. Cassius and Philippa, Bruno and Brutus, and Tyronius and Erastus were at the pools. There were no other visitors, so each pair had their own.

Cassius and Philippa had taken their favorite, the pool next to the big warm rock. The General was lying on it on his back, relaxed, eyes closed. Philippa was in the water. It was still cold, but not as bad as in the springtime. She did a few tiny laps, then pulled herself out. She stood on the edge of the warming rock, and wrung out her hair.

She saw something fly very fast into the pool. *Was that a bird?* She looked up, in time to see that one of the guards was running towards her. He was shouting, but she couldn't hear him over the roar of the falls.

The other guard was pointing up at the sky, gesticulating wildly. She looked up and saw that a shaft was traveling to earth from high above, and was heading right for Cassius Ambrosius.

She flung herself on top of him, landing sideways. Her face hit a rock. She could taste blood in her mouth. Cassius was very startled. She was lying across his chest.
He shouted, "What are you playing at? That really hurt. Get off me!"

He reached around to pull her off. Then he felt the wooden shaft, sticking out of the right side of her lower back.

Chapter Fourteen - Water and a Prayer

Cassius let out a cry that could be heard above the roar of the falls. The men were running. Tyronius and Erastus lifted Philippa and carefully held her, while the Scouts and the General slipped into their shoes. Erastus was sobbing, "No, no, no, no, no." The General barked,
"Bruno, tell the infirmary to prepare. Brutus, find Brian Magnus and tell him to meet us there. Seek him in my back patio. If he's not there, call him, he will come. Now FLY!"
The twins ran.

"Give her to me," said the General. Cassius picked her up, holding her at an angle, to keep any pressure off the arrow. The other two men quickly put their shoes on. They flanked the General who began to run, as gently as possible. As he did, he shouted, "Guards! Find who did this and bring him to me. Alive."

He ran. Up the incline, around the bend, and over the bridge. He was panting and heaving, but he kept up the pace. The other two men ran interference, making sure the path was clear. In between breaths, Erastus kept talking.

"I saw it... the guards were trying... to get your attention. She saw... an arrow was falling. Right towards you. She jumped. On top of you. She saved you. But the arrow... oh, no, no, no, no."
They reached the post. Bruno was waiting with a mule-cart. "Clever lad!" exclaimed Cassius. They helped him climb in with his awkward load, then they raced to the infirmary.

Brutus was there with Brian Magnus. The medics had cleared and disinfected a surgery table. Cassius helped the orderlies to set her down gently on her left side. Philippa groaned in pain.

Brian Magnus had taken charge. He said to the doctor, "Get poppy. And get the salt honey." To the orderlies he said, "Get two stacks of folded blankets." While the medical staff were collecting supplies, Brian Magnus was doing something to the area around the wound. There was a slight whirring sound, like a flock of little wings, then the faint smell of pine sap. He worked on her front, then on her back. The doctor and orderlies returned.

"Prepare the smoke-draught. Set the blankets behind her back, and on her chest, so." Brian Magnus demonstrated. "Put the honey on the wound. Keep applying it."

Cassius had almost caught his breath. He moved to the head of the table and crouched down by her face.

"My tooth is gone!" Philippa said, running her tongue over the bloody hole where her right canine used to be.
"It's alright." He was trying to be stoic.
"Are you alright? Did the point go into you?" She asked.
He looked down at his furry chest. There was a tiny puncture wound, and one small smeared drop of blood. "Hardly at all. You saved my life, Pippa. You were so brave!"
Cassius had been keeping it together, but now that she was in the doctor's care, he began to cry.

The doctor appeared. He gave her a spoonful of something. "This is honey-wine. It will lessen the burn of the smoke."
"What smoke?" she asked.
Brian said,
"It's poppy. It will help you to relax. Then we can remove the dart."
The doctor said, "Breathe this in. Tiny sips of air. Try not to cough." He had a small beaker filled with smoke. He held it to her mouth. She sucked some in. It tasted terrible, and burnt her throat. It almost made her cough.
"Don't cough," said the doctor. He gave her more honey-wine, alternating it with the medicine until the smoke was gone.
"I don't feel so good," she said.
"Let's see if we can do something about that," said Brian. "Keep applying the salt honey." He twisted the dart a little to see if it would move.

"Owwww!" She cried in pain. Brian Magnus said, "Give it another moment for the poppy to take effect." There was a brief silence. Then Philippa suddenly spoke, in a slurred but conversational voice.

"Cassius... if I had let you die... my life would have been... poop... because you're my favorite friend. I'm gonna protect you." She suddenly yawned. "But... what I really wanna know is... where... I mean why don't we... have a pussycat? A black one. NO! An orange one! An orange cat... named... Bootchie." She giggled and said, "Bootchie the Kitty."

Cassius said, "That sounds like a great idea, Pippa. Let's get a cat." Tears were rolling down his face but his voice was calm.
"Alright, hold her steady," said the doctor. They all gripped her tight. "One, two, three-"
Brian Magnus pulled out the shaft. Philippa screamed and passed out.

She awoke to the sound of the doctor talking.

"There's no way of knowing the damage. We'll just have to wait. There was hardly any blood. There didn't seem to be any other substances leaking out. Perhaps the shaft miraculously missed her bowels and organs. At least it was just a dart, not an arrow, and the wood was scraped clean."

Philippa felt groggy and heavy. She was still on her side. She said, "I want to lay on my back." Cassius helped her slowly turn over. She made a little moan, but then she relaxed. She felt her wound. It had been wrapped in loose gauze. "I'm thirsty."
"Just a tiny sip for now," said the doctor. The orderly held up a cup. She sipped it. Then she grabbed it and drank it all.
"Pippa! Please, take it slow," said the General.

"My tooth!" she cried. "I just remembered. It's gone!" She burst into tears.
Cassius said, "I'm so sorry, dearest." He held her. The General looked up. The four men of Ares Mons were standing by, utterly miserable, still in their swimming clothes.

"Men. Thank you for everything. Go and get yourselves changed."
Erastus asked, "What about whoever did this? Can we go hunt him down?"
"Three of the guards have gone to find him," said Cassius. "The other has collected our belongings. Go get your clothes and get dressed. Take a moment, drink some water, say a prayer. We've done all we can for now."

"The same goes for you, sir," said Brian Magnus. "Water and a prayer. I will stay here." Cassius didn't move. "Come on sir, I insist." Brian Magnus pulled him to his feet and gently shoved him towards the door. The five men left the medical tent dejectedly.

Philippa drifted in and out of consciousness. She tried not to moan, because when she did, they made her drink more smoke. Eventually, she fell into a deep sleep.

She awoke again to the sound of voices near the door. The doctor was saying, "You guards can't all come in here. This is a medical facility."

Cassius said, "Take him and get him cleaned up. He's a mess. Mostly from crying, it would appear. Get his face washed. Give him some food and drink. Then bring him right back here. Just one of you bring him in, alright? He really doesn't seem like much of a threat."

Brian Magnus was by her side.

He said, "They caught the fellow who shot you. He's no assassin. He's just a lad. Says he's a Roman citizen. I believe him. He was just testing out darts. He makes them for his sisters to hunt with. Darts with no tips, for shooting birds. He was in the woods above the falls, launching them out over the waterfall to see how they'd fly."

Cassius joined them, adding, "Yes, as much as I wanted to destroy the attacker, I must admit that I felt a bit sorry for him."

"Can I have some water?" Her throat was so dry.

The doctor said, "Yes, but one spoonful at a time. Slowly." He prepared a cup for her.

The General helped her to sit up a bit. He fed her a spoonful of water.

"How do you feel, Pippa?" he asked.

"I think I won't be anyone's pretty queen anymore, with a hole in my teeth."

"You look like a true warrior now," he said. "Real warriors have scars. You were too perfect before. Don't worry, you're still gorgeous. But now you're fierce too."

A guard returned, bringing in a young man. He was freshly washed, but his eyes were red from crying. Bruno, Brutus, Erastus and Tyronius followed him in.

Cassius said, "Pippa, this is Darius Po."

Darius was in his late teens, very thin, with narrow shoulders and shaggy brown hair.

Philippa said, "Come over here, please. Have a seat. Someone get him a chair." Bruno quickly brought one over, and directed the boy to sit.

"Tell me about yourself," she said to him. Darius said,

"Please, I never meant to hurt you. It was an accident. I'm so sorry. Are... are you going to be alright?"

"Don't worry about me. I want to know about you. What's your story, where do you live, that sort of thing."

"I... I live in the woods. With my mother and three sisters. I'm not sure where it is from here."

The accompanying guard spoke up. "Centurion, he comes from a very poor settlement, just a couple of huts, up on the bluff, around two miles east of the falls. They live deep in the woods."

"How many people are in your settlement?" she asked.

"Eight," said Darius. "There's us, and there's a couple with a little boy. We met them in the woods, when we were running away. That was almost three years ago, when he was just a baby."

"Running away from what?" Cassius had joined the conversation, pulling up another chair.
Darius Po was quiet for a moment. "We had a village. A nice one. On the other end of the ridge. There were almost fifty of us. We had some orchards."
His voice was shaking.
"It's alright, son," Cassius said. "Go on."

"My sisters and mother and I went fishing one day," said Darius. "When we were coming home, we saw smoke." He paused. "They were all dead. My father, my brother. Everyone. One of the elders was still dying. He told us what had happened. Men had come out of nowhere and killed everyone. He knew who they were. He said that it was a bunch of renegade soldiers. Enemies of Rome."

Brian Magnus was now standing behind the General's chair. He asked,
"Did he say who their leader was?
"Yes," said Darius, "his name was... Pruntus Dax."
Cassius stood up suddenly, a look of shock and dismay on his face. Brian put his hand on the General's shoulder, but Cassius said stiffly, "Excuse me." He left the room.

It slowly dawned on Philippa.
"Oh, is that... Pruntus the one who led the betrayal of the Auxiliaries?"
Brian Magnus replied, "Yes, it is. We hunted him for ten years. We'd hear of his raids. But they would hit like lightning, and then be gone. We never even came close. Then things got quiet. We'd heard that he had gone to Hibernia. We stopped looking. But now... I'm going to check on the General." Brian left the tent.

At least this has distracted Cassius from worrying about me for a moment, thought Philippa.
"Darius Po," she said, "I want you to know that I am not holding you responsible for my injuries. And no one else should either."
Erastus exclaimed, "Alright, he's suffered. We've all suffered. But he shot our Centurion. He almost shot our General. You can't just let him go."
She smiled. "I wasn't planning to let him go. Darius, is it true that you are a Roman Citizen?"
"Yes."

"Well... how would you like to be a soldier in the Roman Army? You get fed, you get paid, usually, and sometimes you get to fight bad men. Like the ones who slaughtered your people. And we can help your family. They can come live here. There's plenty of room. And provisions."

Darius looked completely caught off guard. "But, I don't know anything about being a soldier."
"My men will teach you," Philippa said. "They didn't know anything either at first."
She shifted slightly, and stifled a cry of pain.
"Think about it," she continued. "I'm not going to force you. As my recruiter, the noble Justinian Justinius said, soldiers enlisted under forced conditions are a liability to Rome and a danger to their comrades."
"I'll do it," said Darius. "Thank you. Thank you for everything, miss."
"Not miss," she said. "Centurion."
"Thank you, Centurion."

Cassius Ambrosius and Brian Magnus returned to the room.
Philippa said, "You're just in time! Someone give me a coin." Brutus reached into his pocket and handed her a gold piece.
She said to Darius, "On your feet, please." He stood, hesitantly.
"Company," she called, "attention!" They all stood up straight.
"Darius Po, repeat after me." She recited, and he repeated each line.

"I will remain at my post until given permission to leave it."
"I will never steal from the Army."
"I will never abandon my weapons."
"I will never flee from battle."
"If need be, I am prepared to give my life for Rome."
She handed him the coin, saying,

"By the command of the Emperor Honorius, by the grace of Jupiter and Mars, Tiro Darius Po is now a candidate soldier of Rome. Congratulations! At ease."
Cassius, Brian Magnus, the Ares Mons soldiers and even the guard came over to clasp arms with Darius.

"I did not see that coming," Brian admitted.
"Well done," said Cassius to Philippa. "We'll add recruiter to your long list of talents."

She said, "Erastus and Tyronius, take care of our new soldier. Outfit his gear, and teach him what to do. Get his people." The medicine had completely worn off now, and she could feel the hole in her side throbbing, as well as the hole in her mouth. She was trying not to writhe in pain.

"Take care of the General. While I'm laid up. All of you. Dismissed. More nasty smoke please. Right now. Hurry!"

She whispered to herself,
"If need be, I am prepared to give my life for Rome."

Chapter Fifteen - Meet Bootchie

"Bring me some fresh vellum, four pieces. And my quill needs some new ink. I could use a fresh graphite stick, too. And grab the template with the chevrons, and the one with the little squares. Oh, just bring all the templates."

Philippa lay on the big bed. The bed was covered with maps, scrolls and other documents. There was a tray table in front of her. It was stacked with writing and drawing materials. There was another tray table set to the side, holding grapes, cheese, bread, and a small vase of flowers.

"Wait! First I have to pee. Come and move all this stuff."

She had been in bed for a month. She had stayed in the infirmary for five days. On her third day there, another doctor was brought in from somewhere. Like the camp doctor, he was short, with white hair and soft hands. He listened to her pulses and her breathing. He peered into her eyes and mouth. He felt her throat, her armpits and groin. He put his ear right up to the wound in the front, and listened for a long time. She turned over carefully and he listened to her back. Then he had her walk around the room a few times. Then she lay back down and he listened again to her front and back. He asked her questions. Was she having regular bowel movements? Did she sweat? He had her take a cup into the hospital privy and pee in it. He looked at it and smelled it before handing it off to one of the attendants.

The doctores had conferred with the General and Brian Magnus. Then they came in to see her with their conclusions, which were basically: so far, so good. Nothing important seemed to be perforated. If her wounds could have a chance to heal, she might turn out just fine. But she would need to keep still.

"So," Cassius had said, "there's good news and bad news. The good news is you get to come home soon. The bad news is, you have to stay in bed for six weeks, minimum."

She slept most of the first two weeks. She was constantly in pain. The doctor would come around with a cup of smoke twice a day, and an orderly would bring one at night. Cassius, Brian, Brutus, Bruno, Artemis and Beni all took turns taking care of her. They brought food and drink to her in bed. She was only allowed to walk to the privy, and only with assistance. They had tried to get her to use a chamber pot, but she said that she'd rather die.

One morning she woke up and the pain had lessened. She politely declined the smoke cup, although she was ready for it by afternoon. By the end of the third week, she was over the smoke cup, and the wound felt much better. But the rest of her felt stiff and weak and out of sorts. She wanted so much to get up and do something. She felt like she was going crazy, and said as much to Cassius. He replied,
"Now that you're feeling better, tell us what we can do for you so you won't be bored."
"Can I use my weights?" She could feel her lovely muscles getting soft and flabby.
"You know that's not allowed."
"Then... I want to work on my book."

Cassius smiled. "That's a fine idea. What do you need?"

From that point on, she had been giving out orders for whatever she wanted. Her attendants were diligent and thoughtful. They brought in bouquets of her favorite flowers. They purchased more vellum and inks. They laundered her nightgowns. She got exactly what she requested for meals. Whatever she desired would be found and delivered.

Erastus and Tyronius began to visit, bringing Darius Po with them. After several weeks of training and eating, he looked like a different person. She told him how much she admired his uniform. She asked after his people. They had all been settled into comfortable civilian quarters. The women had already found work in the gardens. The oldest of his sisters worked there too. The younger children went to the little school that had been set up near the new forum.

She quizzed him on military knowledge. Tyronius and Erastus were doing a thorough job. She gave him marching commands, which he carried out. The room had very little floor space, so it was rather comical for all of them.

Her book had grown into a real project. 'A Military History of the Honorable General Cassius Ambrosius' was coming along. Thanks to the information provided by Brian Magnus, she had documented the Battle of Tameris Bridge, the Battle of the Red Mere, and the Battle of the Gaulish Sevens. She used the templates to organize and ornament the text. She had made notes about his time as Warden of the Weald and the betrayal of the Auxiliaries, but it was all so disturbing that she hadn't written those out yet. She decided instead to focus on the General's victories. Since they had all taken place in or around Gaul, she had to study new maps. Then she decided that she would create her own new maps for the book, featuring the battles and their routes. Then she illustrated the battles with some drawings. She and Brian Magnus spent hours together discussing geography, uniforms, and other details.

Cassius sat for several portraits. They weren't bad. She called on her muse, and made more portraits of him as a young man. She made pictures of Brian Magnus too. It was good to have him around. There was no privacy, so they had ceased their metaphysical discussions, and focused on her project. He found her some bright pigments, which she used to illuminate the scenes. The cover page had the title, and a depiction of the four winds quadrant with the motto Quattro Ventis Potens.

Early in the fifth week, the General came into the tent, smiling broadly. Bruno and Brutus were with him, carrying a basket and a box. Cassius was holding a larger, lidded basket. He set it down on the bed, and opened the top. A little orange and white face appeared. A cat hopped out of the basket.
"Philippa, meet Bootchie," said Cassius. "Bootchie, this is Centurion Pippa Agrippa."

The cat looked at her and blinked. Philippa blinked back. She held out her finger, and he rubbed his face against it. His nose was pink. He sat down, chewed his fluffy tail for a moment, then curled up on the bed purring. Philippa was ecstatic.

"Bootchie is six months old," Cassius explained. "He's accustomed to being indoors. He has his own bed, and his own latrine." The twins came forward, showing her a little cushioned basket and a copper pan filled with sand. They installed the pan in the corner. The cat bed was set on the floor near the stove.

Bootchie was a most agreeable cat. Philippa had been around enough cats to know that wasn't always the case. She praised Cassius for finding such an ideal pet.
He was so cute, even the emotionally detached Brian Magnus was charmed.
Even the Gods, thought Philippa, *can't resist a cute kitty-cat.*

The afternoon of the following day, Philippa was playing with Bootchie. She heard some voices outside. Then Cassius came in and announced, "Centurion, you have a visitor." It was Vela the Celt! He was accompanied by the priest of Mithras. Philippa said, "What a wonderful surprise. It's good to see you, a'Vela." Vela looked at her mouth. He pointed to the hole where her tooth had been, nodding and smiling.

She noticed that he was missing a couple of his own. He said something, and the priest translated- "Vela says it's honorable that Centurion Agrippa has had a tooth knocked out."
Cassius smiled and said, "I told you."

Vela spoke at great length. The priest listened with a look of concentration, then said,
"Vela has heard of your heroic sacrifice to save your General-"
She interrupted. "Really? How?"
"News travels on the trade routes. And a good story spreads quickly. You are famous all over Britannia Prima Sud Est. Anyway, Vela says that he told your story to the God of the West Wind, and that the Wind told him to come here and give you a special gift. He calls it the Arrow of the King."
"If I am understanding correctly, the arrow was made by a Belgic shaman. It was fletched with the hairs of the boar that killed King Magnar the Valorous. The shaman gave the arrow to Vela many years ago, with the instructions that he was never to use it; that someday he would meet the person it belongs to, and now the Wind has informed him that you are that person. It sounds like superstitious nonsense to me."

Says the fellow who worships a man born from a stone, thought Philippa.

Vela was speaking again. The priest listened and said, "Vela would like to see your quiver."
"I'll fetch it," said Cassius, going into her room and returning with her quiver.

Vela took the quiver and inspected it. He set it on the bed beside her. Then from out of his tunic, he brought forth a long skinny bundle. He unrolled the fabric, revealing an arrow. It was a bit longer than the Army arrows. The slender iron tip came to a fine point. It was more like a miniature spear tip than the usual arrow-head. The boar's coarse fur fletching was finely applied. The shaft was white, decorated with rings of black, red and green. There were strange runes painted between the rings. Philippa was amazed. She admired her army issue shafts, but they seemed very plain and ordinary compared to this exotic arrow.

Vela picked up Philippa's quiver and added the Belgic arrow.
He lifted the quiver and sang a chant. Then he spoke at length to the priest, who translated,
"Vela says that this arrow is a talisman. It will protect you. Keep it in your quiver. You may live your whole life and never need to use it. You have to be certain if you do. If you are ever in a situation, and you ask yourself, should I use the arrow, the answer is no. Only use it if you don't have to think about it."

Vela set the quiver back down. Philippa said, "I thank you, most noble Vela. I am honored to receive the Arrow of the King. Will you teach me that chant?" The priest translated her request. Vela sang,

"Borrum Borrum Stribog Borrum
 Borrum Borrum Dogoda Borrum"

She repeated it with him several times. The General joined in too.
"Thank you," she said. "I know Borrum is Celtic for wind spirit. What are the other words?"

It was Cassius who replied, "They are both from the continental Celts. Stribog is the auspicious grandfather of all the winds, much like Jove is. Dogoda is the Goddess of the West Wind. And of love."

Vela and the priest stayed a while longer, and had some refreshments. Then they took their leave. The quiver was put back with her armor.

She was finally approaching the six week mark. The others had decided that this Saturn's day, she could get up and go sit outside on the patio. She had been looking forward to it. Apparently too much. Cassius had said, "Don't get excited. It just means you can get out of bed. You can go sit outside, maybe walk around the garden, that's it. Nothing even slightly strenuous. We're not going to risk losing you *now*."

It was early afternoon. They were sitting on the bed. Philippa was holding a set of maps. The commissariat had recently updated the map inventory, and had sent over some new ones of the continent for her to study. Cassius Ambrosius sat cross-legged next to a stack of old correspondence. Bootchie sat on the bed next to him.
"I'd like to go out now. What are we waiting for?" she asked impatiently.
"We are waiting for... Brian Magnus," he said vaguely. "Besides, Bootchie and I are working here."
"Yes you are!" She laughed. She had been watching them for the past thirty minutes. It was quite entertaining. The General would inspect a document. If it was one of the few worth keeping, he placed it on the bedside table. If not, he set it in front of the cat. Bootchie would push it off the bed. The cat didn't look at the document, he stared at the General the entire time that his paw was moving. He then would turn to see that it had made it to join the pile on the floor before resuming his position, his tail twitching. It was adorable.

By the time Cassius and his assistant had finished sorting the documents, she had begun to doze. She awoke immediately as Brian Magnus entered, followed by Bruno and Brutus.

"Ready to go outside?" asked Brian Magnus.

"Yes." *Some time ago,* she thought to herself. Brutus helped her to stand.

Bruno appeared with her Centurion cloak, not the comfy old brown cape that she was expecting. He balanced it on her shoulders. The silver bosses felt heavy. She had gotten so weak. She wondered, W*ill I ever get my strength back?* Cassius had joined them and was smoothing her hair. He tied part of it back with a ribbon. *They sure are making a fuss,* she thought. But then again, fussing over her had sort of become their occupation, since the incident at the falls.

"Can Bootchie come out with us?" She was torn between wanting the cat to have a chance to enjoy the outdoors, and being afraid that he would run away or come to harm.

"Just you for now," said Brian Magnus. "We'll get the Bootch after you've settled in." She smiled at his nickname for the cat.

They headed to the back door. Bruno opened it. Brutus, Cassius and Brian went through the door. She stepped out into the unaccustomed brightness, followed by Bruno. The twins flanked her. Cassius and Brian stood nearby. She gasped! The patio was filled with flowers. There were cut flowers in vases, blooming flowers in pots, wreaths of roses and lilies, and sprays of flowering sage. The table was covered with an arrangement of fruit, nuts, and honeyed sweetbreads. There was a tray filled with bracelets and hair ornaments.

She looked up. There was so much to take in, she hadn't even noticed the crowd. There were about seventy people, standing quietly, just outside the guard's perimeter. She saw the men from Ares Mons and their families, and the troops who had been their neighbors before the move. She saw Darius Po and his people, Philemones Calla, Paulinus Valinus and Augustus Ionias, the Commissarian and his daughter Justina, and Dimocletus with his wife and son. There were cart drivers and mechanics, gardeners and vendors, and people she recognized but couldn't quite place.

They were all quietly watching her. Flanked by the twins, who monitored her every move, she went over to the steps. Very slowly, they descended to the grotto. Again, she gasped in amazement. The Jupiter shrine had been decorated too. The statue now sat upon a square plinth, painted with the colors of the quadrants. There was a large new brazier. Smaller statues of Mercury, Mars,

Ceres, and Venus had been arranged in front of it. And the stone upon which they all sat had been covered with animal mosaics. It was like a little Mount Temple! She looked at Brian Magnus, who was smiling at her. Supported by the twins, she bowed deeply and reverently before moving on.

She came to the edge of the perimeter, next to the burgeoning garden. The crowd was still mostly silent. It was a little strange. She said, "Hello, everyone, it's so good to see you."

"Louder!" cried a voice from the back. *Oh dear,* she thought, *even my voice has grown weak.*

She filled her lungs with air, and said, "Thank you for everything. Your kindness has warmed my heart, and your presence has lifted my spirits. I look forward to seeing you all again soon." *What was she supposed to do now? Dismiss them? What would the General do?*
"Oh, and one more thing." She took a deep breath, and hollered,
"QUATTRO VENTIS POTENS!"

The crowd roared it back to her. Then they dispersed. The twins helped her slowly back up the stairs and sat her down at the table. Cassius had disappeared, but then he reappeared, carrying Bootchie, who was clinging to him like a baby. Cassius said, "I was afraid that big noise might have frightened him." He set the cat down on the patio floor. The General sat on the top step, blocking the stairs in case Bootchie was too adventurous. Bootchie cautiously slunk around the patio, sniffing at everything. Then apparently satisfied, he climbed into the General's lap, purring. Philippa sat at the table, nibbling at the sweets and examining the trinkets.

After a while Cassius said, "Well, that's enough for the first day out. Back to bed." She didn't argue. As wonderful as this had been, she was worn out. It was clear that she still had a long way to go.

The weeks went by. Philippa was told that the new community hall was to be named after her, in honor of her heroism and sacrifice. Also, that a large crate of pigments were being ordered, and she was expected to oversee the decoration.

It was near the fall equinox. Venus and Mercury were visible most nights. The days were very warm. Philippa longed to go swimming, but that was not going to be allowed, even though her doctor said cool water was good for her. All her baths since she'd been shot had been cool ones.

She tried to make the case for going swimming, but the journey was too long, Cassius had said, and a cart ride would be too rough. Besides, the waters of the beaches were murky, and they had orders to keep her clean.

She kept trying. "The pools at the Falls are always clear. We could go there."
"I'm surprised that you want to return there," said Cassius.
"Why? It's pretty unlikely that we'll be attacked again! As you said yourself, lightning doesn't usually strike the same place twice."
"Anyway, no. It's too far."

One evening, Philemones Calla arrived to see the General. Usually, Cassius would carry on with his business while she was in the room. But this time she and the Bootch were bundled out to the patio to wait with the twins. It had rained, and everything was shiny in the evening sun. The meeting went on, until the long golden strands of sunlight had receded.
"Something's going on, Bootchie," she confided. "I don't know what, but I don't think I like it."

Calla finally left. Brutus and Bruno accompanied her and Bootchie back inside, then they also departed.
Cassius was still seated at the strategy table. Several documents and a map were spread out before him. Brian Magnus was there too, although he hadn't been earlier. *Nulles Ex Nusquam.*

"Sit down, Pippa." Cassius motioned to one of the big chairs.
"What's going on? What did Calla want?" She tried not to allow her voice to betray her anxiety.
"Well... there's good news and bad news. The good news is, we have received a payroll from Rome, and it is being dispersed to the men."
"And the bad news?"
"Now, we don't know that it's bad news," said Brian Magnus. "We're just pretty sure you won't like it. The General and I have received orders. We are to report to the new Provincial Consul of Britannia Prima in a week's time."

"What?" she replied."We have a Consul? I thought they were all in Rome."
"This Consul is the Governor," Cassius explained. "The post was vacant for years and being held by an administrator. But the Emperor Honorius has taken a new interest in Britannia Prima, and the post has been filled by one of his associates. The new Consul is currently in Corinium. We're to meet him there."
"But that's... fifty miles away!" she said, petulantly. "A four day march, at least. Do you really have to go?"
"We have orders, soldier," said Cassius. "What do you think?"

"And, before you ask," added Brian Magnus, "you can't come with us. You're nowhere near well enough."

"Besides, even if you were," said Cassius, "I would not bring you. The last Governor stole two of my best men."

"What do you mean?" she asked, startled.

"They were very capable men," he said. "Like the twins are. He wanted them for himself. So orders came, just like that. No, I am only bringing my most average, uninteresting troops. And Brian Magnus, of course."

"How do you know that they won't try to steal him?" She asked.

"Oh, others have tried, even succeeded, but he's like quicksilver, he slips through their hands. And he always returns to me."

"Like a dog to his master," said Brian flatly.

They both seemed grouchy. She could tell that neither of them really wanted to make this journey.

They spent the next two days preparing. She sat on the bed and watched documents, maps, clothing, and gear grow into piles, which were then packed into trunks. There was a great deal of activity. Bootchie hid under the table.

On the second night the wagons were packed with equipment and provisions. Pippa, Brian Magnus, the Bootch, and Cassius were sitting by the little shrine, burning labdanum incense, for an auspicious journey.

Cassius said, "Gods, I don't look forward to camping. I'm going to miss my comfortable bed. And I'm going to miss Bootchie so much." Bootchie was in his lap, as usual, getting petted. "And you too of course, Pippa."

"I'm glad that I rate in there somewhere," she said, smiling.

"I'll miss you too, little sister," Brian said to her. "Will you work on the book while we're gone?"

Philippa replied. "Yes... but I'll be worrying about you in Corinium. Couldn't you just... pop back and let me know how things are going?"

Ooops! thought Philippa. *I shouldn't have said that in front of Cassius!*

Cassius said, "What do you mean, couldn't he pop back? You said yourself, it's a four day march." He seemed suddenly suspicious.

"Oh... I... " She stammered. "I was just being silly," she said unconvincingly.

"What is this?" Cassius demanded of Brian Magnus. "What does she know? What have you told her?"

"*This* is our sister and friend on Earth. She *knows* everything, because she is far more clever than you realize. And you were the one who *told* her, by insisting on discussing forbidden topics. She figured it out from there."

"WHAT?" Cassius cried angrily.

Philippa rose in the semi-darkness, and recited the words that had burned themselves into her memory.

"Just this once. Find her. It will take you less than the blink of an eye. No, I will not. And we should not even be speaking of these things. I will help you to search again on foot, but I will not break my covenant. You must love to see me suffer! Father, I am just abiding by the rules that you created. Yes, well, apparently I created everything. But what is the point of being all powerful, when I am clearly powerless?"

"Oh." The General's anger dissipated. He seemed somewhat embarrassed. "You did hear that, after all."

"Yes," she said. "But... so what? That was years ago. It didn't change anything about us."

"And it all might turn out to be nonsense, anyway," said Cassius, looking at Brian Magnus.

Brian said, "Right. Sure. But Pippa, please don't ever ask for anything like that again."

She sighed. "I'm sorry. I understand. I'm just really going to miss you both."

They were scheduled to leave at dawn. She woke up and got dressed to see them off. The twins were waiting for her outside the front door. They walked to the road. The wagons were lined up. The last of the trunks were loaded.

Cassius and Brian Magnus appeared from behind the wagons. They were all dressed up, and carried their richly plumed helmets. Brian Magnus was wearing a shiny officer's uniform. It was so strange to see him like that. He usually wore a simple white tunic and grey cloak. Then she looked at Cassius and she shrieked, "Gods! What have you done?" His long hair was all gone! He had been shorn like a sheep. *Who was this stranger?* He looked grim, as she had first imagined he'd be.

"It's alright, Pippa, it's just hair," he said lightly. "It will grow back. We can't give the Consul anything negative to report back to the Emperor." She saw that he had also not worn his Celtic torque.

He gave her a hug goodbye. She touched his head. Where she usually felt soft curls, there was bristly stubble. It was too much. She wept, briefly, pulled herself together, and then they were gone.

Chapter Sixteen - The Virgin Warrior and the General

The time passed uneventfully for Philippa. Her routine was gradually including more and more exercise. The two doctors came to see her one day. They poked, prodded and tested her, then they declared her recovery a success and released her from their care, with a final warning to not overdo it. She began wearing bits of armor again, and started doing some gentle training. She started walking further. One day she walked all the way to the commissary complex, alone. She ate a small meal there and walked back. It felt like a great achievement.

The General's party returned on the evening of the tenth day. The trip had proceeded without incident. It seemed that Corinium was a dull place, not at all like Vindavia Nova. The Governor hadn't really been that interested in them, just in completing his report for the Emperor. They met with him twice.

They'd actually had an enjoyable journey there and back. For all his complaining, Cassius had liked being on the march. It had been a long time since he had traveled anywhere. He said that he felt revitalized. They asked about Philippa's health, and were happy to hear that the doctors had released her.

"And now, we brought something for you." Brian Magnus pulled a scroll from his satchel. The two men looked at one another and laughed.
"We learned a song while we were there," said Brian. "A popular song."
"Listen now," said Cassius, "to The Ballad of the Virgin Warrior and the General."

She was surprised when both of them began to sing-

"Good people of Rome, here's a story to tell
  Of the Virgin Warrior and the General"

Their high and deep voices sounded quite nice together.

"Twas a dark stormy day; the soldiers marched on
  Far from their homes they'd wandered since dawn
  The rains poured down, the ground was sopping
  The soldiers marched on without even stopping"

The two men paused the song, and laughed at the look on her face.
"What? That's not right!" Philippa was aghast.

"Oh, just you wait, it gets better, " said Brian Magnus.
"And by that he means worse," said Cassius.
They continued,

"The General was mighty, the hero of all
  But even the mighty sometimes must fall
  The road grew slick with mud so black
  The mighty General fell onto his back"

"Good people of Rome, here's a story to tell
  Of the Virgin Warrior and the General"

"The great Lord Magnus cried, 'Look at the sky!
  How strangely those long pointy raindrops do fly'
  Cried the Virgin, 'Get up! It's a shower of death!'
  But the poor General had been knocked out of breath"

"The Virgin Warrior, she leaped in the air
  And landed on top of the General there
  The arrows did pierce her, but he was saved
  Because she was so nobly behaved"

"Good people of Rome, here's a story to tell
  Of the Virgin Warrior and the General"

"This is ludicrous!" Philippa cried. They continued.

"The General arose with rage in his heart
  Saying 'I'll find the shooters and tear them apart'
  He dashed up the hill and found seventeen men
  He killed them all dead and then ran down again"

"He ran to the Virgin and cried, 'Do not die!'
  She raised up her head and said, 'I will try.'
  And thanks to the Gods it all turned out right
  They rejoined the ranks, and marched into the night"

"Good people of Rome, here's a story to tell
  Of the Virgin Warrior and the General"

"But that doesn't even make sense!" She was roaring with laughter now. "That's
the stupidest song I ever heard! Are you sure you didn't make it up as a joke?"

"It was written by a professional bard," said Cassius, with tears of laughter rolling down his cheeks. "Everyone's singing it these days."

Later they sat on the patio. Bootchie was overjoyed to be reunited with his General. The neighbors had come over to say a quick hello. Cassius said that he would see them at morning formation. Philippa said, "I'll be there too." They looked at her with surprise.
She said, "What? The doctors released me. And it's just formation."

In the morning she put on her full armor for the first time since the injury. It was so heavy. She almost changed her mind before she walked out the door. But Cassius was waiting for her, so she went with him. By the time they reached the parade ground, she was feeling better. It was good to be moving, even though it was a lot of work. After formation they walked back home.
She undressed and collapsed into bed. But she managed to get up and make it to evening formation too. It was exhausting, but it was making her stronger.

After a week, she was almost beginning to feel like her old self. She began to do light training and sparring, and she spent a lot of time on the archery range. Vela's arrow had reminded her how much she enjoyed using the bow. And it wasn't quite as tiring as the other types of weapons training. She learned to shoot from different vantage points and heights. She became good at reading the wind. She learned to shoot at a moving target, and to shoot while she was moving. Her arms grew in strength. The sword and shield didn't seem quite so heavy. Her side still hurt sometimes, but for the most part she felt recovered.

Virgo had passed, and the scales of Libra had moved into the night sky. She and Cassius were walking home from formation. The General's curls had returned.
Philippa said to him, "I know it's just hair, but I'm glad you're growing it out."
He said, "For now, anyway. I'm going to have to cut it again soon." He looked very serious.
"Listen, Pippa, I have to tell you something. You're not going to like it. At some point, Brian Magnus and I will have to return to Rome. The Governor made it clear that it would be expected of us. Emperor Honorius has ordered that all high ranking officers in the provinces whose time has come to be discharged must go to be released by the Emperor himself."

"No! But why?"
"He is going to personally decommission us. This is his way of exerting control up to the very end, and of ascertaining whether a discharged officer may still be an ally. When the order comes, we'll have to go. I don't dare to antagonize the

Emperor. Rome might be in decline, but he's still the most powerful man in our world, and not very forgiving. I fear that were I to cross him, Vindavia Nova would suffer for it. So I need to keep playing the game, until it finally ends."

"But," she asked, "what if he wants to keep you? What if he won't allow you to return?"
"We won't let that happen," he said confidently.
"Well, when you're there, you mustn't impress him too much! And you were right," she sulked, "I don't like it."

Before she could begin to complain, he suddenly said, "I want to go away for a couple days, with you. Just the two of us. We'll take ponies. Brian and the lads can look after Bootchie. We've both earned some leave. I know a place that you would like. It's just a little over half a day's ride from here. South and slightly east."

"What's it called?" she asked.

"I don't know if it has a local name," Cassius said. "Brian Magnus and I dubbed it High Falls. We bivouacked there once, when we were searching for the traitor Pruntus Dax. We thought that we might be on his trail, but we were misled. The land was completely empty. We never saw signs of any humans at all. Just a vast and scenic river valley. It's an extraordinarily part of Britannia. It was... restorative, just being there. I've always wanted to go back. And I want to take you there. Soon. An adventure together, while the weather is still fine."
Philippa said, "I'm ready when you are, sir."

Two days later, they were on their way. There was great concern among their friends about them going off alone. When Philemones Calla heard that the General was going traveling without any guards, he tried to talk him out of it. Then he complained to Brian Magnus, but he seemed unconcerned. The twins wanted to go with them too. But Cassius was set on it being just the two of them, and wouldn't be dissuaded.

They rode two sleek and well fed ponies called Mika and Ban. They traveled light, well armed but only partially armored. They were dressed like Scouts. No helmets or bright colors; they wore brown leather cuirasses and brown capes, with Celtic trousers and boots. Philippa had her sword, dagger, bow and quiver, and Cassius had a long sword, a dagger and a short sword. They wore no adornment and carried no shield or standard. The idea was to look anonymous, and to blend into the landscape.

They left at dawn and made good time. They followed the road for a while. Around mid-morning they turned and headed up a long grassy incline, dotted with pine trees. Cassius had studied the map the night before, conferring with Brian Magnus on the directions.

"I hope I can actually find this place again," he said as they rode. "It was really remote, and we came at it from a different direction."

Philippa said, "I'm just happy to be having an adventure with you. It doesn't much matter where. And it's really pretty here."

They were on a ridge, following along a clear rushing stream. There were no real paths, but there were numerous deer trails, and the spacing of the trees allowed for easy passage. The hills on either side were covered with old forests. There were wide acres of mighty oak, ash, and larch trees, blazing in a glory of autumn reds and golds. The trees were hung with ivy, and garlanded with flowering trumpet vines. Up on the ridge, where they rode along the water's edge, there were willows, rowans and evergreens. Holly trees glowed in the sun, the deep red berries bright against the glossy green leaves. The air smelled like fennel and mint. The ground was leafy and soft, and large pale mushrooms grew out of the brown furze.

The ridge descended gradually, and they saw a vast green meadow below them. A large herd of red deer were grazing, and flocks of birds were looping through the sky.

The stream broadened and became a rushing river. Mosses and ferns grew in abundance along its banks. The air was fresh, and patches of mist hung in the low areas.
They rode in silence for a long time. Then Philippa said,
"I've read that there are ancient places in Britannia that were already old when the world was young. Full of a history that will never be revealed, and secret names that no one will ever hear. Even the Gods don't know their stories. This feels like such a place. The great achievements of men mean nothing here."
"Some people would find that intimidating," said Cassius. "But I think you and I find it comforting." He rode alongside her, leaned way over, and planted a kiss on her cheek. Mika gave a little kick and trotted ahead.
Philippa smiled and said, "It's alright Mika, he's allowed to do that."

They stopped for lunch at a curve in the river. Cassius hopped off of Ban, but Philippa dismounted slowly and stiffly from her pony. Cassius asked with concern, "Does your side hurt?"

She replied, "No, my butt does! I'm not at all used to riding."

They ate bread, nuts and cheese, and the ponies munched on grass and lichens. The water coursed slower here, and was covered with flocks of ducks and geese. Cassius looked at the sky and the horizon, then referred to his map.

"When we come around this bend, and can see beyond that clump of trees, there should be a waterfall in the distance, over there." He looked at his map once more, then put it away.

They continued. Past the copse of trees, they began to descend. A broad vista opened before them. They stopped, scanning the distance.
"There it is!" exclaimed Cassius.
He almost sounded surprised. She didn't see it.
"Where?"
"See, all that mist hanging over the big rocks?"
Then she saw the waterfall too, distantly shimmering.

They descended onto a moor. The ground was ferny and soft, and littered with great boulders, as if a giant had thrown a handful of stones across it. The sure-footed ponies wove their way through the landscape, which was criss-crossed with streams of water, rushing through mossy beds. There was an abundance of vegetation beside the streams.

Philippa exclaimed, "Look at all the cress!" There were large leafy clumps of tender curly cress growing in and out of the water.

Cassius said, "Whoa." He got off his pony, reached into the saddle bag, and brought out a burlap sack. He took his dagger and harvested a large bunch, from high up where there was no dirt. He recited, "Thank you, local spirits, for this gift."

He gave a small bunch to Philippa, took a sprig for himself, put the remainder in the sack, and tied the sack to the saddlebag. Meanwhile, the ponies had been munching on their own bunches of cress. Cassius remounted Ban, and they resumed their journey.

It was late afternoon when they reached the far side of the meadow. They got off the ponies and led them, continuing on foot. There was a dense grove of trees surrounding the high hill. They could no longer see the waterfall, but they could hear it. Cassius led them carefully through the brambly woods. They climbed gradually, then it became more steep.

The forest came up against a cliff. They turned right. The rock was on one side and the trees on the other. There was just enough room for the ponies. This continued until they were about a third of the way around the hill. They began to see huge jagged boulders scattered all about, and many fallen trees.

"Yes, this looks like it!" Cassius pulled Ban close to the cliff and dismounted. He waited for Philippa to catch up. She dismounted, and he handed her the reins.
"You bring the ponies. I'll clear the way."
He went ahead, clearing away brush. She caught up to him at a place where the cliff split.
He said, "Here's the door. We hid the entrance with this stump."
The giant bole of a tree lay in the crack, piled high with leaves and debris. Cassius cleared it off, and then put his shoulder to the tree stump and pushed. The massive piece of wood shifted to the side with a crunching sound. He walked into the gap.

"Come through," he said. She led the ponies through and waited while he pulled the stump back into place. Then he went ahead saying, "Follow closely. It's a bit of a climb. Mind your step, it might be slippery."

The gap had become a narrow path through the otherwise solid rock. It was dark and close, but there was a light in the distance. They were walking up a steep incline. The sound of the waterfall reverberated faintly through the rocks. As they approached the light, the sound got louder. They reached an opening. It was wide enough to get through in single file. Cassius took Ban's bridle, and went through. Philippa and Mika followed.

Philippa stared in amazement. They were in a cave, a little larger than the General's quarters. The cave was behind the waterfall. A shimmering white curtain of water covered the wide opening. Little gaps would appear and disappear as the water shifted. Through them, she could see tiny bits of the moor they had just traversed. The waterfall pulsed like a living thing. The cave hummed with resonance. Fine water vapor filled the air, and occasional drops of condensation fell from above.
"Stay right against the back wall. Keep off the wet rocks," Cassius said loudly. They hugged the wall and walked carefully past the falling water. Then the cave opened up further into the rock, away from the falls, and there was space to gather.
"This is amazing!" said Philippa. "I didn't know there were caves behind waterfalls." They stood with the ponies in the little chamber, and looked out at the ever-changing flow of water.

"This isn't even the main feature," said Cassius. "But this is where the ponies billet for the night." They unsaddled Mika and Ban and scrubbed them clean with the saddle blankets. Cassius said, "Start getting our things ready to carry to the campsite. I'll take care of them."

Philippa untied their gear. They had a small simple tent and a minimum of bedding, some food and drink, and a change of clothes.

Cassius had brought a cup and basin. There was a narrow trough on the side of the cave that had collected water. He scooped it with the cup, filled the basin, and put the basin in the back of the little room. He unpacked a bale of hay, broke a third of it off, and stashed the rest away. He set the food on the ground by the basin, and the ponies started munching.

He and Philippa picked up their gear and stepped back into the rear of the cave. "One more thing," he said. "The barrier." He grabbed two large branches that were lining the wall. He took some rope from the gear bag, and contrived a fence to keep the ponies from wandering out onto the slippery rocks.

"This way," he said. They continued. It looked like they were against a solid wall. She wondered where could they possibly be going. They reached a small gap.
"Mind your head," said Cassius. They went through, single file. They were on another path through the rock. They walked up a steep incline.
"Careful, there's a drop-off," he warned. "Stay against this wall." She followed close behind him. There was a light up ahead. She couldn't quite see around him. She was sweating from the exertion. They were both panting by the time they reached the light. She could see the late afternoon sky through the opening. Cassius went through it, and she followed.

They were in a small open grassland on the top of the hill, far above the falls. It was completely flat. There were some trees around the edges, but the remainder of it was open. Beyond the perimeter was what looked like the rest of the entire world. Philippa gasped. She turned in a circle. Except for the rocky outcrop they had just come through, it was a full panorama of the landscape. Everywhere she looked, there were endless green hills and meadows, rivers and valleys, forests and fens. It seemed to stretch into infinity. There were low-lying mists beneath them, as if they were above the clouds. She was dumbstruck.

Cassius set down his gear, and relieved her of hers as she stared in awe.
"Impressive, right?" he asked.

"It's the very home of the Gods!" she exclaimed. "It's as if we're on Mount Olympus."

He started walking and she followed. They made a circuit of the perimeter. Every few steps was a new vista of changing landscape. They walked cautiously near the edge. The trees were cedars, spirally twisted from the wind. The edge was not the sheer drop that it first appeared to be, but Philippa and Cassius still stayed well away from it.

They went on. There was a rocky outcropping with a broad flat area. They walked out onto it, about halfway. They were above the waterfall. They could see it pouring down the cliffs below. Philippa's stomach was doing flip-flops. Cassius took her arm and led her back to the upland meadow.

They stood back and looked out. She tried to follow the river into the distance. "Is that the way we came?" she asked, pointing. "Is Vindavia Nova over there?" He stood behind her and looked out. Then he took her shoulders and rotated her a bit to face the setting sun. "That way. West. That's the river we followed. Vindavia Nova is beyond that."

"Where should we set up camp?" he asked.
She turned and looked at the interior. The grasses were green and gold. They glowed in the westering light, casting long shadows. Bees and butterflies flew around blue and purple flowers that she didn't recognize. There were clumps of tall blue grasses which were covered in golden seeds. There was a patch of some short fat plants that were covered in spikes.
"Is that... cactus?" she asked with disbelief. She'd only seen them in books.
"Why, I believe they are," said Cassius. "Best not to set up camp over there." She laughed.

Cassius said, "I think here." He chose a spot near the middle of the highland meadow. He took his short sword, and hewed the grasses. He stacked the cut grass, saying, "For the ponies." This time Philippa recited, "Thank you, local spirits, for this gift."

He inspected the clearing, and then brought out the tent. They set it up facing west. Then they scoured the edges for firewood. They gathered several armloads of sticks. Cassius got out his flint and steel and quickly had a fire going. Philippa took their bedding and folded it to make seats. She began to prepare the food. Cassius took the grass and their water jug, and went back down into the cave. She took out their provisions, portioned them out, and wrapped up the remainder. Cassius returned with the water.

"Poor tired things; they were already asleep!"

"They'll be happy when they wake up and find their treat," said Philippa.

Cassius gathered up some stones and placed them around the fire. Philippa buttered two slices of bread and set them on a stone. She sliced some cheese and layered it on the bread. When it was melted, she carefully pulled the slices off the stone and onto a trencher. Then she peeled and sliced the boiled eggs and added them on top.

"Do you want cress on yours?" she asked him.

"No, thank you," he said. "That was quite enough I had earlier."

She set a huge mound of the curly greens on one the breads, then filled a cup with walnuts, figs and dried grapes. They sat down. Cassius cut the breads in half.

They said their thanks and ate. The world grew dark around them. A wolf raised its voice in the distance. Then from all around, the voices of other wolves joined in. The sound grew into a wild crescendo, and then suddenly all was quiet.

The fire subsided into glowing coals. Philippa yawned. Cassius stood, unfolded the bedding he was seated on, and helped her to lie down on it. She lay on her back. He covered her with her cloak. She watched as he went to bank the fire. Then her eyes closed, and she drifted off.

"Pippa." Cassius was speaking. "Open your eyes."

She did so. The sky was ablaze with stars. She couldn't remember where she was. Then she recalled their journey. She was in a highland meadow over a waterfall.

Like a million sparkling fireflies, the Milky Way spread out gleaming over their heads. Other stars twinkled dimly in the far, far distance. Now and then, one would shoot across the sky and disappear. Above all, Jupiter shone like a glinting gem, colored rays shearing off into the night.

She marveled. *What really was all this? Other worlds? The land of the Gods?* She recalled her vision, and the big red eye in the sky. She thought of Cassius. *Could he really be what Brian Magnus said?* She sat up suddenly and looked at him in the darkness. He was still sitting on the folded bedding. She could see his eyes reflecting the rays of starlight. She almost spoke, but didn't.

"We should move to the tent," he said. "It's tempting to stay out here all night, but we'd get soaked by the dew."

They moved the bedding inside. Philippa lay down and immediately went to sleep.

When she awoke, it was mid-morning. It was very warm in the tent. She shoved off the bedding and went out.
Cassius was standing off at a distance. He came over when he saw her.
"Good morning. There's porridge by the fire. I had mine already."
"Sorry I slept so long," she said. "You could have woke me."
"You needed the rest. Get dressed and have your breakfast, and we can go exploring."

She went behind the rocky outcrop to take care of business. As she was walking back to the camp, she suddenly said, "Oh!"
He came over to her. "What is it?"
"I had a dream. A strange dream."
"Tell me."
"I was... over here." She moved over to a patch of green grass, not far from the tent.
"Was it day or night?" asked Cassius.
"Sort of in-between. There was no sunlight, but I could see. The colors were dim. There was... a hare. A big shaggy hare. I liked looking at it. But as I did, one of its feet came off. The front left one."
"Came off how?"
"It's difficult to describe. It was as if the foot was a bud, tapered at the end, like on a willow branch; it just dropped off and lay in the grass. I was upset and worried about the poor creature. I approached it to see if there was anything I could do. But then it started hopping away. I couldn't see that any of its feet were missing. It seemed fine. I was relieved, but confused. That's it."

"Well, it sounds as though you've had a profound inner vision. Something about loss and gain. Compassion and persistence. That, or you had too much curly cress with dinner." He gave her a reassuring pat on the back. She ate her porridge and finished dressing while he went down and readied the ponies.

Philippa made sure that the fire was out. Then she stowed their gear in the tent and closed it. She headed to the doorway as he was coming up to meet her.
"Ready?" he asked.
She nodded. They went slowly down the incline, skirted the wall and entered the little room. Cassius had been busy. He had mucked out the stable waste and saddled the ponies. Since they were leaving the gear at their campsite, they were traveling light. They had only their weapons to carry, and a few provisions for lunch. Cassius buckled on his sword-belt. Then she put her own sword-belt on

too, and slung her quiver over her shoulder. Her bow was clipped to her saddle. They were ready.

Cassius undid the barricade, and they led the ponies out. They moved carefully through the waterfall cave. She marveled again at the glory of it all. They went down through the other passage and came out at the bottom. Cassius shoved the stump out of the way. They walked the ponies through, then he pushed it back into the gap.

They led the ponies down to the edge of the meadow and mounted.
"It feels good to be traveling light," said Cassius.
She giggled and said, "Like a ray of star shine."
"Eh? Oh, I get it. Traveling light. Iter lucis. Let's see what's over this way." Cassius pointed in a northerly direction. He pulled out the map and studied it as they rode on.

"The map shows nothing beyond that little river," he said. "It's uncharted territory."
"That's... almost daunting," she said. "I hope we don't get lost."
"We'll follow the river to make sure we don't."

They headed for the water. The ground became rockier, and stony cliffs rose high in the distance. There was a pile of scree in the way. They dismounted and led the ponies over it. Then they re-mounted. They came to the river. It was narrow and deep, and the water was blue-green. There was a deer track that ran on level ground right alongside the water, so they stayed with it.

It was another glorious autumn day. Kingfishers were diving into the water from on high. There were fallen leaves of red and gold covering the ground and floating in the river.

Cassius said, "The wind was howling last night. Just for a short while, but it made a big noise. I was amazed that you slept through it. It knocked the leaves right off of the trees. I could hear them dropping like rainfall."

They'd been following the river for a while. The landscape had begun to change. The deer track had veered off in another direction. Now there were willow trees lining their side of the water, so they were obliged to travel a little further away from it, but still parallel. The river widened considerably. The water grew darker. In between the willows, they could see the other side. There was a large empty sandbar, gleaming bronze in the sun, and littered with driftwood.

After a while, the river narrowed again, and the willows thinned out. The ground became hard. They passed great boulders, and strangely shaped large round rocks. The river was now bordered by huge mounds of pebbles that were the size of a hen's egg. The mounds looked like small hills. Luxuriant clumps of grass and flowers grew right out of the stones. Many of the egg shaped rocks were broken, and their insides glowed with muted colors.

Philippa and Cassius dismounted and walked their mounts through this strange territory. The ground shifted disconcertingly. The round pebbles rolled and crunched beneath their feet. After walking quietly for so long on the soft damp leaves, it was very loud.

"Break time," said Cassius. He had spotted a large flat stone amid the pebble mounds. They crunched their way over to it. The ponies grazed on the little bits of grass sticking out of the mounds. Cassius and Philippa sat on the stone bench and undid the lunch sack. They ate figs and nuts, and drank some mint water.

They spent a while there, relaxing on the warm stone, and picking through the pebbles. They were fascinating; like regular rocks on the outside, but the inside was like colored glass. They lined up the most interesting stones on the bench and admired them. Then they each picked out a couple of pebbles, one whole and one broken, to take back as souvenirs. Philippa put them in the bag that the food had been in.

Cassius got up and looked at the sky. They could still see the sun, but it had begun to cloud over. Sol was well past his zenith, and already heading towards the west.
The General said, "It's time to go back. I don't want to get caught in the dark out here."

The ponies had been dozing. Philippa woke them, petting them gently. She gave them the last of the figs as a treat. Soon they were moving again. They walked the ponies back through the pebble mounds, and into the boulder field, where they mounted. The large rocks were casting strange shadows in the slanting sunlight. The air had gotten chillier. They moved at a trot. Dark clouds were beginning to gather. The sun peeked through, here and there, creating long shafts of light. More clouds gathered. Soon the whole sky was dark, and the setting sun was completely obscured. It was getting harder to see. When they reached the place where the river widened, they were relieved. It wasn't much further from here; they would make it back before sundown. They slowed the ponies to a walk.

They were passing the willows near the place where they had spotted the sandbar on the opposite bank.

Suddenly they both stopped their mounts. Over the sound of the river, they could hear a voice. It was a man's voice, harsh and loud. They dismounted and led the ponies, holding the halters so they wouldn't jingle. They picked their way to the water's edge, and found a spot between the trees where they had a clear view.

Across the river, on the broad sandbar, there was a group of four men gathered around a driftwood fire. One of them was a giant, with ragged yellow hair. He was leading a much smaller man by a rope around his neck. Another ruffian was poking at the captive with a burning stick. The big man was laughing, a hard cruel laugh.

Cassius gasped sharply, and said, "Gods! It's Pruntus Dax."

Philippa didn't hesitate. She handed her pony's lead to Cassius. She unhooked her bow and quickly strung it, bracing it against the ground. She reached in the quiver without looking and drew out the shaman's arrow. She nocked the arrow and felt the wind with her face. As she drew and aimed, she chanted,

"Borrum Borrum Stribog Borrum. Borrum Borrum Dogoda Borrum"

She shot the arrow and it flew across the river, burying itself deep in the left eye of Pruntus Dax.

Chapter Seventeen - Justice Served

A loud scream of rage and pain ripped through the air. It ended in a shuddering gasp followed by a muffled choking sound.

They quickly remounted the ponies, and immediately began heading back to camp, past the willows, and back to the deer track. The ponies were anxious to get far away from that horrible noise across the river. They didn't even stop at the pile of scree, but moved nimbly and swiftly over the shifting stones. In what felt like no time at all, they were back at the cave entrance. Cassius leaped off of Ban, threw Philippa the reins and heaved the stump away. They quickly went in, and he replaced the stump.

They led the ponies silently up to the cave and into the stable room. The waterfall glowed like quicksilver. Philippa felt strangely calm. Cassius, however, was visibly shaken. His hands were trembling, but he smiled at her.

He removed the saddles and rubbed Mika and Ban's heaving sides. He fed and watered them, thanking them for being so brave and good. Philippa had been gripping her bow in her left hand this whole time. Now she unstrung it. They had left their weapons with the saddle bags last night. They didn't discuss it, but fully armed, they barricaded the stable door and headed up to their camp. It had been cloudy and almost dark when they had entered the cave. It was hard to see on the final climb, but they clung to the wall.

They reached the top and stepped outside. They were surprised to find that the skies had cleared. The last slanting rays of the setting sun illuminated their little grassland. They were grateful for their peaceful hidden refuge.

Philippa went over to the tent and brought out their bedding to sit on. Cassius was standing on the perimeter, looking out the way they had come, scanning for any sign of activity. There was none. He came over to Philippa and sat down next to her. They sat in silence for a few minutes. Philippa finally said, "Do you think he's dead?"

"Didn't you hear the death cry?" asked Cassius. "Pippa, you vanquished my greatest enemy. One of the cruelest men who ever walked the earth. The Gods rejoice in your victory. Jupiter glories in justice served, and Mars celebrates your perfectly shot arrow."
"I was actually aiming for his throat," she said, "but he moved." She paused. "As long as you're sure he's dead... "

"Yes, Pippa, I've heard many men die. And now he's one of them."
He turned to face her. "First you sacrificed yourself to save me. And now, this."
He put his arm around her shoulder.

After a while, she said, "I've never killed anyone before. If it had to happen, I'm glad it happened while I'm still a soldier. The Emperor ultimately gets the blame for any death caused by a soldier of Rome, as well as the glory. I remember that from training. Civilians are liable for murder, but miletes who kill in service of the Empire are not." She paused, then said, "I wish we could have helped that man they were torturing."

"You helped him by slaying his tormentor. Whoever was performing the abuse, it's a sure bet that Pruntus Dax was behind it."
She asked, "Do you think anyone will come after us?"
"I don't think so," he replied. "Who would want to avenge such a monster? And even if they did, I don't think we're very easy to find here. All the same, we'll have no fire tonight."

She was thoughtful. "Is there something I should do? Or say? Or pray about?"
"Whatever you think is best," said Cassius.
"Now that he is no threat," she said, "I wish him a quick passage to the other side."

She stood, and raised her voice. "I call upon the Psychopomp. Oh mighty spirit of transition, guide the soul of Pruntus Dax from this world. If I have transgressed in any way, I ask forgiveness. May the Gods keep all good people from such bad company."

"Well spoken, Centurion," said Cassius. After a moment he added, "I'd like to be forgiven too. For all the harm I've done. All the enemies that I slaughtered."
"You're forgiven, soldier," she said, smiling, "for the same reason that I am. All glory and all blame belong to the Emperor."

It was dark. Philippa took her bedding into the tent, feeling her way around, and got ready for bed. Cassius put his bedding in there too, but he said, "I'm going to keep a watch on the perimeter."
"Do you think there's really a need?" she asked. "Like you said, who could ever find us here, even if they wanted to?"
"I don't believe that we'll be threatened. All the same it's best to be vigilant. And I'm not ready for bed."
"Should I watch with you?" she asked, yawning.
"No, get some sleep. We'll head out at dawn."

When she woke up, it was just barely light. The General's bedding was next to her. She felt it. It was still warm. *Good,* she thought, *at least he got some rest.* She dressed quickly and pulled the bedding out of the tent. Cassius appeared from the cave entrance.

"Let's leave the tent," he said. "It has served us well, but it's heavy and bulky, and I want to be able to travel swiftly."

They gathered their gear and walked towards the entrance. Then they turned and looked back at their camp.

"This is a hidden jewel," said Philippa.

They walked the ponies past the falls. The water glowed softly in the diffuse morning light. Exiting the cave, Cassius heaved the big stump back into place. They walked down to the long meadow before mounting the ponies.

They made good time. By midmorning they had reached the other side of the lea. They turned and looked again at the falls, barely visible in the distance. They climbed the ridge, and followed the stream. After a while, they stopped to water and graze the ponies. Cassius and Philippa ate the last of their bread and fruit. They traveled on in silence. Most of the leaves had fallen, covering the ground with a mosaic of green, red, brown and gold. The trees surrounding the ridge were almost bare. The distant hills and valleys were visible through the empty branches.

By early afternoon, they had reached the end of the ridge.

"Vindavia Nova," said Cassius, pointing to the settlement.

Philippa smiled and called out, "Quattro Ventis Potens!"

The General echoed her cry, "Quattro Ventis Potens!"

They were on the road, approaching the fort. The guards shouted out a greeting and Cassius returned it. They rode the ponies through the gate, took a left, and continued. Past the parade ground, past the shops and onto the Officers' ring road. When they reached the General's quarters, Tyronius, Erastus, Bruno and Brutus came out to meet them. Tyronius and Erastus unloaded their bags and took the ponies away to pasture. The rest of them went inside.

Bootchie took one look at Cassius and jumped into his arms. Cassius caught him, saying,

"How's my Bootchie!"

"He's been sulking," said Bruno.

"He's glad you're back," said Brutus.

"So are we," they said together, hugging Philippa.

After they got cleaned up, she and the General spent the afternoon resting and eating. They thanked the Gods for bringing them home safe, and they put their strange pebbles on the patio shrine. As they were preparing for evening formation, Brian Magnus appeared, saying, "Welcome back. Did you like the High Falls?" He looked expectantly at Philippa.
"Yes," she said. "It was a journey like no other."

They slipped back into their routine. Several days went by. Philippa and Cassius had both been unusually quiet. It was morning, after formation. They were sitting on the bed looking at documents, when Brian Magnus appeared, saying, "We've had a report from the Outliers that Pruntus Dax is dead. Shot through the eye by a Celt. That's the conclusion, anyway, because the arrow appeared to be of strange barbarian origin. They found him by the river, not very far from the High Falls. One of his hostages managed to escape in the confusion. He told the officers where to look. Is there anything you'd like to tell *me*?"

Brian Magnus and Cassius both looked at Philippa.
"We came upon them quite by accident," she said. "They were across the river from us. Cassius recognized him. The man was a brute; he was having another fellow tortured. I didn't even think about it. I shot him with Vela's arrow."

"And you also didn't think to mention this?" Brian Magnus was indignant.
"We didn't actually see him die," Cassius said. "I felt sure that he had, but we couldn't verify it."
"We haven't even spoken of it since," added Philippa. "It was all so strange. In the midst of our magical holiday, to suddenly discover the enemy. To suddenly... assassinate someone. I think we've been waiting for some kind of sign. And now here you are." She smiled at Brian Magnus.

"Well, then, it's official," Brian said, raising his voice. "Centurion Agrippa has slain the number one enemy of Rome in Britannia Prima Sud Est. With the sacred Arrow of the King, which was gifted to her by a Celtic warrior, because of a shamanic vision. The Gods led her to this task, and she did not fail. It's great news, and a great story too. I'm going to tell everyone." He left the tent.

By evening formation, everyone knew. It was as if a holiday had been declared. The entire post was buzzing with the news that the traitor behind the betrayal of the Auxiliaries had finally been slain. And by their own Philippa Agrippa. The walk to formation was a triumphant procession. Men, women and children followed them, chanting "Agrippa, Agrippa!" When they reached the parade ground, the assembled men all cheered, long and loud.

Cassius shouted, "Centurion Philippa Agrippa, triumphant! She has slain the traitor Pruntus Dax. All honor to her! Hail Agrippa!"
"Hail Agrippa," shouted the crowd.
Some were calling, "Speech! Speech!" Cassius held up his hand, and everyone grew silent. They looked at her expectantly. It was all so strange. She had no idea what to say. So again, she shouted, "Quattro Ventis Potens!"

The crowd roared back, "QUATTRO VENTIS POTENS!"

After dismissal, they went to the dining hall and ate with the Ares Mons. There were congratulations all around. As they were preparing to leave, Philemones Calla showed up. He too congratulated Philippa.

Then he said, "General Ambrosius, I'm sorry to have to bring this up now, but you should know. You and Officer Magnus have received orders to go directly to Portus Adurni. You're to depart for Rome immediately."

Chapter Eighteen - The Secret Plan

It happened very quickly. Like before, there was a flurry of activity. But unlike before, they were going away for a long time. And it had to happen right away. It was late in the year to undertake such a voyage, and they needed to ship out before the weather turned.

The night before they left, the three of them and Bootchie sat together by the fire. Philippa was feeling sad, but she put on a brave face. The men had enough on their minds without having to listen to her complain. And they were counting on her to help keep things on track at Vindavia Nova while they were away. So she tried to be her usual chipper self.

"Traveling by ship sounds exhilarating," she said. "But also, really scary... to be out on the vast ocean in a wooden boat, nothing but water all around. Knowing that the deep sea below is filled with hungry sea creatures--"

"Enough!" said Cassius. "Let's talk about something else."
Brian Magnus said to Philippa, "Don't mind him. He doesn't care for long ocean voyages. They don't agree with him at all."
"I'm sorry," she said. "May the Gods give you good winds and calm seas."
"Speaking of traveling by boat..." Brian Magnus began and then trailed off, looking at Cassius.
Cassius said,
"Pippa, when we come back we'll be decommissioned. Everyone at Vindavia Nova will be discharged. We won't be Roman soldiers any more. We won't even really be Roman any more. We knew that this was coming, and that's why we've tried to prepare as best we could."

"Eventually, we go westward, Cassius and I," said Brian, cryptically. "You seem to be drawn that way too. So, when we return... we're going to take you, if you like, by ship, to Cornouia." She stared blankly at them. "And the Bootch too, of course," he added. "And also Bruno and Brutus."

"Where's... Cornouia," she asked.
"It's what we call Dumnonia, in Britannia Occidens," explained Cassius. "The place with the tin."
She looked at Brian Magnus, recalling their first game of 'Yes or No'.
He smiled and said, "Yes. Will you go with us?"
"Of course," she said. "But... what do you mean, 'eventually you go westward?' Do you mean to Hibernia?"

"No, not exactly," Brian Magnus replied. "The point is, we'll take you to Dumnonia, and we will dwell happily there with you, for as long as we can. It may be that your destiny lies there. If for some reason you don't like it, we'll send you back to Vindavia Nova. But Cassius and I will not be returning. We begin moving west, once we leave Rome."

Cassius said, "You must plan on departing right after we return. We want you to take care of getting things squared away here and making sure that the right people are left in charge. Do it quietly. Nobody need know our plans yet."

"Oh." She was speechless. He continued,
"Pippa, I know that this is a lot to take in. But there's one more thing." He drew a deep breath. "When we get to our final destination, we want you to consider finding a husband. Or, if you like, we'll try to find one for you. Once you're discharged, you are released from your vows, and free to wed." He squeezed her hand. "We won't always be here. We want you to have someone, someone special to you. You're still very young. And you deserve such happiness."

She was silent. Cassius added, "At least think about it, alright?"
"Alright."
Brian Magnus asked, "So Pippa, if you did get married, what sort of man do you think you'd like?"
"A good one," she replied.
"Yes, that goes without saying. But what would he look like? Would he be muscular with dark hair?" He gestured to the General. "Or would he be fair and willowy, like me?"

"I'm pretty sure he wouldn't look like either of you," she said. "That would be too weird." They laughed.
"You've seen a great many men in the Army," said Cassius. "Were they any that you... liked the look of?" Philippa was quiet, then she said,
"There was a fellow in one of the other tents, back at Ares Mons. I served him cake a couple times."
"And, so? What did he look like?" asked Brian.
"He was thin and wiry. He had pale skin. His eyes were hazel colored. His hair was pretty, like a squirrel's tail."
"Thin, strong, pale, hazel eyes and squirrel-tail hair," said Brian, "that's useful information. Very specific. Let's see, what else... how should this man be dressed?"

She thought for a moment and said, "How will *we* be dressed? We won't be in uniform anymore. I'll admit that I won't miss wearing the clanky skirt and the

fussy sandals. Or the helmet, as pretty as it is. But the rest of it, I would wear with other clothes." She looked at Cassius. "Like we do now."
"Then, that is how we'll dress," said Cassius. "I like it too."
Brian Magnus said, "Imagine, then Pippa, if you could wear anything you like. What do you like? What colors and fabrics?"

"May I?" Cassius cut in. He said, "Philippa Agrippa prefers the softest and most expensive fabric available. As a direct descendant of the Gods, she simply cannot abide anything less. She doesn't mind when clothes are worn thin, as long as they were of the very highest quality to begin with. Like my best nightgown."
"You mean my best nightgown?" she inquired.
Cassius said, "Yours? Why, you little thief." They all laughed.

Cassius continued, "She likes muted tones: sage green, slate blue, pale lavender, browns and grays of varying hue. She doesn't really like wearing bright colors. She appreciates elegant ornamentation, and anything made of metal. And after all this time in the Army, she is really tired of red, and will probably not want to wear it anymore. Is that right?" He looked at her.
"Yes," she answered, smiling.

"Then," Cassius continued, "I would assume that she would prefer someone who shares her particular aesthetic."
"So," said Brian Magnus, "someone with the manners and hygiene of a Roman, but the fashion sense of a Celt."
"Sure," she said, thinking that it all just seemed so unlikely.
"Is there anything else we should know about him?" asked Cassius.
"Yes," she said decisively. "He needs to be light enough that I could drag him off to safety if he were unconscious and danger was imminent."
She looked at the General. "Sir, if you and I were ever in that position, I would be unable to help you. I've worried about it ever since I came to work for you."
"A draggable man," Brian Magnus said with a smile.
"That is an unusual criteria for finding a partner," said Cassius, "but we'll add it to the list."
Brian was suddenly serious. "This plan, to go west. Don't share it with anyone. Just carry on. I don't want it to get out ahead of us. It might have a de-stabilizing effect."
She said, "I understand."

They left at dawn, with eight guards, displaying the standard of Vindavia Nova. Philippa held Bootchie and waved goodbye as the cart took them away and into the autumn mist.

Chapter Nineteen - Fulcrum

Two weeks later, the weather turned cold and wet. Philippa prayed that Cassius Ambrosius and Brian Magnus had gotten well underway before the seasonal shift. It was miserable outside. Formations had been cancelled. People stayed busy indoors. Some were grinding grain, making preserves, and preparing for the next planting season. Others used this time for cleaning, and taking inventories of weapons and supplies. The Quaestors were busy reviewing budgets and administrational concerns. Calla was taking care of the General's correspondence. Everything seemed to be going smoothly.

Philippa thought that this would be a good time to finish her book. After all, it was a military history, and the military part was coming to a close.
She and Bootchie parked themselves by the stove. She wrote about the horrific betrayal of the Auxiliaries by Pruntus Dax, and of the death of that outlaw at the hands of the General's Centurion, Philippa Agrippa.

"I'm part of the story, after all. Right Bootchie?" The cat yawned, exposing his long sharp teeth.

Philippa made a few new sketches, and updated her maps with the new landmarks. She drew little pictures, and used her pigments to highlight them. She named the landmarks: Old Forest, Cress Lea, High Falls, Willow River, and Pebble Hills.

A week later, she was done. She assembled all of her documents into the proper order and numbered the pages. She put a blank sheet at the beginning, for an inscription. Then she added a blank sheet to the end, which would describe the honorable discharge of Cassius Ambrosius and Brian Magnus, when they returned. She wouldn't write it yet for fear of tempting fate.
Now it needed a cover. She thought about the recruiter's book. That was a genuine bound codex. The cover was leather. She just had vellum. *I suppose I could commission the leather,* she thought. She spent the rainy afternoon designing the book cover, carefully measuring her document to make it the correct size. It had a band of five bosses, with symbols of Jupiter, Mercury, Ceres, Mars and Venus across the top of the front cover. Then the title, 'A Military History of the Honorable and Heroic Cassius Ambrosius, Legatus of Rome'. By Centurion Philippa Agrippa. On either side of the title was the wind quadrant symbol. Below it was another band of bosses. They displayed an eagle, bull, bear, boar, and cat. The spine just said Cassius Ambrosius in big letters. She tinted the pictures and highlighted the letters.

The next morning she went to the workshops, which were on the way to the cart pool. She was there to see the leather-men. She went into a large building. There was a curtain drawn to create a small waiting area. An apprentice greeted her, took her drawing, and said, "Have a seat." She sat on the leather bench. The smell of hides permeated everything. She didn't care for it. She waited for a while, and then the apprentice returned and said, "It's approved. How many copies do you need in total?"
She hadn't considered that she could make multiple copies.
"Mmm, three please."
"Alright. It will take about six weeks. Is that satisfactory?"
"Yes, thank you." He handed her a receipt and she bid him goodbye.

When she returned home, Bruno and Brutus were there, fussing over the cat. She told them about the book cover, and how she'd spontaneously ordered three of them. "Now I have to copy it all over, twice! What was I thinking?"
Bruno said, "Why don't you get a scribe to do it?"
She smiled and said, "What a great idea."

They were all sitting on the floor admiring Bootchie, who was playing with a string.
"Say, fellows," she said. "I want to ask you something. If I were to go traveling, would you want to come with me?"
They both said, "Yes."
Then Brutus said, "Brian Magnus told us about the secret plan."
Bruno added, "Whenever you go, we'll go with you."

That afternoon, she took a cart to the workshop of the scriveners. Just like at the leather shop, an apprentice greeted her. He took her book and asked her to wait. He returned a short while later.
"Two copies will take about eight weeks."
"Does that include the pictures and maps?"
"Yes, Centurion."
He gave her a receipt and asked, "Are there covers for the books?"
"They are being made at the leather shop." She thought for a moment, then inquired, "Is there someone here who binds codexes?"
"Yes, we have a binding department. When everything's ready, we can assemble your books for you." She thanked him and left.

Scorpio had brought the cold rains. Now in late November they stopped, and the weather became milder. They started having formations again. Philippa was still rebuilding her strength. She walked a lot, and she occasionally trained with the Ares Mons.

One morning, Terranes came by in a cart to let her know that the pigment had arrived, a whole wagonload. Cassius had ordered the delivery when they started to build the new community center. Before he left, the General had told her, "You'll be getting a supply of pigments. Paint the front wall first. Then see how much is left."
"How do you want it painted?" she had asked.
"It's your building," he'd replied. "Paint what you like."

Terranes said, "Oh Pippa, there is so much color! I can't wait until you see it all. We've stored it in the building, just inside the front door. They're still working inside, but the portico section is finished, whenever you want to start on it. It looks very fine, indeed. The braziers have been installed, so you'll have heat. The wagon also brought mixing tubs and dozens of large mixing jars, and water jugs, tarpaulins to protect the floors, and fabrics for cleanup. There are cartons of paintbrushes, and chalk and charcoal sticks with long holders. And some metal containers of liquids that you add to the pigment with the water. There are detailed directions. And a detailed inventory. Very professional."

"I can't wait either!" she said. "Bootchie, I'll be back in a while." Bootchie was asleep on the big bed. He twitched his tail. She put on her cape. They rode the cart to the new development and stopped in front of the big building. Philippa hadn't seen it for a while.
"By the Gods, that is impressive. Very substantial."
The building was large enough to hold around seventy people on the inside. The same number could fit under the portico roof. There were six Ionic columns supporting the portico. The patio floor was made of limestone concrete. The forum itself was made of timber and bricks, then smoothly stuccoed over with white, in the traditional style.

The building's roof was raised, and had been extended over the walls to let light in and keep the rain out. Cassius had designed the building. She had told him about the clever roof on the forge building back at Ares Mons, and he had incorporated that into his plans.

Before he departed, Cassius performed a short public ceremony, and officially named the almost finished new community building the "Forum Philippa Agrippa", in honor of her achievements. There had been some long and tedious discussions between Cassius and Brian Magnus concerning the inscription.

Several different forms of the genitive possessive had been tried out: Forum Philippicae Agrippae, Forum Philippae Agrippae, and Forum Philippa Agrippae. They could think of no other examples of forums named for women with two names, and they could not agree on the grammar. They finally decided to let Philippa herself choose. She declared that all of those inscriptions would be confusing to the many non-Latin speakers who would be frequenting the Forum. She suggested that it should simply be called Forum Philippa Agrippa. Brian Magnus kindly agreed, claiming that since it was no longer just a name, but a title, it would be acceptable. She could see Cassius cringing over the questionable grammar, but he held his tongue.

It was a little embarrassing to see her name displayed largely on the pediment, way up high. But she was proud too, and really happy that this building had turned out so well.

She followed Terranes across the patio. There were two entrances into the hall, evenly spaced. They went in the one on the right. The paints and supplies had been neatly stacked. The jars full of dry pigment were packed in three large crates. Terranes showed her the inventory sheet. There were so many colors! Some of the names she recognized, but many were new to her. Under pigments, she read-

Floridi- Bright colors
Red Lead (vermillion)
Cinnabaris (red dragon's blood)
Armenium (blue azurite)
Chrysocolla (green malachite)
Indigo (royal blue)
Tyrian Purple (murex shell)
Alexandrian (turquoise blue)
Lapis Lazuli (ultramarine)
Haematite (red iron oxide)
Realgar Red (crimson)

Floridi et Austere- Muted colors
Red ochre (hematite)
Orpiment (yellow arsenic sulfide)
Yellow ochre (limonite)
Egyptian Blue (compound)
Yellow jarosite (sulfate)
Green Earth (cretavitridis)

Nigreos et Album- Black and white
Black pyrolusite (manganese oxide)
Wood soot
Burnt ivory
Coal
Ceruse (white lead)
White chalk
White limestone

Terranes lifted the cover off of the crate of the bright colors, the floridi. It was filled with large ceramic and terracotta corked jars. Each of the broad cork tops had been painted with its sample color. Then they viewed the muted austere colors, and the black and white. It was an amazing and extensive collection.

"Centurion, I've got some business nearby to attend to," said Terranes, "shall I leave you the cart?"
"Yes. Thank you." She hugged him. "This is fabulous. I'm going home to think about it. I'll come back later. Give my love to the family!"

She stood and stared at the two entrances. Then she walked across the patio, turned and stared again. Then she got in the cart and went home.

The twins were there, helping Beni and Artemis prepare for lunch. After they ate, the servants cleaned up and departed. The weather was unseasonably warm. The twins dozed. Bruno stretched out on the couch. Brutus spread his cape and lay down in the sun, on the soft grass by the patio.

She sat with Bootchie on the bed, the table before her covered with blank sheets and reference pictures. She had been looking at images of other forums. They all were similarly painted, in bright colors, with stylized foliage and graphic geometric bands. She didn't really care for them, and she really didn't want to have to worry about geometry, and keeping all those lines straight. But she wanted to do something that would still honor tradition. She leafed through her reference material.
There was one image of an ancient forum that she was drawn to. It wasn't just decorated, it was a properly painted mural with scenes of the Deities at play, in luxuriant gardens, surrounded by fluffy clouds. In small neat letters at the bottom, it read - 'Forum Deorum'. The Forum of the Gods. She had liked this one right away, but she didn't think that this much emphasis on all the Gods of Rome would be appropriate for this community hall serving a population of various faiths. Now, staring at this image of a garden paradise, she knew what she would do. Smiling, she set the drawing table aside. She didn't even need to sketch it.

"Bootchie," she said, looking into his eyes, "I'm afraid I am going to have to spend my days away from you for the next couple of months, if I am to complete my task before Cassius Ambrosius and Brian Magnus return." Bootchie blinked at her. "The Scouts will take care of you. Maybe you can come see it when it's done."
By mid-afternoon she had returned to the forum, after first explaining to the twins what her plans were.

"So you don't mind staying here during the day and keeping Bootchie company?" she had asked.

"No," Bruno had laughed, "we don't mind living in luxury, if it will help you out."

She stood just inside the portico and peered at the far wall for a long time. Then she walked slowly towards it. She reached the spot halfway between the two doors. She stood still, then did an about-face. She backed up until she felt the wall behind her. Then she was ready.

It was late in the month of Mars. After that initial burst of cold weather back in November, it had been a very warm and dry season. She had worked on the mural until early January. Then the snows came, and the paintings were covered with waxed tarpaulins.

She hadn't worked alone, far from it, although she'd begun that way. She had sketched out the scene with charcoal, first some of the figures, then some of the backgrounds. It only covered the space between the doors, but it was a start. It was a lot of work, but at least she understood how to draw. She wasn't sure that she really knew how to paint. The directions that came for mixing pigment were not much help. There was so much variation in what to mix in, and when. The directions suggested making small batches at first. Her small batches mostly failed, resulting in paints full of clumps, with the wrong textures. She was afraid that she'd gotten in over her head.

One day, after returning home from morning formation, word arrived that the first copy of the manuscript had been completed, and was awaiting her approval before they made the second one. She returned to the scribes' workshop. She waited in the chair while the assistant went into the back. He came right out again, and stood aside as three elegant civilians wearing paint-spattered work aprons approached her.

"Centurion, this way please," said one of them. She entered the workshop. There were piles of vellum everywhere, and men and women sitting at long tidy tables, making copies. They passed all that, and entered a smaller room, no less full. Rows of shelves lined the walls, filled with containers of pigments and paints. The one long table in here was covered with artwork, paint bottles, quills, rags, brushes, templates, calipers, and rulers. There were racks of painted vellum and parchment, hanging from little clips, air drying.

She followed the men to a podium. Her newly copied manuscript was on it. She looked at the pages. The writing looked so professional! And they had taken all of her rather child-like drawings and maps, and made them look like the real thing.

"It's beautiful!" she exclaimed. "Way better than the original."

"The original is beautiful too," said one of the men, the tallest of the three. "We were very impressed. We look forward to completing your order." The men introduced themselves. The tall man had dark red hair and a short beard. That was Regulus. He copied the text. Of the two shorter men, the one with dark skin and fluffy hair was Xerxes. He did the illuminated letters, and the writing on the maps. The other shorter fellow, with white hair and freckles, was Dod. He made the pictures throughout the text, and illustrated the maps.

Philippa looked around the room, then looked at the three men. "Say, I was wondering," she said, "have any of you ever worked on something... big?"

"Why," asked Dod. "Do you want help with your mural?"

"Oh!" she replied. "You already know about it. Yes! I need help badly. It's such a huge job. I don't think I can do it all myself. I don't even know how to mix the paints. I didn't realize it would be so complicated. I keep getting a big ugly mess of clumps. And one of the yellows smells like it's gone bad."

The three men laughed. "Like rotten eggs?" Regulus asked. She nodded.

"Sulfur," he said. "The smell fades, eventually."

Xerxes said, "We'd love to assist you."

Dod chimed in, "It's been ages since we've worked on anything bigger than a map!"

Regulus said, "We thought about asking you if we could help, but we didn't want to get in your way."

"I'm in my own way!" she had exclaimed. "I would be greatly appreciative of your help and guidance."

"We'll come around later and take a look," said Regulus.

She left for home in a buoyant mood. Not only had the book turned out fine, but more importantly, the mural might stand a chance now too.

She went back to the new building in the midafternoon. As she was walking out the door of her quarters, she had stopped. She'd returned to her bed table, taken the picture of the Forum of the Gods, and put it in her satchel.

As she approached the portico, she heard voices. It sounded like the artists. She went through the door, and stood in awe. The painting equipment had been throughly organized. Part of the entrance area, soon to be a cloak room, was now a paint shop. Waxed tarpaulins covered the floor. The tubs had been set up, and the jugs were nearby. The brushes and the drawing supplies were all on their own shelves, as were the strange chemicals. The pigment crates were arranged against the wall. Two racks of shelves had been installed against the wall too. They were filled with rows of jars. Each had a circle of paint on the side of the jar, as well as on the cork.

"Centurion! There you are," said Regulus. "We've got your paint all mixed. Are you ready to begin?"
"My goodness, that was quick. Umm, sure. I suppose we should begin with the figures?"
"You can start me on the clothing," said Dod. "It's my specialty. Just tell me what you want to see."

Thank the Gods, she thought, *these fellows are here to save me!*
Xerxes said, "Centurion-"
She interrupted, "Please call me Pippa. You're civilians, you don't need to call me Centurion. Besides, this is not an Army project. It's a Vindavia Nova Civic project."
"Well, then, friend Pippa," Xerxes said, "I would be happy to do the heads, just the forms for now, not the features, and the limbs, and the hands and feet. You just tell me what color everyone is."

"Pippa," said Regulus, "do you have a sketch?"
"No, I didn't make one." She suddenly remembered the picture. "But I have my inspiration." She showed them the Forum Deorum. "They're in a garden paradise. So are we. I want it to be like this. But instead of Gods, it's us. Enjoying this beautiful world, like the Gods. But wearing more clothing."
The men laughed. They looked at the picture. Then they looked at her wall sketches. Regulus said, "Perhaps as a start, you could introduce us to the figures."
She went to the central figures, who were gathered below a standard.

"Well," she said, "this is me, in the middle."
"Then you are the fulcrum," said Regulus. "Everything in the scene relates to you."
Xerxes said, "Surely this is the General, and here's Officer Magnus. Is that a cat between them? And these two fellows that look alike are the Marianis twins. Those other men, slightly further back, are the Ares Mons troops. And here's Calla, and the other officers. And there's Darius Po, and his people. What fun!"
"Who are these figures in the far distance?" asked Regulus. She replied,

"They are scenes from the past." There was a little Mount Temple, with Father Florian and Tomasen. There was a scene by the river rest stop, with Justinian and Atticus. There was a depiction of Ares Mons Training Camp, with Aries, Septimius, Senovara, Tristanus, Jacamus, and Master Hestius.

"What goes on the other sides?" Regulus pointed to the blank parts of the wall. "More of the same?"
"That's right," she said. "More of the locals here, soldiers, civilians, wives and children. You three should be in there too! And I want to represent Vela and our Celtic friends."
"Celtic clothing. What joy!" said Xerxes.

"What about greenery?" asked Dod. "Trees and flowers?"
"Yes. Trees and flowers and vines, rivers and streams, stones and shrines and gardens. And I'd like the whole thing to be framed by a border of trees and flowering vines. Not stylized though. Natural looking. And those will be big, right? Because they're in the foreground. Could one of you do that?"
"I can," said Regulus. He picked up a charcoal stick and commenced to sketching.

They worked quickly. She tried to keep up with them. In one week they had gotten things mostly blocked in. The artists brought in a short scaffold, for reaching the high parts. Meanwhile, the tables and benches had been installed on the patio. They were made of timber, and topped with the same smooth polished material as the floor. It was nice to have a place to sit in front of the mural. People began dropping by and watching the work. Mothers brought their children. Soon it was a regular lunch stop for soldiers and civilians. The Commissariat sent trays full of food, no charge. When the Commissary director showed up with his daughter Justina, Philippa put them in the picture.

There was so much white to cover. The artists came when they could, but they still had work of their own to do. She began skipping formations to focus on the mural. She felt kind of bad about it, but she didn't have the time or energy to do both.

One morning, halfway through the third week, she got there early. No one was around yet. She stood back and gazed at the progress. The figures all had faces now, and the backgrounds were taking shape.

"Centurion?"
Philippa turned around. And looked down. There was a group of five children.
"Yes?"

The tallest child was a girl with long blond hair, who asked, "When are you going to paint all the flowers?" Much of the greenery was blocked in, and had taken shape, but all the flowers were still blank.

"I don't know," Philippa responded. "Why?" The other children looked at the tall girl. She said, "Please, we'd like to paint the flowers. We'll be careful and do a good job."
Philippa thought, *I've got three of the finest artists in the land working on this; I can't let a bunch of children ruin it.*
But what she said was, "That sounds like a great idea. We could use the help." She looked at them. "But first, come closer," she said, moving to the wall. They followed.

"Good," she said, "now wait a moment." She went into the building and came out with a drawing stick. "Hold still, please," she said. She quickly sketched the children into one of the blank areas.

"Alright, let's get some flowers painted."

When Regulus, Xerxes, and Dod showed up at mid-day, there were eight children engaged in painting flowers and colored leaves.
"They wanted to help," she said to them. "I couldn't say no. But feel free to direct them if you see that they need it."
"Hello, youngsters," said Xerxes. Dod waved. The children waved back.
Regulus immediately inspected their work, giving helpful advice.

The flowers and leaves were getting done quickly. The children began to whisper and confer with one another. Then the tall girl said, "Centurion?"
"You can call me Pippa."
"Pippa," she asked, "May we paint some animals? Birds and squirrels and bunnies and hedge-pigs and foxes and frogs?" By the end of the day, the mural was alive with creatures. The children went home. Then Dod, Xerxes and Regulus went around tidying up the children's work, just a little.

Then they'd all stood back and admired it.

They had worked on it for two more weeks. The weather had gotten colder, but they'd lit the braziers, and it was still warm enough to paint. A small stove had been installed in the pigment room, to prevent freezing if the temperature fell. The last days of work had been chilly and hasty, concluding in semi darkness. Finally the mural was covered with waxed tarps, and the paint was put away.

The calendar had started over. It was the year 404. By the end of March, the snow had melted. They were going to reveal the wall. She arrived there just as Regulus, Xerxes and Dod were undoing the cover. They untied it, and the tarp fell to earth. Pippa gasped.

It was glorious! She prayed that Cassius Ambrosius and Brian Magnus would come back soon and see it.

It was late May. The air had grown warm. The Forum Philippa Agrippa had been completed. The mural was finished to the last detail. The inside of the building was left undecorated, except for a quadrant of the four winds over the fireplace. The interior had been furnished with seating and dining areas, a market space, civic offices, some exercise equipment, and a small library.

The patio was a popular spot. The gardeners had brought in flowerpots and hanging baskets. Food vendors had set up shop on the perimeter. People would buy their food, and dine under the portico, or in the building.

The troops held formation in the morning only. The men still trained, and guard duty was always a serious matter, but drilling and marching were no longer routine. Most of the soldiers of Vindavia Nova had civilian occupations now too. The village was thriving. The crops were in the ground and were starting to grow. Babies were being born, both human and animal. The gardens and orchards had been expanded. A new school was being built. So was a Christian chapel, but the anchor of hope was gone; their new symbol was the grim cross of death and suffering.

The economy was stable. The administrators were pleased. Coins were spent, and goods were bartered. The Celts had brought a load of new clothing and accessories soon after the snow melted. Philippa told Vela how the shaman arrow had been used to slay the enemy. Vela was delighted to hear it, although he didn't really seem surprised.

Meanwhile, Philippa and the Scouts had been quietly conferring about the future, and she had been getting her things in order.

It was a fine day. She was in the orchard, making a new map of the fruit and nut trees. She was concentrating hard. People were coming and going. She heard a commotion.

She finally looked up and there they were, Cassius Ambrosius and Brian Magnus, back from Rome. The General's hair had grown long again. There were some white streaks among the dark wavy curls. Despite that, he looked youthful. He had lost some weight. He was wearing new clothes: pale blue trousers and brown boots, and a dark blue tunic under cream-colored leather armor. Brian Magnus also had some new clothes: close fitting grey trousers shot with silver thread, and a white linen tunic under a blue and silver vestment.

The General hollered, "PIPPA!" He bounded over to her and lifted her in his arms, squeezing her tightly, saying, "It was unbearable, being separated from you for so long." She held on to him, crying tears of happiness and relief.

"Hello, little sister," said Brian Magnus. She turned to him. He embraced her briefly, then he held her at arm's length and said quietly, "Are you ready for the next adventure?" She nodded.

Cassius exclaimed, "We saw your Forum. It's a masterpiece! And a popular lunch spot, apparently. In fact... let's go have lunch."
The three of them departed the orchard. They used the shortcut that backtracked up a brushy hill and came out behind the shops.
"Have you two had a chance to see Bootchie yet?" she asked as they climbed.
"Yes," said Brian Magnus, "he greeted Cassius and ignored me, as usual." They approached the Forum.
Cassius said, "Let's get food and you can tell us everything. Then we can go home, and we'll tell *you* everything."
They stopped at the stalls and bought barley and hazelnut cakes, with cress, and plum sauce.

"Hail to good simple food," said Cassius. "You can't get that in the City. Outside it, yes, but Rome itself... it's just absurd. Everything's crumbling, but they're still feasting on flamingo tongue and the choicest pig-womb."
"Why?" said Philippa. "What's the matter with them?"
"So many things," said Brian Magnus.
"Did you visit the temple of Jupiter Optus Maximus?" she asked.
"We did go to the Capitolium," said Brian, with a sideways glance at Cassius. "The General had some sort of episode there. He briefly lost consciousness."
"It was the heat," said Cassius, "after climbing all those stairs."
"Heat doesn't cause your nose to bleed like that," said Brian flatly.

Cassius had finished eating. He got up and went to look at the mural.

"Anyway," Brian continued, "I brought you some cards." He reached in his satchel and pulled out a small bundle of souvenir renderings, showing the temple, statues of Jupiter, Venus and Mars, and a portrait of Marcus Aurelias.

"Thank you," she said. "I love them!" And then more quietly, "What really happened? Is he alright?"

"Oh, sure." He stood. "I want a closer look too." They gathered in front of the mural, examining the details. Regulus had written the name of every character in small fine gold script underneath them. Cassius read each one aloud.

"Altheia Ilithia. That's your mother." He stared at the tiny figure way in the background. "And that's where you lived before the temple. In a little garden house. That's sweet."

"Is it just me," asked Brian Magnus, looking at his depiction, "or am I see-through?"
Pippa said, "That color we used on your skin, it turned out to be a little transparent. I didn't plan it that way. We should have added some of the sulfur yellow to give it some body, but I didn't want to use it too much. It smells just like poop."

"It seems appropriate," Brian said. "And I suppose I'd rather be transparent than poop-faced."

They left the Forum. Word had gotten out that Cassius Ambrosius and Brian Magnus were back. Friends came out to see them. When they reached the General's quarters, Darius, Erastus and Tyronius were waiting outside.

After greeting them, Cassius said, "I want to have evening formation. Let everyone know."
Then the three men left. Philippa, Brian, and Cassius went inside. Bruno and Brutus were standing by. Bootchie was on the big bed.

"We'll be in our billet," said Bruno.
"Let us know when we're needed," said Brutus.
"Bye, Bootchie," they said together.

Pippa, Cassius and Brian walked out to the patio. The cat followed, rubbing against the General until he got picked up. They sat down at the table. The others had left bread, cheese, berries and wine for them.

"Alright, Pippa," said Brian Magnus, "let us tell you all about it."
"Hang on," she said, "I'll get my notebook."

Chapter Twenty - A Draggable Man

"Well," said Brian Magnus, "we can tell you that from here, it's a clear path to the coast, via Novio Magus, to Portus Adurni. The roads are still good. The settlements are in decline, but they're interesting. Lots of mosaics."

"On the fourth evening, we met our ship. It was like a traditional lusoria, but with more of a fore and aft deck. A fast little ship. Named the 'Augustina'." He grinned. "Cassius would have been content with something bigger and slower. It was a choppy ride to the continent. Once we crossed the channel, we hugged the coasts all the way around Iberia. We stopped in Brigantium for supplies, then again in Gaddes. The journey was mostly uneventful. The most exciting thing was that two young camels came on board at Brigantium. A fancy pair of females, name Uma and Dona. The eyelashes those girls had! They had two servants. One fellow walked them around all day, and another fellow went behind to clean up after them. They left us at Gaddes. Then we went past the Pillars, and we were in the Mediterranean."

"We were in open water for a couple of days. Then we reached Rome. We disembarked at Portus. That's the main big port. What a mess! It took forever to collect our gear and get out of there. We decided that when we departed Rome, it would be from Ostia, which is much nicer than Portus. In fact, we wound up staying in Ostia. But more about that shortly."

Philippa had been scribbling notes. She marveled at the narrative vigor of Brian Magnus. *He never even stops to take a breath,* she thought. *Does he take breaths?* She'd never noticed. But he was continuing.

"We reported to the Palatine the next day. Palatine Hill, where the Emperor stays. That's near the Circus Maximus, you've probably heard of that. We'd been ordered to report to the Emperor immediately upon arrival. So naturally it took five weeks before he got around to seeing us. The great Emperor Honorius. He didn't really want to see *us*, he wanted to see what we'd brought. Evidently the small fortune in tax revenues we'd given him was satisfactory. He thanked us for our service to Rome, stamped our decommission orders, gave us a chest of coins, and we were done in ten minutes."

"After waiting around for five weeks, we traded boxes of coins, and that was it. We are all officially decommissioned as of the twenty-eighth of May. Which just happens to be tomorrow. This is your last day as a soldier, soldier." He smiled at Pippa. Before the enormity of that could even sink in, he continued the narrative.

"There were a number of folks in our situation, high ranking British Roman officers from Londinium and Dubris and Camelodunum, waiting around in Rome for their careers to end. There were officers from western Gaul and Brittany in the same situation too. Everyone just wanted to get out of there. The main topic of conversation was the availability of boats shipping out towards home. Rome took care of getting us to the Emperor. It looked as though getting back was going to be our own problem."

"There was an Army Transport Dispatch office in Portus where you could apply for passage back, but it was reputed to be slow and unreliable. So most of the ex-soldiers were finding their own way back. All of the officers we met had at least twenty soldiers returning with them. One had brought fifty men! The eight guards we'd brought with us were planning to stay in Rome. We just needed passage back for the two of us."

"So, while all the other officers wound up in Portus, where the big navy and merchant ships harbored, we went to Ostia, which only got smaller merchant ships, and almost no military boat traffic. And it was a pleasant place to be. But unlike Portus, there was no schedule, no roster, no timetable for arrivals and departures. It was just a matter of finding the right ship with the right skipper at the right time. We walked up and down the docks, asking around. We went to taverns and squares and talked to the locals. We were not having any luck. So we decided to take a thorough walk around all the shops. We thought if we saw some goods from Britannia, or Brittany, or even Hibernia, we could find out if those trade ships might be through soon."

"So that's what we did; girl, you would have been proud of us! We diligently went shopping every day. And then one day we found a shop in Ostia that sold tin items from Britannia Prima. They were even advertised that way. And when we asked the shopkeeper, Argentio, he said that he was expecting the tin merchants in about three weeks. He said that they were very friendly."

"We kept up the search, just in case something else came up, but we'd pretty much pinned all our hopes on Argentio knowing what he was talking about. We went to see him every day, and brought him wine and cheeses, and told him stories. We even brought flowers for his wife, Catalina."

"We unabashedly ingratiated ourselves, hoping that he would be charmed enough to present our case persuasively when the sailors arrived from Dumnonia, from the Tre-ve-na, on the far west coast of Britannia Prima, where they came from. Trevena, by the way, is the kingdom of the shiny tin."

"Two and a half weeks later we showed up for our daily visit, and Argentio was very excited. The tin men had arrived ahead of schedule, and he had already spoken to them about arranging our passage back to Britannia. They were bringing their first load to his shop that afternoon, so we stayed to meet them."

"There was an older man with short grizzled sandy-colored hair, and there were two younger fellows. The youngest resembled the older man, with a thin face and sandy hair. The older lad was more full-faced, with golden hair. We helped them unload their wares when they arrived. Well, Cassius did anyway. Turns out tin is actually quite heavy. Then we made proper introductions. The older man is Branok a'n Ros Dowr - that means Crow of the Wetlands. His son is sixteen, Costentyn a'n Ros Dowr. Constantine, in Kernowek. That's their language. The other lad is Auryn a'n Ben Avalen, age twenty-two. That means Gold of the Apple Hill, Pen Avalen. Apples again!"

"We went to a tavern to talk about it. Branok had a map showing the shipping routes. He asked us if we were wanting to return to our point of origin, Portus Adurni. We said yes, but just briefly; then we were actually hoping to get passage to Dumnonia; now that we were released from service, we wanted to head west."

"Cassius told him that our younger sister Philippa had always wanted to go there, and now we were planning to take her there to live. Costentyn asked if she was pretty! Cassius and I both said 'yes'. Then he asked, 'And which one of you gentlemen does she most resemble?' "

"Cassius said, 'Young man, are you suggesting that one of us isn't as pretty as the other?' And our General got all puffed up, like he does, muscles bulging. The poor lad stammered and said, 'No, I'm... sure you're both very attractive gentlemen'."

"Then Cassius had laughed. Everyone laughed. I said, 'Don't worry, she's not actually related to either of us. And she's prettier than both of us combined.' "

"Then Auryn asked, 'How old is she?' I said you were in your mid-twenties. Costentyn asked him, 'Why do you care? I thought you were in love with Merryn a'n Bol Gwynne.' Her name means Sea Born from the White Pool, Pol Gwynne. Sometimes the first letters change sound. I'm really enjoying this language, in case you hadn't noticed. Then the lad Auryn said, 'Not for me! For Arghan.' Costentyn said, 'Oh yes. Uncle Arghan needs a wife. He's getting really old. He's nearly thirty!' That got a laugh too."

Brian Magnus paused. He looked at Cassius, then at Pippa, and asked, "Am I talking too much?"

"Never," said Pippa.
"Always," said Cassius at the same time.
He smiled and shrugged, then continued.

"Arghan a'n Ben Avalen, that means Silver from the Apple Hill; isn't that lovely? He is the older brother of Auryn. And they are both nephews of Branok. They live in the castle. Arghan isn't just a trader, he is a Master Smith. To the King and Queen! Arthek Gallósek, Ruifadur, ha Elowen Glas Lagas, Ruifanes Teg, Rowlyas a'n Ruvaneth ahan' Dre Van Venydh, Tre-War-Avana - Trevena!"

"Which means, The Great Bear, King, and The Blue Eyed Willow, Lovely Queen, rulers of the Kingdom of the Shining Tin: Trevena. Merryn a'n Bol Gwynne is the Princess. Auryn has very high hopes."

"Anyway, we accompanied them back to their ship. Arghan was coming down the gangplank as we approached. He was wearing a lovely blue and grey tunic over light brown trousers. He looked slim and graceful. His hair was fluffy, and sort of grayish brown."
"Cassius said to me, 'Does that look like a draggable man?' 'Yes,' I replied, 'a draggable man if ever I've seen one.' Anyway, to make a long story short- we found you a husband. If you like him. We think you will. We do."

"But," said Pippa, "do you think he'll like me? Did you tell him about the hole in my teeth?"
"Yes," Brian said, "and the hole in your side. And everything else about you. There was plenty of time to talk on the voyage back. Oh, and he sent this for you."
Brian reached into his satchel.
"He actually created it during the voyage. While the ship was rolling, and Cassius was heaving, Arghan of Pen Avalen made this for you, Pippa." He handed her a long box, made of stiff fabric.

"He asked us if you like adornment," said Cassius. "I said yes, but nothing too girly. That you'd been wearing armor most of your life."
She opened the box. It was a neckpiece. There were three panels of delicate chain mail. The mail was composed of many tiny gold and silver rings, arranged in an intricate pattern. The panels were connected by slightly domed lozenges of tin, which were set in bezels of gold. The outer panels tapered gracefully

towards the neck, and were attached by silver chains that hooked together. She held it up and examined it.

"Look at the back," said Cassius. He helped her turn it around. On the reverse side of the two tin lozenges were tiny engraved inscriptions. The first one read- 'For Philippa', and the second- 'From Arghan'. He held it up for her to try on. She lifted up her hair and he connected it in back. It felt solid but lightweight. Cassius brought her Celtic mirror so she could see it. It fit perfectly. She moved back and forth. The neckpiece stayed in place, while the chain mail gently rippled.
She smiled broadly. "It's... just right," she said. "Thank you, brothers."

"The tin men will wait for us at Portus Adurni," said Brian Magnus. "How soon can you be ready?"
"I'm ready," she said. "Except for a couple of things I can take care of this evening. The Scouts are ready too. They've even made a new carrier for Bootchie."
"Right then," said Cassius, "it looks as though we'll be able to leave tomorrow. I'll announce all the news at formation. And then we will host a feast. At the Forum Philippa Agrippa."

"And now, we have some things to attend to," said Brian. "We'll meet you back here before formation." They left. She retrieved the three beautifully bound Histories, which had been stashed in her room. She spread them out on the bed, and began to write on the last page of her original book:

By the year 400, the Empire was withdrawing from Britannia Prima. Selected commissioned officers who planned to stay in the country were ordered to report to the Palatine in Rome, in order to be personally discharged by the Emperor Honorius. In the autumn of 403, Commander Legatus Cassius Ambrosius and Securitor Preceps Brian Magnus journeyed to Rome by Army transport ship. There they were thanked by the Emperor and awarded for their service. They, along with the entire cohort at Vindavia Nova, were honorably discharged, pending the date on the orders, May 28th, 404.
That spring, Cassius Ambrosius and Brian Magnus returned to Britannia on a ship that originated in Dumnonia, from Trevena, along the far west coast of Britannia Prima. They returned to Vindavia Nova on the 27th of May, in time to discharge the ranks.
Upon their return, a plan was formed between Cassius Ambrosius, Brian Magnus, and Philippa Agrippa. After officially discharging the service members and thanking everyone, the entire post would be invited to a great feast. Vows of friendship would be made, and many fond farewells would be said, for upon

the next day the three of them, accompanied by Bruno Marianis, Brutus
Marianis, and Bootchie the orange and white cat, would be departing from
Vindavia Nova and heading west. They would be returning to the ship which
would take them to live in Trevena, the shining sea kingdom of the tin people.

Written by Centurion Philippa Agrippa, in the year 404. May the Gods bless
and protect all who read this history of the great General Cassius Ambrosius.
Quattro Ventis Potens. Finis.

She read it back over, then proceeded to copy it into the other two books. She
was trying to be careful, but also trying to be quick. Her hand was cramping
badly by the time she finished. She rested for a moment, then commenced to
write the inscription. She had considered various dedications. Finally she had
decided on what had become her favorite quote. She carefully wrote on each
blank first page-

"Gain is loss and loss is gain. People come and go. That's the Army, that's life.
Like the Big Man said, let's enjoy it while it lasts." Tyronius Danu, 392.

That was it, they were done. She set them on the table, and went to finish her
final packing. After a while Cassius and Brian returned, with the Scouts.
"What's this?" Cassius asked, picking up the top book from the stack.
"It's your book," she said. "I just finished them. I'm giving one to the men, and
the other two are to take with us. The original one is yours."
Cassius said, "My history! In a real codex! Oh, Pippa, this is gorgeous." He sat
down and started looking at it.
"You'll have time later," said Brian. "We have to get going now." Reluctantly,
Cassius closed the book. He got up and hugged Philippa.
Then he said, "Right. One last formation. One last time in full dress. One last
night as a soldier of Rome!"

Everyone was there at formation, almost the entire post, soldiers and civilians.
The officers were in their finest armor. There was a sense of nervous
anticipation from the crowd.

Brian Magnus made the first announcement. He said loudly,
"Soldiers of the Army of Rome. Troops of Vindavia Nova. The Emperor thanks
you for your loyal service. You are hereby honorably discharged as of May 28,
in the year 404. Your duties to the Empire have come to an end. May the Gods
reward you all for your many years of service with many more years of health
and prosperity." He shouted, "Quattro Ventis Potens!"

"Quattro Ventis Potens." The return cry was thin. People seem uncertain. Brian Magnus continued.

"Friends, Quattro Ventis Potens is *your* motto. It never belonged to the Army. It belongs to this place, blessed by the mighty four winds, and to all of you who made it grow and prosper." He raised his voice and it rang through the air.

"Vindavia Nova was once a fort. Now it's a town. Your town. And one of the finest in all Britannia. WHAT IS THE MOTTO OF YOUR TOWN?" This time they were ready.

"QUATTRO VENTIS POTENS!" The cry rang through the air.

Cassius came and stood by him, saying, "Soldiers. Townspeople. Friends! It has been the greatest of privileges to serve you and work alongside you all these years. Vindavia Nova saved my life, and I hope that I have given something back in return. But my work here is done. Our work here is done." He motioned to Pippa, Brutus and Bruno.

They came and stood with him and Brian Magnus.

"It has long been our intention to travel to the west. It is the physical and spiritual fulfillment of our destinies. Please understand that if we were not compelled westward, we would live here with you all in contentment for the rest of our days. There was never a finer place or people. It grieves us sorely, but we must tear ourselves away from you. Tomorrow... " Cassius was trying to not be overcome with emotion. "Tomorrow, Brian Magnus, Philippa Agrippa, Bruno Marianis, Brutus Marianis and myself depart for Dumnonia. There is a ship waiting at Portus Adurni to take us."

There were cries of outrage and wails of despair from the crowd. Pippa cried loudly,

"I know. Change HURTS! But then we grow. If you weren't ready for us to leave, we wouldn't be able to. When you look back at this night, we want it to be with gladness. And so everyone is invited to a great feast, at the Forum, and there we will say hail and farewell to all of you."

"And so, to the Forum!" Shouted Cassius. "QUATTRO VENTIS POTENS!"
"QUATTRO VENTIS POTENS!" shouted the crowd.

"And for the last time... soldiers of Vindavia Nova, soldiers of Rome." He couldn't hold back a tear. "You are dismissed."

It was several hours past midnight when they returned to their quarters. Philippa was not at all used to being up so late. She was physically and emotionally exhausted, her voice was tired, and her head ached from all the noise and excitement. But it had been worth it. By the end of the night, after the talking, toasts, cheers, tears, hugs, and vows of friendship, everyone seemed happy. The men of Ares Mons, seated at a table together, were quite disconsolate, and silent at first, until she presented them with her book.

"It's the Military History of Cassius Ambrosius," she had told them. "And you're all in it. By name." She had devoted a chapter to them, and a short history of the training camp.

"And see," she said, "Tyronius wrote the inscription!" After that, they couldn't remain upset with her, even though several of them were reduced to tears many times throughout the evening.

The travelers had only slept for a few hours when the drivers showed up with the wagon and pony-cart, and the guard assembled. They would be escorted to the port by eight soldiers. The trunks and luggage were loaded onto the ox-wagon. Bruno and Brutus were riding ponies. Cassius, Brian, and Pippa loaded the last of their belongings onto the cart, including the box of scrolls and Bootchie. His new carrier was roomy, with a selection of toys, and all the comforts that he was accustomed to.

They went into the tent, to have one final look around.

"Gods," said Cassius, "it breaks my heart to leave this bed behind." He patted it and sighed. "But it belongs here."

They went to the patio. They kneeled before the Deities and thanked them. Philippa had packed her little old Jupiter; they were leaving the rest of the statues to look after their friends. They asked them to continue to shower blessings on Vindavia Nova. They prayed that the Old Gods would not be forgotten in this new world they were leaving behind. Then they said goodbye to Artemis and Beni, who had come to see them off, and they got in the cart.

The cart and wagon began to roll through the semi-darkness. They drove past the parade ground, the Forum, the shops, the tents and stables, the gardens and barricades, and then they were out of the gate. The soldiers at the gate saluted them, one last time. As they turned on the road that would take them to the port, the sun rose behind them, giving them all halos of light, and sending long shadows ahead of them.

"Farewell to Vindavia Nova," said Cassius. "Farewell to Quattro Ventis Potens. May the mighty four winds continue to guide us on our travels, but... the grandeur of that motto no longer seems appropriate. It doesn't reflect our... diminished state. We need a new saying."

"We already have one," said Brian Magnus, looking at Pippa. At the same time they both exclaimed, "Nulles Ex Nusquam!" Cassius shrugged. "Nulles Ex Nusquam," he repeated.

They camped in tents the first night, at a parkland between the road and a stream. There were several other groups camped there too, mostly local traders. It rained during the night, but by dawn the sky was clear again. In early afternoon, they reached Novio Magus. Camp was set up on the green for the guards and wagons. Cassius, Brian Magnus, Pippa, Bootchie, Brutus and Bruno were jammed into two small rooms at a nearby inn. They put their overnight bags in the rooms.

"Ready to explore?" said Brian Magnus to Pippa and the twins.
Cassius said, "I'll stay here with Bootchie. I saw it all last time. I'm going to read my book, then take a nap. See you at dinner." He did look tired, and his eyes were red. They said goodbye and departed.

The area right around the inn was fairly well populated. Brian Magnus led them up a side lane and into a neighborhood that looked deserted. What were once well-to-do homes were now crumbling in disrepair. One house was particularly grand, with corinthian columns supporting a big and lavish portico. Part of the roof and wall had collapsed. The garden surrounding the house was overgrown with dendrons and brambles. A high trellis across the top of the courtyard created a cover of flowering vines.

He picked his way over the rubble. They followed. They entered the courtyard. Philippa stared. It was covered by a huge mosaic, like the one at Mount Temple, but three times the size. This one had fish and animals too, but it also had geometric bands and borders. The center was a medallion, with two dolphins arranged like the Pisces. The colors were still bright and vibrant. A breeze was blowing, and the vine-covered trellis overhead cast a rippling shadow that seemed to activate the images. Some of the tesserae were metallic, and sparkled like gems.

They stayed there for quite a while, enjoying the peaceful ruins. Then they walked back down the lane. They stopped at a vendor and bought lemonade, and barley cakes with fire-roasted shrimp and baby onions, covered in dill sauce.
They returned to the inn. Cassius was asleep. The book and the cat lay beside him. Bootchie was sleeping too. It seemed like a good idea. They all napped until dinner, after which they went right back to bed.

The next day, the sky was clear. The road was good, and they made excellent time to Portus Adurni. On the outskirts, they stopped for lunch at a charming little popina. It was in an old villa, but one that had been kept up. It was elegant, and filled with mosaics and fine artwork.

While lunch was being prepared, they explored the rooms. Pippa was staring at yet another scene of dolphins.
Brian Magnus approached, saying, "You like dolphins? You'll see them on the voyage. They swim in front of the ship."
Pippa thought that sounded dangerous. "They don't get hit?" she asked.
"No, they love it. It's a game to them, and a fun way to travel."

They sat down to eat on the elegant patio. Food was delivered to the guards, who stayed with the gear and took care of the oxen and ponies. A spot was set up for Bootchie to have some lunch, stretch his legs, and use the box. The twins cared for him as if he were royalty. They carried his box between them, like a palanquin, and they had a portable enclosed playpen which was set up for him wherever they went. They were not taking any chances of him wandering off, getting stolen, or grabbed by a dog or a falcon.

"How far to the port from here?" asked Philippa. Lunch was almost over. She was beginning to get a bit nervous.
"Just a half a mile; we're nearly there," said Cassius. He looked better. His eyes weren't quite so red. She gazed at him fondly. Then she rose, went to the back of his chair, put her arms around him and kissed him on the top of the head.

"I'd have told you that myself," said Brian Magnus, "if I'd known there was a hug and a kiss involved."

She laughed and moved to where Brian sat, his plate of food untouched except for where Cassius had been nibbling at it. She gave him a tingly hug and a planted a kiss on his head. His hair was as soft as her own.
"There," he said, "now I feel better." Philippa smiled. *This is my family,* she thought. And now she would be part of another family too. *It's uncharted territory.*
"Let's go get this over with," she said. "The less time I have to get nervous, the better."

They left the inn, after congratulating the proprietors on having the best establishment in Britannia Prima Sud Est. The road began to climb, gently at first, and then much more steeply. Their cart was in front, keeping pace with the forward guard. Philippa could hear the soldiers' deep breathing, and the shrill creaking of the wagon's axles. They crested the ridge. Philippa let out a sharp little cry, "Ahhh!"

"Hold!" called Cassius. The convoy abruptly stopped.

"What is it?" he asked her.

She was standing up in the cart, transfixed on the horizon. There was a colossal blueness, sparkling with tiny stars, rising above the hills and reaching half way up to the sky.

"It's... the ocean. I didn't expect to see it like this. It's overwhelming. I thought it would look flat, but it's... I don't know how to describe it."

Brian offered the word, "Liminal?"

"Yes, sure, liminal." *I'll have to look that up,* she told herself. "Sorry, I didn't mean to startle everyone."

She sat back down. Cassius called, "Go!" and they continued.

"It may seem... liminal now," he said, "but wait until we're on it. It'll be flat enough alright. But no less overwhelming."

They rode down the hill and approached the port. Portus Adurni was a small settlement. It had once been larger. The harbor was one of the finest on the coast, wide but sheltered. There were strong sea-walls, but the land had flooded anyway, and then receded again, leaving ruined settlements along the water's edge. Several rivers fed into the area. The village was surrounded by mudflat and marshland on either side, teeming with seabirds. They passed some canals, filled with boats and barges. The air smelled marshy and fishy. Then they reached the docks. Ships were being loaded and unloaded. There were pallets of lumber and hay, crates of amphorae, tubs of fresh shellfish, and racks of dried whitefish.

They got off the cart. Philippa was wearing a slate grey tunic over cream colored trousers, dark gray boots, a silver mesh belt with a long dagger, and the neckpiece that Arghan had made for her. Her hair was loose and hung to the middle of her back. Cassius fiddled with it for a bit, smoothing out some of the tangles.

They walked along the row of ships and stopped in front of one. The wagon was unloaded. The guards were dismissed for the last time.

This is really happening, thought Pippa.

Philippa looked at the ship. It was a pretty vessel, not as big as some of the others, but solid, and elegantly crafted of shiny dark wood that was highlighted on the rails with silver leaf. The well-worn hull was meticulously straked, and strapped with metal stays. The green and white sails were neatly furled. The ship had the carved figurehead of a woman holding a sword whose blade looked like a narwhal horn, pointing downwards with both hands. Her hair surrounded her in swirls that looked like the wind.

Brian Magnus had gone ahead to announce their arrival. As Pippa stood admiring the ship, he came down the gangway, followed by a group of men.

From Brian's descriptions, Philippa recognized Branok, Costentyn and Auryn. Then Arghan. He looked just like Brian Magnus had described him. He was wearing a tunic of light brown with silver thread over trousers of muted forest green. His cloak was a slightly darker green. He wore a simple silver collar, and his belt had silver buckles. So did his boots, which were of soft brown leather.

Philippa and Arghan were brought face to face. Introductions were made. He was taller than Cassius, but not as tall as Brian Magnus. He bowed and extended his hand. She took it, smiled at him, and then gave him a big hug. He was surprised, but he hugged her in return. Everyone smiled at that. Brian Magnus introduced her to the men. Besides Branok, Costentyn and Auryn, there were three others. The first fellow was small and stout, with a kind, weathered face and a receding hairline.
"Santo a'n Bol Sten, Little Alexander from the Tin Pool," said Brian. "And this is Piran Glowbrenn. What a fine-sounding name. It means Little Dark Coal Man." Piran was slightly built, with cropped black hair.
"And this is Edern Pinbren. Eternal Pine. Very poetic. His family are Roman Britons. He's Arghan and Auryn's second cousin." Edern Pinbren was very tall and lanky. He had hazel colored eyes and sandy brown hair.

Philippa greeted them all and they bowed. Then the others all found something to do or look at nearby, leaving the two of them alone. They stood in silence.

"Is this your ship?" she asked. She couldn't think of anything else to say.
"My brother's and mine," he replied. "Uncle Branok pilots it. Costentyn and Auryn help the crew. The ship has a shallow keel for easy maneuvering along the shore. But she still handles well on the open sea. She's got a hull of stout Britannic oak."
Philippa read aloud the name that was written on the bow in white and gold letters. "Awel Glor."
"It means breeze. It's also our mother's name."
"And your mother... is she well?" Pippa asked.
"Yes. And father," he replied.
"Sten a'n Ben Avalen," she said, grateful for the tutelage of Brian Magnus. "That means tin, right? Tin from the Apple Hill?"
"That's right! But unless you're being poetic or formal, you can skip the a'n, which means from the; we just say Pen Avalen."
"Pen Avalen," she repeated. "Do your parents live at the castle too, Arghan?"

"No, they did for many years, as did their parents before them. But they have retired back to our family estate in the orchards, and I have long since taken my father's place as the Angove, the royal goldsmith to the King and Queen."

Philippa was silent. That all sounded really impressive.

They walked up the gangplank and stepped onto the deck.

"Welcome aboard," he said. She stood uncertainly for a moment. It felt solid enough, but there was an underlying sense of constant movement which was very disconcerting. Arghan asked, "Have you never been on the water?"

"No, just in it. In the river when I learned to swim."

"Well, it's good to know that you can swim. And don't worry, it feels wobbly at first, but once we're underway you'll get your sea legs." They proceeded to the stern, staying close to the top rails.

"When you walk on the ship, you have to take care. The main thing is, stay away from the sails. Stay close to the railings. There's a safe zone, where the boom doesn't reach, but it's just a few feet wide."

He stopped and looked at her.

"It's very dangerous. The boom can take a person's head right off. You understand?"

"Yes... thank you for the warning."

They reached the stern. The aft deck was an open area, densely packed with crates, and covered with tarpaulins. The remaining space was taken up by a small enclosed stable, which currently housed three recently shorn sheep and a small pony. Arghan opened the outer door. The animals all came running to the gate, the sheep baa-ing loudly.

Philippa laughed in delight. "Oh, how adorable!"

"The sheep are breeding stock for the King's flock, and the pony is a gift for the Princess." He scooped some grain from a barrel. "Here, do you want to feed them?" They fed the animals through the slats from their cupped hands. Philippa thought for a moment and recited, "Merryn a'n Bol Gwynne, Pennsevigis. Sea-born from the white pool, Princess."

"How did you learn all this so quickly?"

"You've met Brian Magnus?" she asked.

He laughed. "Yes. The good fellow likes to explain things in detail."

"Follow me, please." He went all the way back to the stern. "This is the privy." It was an outhouse, built on the stern overhang. She peered inside. There was a rudimentary latrine set above a lattice of slats. The open water was below. She said nervously, "It just... hangs out over the ocean."

"Sorry," Arghan said. "You get used to it. Sort of."

She thought about the vast ocean and all the creatures it must hold. Pippa asked, "Is it true that dolphins swim at the front of the boat?"

"The bow of the ship. Please don't call her a boat. The ocean's big enough as it is. And yes, they will swim with us, the porpoises too, all smiling happily the entire time."
"I look forward to seeing that."

"What kind of ship is this?" she asked.
"Mm? The kind that floats, I hope," he said smiling. She laughed.
He said, "You mean does this style of vessel have a name? I don't think so."
He looked her in the eyes. "You Romans," he said, not unkindly, "you really seem to enjoy... classifying things."
"I suppose we do," she replied, "we're meant to be curious. To develop critical thinking."
"That's good," he said. "Ignorance is a dangerous thing. And easily avoidable through proper education."

Pippa liked what she was hearing. She asked him, "Do all your people speak Latin?"
"The King doesn't, but the Queen does. And the counselors and advisors. And the traders and merchants. And all the artisans and sailors. And the farmers and builders." He paused. "And the servers and the kitchen staff. Come to think of it, anyone who works for a living knows some Latin." They both laughed. She was relieved that he didn't seem to take his exalted position too seriously.

"Come back around here," Arghan said. They walked to the other side of the stable, which was covered by a shed.
"This is our floating workshop. We keep a small forge and anvil in case we need to make a replacement piece of hardware for the ship. I make adornments, to pass the time. You can only watch the dolphins for so long." He smiled. There was a tiny workbench with a rack of tools, coils of wire, a blow torch and a pitch bowl, all held in place with straps. The workbench had drawers underneath. He opened the first one. "Do you know your metals?" She looked.
"Copper," she said instantly.
"Good." He opened the second drawer.
"Silver. Probably coin silver, by the look of it."
"Very good!" He opened the third drawer.
"Iron. Not the best-looking," she said, peering at the oxidized ingots.
"It's good iron," he replied. "Or at least it was, before it came on the ship. The salt air corrodes it."
"No gold?" She was a little disappointed.
"Oh, there's gold," he said. "In one of these drawers. Do you think you can find it?"

"Yes," she said confidently. The iron drawer was still open. *You wouldn't want to hide pure gold near this rusty iron,* she thought. *It might get contaminated.* She closed it. She opened the silver drawer. The silver was in a long deep tray, easy to lift out. *That could be a decoy. Make the silver easy to grab, and hope that a potential thief will be satisfied.* She closed it and opened the copper drawer. There were about two dozen long copper ingots. She removed them all, stacking them carefully on the workbench. Philippa thought about the temple, and the mosaic tools. She put her hand into the now empty drawer, and felt around. At the back, up in the right hand corner, there was a tiny hook. She fiddled with it. She put her face close up, and peered inside. Then she put her hand back in, released the catch, and removed the back of the drawer.

There was a bundle, wrapped in waxed linen. She pulled it out. It was the size of the palm of her hand, and it was very heavy. She handed it to Arghan who exclaimed,
"You are just as sharp as Brian Magnus said you'd be!"
He unwrapped the cloth and revealed the contents to her. There was a shallow wooden box with a lid.

"Open it," he said. She removed the lid. Inside the box were perfectly cut and stacked little squares of gold. It reminded her of one of the boxes of sweetmeats which had been handed out at the wedding of Terranes and Julia.

"They look good enough to eat!" she said.
Arghan laughed, saying, "You must be hungry!"
He put the gold away. Pippa handed him the copper, and he replaced it in the drawer.

"Do you use lead?" she asked.
"No!" He exclaimed. "Lead is poison. The Greeks figured that out hundreds of years ago. Some people still use it, to make cheap white metal. Amateurs like it because it's soft. They don't understand that the convenience comes at a cost."

"How is it poison?" Philippa asked, startled at this revelation.
"There's something... unwholesome about it. Tin is the angel of the earth, and lead is the devil. It's a contaminant. It sickens the body and mind, kills plants, and makes the earth and water toxic. It doesn't interact with the air. Tin corrodes. It's a living element. Lead doesn't break down. It's already dead. It just gets dark and ugly and greasy looking."

Pippa said, "One of the Centurions at Ares Mons always drank from a lead goblet. I remember it was dull and shiny, but not in a nice way like tin."

"Then he's permanently poisoned," said Arghan. "There's no antidote or treatment. It will eventually destroy the blood and organs, but first it makes a person angry and bitter and completely ignorant of his condition. Was this centurion a pleasant fellow?"

She thought of the red haired centurion at Ares Mons, the one who said he didn't want her. The other centurions had treated her respectfully after the initial encounter, but the red haired one was always a brute.
"He was by far the most consistently unpleasant and hostile person that I met in all my years of service."
"Well, it might be that some of his bad behavior was due to lead poisoning. I'm sorry you had to deal with someone like that."

They stood together in silence for a moment. Then Arghan said,
"Let's finish the tour, and then we can get some food." They came back up the other side of the ship, staying close to the rails.
"Our quarters are below the aft deck," he explained. "We're jammed in there pretty tight. Yours are below the fore deck. They're a little nicer."

They continued up to the fore deck. On it, there was a big ship's wheel, attached to a long apparatus that connected it to the rudder. There were navigational tools and scopes mounted on stands. The stands were attached to tracks on the ground, and locked into place. There was a small chart-room that displayed nautical maps. Arghan pointed to a chart, saying, "Here's our route. The Awel Glor is good at navigating close to shore, and can go up rivers where deeper keeled ships of the same size can't."

Arghan and Pippa left the foredeck and went to the bow. They stood looking out. The ship was docked in a canal, so there wasn't much to see. Her eyes followed the bowsprit to its point.
A sea voyage, she thought. *With my soon-to-be betrothed. This is all going to be very different.* It was a bit overwhelming. For a moment she was almost sorry that they had ever left the cozy confines of Vindavia Nova.
"Shall we go below?" asked Arghan. "Mind your step."
She went cautiously down the steep stairs. It was dark, and there was a pleasant scent of aged wood. Her eyes adjusted.

"In here, our bunks," he said. She looked into the back room. It was jammed with cots, hammocks, sea chests and lockers. There was a tiny table with two narrow benches. Clotheslines crisscrossed the room, covered with trousers and jackets. "I'd invite you in, but I think you can see from here that it's a disaster."

He turned around and motioned for her to follow.
"Here you are, the aft quarters. Oh good, they've already brought your things aboard."

She saw her trunks and scroll library, neatly secured against the wall, next to the luggage of Cassius and Brian Magnus.

Arghan continued, "You can have have one of these berths."
Following the curve of the ship, there were six cozy beds built into the walls of the hull, two deep. "Cassius has been bunking at the front starboard, and Brian claimed the one above him."

"I'll take this one," she said, going to the low port-side bunk opposite Cassius. She sat for a moment. Then she got up and went to her gear trunk, unstrapped it and opened it.
"You might like to see my cuirass. The master smith made it for me." She unwrapped the shiny bronze breastplate.
"Oh, my!" he exclaimed. "They made this at Ares Mons? That's brilliant. And... you wore it?"
"Every working day for nearly ten years. Shall I model it for you?"
"Please," he said. "May I assist you?"
"Just help me take off my beautiful neckpiece. I don't want it to get damaged. Thank you for that, by the way." She lifted her hair.
"You're very welcome." He unclasped the neckpiece and set it on her berth.

She slipped on the cuirass, deftly buckled it, and pulled her hair free. Arghan gazed in admiration. "That is glorious. I've never had any desire to be a soldier, but this makes me want to follow you into battle."

He ran his fingers along the curves. "What a fine finish. It shines beautifully but you can still see the planishing marks..." She couldn't help giggling as he caressed her metal chest. "Oh! I'm sorry," he said, suddenly flushed. "I didn't mean to... "
"That's alright," she said, "it's not as though I felt it!" They both laughed. She unhooked the cuirass and slipped it off. She replaced it in the trunk, adding, "I've got something else."

She brought out her bundle. She opened it, took out the Jupiter statue, and stuck it in the corner of her bunk. "Hello, old friend," she said. "We're on the water!"

She returned to the bundle and took out her Army nails, which she had bound with twine, and handed them to Arghan.

"I made these. At the Ares Mons forge. Soldiers were required to help out around the post and learn new skills. Metalwork was one of my vocations. That and farming."

He held the sleek iron nails in his palm. "Roman nails," he said. "Very fine quality. And these have never been used." He smelled them. "They still smell faintly of the forge."
"I noticed that too," she said. "I like the smell." He was still staring at the nails.
"They're yours if you want them," she said. "They've been sitting on my little altar all these years. Maybe you can think of something interesting to do with them."

"Yes," he said. "Thank you. They're very special." He put the nails in his pocket. She picked up the neckpiece from the bed, handed it to him, and lifted her hair. He carefully placed the neckpiece on her and connected it.

They went back topside and exited down the gangway. They could see the others in the distance.
"I wonder what they've been doing?" she mused.
"You mean besides worrying about whether we're getting along?" he asked.

She laughed and said, "Let's put their minds at rest." She reached out her hand and he took it.

Chapter Twenty One - Domini Domini

"Listen to this," said Brian Magnus. He was holding a small codex that he had purchased from a bookseller in Portus Adurni. "This is a history of Britannia by Diodorus Siculus. He was a Sicilian Greek historian, in the first century of the current era."

"He writes of 'the inhabitants of that part of Britain which is called Belerion'. Shining Country. That's in the far west of Dumnonia, in a place where the land appears to end. Diodorus says that 'the inhabitants of Belerion are very fond of strangers and from their intercourse with foreign merchants are civilized in their manner of life. They prepare the tin, working very carefully the earth in which it is produced. The ground is rocky but it contains earthy veins, the produce of which is ground down, smelted and purified. They beat the metal into masses shaped like astralgi (knuckle-bones) and carry it off to a certain island called Ictis. During the ebb of the tide the intervening space is left dry and they carry over to the island the tin in abundance in their wagons.' Then he says, 'Here then the merchants buy the tin from the natives and carry it over to Gaul, and after travelling overland for about thirty days, they finally bring their loads on horses to the mouth of the Rhone.' That's up in the Montes Alpes."

"Diodorus is quoting from the writings of Pythias of Massalia," Brian Magnus continued. "He was a Greek explorer and map-maker from the fourth century B.C. He was the first to go all the way around Albion. He called it Prideni. It means 'land of the pretty ones'. Very fitting. That's probably where the word Briton comes from. Pythias also described the frozen land further to the north, called Thule."

They were all sitting up in the bow on the little deck benches. It was a clear sunny day and the sky was a brilliant blue. On the starboard side, the southern coast of Prideni slipped by at a leisurely rate. On the port side, they were passing a long island, covered with cliffs and dunes, and dotted with scrubby vegetation.

The Awel Glor had departed with the morning tide. They had almost missed it. It took a while to navigate their way out of Portus Adurni. It was not the same way they had come in. They tacked hard up a channel which soon bent sharply southward. Making the turn was problematic. Apparently there was a shallow point somewhere that needed to be avoided. It was unclear exactly where it was. The sailors heaved and hauled, shouting loudly to each other. When they finally managed to come tightly about, they had sailed slowly back down to the bay. Then they were finally headed west, picking up speed. They still hadn't viewed the open sea. No dolphins had shown up yet, but the little bow-deck was a nice place to relax.

Cassius and Arghan were sitting in the sun. Brian Magnus and Pippa were on the shady side. Bootchie was sleeping in his playpen, which was set up between them. The twins were stretched out on either side of the foredeck. Branok was piloting the ship, and Costentyn and Auryn were sitting on the foredeck with their backs against the chart-room, playing a dice game. Piran was on lookout. Edern and Santo were tending to the animals on the aft deck.

"What is Ictus?" asked Cassius.
Arghan replied, "It's a tidal island. It's in the Baya Ronda. The Rounded Bay. About halfway between here and Trevena."
"What's a tidal island?" asked Pippa.
"At high tide it's an island surrounded by water," Arghan replied. "But at low tide you can walk there from the mainland. The name Ictis is foreign. We call it Karrek Loos y'n Koos. That means the Grey Rock in the Woods. If you think that name doesn't make sense, you're right."

"Then why is it called that?" asked Cassius.

Arghan replied, "There was a mighty flood, long ago. Folks say that it happened in our great-grandparents time. There *was* a flood during that time, but I think the big flood that changed it must have occurred much earlier. Anyway, they kept the old name, even though the rock is now in the water, not the woods."

Pippa asked, "Do the floods happen very often?"
"Well, yes," he replied. "It flooded when my father was young, but not too badly. It also flooded when I was young. That was worse. The seawalls helped, but some coastal farmlands and livestock still got washed away. Afterwards, some of the harbor entrances along the south coast had changed. Rivers shifted position too. Some coastal areas grew. Others shrank, or disappeared. The beach below Trevena used to be much wider at low tide than it is now. It's all constantly changing. Some of the navigational charts are way out of date."

"Not the one we're using today, I hope!" said Cassius. Arghan laughed, then he called to Auryn in Kernowek. Auryn rose, went into the chart room, and returned holding a navigational map, which he brought to his brother. Arghan thanked him, saying, "Meur ras."

Arghan set the map on the deck between them, next to Bootchie's pen. They gathered around to see. Bootchie woke up and looked at them all. Then he stretched, yawned, and plumped against the wall of his pen, purring loudly. Auryn petted the cat very gently through the slats.

He asked Brian, "May I come to your quarters sometime and play with Bootchie outside of his pen?"

"Of course," said Brian Magnus. "Come today. Bootchie would like that."

"Here we are," said Arghan, pointing. "We just turned to the west. Vectis is south of us. The Bar. It's a large island. We're passing along the north edge of it. We'll come out here before too long." He pointed to a spot where the narrow waterway that they were following opened up onto the sea. "We'll cut across this bay here, if the wind is right." He pointed to the next western promontory. "Then we'll come 'round this headland and follow the cove. It's very pretty."

"Our destination for tonight is here." He pointed to the far side of the cove. "Tomorrow, we have to make a delivery, and pick up a shipment, all the way up here." They followed his finger as it pointed to the western edge of a long lake. "There's a big trading post, on the Durnovaria Road, right by the docks."

"It's not the usual sort of harbor. First there's a narrow river. It feeds into a lake. The Ratha Pol."
"Pol is pool, right?" Pippa asked. "What's ratha?"
"It means scratchy," said Auryn. Seeing her puzzled look, he added, "It will make sense when we get there."

"We go quite a ways inland," Arghan continued. "It's a complicated process. There are several big grain mills along there, and they need just the right level of water to work, so the river-masters control the flow with watergates. We won't be able to go in until tomorrow, and it's really not that far from here. We have time for some sight-seeing. If you're interested. We could stop for lunch... here." He pointed to a spot about halfway along the wide cove. "Just beyond Klog Eythin, the Furze Cliff, there's a small settlement. I thought you might like to see the Roman Temple there. It's pretty impressive, even if it has seen better days."

"A Roman Temple!" cried Pippa. "What a surprise."
"That would be lovely," said Cassius. "It may be the last one we see for a while."
"Or ever," said Brian Magnus.

Just then, the southern bank was gone, and they beheld the open sea on their port side. *That's more like it,* thought Pippa. *Flat and wide.* The wind picked up and they flew along the water.

The starboard shore came close and then receded as they passed by inlets and promontories. They could now see that Vectis extended south into the far distance. The large island gradually disappeared from view.

After a while, Arghan said, "There's the Sea-Door." They were approaching a great freestanding stone portal, rising out of the water. The opening was as wide as an ox-wagon.

"That's amazing!" cried Pippa.

More strange rock formations appeared along the coast. There were tall freestanding cliffs that looked like sliced loaves of bread. Some of them had collapsed in heaps.

Then the cliff face grew massive, dotted here and there with occasional scrubby plants. Before long, it was entirely covered with vegetation of green, brown and gold.

"Klog Eythin," called Piran from up on the lookout. The sailors prepared to dock. The rest of them went below and closed the door. Bootchie was let out of his pen. He stretched, then jumped on Pippa's bed and began grooming his fluffy tail.

"I think that I'll stay behind this time," said Brian Magnus. "The Mighty Bootch is expecting company." He smiled at Pippa. "And I've got some reading to catch up on."

The others got ready for their outing, said farewell, and went back topside. They were entering a tiny but bustling port. The Awel Glor had dropped her mainsail, and Branok was slowly coaxing her up to the dock. He whistled. A man appeared. Edern Pinbren threw the line, and the man on the dock caught it and tied them off. They repeated the process with another line. Meanwhile Santo and Piran lowered the headsail. The ship stopped with a tiny shudder. Arghan and Auryn dropped the gangplank.

After the vessel was secured, Pippa, Arghan, Cassius, Edern, Bruno and Brutus exited the ship together for the tour of the temple. Santo, Piran and Costentyn also left the ship. They were not going to the temple, they were heading towards the heart of the little settlement. Auryn and Brian Magnus stayed on board. Branok stayed aboard too, declaring, "I'm getting some rest. Coming about this morning was exhausting. And I'm afraid that tomorrow's delivery will be filled with challenges too."

They were docked in a sheltered cove. Along the port were vendors and traders. Arghan pointed to a trail and said, "We go up this lane to reach the road. It's only about a mile to the temple, but it's a bit of a climb. We can catch a ride up, and then walk back down."

They headed up the lane and onto the road. Mule carts were lined up along one side. They hired two carts to carry them to the temple. They travelled west on the smooth road for about half a mile. Then they turned north onto a smaller track and began steeply ascending. The hill flattened out on top. The temple was shining in the sun. It was made of white and grey stones, and red bricks bearing traces of white lime wash. It had a high-story thatched roof with tiny recessed windows.

They paid the cart-drivers and entered the complex, which was surrounded by a low stone wall. On the way, they passed several small brick buildings.
"Those would be the priest's quarters, and the offering vendors," said Cassius.
"There's no priest here anymore," said Edern, "but sometimes one will come from Durnovaria. My family attended a wedding here, about thirty years ago. I was young but I remember it. Several priests came for that, and the booths were selling offerings. Incense and birds."
"Birds?" asked Pippa.
"Birds, to sacrifice," he replied. "Sorry, I know its traditional, but I think it's barbaric."
"I agree," she said. "Surely the Gods prefer the sweet smell of incense."
Said Cassius, "I'm sure they must."

They passed a well. Looking down into it, they saw no water, just a pile of coins, greenish-black with age.
"The well dried up years ago," said Arghan, "but people still throw coins in. Every now and then you hear about some poor fool who got stuck down there, trying to collect them."

Blue lupins and yellow roses were growing on either side of a white pebble path that led them to the entrance. The outer wall, the peristyle, was made of white stone, five feet thick. Each side of the square was about thirty-five feet long, just a bit shorter than the length of the Awel Glor. A clay-tile covered portico extended inwardly, supported by four plain white columns. Cassius called the material 'lapis alba', white stone, and praised it's quality. Edern said,
"The white stone comes from the isle of Puirbeag. It must have been a lot of work to haul it up the hill."
The colonnade extended around all four sides of the inner building. A short flight of steps led to the entrance, which was on the south wall, facing the sea. The companions went up and stepped into it.

"This is similar to Mount Temple," said Pippa, "but that temple was rectangular. And the colonnade was much narrower. And it had a slate roof. Also, it faced east. I thought that most Roman temples faced east."

"I'm pretty sure that this is not like most Roman temples," said Edern. "I understand that traditionally, only the priests were allowed inside to view the Gods. It's never been like that here. It's always been open. And the temple serves local gods as well as Roman."
Cassius said, "That is so very... Britannic. I like it."

They walked around the colonnade one time, returned to the south entrance, and looked out over the ocean. Then they went into the cella. There were recesses in the wall of the shrine, creating niches which held small bronze icons: the Wheel of Taranis, the rearing Horse of Epona, the Triple Leg of Manannán, and the Crane of his sea-father Lir. In the center, upon a white stone plinth, was a bronze statue of Poseidon. He was reclining on a wave, his hair flying around him. He was holding a trident. The sun came through the door, lighting him brightly, and gently illuminating the other icons.

"Neptune," said Bruno and Brutus, bowing. "God of the sea."

"The temple is also dedicated to Aesculapius," said Edern. He led them back to the south-east corner. There was a large staff with a snake wrapped around it carved into a niche in the wall.

"From the time of the first pox. The priests convinced the people that Aesculapius would save them if they sacrificed enough birds. My grandsire told me about it. He said it was ridiculous. The temple was surrounded by greedy merchants. They and the priests were getting rich selling offering birds. For an additional fee, they would put your sacrificed bird into the maggots and retrieve the skeleton. Then the skeleton would be displayed on the temple wall. Here in the corner, on both sides of the wall, were rows and rows of bird skeletons. Accented with decorative tiles. Of course, the pox came and people got sick and died anyway. My grandsire lost three of his brothers. Anyway, that brought an end to the big business of bird offerings."

"And the wall display?" asked Cassius. "Did the people finally realize that it was in bad taste?"
Edern laughed. "No, but when Emperor Theodosius militarized Christianity to persecute those who worship the Old Gods, the people cleared out the temple. He was executing our relatives back on the continent. Faithful Roman citizens. Folks were scared. They hid the statue and the icons in a cave. And they removed the birds and tiles from the walls, and buried them deep, along with all the sacrificial weapons. The temple stayed that way for a generation."
"But no Roman official ever came to check if they were pagan or not. It was becoming pretty clear that the Emperor had other things to worry about. And

then, they heard that in his old age he had repented betraying the Gods, and rescinded his punishments. So the locals put the statue and icons back in the temple, and got some new bird sacrificing tools. They don't display the bones anymore, although they still make offerings to Aesculapius on special occasions. But there haven't been many of those lately."

They went outside. "There's a really old cemetery over there," said Edern, pointing. "It predates the temple."

They wandered across an open space until they reached the edge of the hill. There was an old burial ground. It was also square-shaped. Memorial stones were sticking out of the ground at various angles, half submerged in the earth. There were piled up cairns, some large slabs, and several beehive tombs. An ancient Hermes-stone stood in each corner, guarding the site.

Cassius sat down to rest on one of the benches. Edern and the twins were exploring the perimeter.

Philippa and Arghan were wandering among the ancient graves. The ground was very uneven. She suddenly tripped and fell. "Ow!" she said, more in annoyance than pain. Arghan was there immediately, looking very concerned.

"I'm alright," she assured him. "I just need to watch where I'm going."

He extended a hand to her and she took it. She put her other hand on a small stone to push herself up from the ground. As she was positioning herself, she realized that the stone felt strange. "Wait a moment," she said, examining the object. "What is this? It feels like armor."

Arghan felt it too. For a moment both their hands were on it, touching. They smiled at each other. Then he took out a knife and began cautiously loosening the object from the earth. He ran the blade beneath it and it popped loose. He cleaned the dirt off and they looked at it.

It was a bronze rondel, the size of half of a large apple. The rim at the bottom edge was corroded, otherwise it was intact. The face of it showed two human figures intertwined. They had roots and branches like trees. Above them was the sun, and in the sun was the front-facing head of a lion. There was a border of acanthus leaves around the rim. They gazed at it in wonder.

"Do you think it's alright if we keep it?" Pippa asked.
"Yes," he replied, "I think it was a gift from the earth."

"Let's show Cassius," she said. They walked over to where he was sitting. He smiled, but didn't get up. *He looks tired,* she thought, *and his eyes are red again.* They sat on either side of him.

"Look what we found." She handed it to him. He looked at it for a long time. Then he said,

"This is very old. It's auspicious that you found it."

"Pippa found it," said Arghan. "She fell on it."

Cassius laughed. "That doesn't surprise me."

Pippa asked, "What do you think it means?"

Cassius replied, without hesitation, "I think it means that you two are betrothed. Can we say that's what it means?"

Pippa and Arghan leaned forward and looked at each other. She said, "It's alright with me."

"Me too," he agreed. And just like that it was done.

Cassius smiled brightly. "Congratulations."

"Cassius, when the time comes," asked Pippa, "will you perform the ceremony? Like you did for Davines and Keli? That was lovely." She turned to Arghan, saying, "If that works for you, of course."

"I would be honored," said Arghan.

"As would I," said Cassius. He rose. They stood too.

Cassius said, "I feel better now, knowing that this is resolved." He smiled.

Arghan put the rondel in his pocket. Then he looked at Cassius and said, "Sir, your nose is bleeding." Pippa stared apprehensively at the little trickle of blood making its way to his chin. Arghan pulled out a hand-cloth and gave it to Cassius, who wiped his nose.

"Thank you," he said. "Roman temples. They seem to give me nosebleeds."

The bleeding had stopped.

Cassius turned to Pippa and said, "Don't look so worried. I'm fine. Enjoy this happy day."

The others joined them. They went back to the temple area and started down the hill. They took a different trail this time, and soon they found themselves at a small trading post. There were vendors selling smoked fish, grain cakes, and fruit. They made a picnic by the side of the road. Then they headed back to the harbor.

When they returned from their outing, Auryn was in their room, sitting next to Bootchie on the floor. Brian Magnus was lounging up in his berth, reading a document.

"Look, we have a game," Auryn said. He had one of the cat's toys, a bundled up ball of yarn. Auryn slid it to Bootchie. Bootchie slid it back, staring at Auryn the entire time.

Cassius laughed and said, "I know this game. From when Bootchie used to help me with my work. If you ever need to get rid of unwanted correspondence, he's an expert."

Soon they were underway again. Most of the companions were resting. Cassius and Brian Magnus were down below. Arghan went with the sailors to prepare for tomorrow's delivery. Philippa wandered to the bow and sat alone, studying a list of Cornish phrases that she had scribed. She was trying to sound out the strange words.

Hello - Dydh da
Goodbye - Dyw genes
Please - Mar pleg
Thank you - Meur ras

Bruno and Brutus approached. Bruno sat down next to her on the bench. Brutus sat down in front of her. They both looked at her expectantly.

"Dydh da," she said. "Good day."

"Hello," they said in unison.

They're acting strangely, she thought. "What's up?"

Neither of them answered. They looked at one another. They seemed uncertain. It was very unlike them.

"Well?" she asked.

Bruno said, still looking at his brother, "It's about Brian Magnus. We just want to understand."

Brutus said, "We're concerned. We've been observing him. For a very long time. He doesn't eat, or drink. I don't think he even sleeps."

Bruno said, "That can't be good for a person."

Brutus added, "Unless somehow he's not a person."

"What do you mean?" asked Pippa cautiously.

Brutus responded, "Well, what sort of person doesn't eat or drink or sleep?"

Bruno said, "We finally asked him to please explain, but he said that we should ask you instead... that we should ask you some... "

Together they said, "... yes or no questions."

Philippa was shocked. In her mind, the deep conversations with Brian Magnus had a dreamlike quality that kept her from having to scrutinize them. The thought of hauling them out into the light of day was discomforting. But if that's what Brian Magnus wanted her to do, she would of course comply.

She said, "I'll tell you about Brian Magnus. And about Cassius Ambrosius. Their stories are connected. But I can only answer yes or no questions. Alright?"
"Alright," they said.

A short while later, Pippa was sitting on her bunk. She had answered the twins' barrage of questions as well as she could, and then she had retreated to quarters. She had greeted Cassius, Brian Magnus, and Bootchie. Then she quietly began putting the finishing touches on her new cloak. Cassius had helped her to fashion it out of one of her pieces of elegant plaid Celtic fabric. He had sewn the edges with fine little stitches, and helped her remove the ornate silver bosses from her centurion robe, and attach them to the new one.

Brian was on his bunk, reading a document. *Curious,* thought Pippa. *It looked like the same one he'd been staring at all day.* Cassius was stretched out on his back, eyes closed. Bootchie was lying on his chest. Occasionally the cat would put out a paw and rearrange a lock of the General's hair.
Bruno and Brutus entered, closing the door behind them.

"Salvete, Domini," they said, bowing to Brian Magnus and Cassius Ambrosius. Cassius was startled out of his doze. He sat up. Bootchie slid down to his lap and stayed there.
"What's all this about?" Cassius asked.

Brian Magnus said casually, "They know our secrets." Before that could even sink in, he continued, "But I know theirs!" He sat up. "And we should be calling *them* Lords."

Bruno and Brutus looked at each other in confusion.
"What? What are you going on about *now*?" Cassius asked.

"Pippa, what do you know about the Marianis brothers?" Brian Magnus asked, grinning. "About their background?"
She was caught off guard by the very sudden change of subject. "Well... Brutus and Bruno are the only children of an upper-class Roman couple. They never knew their mother. Their father died when they were young. They were raised by their cousin, in the Wealas of Cymru, on a big farm."

Brian said, "My friends, these two dear comrades of ours are actually noble lords. They are the youngest sons of Magnus Maximus, the rogue Emperor of Britain and Gaul, also known as Macsen Wledig, the legendary hero of the Kombrogian Wealas."

Cassius said, "That's absurd. Magnus Maximus had one son, Victor. He was just a lad, but Maximus named him co-emperor. Victor was assassinated in Trier by General Arbogast, on the orders of Theodosius, after Magnus met his end."

"Secrets are secret no more," said Brian Magnus, raising the pointer finger of each hand. "These two were born a year after Victor was, in a rural coastal area of Gaul. When they were nearly two, they were quietly transported to a remote farm in the west country of Britannia. For their own protection. Maximus was popular, but he was a usurper, and had many enemies. He was engaging in a long campaign on the continent, and he wanted to protect his dynasty. Which only lasted a few years. Maximus died in 388."

The twins stood as if in shock. Philippa got up and guided them to sit on her berth. They sat. She wriggled between them and put an arm around each one.

"Gods. That must be a lot to take in," she said to them. "Did you know any of that already?"

"No," said Bruno. "We just grew up on the farm. Nothing out of the ordinary."
Brutus said, "The cousin who raised us told us that our father died in a hunting accident."
"That's true in a way," Brian laughed. "He was hunting for glory when he met his end." Pippa scowled at him. "Sorry. Your cousin was the only one who knew the truth. And she died without telling you."

"Well," Cassius said, setting Bootchie aside and heaving himself to his feet, "I'm honored to meet the secret sons of Magnus Maximus. I'm not surprised. You've always been very noble fellows. A cut above the rest."
Cassius bowed deeply, then sat back down. Bootchie moved back to his lap.

"You know, many of us in the Army supported Maximus," said Cassius. "At first, anyway. Rome had split, and the western empire was clearly failing. We needed a leader. He was bold and charismatic. But Britannia and Gaul were not enough for him. He wanted to keep expanding and invading. His campaigns and his reign were both fraught with disaster and poor judgement. Most of his legions were destroyed or dispersed. That was around twenty years ago. You want to know why the population here suddenly declined? Maximus is the real reason why. He took the finest men in Albion away, never to return. As a military leader, I understand his decision, but as a Briton, it's unforgivable. Although technically, he was not a Briton himself. He was born in Hispania."

"Oh," said Pippa, "that would explain why Bruno and Brutus are so tall, dark and handsome."

There was a knock at the door. "Yes," called Brian. Arghan opened the door and said, "I just wanted to let you know that we're at the entrance to the Ratha Pol. We're waiting our turn to dock for the night. And dinner is nearly ready."

"Thank you," said Pippa. "We'll put Bootchie away and come up."

Arghan smiled and shut the door. The twins put Bootchie in his pen. Pippa slipped her shoes on. The five of them headed for the door. *Just like everything was totally normal,* she mused. She thought about Arghan. His family seemed refreshingly ordinary. Suddenly a thought occurred to her and she giggled.

Cassius had been reaching for the door. He stopped. "What's so funny?"
"Nothing," she said.
"You laughed out loud," said Brian Magnus. "It must be *something.*"
"No really-" she protested.
Cassius folded his arms and blocked the door.

"Alright," she said, "I was thinking about Arghan's people. They all seem so normal. Like a regular family. Father, mother, brother, and cousins. Then I thought about my people. My family." She smiled broadly at them.

"Two earth-bound gods, two rogue princes, and a cat."

Chapter Twenty Two - The Lost Wind

The Awel Glor had taken its position along the entrance to the Ratha Pol. The sun was beginning to set. The lanterns were lit on board the waiting ships, and all along the harbor. It reminded Pippa of the first time she saw the Ares Mons camp all lit up. Only here there were flickering lights on the water too.

They all gathered up in the foredeck and ate a simple meal. After dinner, Cassius said, "Your attention, please." He rose.
"I am delighted to announce that this auspicious day marks the betrothal of Arghan Pen Avalen and Philippa Agrippa."
They were congratulated all around. Cassius told the group about the talisman that the couple had found. Arghan took it from his pocket and showed it to everyone.
The metal glowed in the lamplight. They were all suitably impressed.

Arghan walked Pippa to her room and kissed her goodnight. Happy but exhausted, she fell asleep the moment her head hit the pillow.

The ship was moving again. Philippa opened her eyes. It was morning. She looked around the room. The others were gone, except for Bootchie, who was asleep at the foot of her bed.
She got up and dressed. Then she put Bootchie in his pen. She took his litter box and scoop with her to the latrine. She could hear the men talking up on the foredeck. After she had taken care of business, she returned to the room and replaced the box. She cleaned her hands, and then went back upstairs to join the others.

A pilot boat appeared and signaled to them. It was time to enter the Ratha Pol. Piran and Santo turned the headsail so that Branok could sheet to windward. They entered a broad channel. It was wide and clear. Ships lined the sides. They passed several canals. Some were open, and others were blocked with heavy gates. In the distance, they could see three grain mills. They all had waterwheels, and the largest one also had a windmill.

The Awel Glor was picking up speed. They were still only going under the headsail, but the deep current seemed to be moving them along as well. They could see the road running parallel to the river. Then the waterway suddenly narrowed and they could only see dense trees and bushes.

Branok called some orders. The crew adjusted the sail so that they were heading up the breeze. They began to slow down. Branok made little back and forth motions with the wheel to slow them further. The waterway grew narrower. Trees and bushes crowded in on them. It got even narrower. The trees and bushes gave way to tall prickly hedges, on both sides of the channel.

Suddenly Philippa heard a terrible sound, a harsh screeching that grew louder and louder. Then she realized that the boat was being scraped on both sides by the heavy brush. She covered her ears. It barely helped. Just when she thought that she couldn't take any more, they were through.

"See?" grinned Auryn. "Ratha Pol. Scratchy pool."
"Why don't they cut back the hedges?" asked Philippa.
"They do," Auryn replied. "Constantly. But they're everywhere, and they grow back fast and thick."

They had come into a settlement next to the Durnovaria Road. There was a series of small docks. Beyond them were shops, market stalls, some sheds, an outdoor cafe, a small inn called a mansio, and a bath house. On the outskirts were a few Roman-style huts and some big Army tents. There were wagons and trolleys lining the side of the road. Some were in use, and supplies were being loaded and unloaded.

They proceeded to the third dock and brought the Awel Glor around. Lines were secured. Then the men from Trevena sprang into action, while the rest of them stood on the deck and watched. Trolleys were brought from the road and crates of wine and oil were taken off of the ship and loaded onto them. Branok walked around with an inventory list, checking the loads. Then they were trundled to one of the nearby sheds and brought inside.

The trolley was then hauled to a different cabin, which housed sacks of grain. The men loaded the grain. They stopped at one more cabin, and loaded up six water barrels. They headed back to the ship to store the supplies on the aft-deck. When the deliveries were complete, they tightly covered the grain bags with waxed fabric.

"This is our last scheduled stop," said Branok, "if you need to pick up more supplies. We can spend the afternoon here, so there's time for lunch and marketing. Be back at the ship at least two hours before sunset. We'll be sleeping on the open water for the next night or two."

Arghan pulled out a sea chest. It was full of sacks. "Help yourselves."

Everyone grabbed several bags except Branok, Edern, and Brian Magnus, who were staying on board.

"Bring us lunch, boys," Branok said to Costentyn and Auryn as they departed.

"Have fun shopping," said Brian Magnus to Pippa. She gave him a quick hug. She was a little concerned about him, and also a little curious. He had been spending so much time in his bunk. He was ostensibly reading, but he seemed to always have the same document in his hand.

What else is he doing as he lies there? It must be exhausting, being Brian Magnus.

They exited the ship. Cassius, Pippa, Arghan and the twins stood on the dock and looked around.

"Something smells good," Cassius said. "Arghan, where do you like to eat around here?"

"This way," he replied. He led them past the inn. There was an open courtyard, with several food vendors.

"It's all good here," he said, "but I like this one best."

He pointed to a stall near some benches, where a short, dark-haired man was cooking vegetables and prawns in a huge sizzling skillet. Next to the skillet was a big covered pot that was gently steaming.

Cassius smiled. "Cibus Orientalis. I haven't had that in a while."

It did smell good, Pippa thought, breathing in the strange but enticing aroma of exotic spices.

They gathered around the vendor's stall. Cassius smiled at the man and held up his hand, indicating five orders.

The man nodded. He took five ceramic bowls from a stack and set them in front of him. He put spoons in each bowl. Then he opened the covered pot. A rush of steam poured out. He scooped noodles quickly into the five bowls. Then he added a portion from the skillet to each one. He topped them off with some red sauce. Arghan then pointed to a large ceramic jug, and held up his hand. The man set out five cups close together, and filled them from the jug.

"Hibiscus infusion," said Arghan. He handed the man some coins. The man looked very pleased, and bowed to them repeatedly.

They took their meals to the bench. The food was very hot. While it was cooling, Pippa tried the infusion. It was different, floral yet earthy. She didn't love the taste, but it was refreshing.

She wasn't sure about the food. The men ate the steaming noodles quickly. There was a lot of slurping. It was a little off-putting. She ate a small bit of the vegetables. They were spicy! Her mouth was burning and her eyes watered.

"How can you all eat this?" she asked. She put the bowl on the bench, picked up her cup and drank the contents.
"Is it too spicy?" asked Arghan. "I'm sorry."
"That's alright, I'll eat yours." Cassius took her bowl. "And then we can find something you like, Pippa."

After they were all finished, they returned the dishes to the man in the stall and thanked him again. They wandered around among the food vendors. Pippa found one that sold a turnip cake with cheese on a slice of bread. She ate one, even though her mouth was still burning from the spices. It was good. Then Arghan treated everyone to strawberries with cream.
"The cream will help the burning," he said to Pippa. It did.

They wandered around. There were many shops. They bought bread, cheese, olives, and grain cakes. The twins bought several smoked hens for the cat, and some sausages for themselves. Cassius got a package of the stinky little dried fish that he and Bootchie both enjoyed. Pippa found a clothing shop. She picked out a kirtled tunic and some new trousers. She saw some Celtic fabrics that she liked and bought some large pieces. Cassius and the twins bought a few new items too.

They wandered on. They found a shop that sold reed flutes. Pippa seemed interested, so Arghan bought one for her. They went into an incense and spice shop. She was not expecting to find cinnamon, but happily, she did. It was 'only recently available again', the shop-keeper told her. She bought a small fortune's worth, and a jar with a lid to keep it in. Cassius bought some amber-colored pebbles of incense. They found a shop that sold chunks of honeycomb, neatly contained in beeswax shells, and they all bought some.

"Let's see what's in the Army tents," said Pippa.
They walked past the bustling little mansio to the tents. They were open on both ends. The shelves were full of Roman goods. It was like the commissary. One tent had racks full of pottery, dishes, cups, bowls, and utensils. In the other tent was the shopkeeper, standing behind a counter that featured a large scale. There were pallets covered with bags of grain, flour, hazelnuts, dried apples, and dried grapes. The twins said simultaneously, "Apple cake!"
"Yes, we should get ingredients while we're here," Philippa said. "It's been awhile since I've baked. And now we have cinnamon again!"

Arghan said, "I've heard about your apple cake."

She smiled. "When we get to where we're going, I'll make one."
Bruno and Brutus had already begun to gather the ingredients. The shopkeeper came over and began portioning out their order. He called out, "Diadonis!" A dark-skinned young man appeared and began to help pack the items. Bruno and Brutus stared at him.

Then Bruno said, "Ares Mons?" The young man looked up in surprise and said, "I know you. You're the Marianis brothers. Scouts of the Virgin Warrior. I'm Diadonis Garhus. I was in the training group before yours."

"Pippa," cried Brutus, "here's someone from Ares Mons!" Pippa had overhead the conversation, and was already on her way to join them, followed by Cassius and Arghan. "This is Diadonis Garhus," said Bruno.
"Decanus Agrippa!" said Diadonis. "I am honored."

"I'm delighted to see you again, Diadonis," she said. "This is Arghan Pen Avalen, my betrothed." The two men bowed to each other. "And this is Cassius Ambrosius, my General." Diadonis saluted, and Cassius returned it. "And I haven't been a Decanus for a long time. I was discharged as a Centurion." He saluted her also, and she saluted him back, saying, "I've often wondered what became of you fellows. Ares Mons was lonely after you left."

Diadonis told them his story while he packed up their goods.
"We were sent to the Durnovia Fort," he said. "It's north of here."
"I remember," Pippa replied, "by the order of the Emperors, to defend against the Hibernian incursion. Your Centurions were very disappointed that they weren't heading east."
"Right," he said. "But by the time we got here, the troops were gone! Back to Rome, apparently. Our Centurions couldn't wait to follow them. They said they had gotten orders. They left us there and and we never saw them again."
"What?" cried Cassius. "Abandoning their men. It's disgraceful."
"Well, yes," Diadonis continued, "but it worked out alright. We never met any Hibernian invaders. Some of the lads eventually went off on their own, but most of us stayed here. We had enough supplies to trade with the locals. Then we... became the locals. I've got a wife and five children now. This is my father-in-law," he said, indicating the shopkeeper.

"You've done well," said Cassius. "You should be proud of yourself, Diadonis Garhus. May the Gods favor you and bless your family with health and prosperity."

"Thank you, sir," said Diadonis.

"And thank you for your service, soldier," Pippa said. "You and your comrades should consider yourselves retroactively honorably discharged from the Army of Rome." He saluted and she saluted back.

They paid for the goods, and gave the shopkeeper a very large tip, in honor of Diadonis. They said their farewells and headed back towards the dock to unload their heavy sacks.

The others had already returned. The supplies were stored under the tarps, in the chartroom, and downstairs. The ship was filled with strapped down crates and bulging sacks. Branok was sleeping in the aft bunk room. Brian Magnus and Auryn were at the bow, with Bootchie in his pen. The other men from Trevena were feeding the pony and sheep. Arghan was carrying one of Pippa's sacks for her. He accompanied her to the forequarters. No one was there. He set the sack inside.
"I've got some work to do," he said.

"Thank you for taking us around," she replied. "It was lovely."

He kissed her and went back topside. She put on her comfortable tunic and soft shoes and went up to the bow. Auryn was feeding Bootchie pieces of chicken and fish through the slats of his pen while Cassius and the twins watched. Cassius had set some of the incense on an oyster-shell and lit it. It fizzled slowly, releasing dancing wisps of smoke. The odor was pungent and sweet. Brian Magnus was sitting next to it, intently watching the smoke curl.

After a while, Arghan joined them. He took a turn feeding Bootchie, then said, "We're about to get underway. The skipper wants me to remind you to secure your belongings, if you haven't already done so."
"Do we have to go back the way we came?" asked Pippa.
"Yes, we'll depart as soon as the pilot ship arrives."
"I need to secure my bags," she said, "and I think I'm going to stay downstairs until we're through the screeching hedges."

She went down below and strapped up the loose luggage.
She sat down on her bunk. Then she got up and went over to the berth of Brian Magnus. The document was lying on it. She climbed up onto his bunk and picked it up. It looked like a very old and tattered scroll which had been adhered to a newer piece of vellum. In small elegant script, it read:

From the Celestial Archivist, in gracious acknowledgment to the All Mighty Father God, who proclaims his son, the Messenger of God, as leader and commander of all in these verses:

Ye mortal men and fleshly, who are naught,
How quickly are ye puffed up, seeing not
The end of life! Tremble now,
And fear God, who watches over you,
The one who is most high, the one who knows,
The all-observant witness of all things.

Almighty and invisible, himself
Alone beholding all things, but not seen
Is he himself by any mortal flesh.
For what flesh is there able to behold
With eyes the heavenly and true God divine,
Who has his habitation in the sky?

Not even before the bright rays of the sun
Can men stand still, men who are mortal born,
Existing but as veins and flesh on bones.

He who alone is ruler of the world,
Who alone is forever and has been
From everlasting, reverence ye him,
The self-existent one, unbegotten and reborn,
Who rules all things through all time, dealing out
Judgement unto all mortals in a common light.

All-nourishing Creator, who in all
Sweet breath implanted, and made God the guide of all.

She read it again. Then she went back to the part that asked, 'For what flesh is there able to behold with eyes the heavenly and true God divine, who has his habitation in the sky?'

It suddenly occurred to her that Brian Magnus had been carrying this document around because he wanted her to read it, only he couldn't say so directly. *But what does it mean?* she wondered. *Is he trying to tell me something?* Suddenly her head felt heavy. She was so tired. She replaced the document, slid off the bunk, and climbed into her berth, pulling her cape up over her head, leaving just a little hole for air.

She was awakened by the screeching sound. Still snug under her cape, she didn't move, except to cover her ears. The noise was muffled down here below deck, but somehow even louder. She cringed. Then it stopped. She could feel the ship moving freely. She pulled off the cape and sat up. Cassius was sitting on his bunk. Bootchie was clinging to his chest, his tail still fluffed up in alarm. Bruno and Brutus were stowing some more gear.

"Ow!" said Cassius. "It's alright Bootch, you can let go now." The cat relaxed and Cassius set him on the bed.
"There you are," said Brutus to Pippa. "You were sleeping very soundly."
"You were snoring," said Bruno, smiling at her.
"Never!" exclaimed Pippa, smiling back at him. She pushed the cape all the way off. Cassius brought her a cup of water. She drank most of it, then used the last bit to splash her face with.
She stood up, and looked at Brian's bunk. The document was gone.

"Did Brian Magnus come in while I was sleeping?" she asked.
"No, he's still on deck. Why?" said Cassius.
"Nothing," she said casually, "it must have been a dream." She looked again. The document was not there anywhere. She asked, "Did one of you take a document off his bunk?"
"What document?" said Bruno.
"The one he's been reading for the past day or so," she said.
Brutus shrugged, saying, "I haven't noticed him reading anything."
Bruno shook his head. Cassius said, "Maybe that was part of your dream."
"Um... yes, I suppose it was."
Changing the subject she asked, "Are we under way?"
"We must be by now," replied Cassius. "Let's go see."

By the time they were back up top, the ship had come about and turned south. Land was passing by on their starboard side. They joined Brian Magnus and Arghan at the bow. Pippa looked at the marshy headland.
"Is that Vindeles?" she asked.
"Yes," said Arghan. "It's a tidal island too. Known for its white stone."

They began tacking southwestwardly, rounding the island, which cast a long shadow over them. Then suddenly they were past it. They were on the open sea, facing the sunset. Everything was illuminated with red and gold. The water shimmered like molten metal. The land had receded and could be seen no more. Pippa stared. She thought she could detect distant hills to the west, but it was hard to be sure. They might just be clouds. She turned all the way around. There was golden sparkling water in every direction.

"Here they are!" cried Brian Magnus excitedly. "The dolphins have found us."
They all went to the bow to look. They peered over the rail. The dolphins were swimming with them, diving and rolling along the point of the bow. Every now and then one grinning dolphin would flip itself up into the air, tail flapping, and signal to them with little head movements before it splashed back down. Pippa was enchanted.

"Oh! They look so happy," she said. "Hello friends!" They stood and watched the dolphins until the light had faded, and they were just dim moving shadows below.

Branok called out some orders to the crew. "Dropya golyow."
"Is that drop sails?" Pippa asked Arghan.
"Yes," he replied.
The main sail collapsed with a whiffle and a thud. Piran was going around lighting the ship's lanterns.

"Are we stopping for the night?" asked Bruno.
"No," said Arghan. "We're waiting for the stars to appear so we can track our course. Hopefully the night stays nice and clear. Otherwise we could end up in Brittany."
Cassius laughed, and asked, "Has that ever happened?"
"Sadly, yes," Arghan replied. "Twice."

Pippa peered down over the edge. "They're gone," she said. Arghan put his arm around her.
"They'll come back when we move again. They are going to find some dinner. Meanwhile, I think we're nearly ready for ours."

The aft-deck had been cleared, and there was a small table with two benches set up between the cargo and the paddock. The furniture was put together from long boards and barrels. There was a large empty area on the deck nearby. Costentyn appeared with a bucket on a long line. He dropped it over the side, and pulled it back up full of sea water. Then he poured it on the open space. He put the bucket back overboard and then poured it out onto the deck again.

Philippa was wondering if it was some sort of ritual. Then Branok and Edern showed up carrying a big bronze box on a stand. Piran was carrying a large bronze tray that looked like it had oar locks. Santo was holding a folded blanket. He put the blanket down on the wet area. Costentyn soaked it with another bucket of water. Piran set down the tray, and Branok and Edern put the box inside it.

Pippa suddenly realized that it was an oven. Auryn arrived, carrying a bundle of sticks and logs. He set them on the deck, and Arghan organized them in the tray, added some dried grass, and lit the fire with flint and steel. Then the twins arrived, carrying a plank that was covered with cookware and supplies. Two more barrels were set up near the table, and they set down the plank. Branok had returned with a spit of fish, which he set into the locks.

"Is that my cake pan?" Pippa went over to the plank. "And my bowl?"
It had not occurred to her that she could bake a cake on a ship.
"And your spoon and spatula, trivet, knife and hot glove," said Bruno. "And your ingredients, all measured out."
Brutus said, "We wanted to make it easy for you. We already chopped the fruit and nuts. And we soaked the dried apples in honey water."
"Thank you," she said. Pippa moved over to the board and began mixing dry ingredients. Bruno cracked the eggs while Brutus buttered the pan. She mixed the wet ingredients and added them to the dry. She gave the mixture several vigorous stirs and poured it in the pan. She combined honey, butter, cinnamon and chopped nuts together in the bowl, spread it across the top, and covered it with the lid. Brutus opened the oven door, Bruno put the pan inside, and Brutus closed the door.

The fish was ready, and there was bread, butter, tiny onions, capers, and pickled cabbage to go with it. A jug of white wine was brought out, and everyone got a cupful. They ate and drank in silence at the makeshift table. Brian Magnus stayed up at the bow, staring into the darkness.

The fire was dying down. Arghan banked the coals. Pippa used her hot glove to open the oven a little way. She peeked in. "Almost," she said, closing it again. She sat down and took a sip of wine. The twins watched her expectantly. After a couple of minutes she said, "Now."

Bruno and Brutus retrieved the cake pan from the oven, set it on the iron trivet, and removed the lid. She carefully ran the knife around the edge, loosening the steaming cake.
Philippa silently waited for it to get cool enough to slice. As she did, the words on the scroll came back to her.

Almighty and invisible, himself
Alone beholding all things, but not seen
Is he himself by any mortal flesh.
For what flesh is there able to behold

With eyes the heavenly and true God divine,
Who has his habitation in the sky?

"Apple cake. Apple cake. Apple cake."
She was distracted from her reverie by the old familiar chant. Bruno and Brutus had begun it, Cassius had chimed in, and now all the men had added their voices. Pippa smiled and reached for the spatula.

Brian Magnus came over and crouched by her side. He inhaled the steam from the cake, and recited, "All-nourishing Creator, who in all sweet breath implanted, and made God the guide of all."

She cut the cake into sections. The first piece broke trying to get it out, but then the others came easily. Everyone except Brian Magnus enjoyed a piece or two. The men praised her baking skills.

Branok stood up. "Thank you," he said to Pippa. Then he went to the wheel, calling, "Sevel golyow."

They were raising the sail. She looked up. While they'd been eating, the sky had filled. It was like the sky that they had seen at High Falls: an endlessly vast array of lights.
The fire was quickly extinguished. They were moving again. The ship thrummed with energy.

"The dolphins are back," said Brian Magnus.

All through that night and well into the next day, the Awel Glor flew along. In the early afternoon, Philippa and Arghan were in the chart room. It had become their favorite place to escape to for a little privacy on the crowded vessel.
The ship had come across the open water, bypassing the coastal areas. They were looking at the map, as Arghan tracked their progress.

She pointed to a town labeled Isca. It was at the mouth of a wide inlet.
"That looks like a big place," said Pippa. "Do you trade with them?"
"No, we don't go to Isca," Arghan replied. "It's the realm of Lord Trevelghorm. Best avoided. He and King Arthek have a contentious relationship."
He moved his finger to the west end of the peninsula.
"When next we see land, it will be this promontory, the Lys Ardh, the High Court. Also called Bridanoc. It will be on our starboard side. Then we'll pass

another promontory, Portha Kernow. The Port of the Horn. From there we'll able to see Ennor on the port-side."

Pippa had gotten out the long list of of Kernowek words she kept with her and was making notes. Arghan explained, "En Noer, shortened from Enys Meur, meaning great isle. It's not far from the coast. It was once connected by land. You can see the remains of the surrounding forests at low tide."

She traced her finger westward along the narrow stretch of water, and said, "Then, once we pass through here, all we have to do is turn north. We're nearly there."
"Yes... " he slowly replied.
"Why do you sound so uncertain?" she asked.
"I hope that everything goes smoothly. But I've made this journey every year since I was a lad. The last leg of it has been difficult. Not every time. But most of them."
"Difficult how?" she asked.
"Too much wind, no wind, strange currents, sudden storms... and once we were attacked by sea raiders."
"No!" Pippa was aghast.
"Fortunately the wind blew us away from them. But not before they landed a flaming arrow on our deck, and we had to put out the fire. You can still see the scorch marks."
"Should we be armed and ready?" she asked. "In case they come back?"
"King Arthek had them hunted down and destroyed. Very publicly. I don't think anyone else would be foolish enough to try it. Anyway, let's hope for smooth sailing."

They sat for a while, snuggled together, looking at the map. Then they heard some shouting. They got up to see what was happening. The shouting had come from up high on the mast, where Piran was in the lookout.

"Lys Ardh has been sighted," Arghan said. "We'll be passing by Ictis soon, but not close enough to see it."
They went to the bow, where the others were gathered. There was a great deal of sea-mist. The land drifted slowly into view. Craggy cliffs and sheltered bays passed by. Then the land receded and was gone again. After a few moments, there was a new cry.
"Portha Kernow," called Piran. The land had reappeared on the starboard side. Then, "Ennor."
On the port side, they could see a distant land mass through the haze. The breeze blew them along swiftly. The faraway land disappeared from view.

They sailed alongside the coastal promontory. The wind blew them past coves, inlets, craggy beaches and little islands. Then they came out again into open water. Branok shouted orders to tack to starboard. They turned northward. The sails rippled noisily. Then they suddenly stopped.

The ship wasn't moving. They all waited. It was eerily quiet. The dolphins were gone.
An anguished cry came from the lookout. "Awel kellys!"

Philippa looked at Arghan. He sighed and said, "The lost wind." They were becalmed.

The rest of the day brought more mist. By mid-afternoon it had turned into a light rain. The companions watched as Santo and Piran fed and watered the pony and sheep, then took the pony for a walk around the deck. They dried him with a blanket and put him in his pen. Then they all went below, except for Branok, who was camped out in the dry chart-room.

Philippa was in the forequarters, with Cassius, Brian, Bruno, Brutus, Arghan and Auryn. Auryn had discovered that Bootchie like being groomed. He was combing his face gently with one of Pippa's decorative Celtic combs.
"At least we have plenty of food and water," said Auryn. "I wouldn't want Bootchie to go hungry."
Cassius laughed. "I'm glad you have your priorities in order."

"This has happened before, right?" Philippa asked Arghan. "How long was it until the wind came back?"
"It's happened three times that I recall. Usually it comes within a couple of days. Once, it took a week."

The evening dragged by. No one had much appetite. They ate some grain cakes for dinner. Pippa practiced playing her reed flute. Brian Magnus showed her how to finger the notes.

Darkness fell. The rain had stopped, but the air was still heavy with water. The lanterns on the top-deck were little blurry points of light. They slept.

The next morning dawned clear and bright, but there was still no wind. The sun was warm and the air was humid. Below decks, the temperature was getting uncomfortable. And it was beginning to smell like unwashed men. Philippa didn't stay in bed as long as usual. When she came up topside, the light was blinding.

Everyone was on deck, hiding in the shade. Pippa went to the stern to visit the privy. Then she stopped at the animal pen and used some of the water in their barrel to wash up. The sheep were lined up in the shade, panting slightly. The little pony was sweating.

"Poor hot creature," said Pippa. Edern came and took him out. "At least the sheep were recently shorn," he said. "They're not too uncomfortable." He walked the pony out onto the aft deck. Santo and Piran were hanging some tarpaulins, creating a shady area in the space where they had made their fire. The twins brought Bootchie under it and set up his covered playpen. Cassius and Brian Magnus came over to sit in the shade with them.

"Seen Arghan?" she asked.
"He's in the map-room with Branok," said Cassius.
"Then I won't bother him," she said. She went over to pet the pony.

Cassius said, "I'm taking Bootchie out. He's been penned up for too long. There's no danger from dogs here, the sky is empty, and I don't believe he would jump overboard. If he does, I'll jump in and rescue him. Alright, Pippa?" She nodded.

The twins removed the playpen cover. Cassius scooped up the cat and held him. They were face to face.
"Now, Bootchie," said Cassius, "I think by now you realize that we are floating on the water. The number one rule is: stay on board the ship. Understand?" The cat put his pink nose up to touch the General's nose. They blinked at each other. Cassius set the cat down on the deck. Bootchie immediately began sniffing around. He found a spot to roll in. They all watched him protectively. He stood up and shook himself.

Bootchie approached the pony with halting steps. The pony put his nose to the ground. The cat sat down in front of him, and put his paw on the pony's muzzle. Bootchie moved his paw up and down.
"He's petting the pony!" said Auryn. "That's the sweetest thing I've ever seen."

By the time Arghan and Branok joined them, the cat was perched on the pony's back, kneading the back of his neck and grooming his mane. The pony looked happy.
"Bootchie," said Arghan. "You are so talented!"

"That's a cute cat," said Branok. "Even so, I've never seen a group of soldiers make such a fuss over a cat. What's so special about this one? Aside from riding a pony?"

"Why, this is the great Bootchie of Vindavia Nova," said Brian Magnus in his fine orator's voice.
"When the darts rained from on high, and would have pierced our General's heart, the Virgin Warrior threw herself in harm's way to save him. The dart that entered her side pierced her all the way through, and entered the skin over the General's heart, drawing one drop of blood. He carried her, running all the way to the doctores. She was placed on the surgeon's table to have the shaft removed. She inhaled the poppy smoke. As it was beginning to take effect, she asked the General for a cat. An orange cat named Bootchie. Then she screamed and fainted as the shaft was pulled from her side."

"Would she recover? We didn't know. Our General focused his energy on granting her request. He sent the Scouts to scour the region for the right cat. It took nearly a month of searching before Bootchie was discovered and brought home to the ailing warrior, who went on to make a full recovery. That's what makes him special. That, and riding a pony."
Pippa applauded the speech. "I didn't know that finding Bootchie had involved so much effort," she said. "Thank you."

They had a light lunch. Afterwards, Bootchie rode the pony as he was walked around the ship a few times. Everyone watched. Then the cat dismounted, bounded into his open playpen, and purring loudly, curled up and went to sleep. The twins replaced the top.

Playing with the cat had helped to pass some time. It was early afternoon. There had been no hint of a breeze all day. Piran and Santo were sleeping downstairs in their bunks. Branok and Costentyn were resting in the chart room. The others remained under the tarp in the shade.

Pippa was restless. She went and stood under the mast, gazing up at the slackened sails. *Awel Glor,* she thought. *How about a breeze?* She went back to the aft-deck and plopped herself down.
"This is maddening," Pippa said. "Doing nothing on land was never this exhausting! Do you think we should pray? To Quattro Ventis Potens?"

"We just need one wind, Pippa, not all four," Cassius said with a smile.
"Philippa," said Arghan suddenly, "I was wondering. Does it matter to you that I don't worship the Gods? Or even believe in them?"

She thought for a moment, then she said, "I needed the Gods. They gave me guidance when I was a child, and support as an adult. I need them still. They're part of my family. But you seem fine without them, or without being conscious of them. Maybe because you grew up with an actual family. I think that some people need the Gods because they're lost and alone, as I was. And some need them because they cannot trust themselves to know right from wrong, or they would be inclined to be evil except for fear of God's punishment. You're not like either of those things."

"I'd say that Arghan is a Stoic," said Brian Magnus. "Like you, Pippa."
"What's a Stoic?" asked Arghan.
"Stoicism is a philosophy of life," said Cassius. "It's based on moderation and critical thinking. The Stoic is even-tempered and contemplative. Someone who enjoys what life has to offer, but is not overly attached to it. A Stoic hopes for the best, but is prepared for the worst."

"If the Stoic is attached to anything," added Pippa, "it's to the duty of living a virtuous life. Not letting down others, and not letting down oneself. Never diminishing others with hurtful words or thoughts. And never disparaging oneself, either."

"That's intriguing," said Arghan, "but you didn't really answer my question. The people of Trevena have superstitions, as do all seafarers, but we don't really have a religion. Are you alright with that?"
"Of course," she said. "I honor you as you are. And I consider my relationship with the Gods as spirituality. Not religion. I don't believe that I trust religion. I think it gets easily corrupted."
She looked at Edern. "Edern, you were raised Roman, what do you think?"

"I grew up with the Gods," said Edern. "They're like my oldest friends. It's a personal relationship; a conversation between me and them. I don't have to report to anyone else, or justify my spiritual life to some official representative. I think that's where religion comes in at its worst, forcing other people to adhere to beliefs they don't actually have. Like the followers of the Christ, who want to destroy anyone who doesn't swear loyalty to the one that they call the Prince of Peace. How is that right? The old Gods aren't perfect, but they love us all. Not just a chosen few. And they love each other. This new one only seems to love Himself. That, or his followers have corrupted his message beyond recognition."

"They have," said Brian Magnus. "His message was clearly about universal love. And hope. But the authorities made it all about power. Both Constantine and Theodosius saw it as a way to control people throughout the Empire. If Rome hadn't institutionalized it, the cult would have likely died out. It has already changed the psyche of humanity, and not necessarily for the better."

"Before the forced imposition of Christianity, there was the threat of earthly punishment, but as long as you weren't an obvious criminal, at least you could live whatever life you chose, and your relationship with the afterlife was your own business. Now, there's also the threat of being persecuted and tortured forever in the afterlife. Your thoughts are no longer your own. They belong to the institution. It's a sort of mental incarceration. It leads to the suppression and destruction of creative thoughts and original ideas."

"I read the teachings of the Christ," said Pippa. "I liked his words, all about peace and love. Then I met some followers. They seemed blindly hypocritical. And tiresomely fanatical. And they changed the symbol from the anchor of hope to the cross of death. I don't understand." She looked at Brian. "Brian Magnus, you know so much, can you enlighten us?"

"I won't guarantee that," he said, smiling, "but I will tell you what I know."

"The Christ was a very great man. He was of a high noble lineage, but an earthly one, not divine. He was good and kind, charismatic, courageous and clever. He was highly critical of both the Jews and the Romans. And deservedly so. It was a real low point in human history. With a few exceptions, the Romans treated the Jews very badly. They were asking for trouble. But the Jews also behaved cruelly, and were corrupt, and willfully ignorant."

"He was taken to Egypt as a boy. There he studied old scriptures, from Greece, Etruria and the far East. He became a master orator. He learned Coptic sorcery techniques; the things that allowed him to appear as if he were performing miracles. There were drugs that would induce a sick appearance or even a deathlike state, but leave no long-term effects. He used them on his followers to help make his points. The followers took them willingly, competing with one another in fact, for a chance to be in the performances. He also studied the machinations of Heron of Alexandria and used them in his presentations. Water to wine, that sort of thing. He found inventive and creative ways to inspire people to be compassionate, virtuous and kind."

"After traveling, he came back to Judea and was baptized as the Messiah. He told parables and made proclamations. His sermons were full of ideas from various ancient texts and traditions. He recast himself in old tales of Mithras, Osiris and others. His parable of the mustard seed, for example, is straight out of the tales of the Krshn, from the Sindhu. And the original good shepherd was Hermes, of course."

"His followers were poor and desperate. But he was only there to provide hope, and not rescue. And when they discovered that he was actually a pacifist, most of the Jews didn't want him as their savior anymore. Only his most fanatical followers stuck with him. They worshipped him. They wanted to believe he could save them from their wretched existence. Eventually, he became overwhelmed by the role he was playing. By the time he was executed, he was fully committed to his destiny."

"His followers were obsessed. Four of them stole his body from the tomb. It took a conspiracy of that many to shift the stone. They took his corpse up into the desert hills and cremated it. Then they scattered the ashes."

"They went home and waited until the Sabbath had passed, and then returned with the others to prepare the body for burial. Miraculously, it was gone. They declared him risen. They didn't care that they were deceitful, they only cared that their dead Messiah wouldn't be forgotten. That is the danger of religion: truth is sacrificed in the service of the message. His followers claimed to have seen him and spoken to him. Just as they were competing during his life to be near him, they were competing after his death about who had been contacted by him from the afterlife."

"The followers began breaking Roman laws, on purpose. They made themselves outlaws. They were willingly setting themselves up for persecution. It was becoming a suicide cult, as members went out of their way to provoke the authorities. Martyrdom became the new form of competition among the followers."

"And then it all turned around. The followers became the leaders, and then they themselves began persecuting anyone who wouldn't comply. That's the legacy. It's not going away. And as it spreads, fanaticism, corruption and cruelty go with it. Not among all Christians of course. There are a great many who are devout, reasonable, peaceful people living lives of charity, simplicity, and tolerance. But they're not the ones you hear about."

There was silence for several moments. Then Brian Magnus said to Cassius, "Do you have anything to add to that, sir?"
Cassius said, "When god comes to earth as god, it's in aid of humanity. When god comes to earth as a human, it's in aid of divinity."

Suddenly there was a swooshing sound. The wind was back. The sails filled with air. Branok was at the wheel, shouting orders. The crew were dashing about. The others stayed out of the way. The sails flapped wildly, and then filled completely. The ship completed the turn to starboard it had begun two days before. They were moving again.

The sea was different on this side of the mainland. The water was darker, and rougher. It was no longer smooth sailing. Choppy little waves pounded at the side of the ship. The starboard land looked imposing and rugged. Great dark cliffs were interspersed with glittering sandy beaches. As they made their way north, the air grew cooler.

This constant chopping of the waves is getting annoying, Pippa thought. She felt tired, and a little dizzy. She excused herself and went below to lie down. *I won't be able to sleep,* she thought, but she drifted off right away.

She awoke suddenly. She had been dreaming about Cassius. In the dream, he was going on a journey. She suddenly wanted to see him. She looked around. He wasn't there. It was late afternoon. The light was fading. She could see that the twins were asleep in their bunks, and Bootchie's pen was secured.

She realized that she had a gut ache. She didn't want to move, but she got up to head to the latrine. As she came out on deck, the sound of the choppy pounding surf made her head hurt. The ship was rolling. Her feet were unsteady. She was almost to the latrine, when she suddenly leaned over the rails and vomited. Then again. And again. Surely she was empty. But she still felt sick. She moaned.

"Salve, Pippa." It was Cassius. He had been there all along, against the rail.

"Welcome to the ocean," he said. There was a jug of water nearby. He poured her a cup. He gave her the water. "Rinse and spit. Don't drink any yet." She did as he said. He took a cloth from his pocket, dampened it, and wiped her face with it.

"Here, this is Arghan's. You might as well take it." Even in the semi-darkness she could see the blood stain. She moved close to him and he put his arm around her.

"The Virgin Warrior and the General," he said. "Not our finest moment."
"Oh, Cassius!" She wanted to tell him everything that was in her heart, and all that he meant to her. Instead, she leaned over the rails and heaved.

Chapter Twenty Three - My A'th Kar

The western sea had turned golden in the light of the sunset. The sky was dark blue, with purple and pink clouds hovering on the horizon. The pounding of the little waves had mostly ceased, and she and Cassius were feeling better. The evening was warm. They were up in the bow, with Arghan and Brian Magnus, watching the dolphins. Suddenly the dolphins all waved their tails, and they were gone. Pippa heard the sound of a horn.

A cry rang out from the ship's mast, "Trevena!"
Then a cry rose from off in the darkness, "Trevena!"
The land on the starboard side had become very tall. There were still coves and beaches, but the cliffs rising above them were massive. Pippa couldn't see the top. The ship was heading towards a large harbor, bounded by high cliffs, and guarded by four curved rows of seawalls.

The seawalls were staggered, so it took some maneuvering to get through them. The Awel Glor zig-zagged slowly and carefully through the stone edifices. Fishing vessels, all hung with nets, had their own little port and pier, just behind the innermost seawall. On the opposite side, there was a boat landing. Skiffs, rafts, and coracles were leaning against a big wooden frame. Ships were hove to at anchor, and lined up in columns on the deep bay. Smaller boats were tethered along a broad pier. It was very orderly.

Lamps were being lit, all up and down the piers, along the docks, and on many of the vessels. Pippa's eye followed a row of little lights going up the cliff.
"Are those stairs?" she asked Arghan.
"Yes," he replied, "all the way up to the castle." She looked up. She couldn't see anything but cliffs.
"Please tell me there's another way up!" said Cassius.
Arghan laughed and said, "There will be carts waiting for us."
"How do they know we're coming?" Pippa asked.
"Word has already spread," said Brian Magnus. "The king has eyes and ears everywhere. We were spotted well before the watch cried out."

They moved slowly up to the biggest pier and came alongside. As they did, the castle loomed into view. Perched atop a nearly vertical ledge, far above the water, was their destination. Philippa gasped. It was so far up! Much higher than High Falls. In the semi-darkness, it rose like a continuation of the rugged cliffs. If not for lights twinkling in the windows, and around the grounds of the castle, she wouldn't even have known it was there.

The Awel Glor was tethered, and disembarking began at an efficient pace. The sailors called out, and the men on the shore called back. The passengers gathered their belongings. Pippa was packing her last bag, and Brian and the twins were preparing Bootchie for the journey. Cassius was sitting on his bunk. "This is a good ship," he pronounced. "Hail to the Awel Glor, and to the winds and waves that brought us here!"
"Hail!" they all responded.

They came topside. Most of the activity was at the stern, where the pony and sheep were getting prepared for the trip up the hill. There was a group of young men bustling around. They were wearing tunics of crisp white linen, bordered with crenelated appliqués of silver argent and blue azure. Some were carrying away the cargo. Two of them led the pony away.

A huge man in a dark blue tunic and trousers appeared. He picked up one of the sheep, carried it down the gangplank, and put it in a cart. The sheep didn't seemed to mind. He repeated it with the other two sheep.

Their luggage was all loaded. Pippa was just wondering where Arghan was, when he appeared from below decks with Auryn, Branok, and Costentyn. They were dressed in white tunics with blue and silver trim. They were also wearing tin neckpieces, and silver mesh belts that held short daggers.
Pippa said, "Oh, you all look nice. Should we have changed already?"
"No," Arghan replied, "we're obliged to dress this way upon arrival. You'll have time to settle in and freshen up before you're received in court."

They stood on the leeward side of the foredeck and watched the activity. The uniformed men had loaded the cargo and luggage onto three large ox-drawn wagons. Piran, Edern and Santo were securing the sails and tack, covering hatches, and pinning down tarps. Then the three men joined them, and they all went down to the dock.

As Pippa stepped onto the pier, her legs went out from under her. The land was rolling like the sea. Arghan was waiting to catch her. She steadied herself.
Cassius took her arm and said, "Walk with me. My land legs are wobbly too." They went from one end of the dock to the other and back.
"Alright now?" asked Arghan. She nodded in relief.

One of the guards, wearing a broad blue sash, came to meet them. Branok handed him a messenger satchel. The man bowed and retreated. Another man came forward, wearing a silver sash. Arghan handed him a document. The man put it in his pocket, bowed and scurried off. The fellow in the blue sash called out, "Ni yskynna!" Pippa understood. 'We go up'. The wagons trundled off up the road, creaking under their heavy loads.

"First, we go to reception," Arghan said. "You can put your bags in the carts." There were four pony-carts parked beside a stone building with a broad covered wooden porch. The porch was filled with tables and benches, and lit with candles. There were trays set out with jugs of wine, bread, cheese, fruit and fish. Several people were sitting and talking quietly.

They stowed their gear, then followed Arghan onto the porch and around the side of the stone building. There was a table set up with water in pitchers, wash-bowls, and soft towels. They cleaned up and came back around. Piran, Edern and Santo bid them a good meal, and went and sat at one of the tables. The rest of them went into the stone house.
Auryn said, "Usually we'd be outside too. But because we are escorting such esteemed guests, we get the special treatment."

They were greeted by a female attendant in silver and blue. She bowed to Arghan. She led them through a corridor, and into a spacious room. It was lit with elegant tin wall-sconces and one large candelabra, which was on a big round wooden table. The table was set with dishes and cups of fine silver and blue enamel. There were thick carpets on the floor, and tapestries on the wall depicting woodland scenes. There was a large ornate fireplace, carved with interlocking spirals. It was not lit on this warm night, but the mantel was covered with glowing lamps.

While they stood there taking it all in, a door opened, and a team of servers brought in a feast and laid it on the table. On one tray were lobsters, scallops, prawns, fishcakes, sea cress, and cabbage relish. On the next was a wide variety of cheeses, with bread, honey and butter. On the third were trays of figs, olives, grapes, candied walnuts, and crystalized orange rind.

The servers disappeared through the door and quickly returned with pitchers of wine and water. Then they bowed and went away, except for one, who returned, put a bowl of cream on the table and said, "For the cat."

"How did they know we had a cat?" asked Bruno, as he and Brutus undid Bootchie's pen and set him on the bench. Bootchie immediately put his paws on the table and began lapping up the cream.
"Arghan submitted his report, and it's already being acted upon," said Brian Magnus.
"Wo," said Pippa. "That was fast."

The group sat down and began to eat and drink. It was all delicious, and perfectly prepared.

"This is so fancy," said Pippa. "And it's just the reception. The castle must be really amazing."

"It is," said Branok, "but some of the nicest things are in here. It's meant to make an opulent first impression."

"Life with the royals is all about making an impression," said Arghan. "The King wants to impress you, and he expects you to impress him. It's just the way it is." He said to Pippa, "When you worked for the General, you wanted him to be impressed with you, right?"

"I still do," said Pippa, smiling at Cassius.

"And you, sir," Arghan continued, looking at Cassius, "you wanted to live up to her expectations, right?"

"I still do too," said Cassius, smiling back at her.

"Well," Arghan concluded, "it's like that. There's a high standard of expectation on both sides."

Their meal was concluded. They left the stone building, rejoined the three sailors, squeezed into the carts, and rode up the hill into the darkness. Pippa was sitting between Arghan and Cassius. Brian Magnus was on the other side of Cassius.

"It takes a while to get up the hill," said Arghan. "Try to get some rest. The King will expect you to be alert. He doesn't like it when people fall asleep in court." Pippa closed her eyes.

The cart stopped with a jolt. Pippa woke up. They were there. They got out and joined the others.

They waited at a back entrance to the large building. Branok bade them farewell and left with one of the guards. Philippa looked around. She could see lights in the far distance.

"What's that?" she asked Arghan.

"That's the village of Trevena, called Tintagel," he said. "Over on the other cliff. We can go there sometime. But it's a long way down, and a long way back up again. There's been talk of building a footbridge. The King wants to hire some Roman engineers for the job, if there are any left."

A silver-sashed guard bowed and moved aside for them. Arghan led them up a stone staircase. They climbed three levels, then went through a wide arched doorway.

"We're down this way," said Piran. "See you all in court." He left with Santo and Edern and went down a corridor. The rest of them followed Arghan in the other direction.

"This wing is yours," he said. "Here's the common area." He motioned to the broad room that stood before them, minimally equipped with table and chairs, a couch, rugs, lamps and shelves. There was a large fireplace, unlit but covered with lamps, like the one in reception. There were jugs of wine and water and baskets of victuals on a counter near the table.

"There are six rooms," he continued. "Some of them are connected. Take your pick. The bathroom is through there." He motioned to a door in the far corner. "There are two tubs, and the attendants have put hot water in the tanks, if you want baths. Court will begin in about two hours. I'll come get you."

Their luggage was all lined up in the hall. Philippa asked, "How should we dress?"
"Dress to impress," he replied. "I think you should all wear your cuirasses. The king would like that. He loves metal. No weapons, though."
He kissed Pippa, saying, "I have some things to attend to. See you after a while."

She went to the bathroom. The bathtubs were side by side in a tiled room, next to two benches. The tubs looked like little wooden boats. There was a curtain tied up against the wall in-between them, and a privy on each side. There were big towels, scrub cloths, and several jars of bath soap.

Cassius came in saying, "You bathe first. But don't stay too long, I want to use the water while it's still hot. Bruno and Brutus can have the other tub."
Cassius pulled the curtain shut, stoppered the tub, and released the tank valve. The bathtub began to slowly fill with steamy water. "That's a clever setup," he noted.
"We'll pick a room for you and put your things in it. Go ahead and bathe. I'll find your robe." He went out.

She undid her neckpiece and set it on the bench. Then she quickly pulled off her dirty clothes and slipped into the warm shallow water. It felt so good. But she didn't want to use too much, or get too relaxed, so she turned off the valve. She lay back and wet her hair, then washed it and the rest of herself with a little bit of the soap. It smelled very faintly of lavender and mint. She lay back and rinsed. Then she pulled the plug and let out the soapy water. She replaced the plug and let in just enough for a final rinse. Then she drained the water.

She got out, drying herself with a large fluffy towel. She could hear one of the twins on the other side of the curtain, starting to fill the tub. Her door opened partway. Cassius stuck in his arm. "Here's your cloak," he said, handing her the soft brown one.

She wrapped herself in the cloak, and spent some time drying and combing out her hair. Then she hung up the towel, picked up her things, and went back out into the common room. Cassius had stripped down to his tunic trousers. "Brian's in your room. We've put together an outfit for you. See if you like it."

She went down the hall and stopped at the first room. Bootchie was in his playpen, enjoying a meal of chicken, curly cress, and a bowl of milk. The General's copy of her book was on a shelf. She saw his clothes laid out on the bed: A blue-gray tunic of soft wool, cream colored trousers, high grey Celtic boots with silver buckles, his battered but still elegant cuirass, and a brown cloak shot with silver. He too had re-used his Vindavia bosses on a new cloak.

There was a door on the other side of the bed. She went through it and found her own room. An outfit was laid out on her bed. Brian Magnus was standing and looking at it in the lamplight.

"You have some pretty clothes," said Brian. "I've not seen this tunic before."
"I've never unpacked some of the things from our last shopping trip," she said.
She looked at the outfit: Her new kirtled tunic, deep blue, bordered with tiny silver chevrons, and cut longer in the back than in the front. Beneath it, a pair of dark grey trousers, and her greenish-black Celtic boots with the silver buckles. Over the tunic was her white-bronze cuirass, shiny as ever. The ensemble was all laid out on top of her new Celtic cloak, which was a plaid of blue, green and silver. The bosses were flipped over, and gleamed brightly against the dark blue fabric of the tunic.

"That looks perfect. Thank you." He left the room. She set her neckpiece on the dresser. Then she pulled her small clothes out of the trunk and got dressed. She remembered Jupiter, and put him on his tray atop the mantel. She walked out of the room. The cuirass felt heavy. Maybe she was getting too used to civilian clothes, but they sure were comfortable after all those years of wearing a uniform.

She went out to the common area. Brian Magnus was now wearing his white tunic over silver and blue trousers, with cream colored boots. He wore a silvery grey cape with securitor bosses. His fine white-metal cuirass gleamed. The twins appeared, dressed identically. They also wore their securitor cloaks and bosses, over light grey tunics and trousers, with their Army cuirasses and sandals. Cassius was dressed and seated at the table, eating from a large platter of bread, cheese, olives, and grapes. Pippa sat down next to him and helped herself to some grapes. The twins had rebuilt Bootchie's original small travel case. They showed it to him. He quickly used his litter box, and then hopped into the case expectantly. They were all ready to go.

Philippa said, "I just want to tell you all, my a'th kar."
"What's that?" asked Cassius.
"It means 'I love you'," said Brian Magnus.
"Well then, my a'th kar," said Cassius.
"My a'th kar," they all repeated.
Brutus leaned over the cat carrier. "My a'th kar, Bootchie."

Arghan arrived. They rose.
"You all look spectacular," he said. "We should head down now. Last chance to use the privy for a while. And don't forget your tributes."
He had explained on the ship that it was necessary to bring gifts, special gifts, to the King. The men of Vindavia Nova were giving him the cask of gold and silver coins that had been presented to Cassius and Brian Magnus upon their discharge back in Rome. Arghan had mentioned that the king was well read, and proud of his library. Pippa was giving him the old scrolls, and the scribed copy of her Military History of Cassius Ambrosius. Brutus and Bruno carried the library box, and Pippa carried the book. Cassius carried the cat, who was also expected, as a new visitor, to be at court.

They went down one flight of stairs, entered a corridor, and went down a shorter flight of stairs. "Here's the dining room," Arghan said, pointing to a large hall filled with tables and benches. "The court is on the other side." They crossed a railed terrace, lit with tiny lamps. "There's a good view from here," said Arghan. "Maybe later when the moon's out you'll be able to see it."

They came to the entrance of a large hall. At the other end was a carpeted dais, and on it were three very ornately carved chairs, surrounded by some that were lower and simpler in design. On the wall behind the dais was a great shield. Against an azure blue background there was a triple spiral in silver argent. At the center of each spiral was a lozenge, showing a bear and a willow tree in the bottom spirals, and crossed hammers in the top. The walls were covered with lush tapestries, depicting castles and hills, fluffy clouds, ships and peaceful sea-scapes. Massive pieces of driftwood had been artfully suspended from the high ceiling. They held dozens of tin lamps. There were simple benches set up in angled rows on both sides of the room. There were two other benches that were right in front of the dais, facing the thrones. They had carved backs, and were cushioned.

"People will get settled in soon," Arghan explained. "The crier will announce the court. Then everyone stands. The lesser nobles will enter. Then the seneschals and advisors, and then the royal family. Everyone waits until all three royals are seated. Then we all sit. The crier will call us to come forward; the crew of the Awel Glor I mean. He'll call us individually by name. We'll stand in the aisle until everyone is called. Then we will go up together, and present our gifts. We have gifts for all three Royals. Don't worry, you are only meant to have gifts for the King at the initial meeting. Anyway, first we stand at attention, then we bow, then we stand at our ease. You all do the same when it's your turn."

"When we are dismissed, the crier will call for you. Brian Magnus composed your introductions. They sound very impressive. Give your tributes to the attendants now. They will bear the gifts." The attendants were standing by. They took the chest, scroll-box and book. "When the time comes, hand Bootchie to Auryn. He'll bring him when he's called for."

"The Royal Family will greet you. I've briefed them, so they know some things about you. I'll stay with you to translate. There's a blue line on the floor. I'll be standing there the whole time. When you approach, don't go past it. But try not to stare at it either. Oh, and do not look directly at the King when you are in front of him. It's perfectly fine to gaze upon him from anywhere else in the room, including the benches, just not while standing at the front line. The Queen, though, she'll want to make eye contact. She may even come up to you. It's alright. She's very kind."

"If they invite you to sit, take the nearest spot on one of the front benches. They will probably ask you some questions. Some of them may be quite personal. Just answer calmly. And diplomatically. When they're done, they'll dismiss you. Get back in line where you began. Come back to attention. Bow again. And take two steps backwards before turning around."

He smiled at Philippa. "Kemmer with dout ty dhe godha."
Pippa said, "That means 'mind you don't fall'. My lovely tutor thought I should know that phrase, after I fell over in the cemetery." The others laughed.
Arghan smiled, "Don't be nervous, Pippa." *Too late,* she thought.
He stepped back and viewed them. "You all really do look glorious."
He looked up the hall and said, "I would suggest that you approach side by side. There's enough room. If you could do some ordered marching, the King would be impressed. He admires efficiency. And he respects military rank."

"Agrippa, will you lead us when the time comes?" asked Cassius.
She swallowed her nerves and said, "Yes, sir."

The five former soldiers sat in the very back row on the right. Arghan had arranged them in the order that they would be called. He stood behind Pippa. The hall was filling with men and women. Many were stopping by to have a look at the newcomers. Some called greetings to Arghan, "Angove!" Pippa knew that meant 'The Smith', meaning the Royal Smith, but that it also meant the Master of Trades, and it came with a duty to travel, and to establish trading partners.

The people were very dressed up. They paraded up the aisle and took their places on the benches. There was a lot of finely crafted adornment.
"Did you make some of those things?" asked Pippa.
"Yes," Arghan replied, "and some were made by my father, and grandfather. And some by my brother. He will be the next Angove, if all goes to plan."

Auryn, Branok, Costentyn, Edern, Piran, and Santo came and sat on the other back row. They waved. It was good to see familiar faces. Some people called to them, shouting, "Awel Glor!" Pippa noticed the guards holding tight to the leads of the pony and sheep out on the terrace.

"I'll be right over there," Arghan said, patting her shoulders. He went and sat down with the sailors.

Two heralds, wearing tall blue cylindrical hats with silver ribbons, appeared in front of the dais. They blew on conch shell horns. It was a loud dissonant sound. A growl of complaint came from the cat carrier.
"It's alright, Bootchie," Cassius said soothingly.

Everyone stood. A crier appeared between the heralds, shouting, "Pobel ruvaneth!" Kingdom people. He read off a list. People entered one at a time from the rear, ascended the dais, and stood by a chair. The titles and names went by so quickly Pippa didn't catch them. The last title she recognized because Arghan had told them about him. "Kussulyer Bretonek." Councilor, of the Breton. The King's closest advisor. He was an elderly man, wearing a black robe trimmed with white fur, and an enormous chain, made of heavy links of silver. He stood by a chair close to the thrones.

Two musicians appeared, playing a stately tune with a bowed harp and a small drum. It sounded nice, especially after the conchs. The royal family appeared at the front of the dais.

The crier announced,
"Arthek Gallósek, Ruifadur!"
"Trevena!" shouted the crowd.
"Elowen Glas Lagas, Teg Ruifanes!"
"Trevena!"
"Merryn a'n Bol Gwynne, Pennsevigis!"
"Trevena!"

The King, Queen, and Princess all took their places in front of their thrones. The King was accompanied by a page who led the leashes of two great hounds. The dogs were extremely tall.

Philippa had expected Arthek the Bear to be massive, but he was small and wiry. He was dressed in bright silver, blue and gold. He wore a coronet of gold, with silver and tin rosettes, over a mop of red hair.

She gazed at the Queen. She was tall and willowy, dressed in deep green velvet. Her waist-length auburn hair was held back by a delicate crown of gold set with little blue stones. The Princess was petite and adorable, with a sweet pointed face, and a fluffy crown of red-gold curls. Pippa could see even from the back row that she had brilliant green eyes. She wore a simple gold headband and a gown of sky blue with a silver girdle.

The crowd was cheering. The King held up his hand. The crier spoke some more. The three royals sat. Everyone else sat. The crier went on. He spoke so quickly, Pippa didn't catch any of it, except 'Awel Glor', which was repeated several times.
Then the crier began calling names:

"Piran Glowbrenn, Edern Pinbren, Santo a'n Bol Sten, Costentyn a'n Ros Dowr, Auryn a'n Ben Avalen- Golyoryon vryntin!" Splendid sailors.
The crowd called, "Golyoryon vryntin!"

"Branok a'n Ros Dowr - Lewyader bryntin!" Splendid pilot.
"Lewyader bryntin!" They all replied.

"Arghan a'n Ben Avalen- Angove!"
The crowd called,"Angove! Angove! Angove!"

Arghan and the others approached the dais in a group. They spread out before the blue line and stood at attention. They bowed, more or less together, then stood at ease.

The king spoke to them. Pippa recognized the phrase 'gwrys yn ta'. Well done. The season's trading had been profitable.

Arghan spoke. She heard the words 'royow'. Time for the gifts.

He signaled to a guard, who handed Arghan the gift for the queen, two large bolts of fabric: jade green silk and dark blue velvet. Arghan showed them to her. Then a guard brought them up to her. The Queen touched the materials. Then she smiled and nodded. A murmur of approval went through the crowd. The fabric was set upon the dais. "Meur ras," said the queen.

Next it was time for the King's present. Three guards appeared. Each had a sheep on a leash. The sheep's fur had grown out in short pretty curls, and they had bright blue and silver ribbon bows around their collars. They walked nonchalantly up to the line and then, as if on cue, they all baa'd loudly at once. The King burst out laughing, then everyone laughed. "Meur ras, meur ras," he said. The sheep wouldn't stop baa-ing. The King, still laughing, signaled for them to be taken away.

Then it was time for the Princess. The pony was brought in. The Princess said, "Ah! Hobba teg." Pretty pony. The crowd went, "Awww!"

The pony had been immaculately groomed, and there were tiny silver and blue ribbons braided into his mane. He was brought up, and the reins were handed to Auryn, who offered them to the Princess. The Princess came to the edge of the dais and took them.

"Meur ras," she said, smiling. She handed the reins back to the guard. The crowd applauded. The pony stood contentedly by. Auryn went back to his place, looking flushed and happy.

The King waved his hand in dismissal. The men came to attention and bowed. Arghan stayed, while the others took two small steps backwards, then turned around and went to their seats.

The crier continued. "Kothmans nowydh!" New friends. *That's us,* thought Pippa.

"Praefectus Securitor Bruno Regulus Marianis," *That sounds impressive,* thought Pippa. Bruno went and stood on the far side of the wide aisle.

"Praefectus Securitor Brutus Julius Marianis." Brutus stood next to him.

"Princeps Securitor Brian Volatilus Cursor Magnus." Brian stood by Brutus.

Philippa smiled. *Back east,* she thought, *Brian meant 'noble', but here, it refers to the throat. He is the Great Noble-Throated Flying Runner.*

"General Cassius Omnes Deos Ambrosius, Commander Legatus of Britannia Prima, Sud Est."

A Chance All Gods Immortal, Pippa thought. It had somehow not occurred to her before. Cassius meant chance, or an empty vessel filled with potential.

Cassius moved up. Auryn came and took Bootchie from him.

"Centurion Heroina Philippa Soror Deorum Agrippa." *And now she was Sister of the Gods!* She moved out to take her place with the men. She looked up at the dais, then at Arghan. Arghan nodded at her. She looked down the line of soldiers.

"Company, cover left." They straightened up the line, putting their left arms out to create even spacing.

"Company, at-ten-tion!" They clicked into place.

She called out, "Forward... march. Dex-sin, dex-sin." They continued marching in silence until just before they reached the line, where Arghan stood. She called, "Company, halt."

They stopped all at once, still at attention. "On two, company bow. One, two." They bowed in perfect sync and came back up.

"Stand at... ease." They all did so. Pippa tried to breathe normally. She looked up. She almost looked at the king, then she remembered not to. She looked at the shield on the wall. Then she realized that the Queen was watching her, smiling. She smiled back. The King gestured for them to sit. They moved over to the benches and were seated. Now it was alright to look.

The King was speaking to the Twins. He had bright twinkling blue eyes. His craggy and weathered face was clean-shaven except for a long red fringe around the edge, like a mane.

Arghan translated. "The great King Arthek has heard of the bravery and skill of the twin Scouts." He listened as the King spoke. "Bruno, he's asking how you got your scar."

"We were harvesting hay," said Bruno, "when we were ten years old. It was an accident. I got in the way of a big man with a scythe."

Arghan translated. The King nodded thoughtfully. The Queen smiled sympathetically.

The King looked at Brian Magnus. He spoke. Arghan said, "The great King Arthek is honored to have such a great expert of intelligence-gathering in his court." The King spoke some more.

"Sir," said Arghan, "the great King Arthek would like to know where you where born."

"Arcadia," said Brian Magnus. "In Greece." Arghan translated. The King nodded, looking impressed.

Moving on to Cassius. The King bowed his head while speaking. Arghan said, "The great King Arthek is honored to have the mighty chief of the Roman Army in his court. He says that we have always cherished the Romans as trading partners, and admired their culture." The King smiled at Cassius, and Cassius smiled back.

He looked at Philippa. He spoke. Arghan said, "The great King Arthek has heard of the Centurion Heroina and is honored to have such a warrior at court." The King squinted at her cape bosses, and spoke some more.
Arghan said, "He is also pleased to see that you have a bear on your insignia." The King made a scary face, put up his arms and roared like a bear. Pippa smiled broadly. Everyone laughed. The King spoke.

Arghan translated, "Philippa, the great King Arthek wants to know how you lost your tooth."

She was surprised, and not sure where to begin.
Arghan quickly said, "I know this story, if you'll allow me."
He began speaking very rapidly in his native language. Aside from the mention of her and Cassius's names, she didn't understand any of it. At several points there were gasps of astonishment and murmurs of sympathy from the royals, and from the crowd.

The King spoke to Arghan. He translated. "Philippa, the great King Arthek requests that you point to where the shaft pierced you." She stood hesitantly, and touched the spot on her right lower back, and then the corresponding exit on the front. The King nodded. The Queen looked visibly moved. Pippa sat back down.

The King was speaking again. Arghan said to Cassius, "Sir, the great King Arthek requests that you point to where the shaft barely entered your breast." Cassius stood and touched his breastplate over his sternum. He sat again.

The king was talking to Arghan again. Arghan said to Cassius, "The great King Arthek understands that Cassius Ambrosius was lying on his back, unarmored, and that when shafts fell from above, Philippa Agrippa bravely threw herself in harm's way to save him. What the King wants to know is, why was the great General lying on his back unarmored in the first place?"

Cassius replied, smiling, "We were bathing under a waterfall." Arghan translated. The King smiled and shook his head, saying, "Peryl anwaytys. An gwettha." Arghan translated. "Unexpected danger. The worst."

Arghan now addressed the King and Queen. Pippa heard her name mentioned, and then she heard the phrase 'mos ambosys'- betrothed. He was telling the court of their engagement! The King clapped his hands, the Queen smiled broadly, and the Princess squealed with delight. The King announced the engagement to the crowd, and they cheered. Then the King spoke to Pippa again. Arghan and the crowd laughed.

Arghan said, grinning, "The great King Arthek says if you can command our Angove like you do these mighty soldiers, you'll have him shaped up in no time."

The gifts were brought. Four guards arrived carrying the chest of coins. Cassius, Brian, Bruno and Brutus took the box from them. They carried it to the dais. Cassius opened it.

"Great King," he said, "this cask of silver and gold coins was granted to us by the Roman Emperor Honorius upon our discharge from the Army. We offer it to you as a tribute of our respect and friendship." Arghan translated. The King came forward, examining the coins, speaking rapidly.

Arghan said, "The great King Arthek says, of all the tributes he has received during his reign, this is the richest and most noble."

Then it was Pippa's turn. A guard brought the library forward and handed it to her. She walked up and hefted it onto the stage, saying, as Arghan translated,
"We have heard of the fine library of the great King Arthek, and of his love for learning. I present this collection of scrolls, many of them ancient. This was the library of Father Florian the Red. He was my teacher and friend at Mount Temple, the Britannic hilltop shrine of Jupiter, where I lived and worked, from when I was orphaned at age six, until I joined the Army. He entrusted these rare documents to me, and now I offer them to the Great King Arthek."

One of the guards on the dais opened the box. The King came forward. So did Kussulyer Bretonek. They examined the scrolls. Then the King closed the box. He spoke at length. He seemed visibly moved. Arghan translated.

"This is an astonishing and unexpected treasure. A wealth of rare ancient knowledge. We are humbled by this great gift. We just said, of all the tributes received during our reign, the cask of Roman coins was the richest and most noble. But this surpasses even that."
The King was smiling at her. The Kussulyer whispered to the King. The King spoke to Philippa. Arghan translated.

"The King asks, how is it that a female was allowed to serve in a Jupiter Temple?"

Pippa smiled. "The same reason that a female was allowed to join the Army. They had run out of men."

Arghan translated. The King laughed. Everyone laughed, including Kussulyer Bretonek.

Then the guard handed Pippa the book. She said,

"This codex is also for your library, Great King. It is the Military History of the Great General Cassius Ambrosius. I wrote it with the help of Princeps Securitor Brian Magnus."

The guard held the book, while the King opened it and turned the pages. He spoke. Arghan translated.

"We treasure this volume. I am so interested in this, perhaps I'll finally learn some Latin."

Pippa smiled. The codex was set upon the scroll box.

King Arthek looked thoughtfully at Cassius. He spoke. Arghan translated.

"Only the greatest of men would give such a tribute. Only the greatest of men would inspire such a following. Great Warrior, what is it that we can do for you?"

Cassius seemed surprised by the question. He thought for a moment, then said, "We would all like to stay here with you. One day, Brian Magnus and I will go away, across the Western Sea. It is our destiny. Until then, we will be your loyal subjects. We want to be sure that our comrades are always well looked after. The noble Marianis brothers." He stopped for a moment. His big brown eyes were shining. "And our Philippa. She has suffered so much and worked so hard. We want her to have a good life, among good people. We rejoice that she has found love. We ask that you keep her always under your royal care and protection."

Arghan translated. Towards the end, he could not hold back the tears. He wasn't alone. Pippa was bawling. Even the King was weeping. The Queen suddenly left the dais and came before them. Two guards followed. The five companions stood. The Queen embraced Pippa and held her for a long time. She went down the row. She embraced Cassius, who gave her a big hug in return. She embraced Brian Magnus, who briefly returned the gesture, giving the Queen his most charming smile. She embraced Brutus, and then Bruno. They both were in tears. She embraced them once more, at the same time.

Then she said loudly, to all five of them, in Kernowek, "Dynnargh teylu." And then in Latin, she said, "Grata familia." Welcome family.

The King came to the edge of the dais. He escorted the Queen back up to her seat. He was preparing to dismiss them. The Princess suddenly spoke. They all turned to her.
Arghan translated, "Her Highness says- Hold! There's one more visitor we haven't met yet."

All five of them at once said, "Bootchie!"

Auryn brought the cat carrier and opened it so Cassius could get Bootchie out. He put the fluffy little orange cat on his shoulder. Bootchie casually groomed the General's hair, oblivious to the crowd. The Princess let out a little squeal of delight, then began speaking to Arghan.

Arghan said, "Her Highness wishes to know if it's true that Bootchie and the pony are friends." Cassius carried the cat over to the pony and put them nose to nose.

The pony thrust its head up, whinnying joyfully. Cassius set the cat on his back. Bootchie began petting the pony's mane. Cassius took the lead from the guard, and walked the pony across the court. Bootchie sat perfectly still, looking pleased with himself. Cassius returned the pony, and picked the cat back up.

The Princess said, "Dynnargh Bootchie. Dynnargh teylu."

Everyone cheered. The King rose and summoned his dog-handler. Arghan translated. "Bring Orrys and Ulna to meet our guests."
The two tall hounds came forward to be petted. Pippa stroked the silky fur on the back of their long pointed heads. Cassius held Bootchie up for each dog to politely sniff. Then he handed the cat back to Auryn. The King made a gesture of dismissal. The dog-handler retreated with Orrys and Ulna.

The five of them automatically snapped to attention.
Pippa said, "Company, on the count of two, bow. One, two." They came back to attention. Agrippa glanced over her shoulder, to make sure there was room. "Company, two steps backwards. One, two." They stepped back in unison. "About... face. Forward march."
They crisply turned and marched back to their places.

The royal family rose. The conchs blew once more. Everyone stood quietly. The royals exited the dais, followed by the councilors and lesser nobles. Then the room erupted in conversation.

Philippa suddenly yawned. Arghan said, "It's late. We can go now if you like."

They turned around and walked out on the terrace. A nearly full moon lit up the scene. The sky was deep purple, with scattered billowy pink clouds. It was met at the far horizon by the sea, a seemingly endless stretch of midnight and slate blue, sparkling with rippling lights, disappearing into the distance.

Chapter Twenty Four - Walking with Giants

Pippa was bored. It was a new concept, so it had taken her a while to realize that her restlessness, and the sensation that time was dragging by, could be equated with boredom. It made her feel a little guilty, considering the honored company she kept. For the past couple of days, she had spent most of her time with the women in the ladies' wing. It was a well lit area, with broad curved benches, covered with what seemed like an excessive amount of embroidered cushions. Needlework frames lined the wall, and a polished wooden table held cut flowers and a pitcher of rosewater. She was with the Queen and the Princess, and their female attendants.

The first time with the ladies had been alright. Auryn had brought in the pony. Hobba was sequestered on a tarpaulin, out on the porch, just in case. While Hobba and Bootchie spent time together, Auryn sat with the Princess and watched them. Meanwhile, the Queen had asked Philippa polite questions, which she tried to answer politely. The next day, the ladies decided that she should join them at the needlework frames, which is how they spent the majority of their daylight hours: poking a needle in and out of fabric while engaging in light conversation. It was all very proper. And rather dull.

The day after arrival, she and her comrades had gotten a tour of the estate. The grounds were beautifully terraced and landscaped. There were familiar trees and flowers, plus many she had never seen before. On one sheltered terrace there was a small orchard of apple, apricot, and pear trees. On another was an enchanting trellised vineyard. A broad path led gradually down the stone terraces, until it finally joined the stairs that went down the cliff. From this vantage, two bays could be seen, down below, one facing south-east, and one facing west. Most of the ships, including the Awel Glor, were anchored in the southeastern harbor. The western side had fewer ships and higher seawalls.

Pippa had stared westward. *This could be the end of the world,* she thought, *or the edge of the known world.* Out there somewhere was the isle of Hibernia, a wild and beautiful place. Beyond that... nobody knew. There were legends of mysterious islands, sunk beneath the waves, that would reappear as ships approached, rising high above the sea mist.

In the daylight, the stone steps from the castle to the bay were not quite as forbidding. The broad stairs were well maintained, and there was a good rope handrail all the way down. The morning after their arrival, the group had descended from the dizzying height to the golden sandy beach. Looking back up, the far-away castle seemed precariously placed. Pippa had gazed at the surrounding cliffs. She could see sections of a winding cart-road in between high grassy meadows where sheep grazed. There were long poles with davit arms and pulleys along the cliffs. Some were being used to shift large stones into place in an attempt to hold back erosion.

Strange towering rock formations rose from the cliffs, and out of the water, like precarious stacks of massive griddle-cakes, made of stone.

The tide was going out. The seawalls gleamed in the sun. Bright sails could be seen on the water. They walked along the beach. The receding waves left sparkling swirls of shiny black sand on top of the gold. Philippa felt the cold water with her hand. It left her fingers sticky. She put a finger in her mouth. The water tasted bitter and harsh.
"We'll have to go swimming, Pippa," said Cassius.
"Sounds good," she had replied, although she had her doubts. She could feel her eyes and nose burning at the very thought of it.

They started back up the steps. Brian Magnus and the twins had gone up first, and were soon out of sight. Arghan climbed patiently with Cassius and Pippa. They had to stop more than once. By the time they'd reached the top, the two of them were heaving with exertion. They collapsed together, panting.
"How did we get so out of shape?" Pippa had gasped.
"It's from being cooped up on the ship," Arghan had suggested.
"You all were on the ship too," Cassius exclaimed, indicating the others, "and look at you. Not even winded."
"Yes, look at them," Pippa had said, gazing at the group of trim and handsome men. "They look like... young gods."
She turned to Cassius. "And we look like..."
"Old gods," said Brian Magnus with a grin.

The castle was impressive, and the views from it were spectacular. Especially from the Angove's luxurious suite of rooms; Arghan's home, which would eventually be her home too. It was certainly large enough, with three bedchambers, two bathrooms, a small kitchen, and a big open common space. There were fireplaces in every room, and decorative tin ceilings. The furniture was comfortable, and the accessories were elegant. The most impressive feature of the main room was the broad terrace that opened up onto the vast ocean, with views of both bays. It was almost overwhelming. Standing at the railing, Pippa felt as though she was floating in space.

They had all visited the lowest level for a tour of the workshops, which were separate from the castle. A covered walkway led to a large stone building. Inside was a long open hall with many high windows. The room was divided by latticed screens, covered in sailcloth. At one end of the hall was a woodworking shop, with stacks of planks and stumps. Men were milling boards. The air was filled with sawdust. It smelled good.

Next there was a paint room, filled with tubs of lime-wash and mixed pigments. It didn't smell very good, but it reminded Pippa of working on the Forum mural. There was a ceramics room, with shelves of clay items drying on racks. Potters were working on wheels, and at a long table.
Then they reached an interior stone wall, with a timber door clad in decorative hammered tin, and entered the metals studio.

It was extensive, like a smaller version of the one at Ares Mons, but not nearly as tidy. There were tools everywhere, and the floor was covered with a clumpy mix of metal dust and regular dust.

"Sorry about the mess," Arghan had said. "I haven't been in here since our voyage. And we left in a hurry."
It was still very impressive. Shiny hammered shields of tin and bronze adorned the wall, and there were large platters with repoussé and chased scenes of ships, castles, animals, fruit and flowers. The shop led out onto its own partially covered terrace, where there were forges, kilns, and crucibles. The end of the terrace jutted out over the edge of the cliff. Just outside of the covered portion was a row of full rain barrels. Cassius stood at the railings, soaking up the sunshine. The rails were covered with flowering trumpet vines. A single hummingbird methodically flew from blossom to blossom. The sea sparkled in the background. *A nice place for a workshop,* Pippa had thought.

Arghan had said to her, "Once we get a chance, I'll set up a bench for you, if you like."
"But first," he'd added, "I have to go to meet with the king and his advisors. In fact, we all do."
He indicated Cassius, Brian, Bruno and Brutus.
"Everyone but me?" she'd asked.

"The ladies of the court want to be your friends," Arghan had explained. "And they're expecting you to spend some time with them."
Cassius added, "I would think you might appreciate female company for a change."

"Anyway, we're engaged in negotiations concerning the future," said Brian Magnus. "There have been some... lively debates. There's a lot going on. And a lot at stake."

"It isn't that we don't value your input," said Cassius. "And enjoy your company. We just want to spare you for now."

"The King is... challenging to work with," said Arghan. "Demanding. When we know more details, we'll share them with you."

She didn't know what to make of that, but she trusted them.

And so, here she was, surrounded by lovely ladies, and bored. She was staring out the window, daydreaming.

The Queen noticed. "Philippa, does needlework not suit you?"

"I'm afraid that I'm not used to it," she admitted.

"Don't bother, if you don't care for it," said the Queen lightly. "It isn't as though there's a shortage of embroidered cushions around here." The ladies giggled.

"So, my dear," asked the Queen, "what sort of pastimes are you used to? That you could do in our company, I mean. No swords." More giggling.

"I like to draw," she said. "And color. I could make your likenesses, if you care to pose."

"That sounds fun," said the Princess.

"What would you need for that? Vellum?" asked the Queen. Pippa thought. She was tired of vellum. It was limiting. She had enjoyed working on the forum, creating directly on a hard white surface. She remembered seeing lime-washed slates in the artists' workshop back in Vindavia Nova.

"I'd like to use white-limed slates or boards. I could probably get something like that down in the shops."

"I'm sure you could. Let's have our lunch now, then you can go see."

After a dainty lunch of prawn salad, sea cress, and tiny rolls, Pippa excused herself and went to the workshops. She entered the wood shop, and walked up to one of the workers. He bowed. She told him what she wanted, ten smooth lime-washed slates or planks, some new chalks and graphites, and a small assortment of pigments. The least smelly colors. He assured her that would be no problem, they would be delivered to her quarters in three day's time.

That was easy, she thought. She decided to poke her head into the metals studio and see if Auryn was there. She opened the door. She saw a broom, some bins, rags, and a dustpan. He was sitting at one of the workbenches, sorting through the items.

"Dohajydh da. Good afternoon, Auryn," she said, and went inside. He got up and greeted her.
"I'm on cleaning duty," he said. "And I'm not supposed to stop until I'm done. Unless you need something. Do you need something?" He looked hopeful.
"Umm. I don't think so," she said. "But I could help you clean the studio if you like. I'm good at that sort of thing."
"Oh, no, that's alright, it's my job," he replied.

She had wandered towards an open door that led to a smaller room. "Don't go in there!" Auryn suddenly cried, leaping ahead of her, and shutting the door.
"Alright!" she said. "Goodness, what drama!"
"Sorry. It's off limits. Are you sure there isn't something I can help you with?"

She thought for a moment, then said, "Actually, yes. I want to know where I can make apple cake. Should I go to the kitchens? I've never used an indoor oven."
Auryn smiled. "I can help you figure that out. Anything else?"
He stared at her with his big blue eyes, looking expectant.
"Yes. The instrument that played before the court came in. With the drum. What is that?"

It was a type of harp called a telyn. It had six strings, set up in three groups of two. It could be played with or without a bow. Auryn had taken her to meet the musicians. They were three brothers and a sister, Govenek, Gorwel, Growen, and Gras a'n Bol Pri: Hope, Horizon, Granite and Grace, of the Clay Pool, Pol Pri. They all had shaggy dark hair. The sister had hers cut in a fringe that hung down over her eyes. They had a room full of harps, horns, flutes, drums, and other things Pippa didn't recognize. The musicians had been very helpful. They were interesting people. They gave her a harp, a short lesson, and invited her to come and play with them once she'd had some practice.

It was late in the afternoon. She was sitting on the floor with Bootchie, bowing long tones like the musicians had showed her, when Cassius, Brian, and the twins came in.
Bruno said, "A bowed harp!"

"What's this?" cried Cassius. "Have you found a way to punish us for deserting you today?"

"I invented the harp, you know," said Brian Magnus. "Presented it to Apollo back in the day."

Bruno and Brutus looked at him, wide eyed.

"Sure you did, son," said Cassius, patronizingly. They all laughed.

"I'll believe you, oh ancient one, if you can tune it for me," said Pippa, offering him the instrument. That seemed to be her biggest challenge so far. He took it, made some rapid adjustments, and handed it back. She gently plucked the strings. They sounded a lot better.

"Gratias, Dominus meus," she said.

"I'm surprised Bootchie is alright with this," said Brutus.

"He likes it," Pippa replied. "Look, he's made a game." She set the harp gently on the rug in front of the cat. She plucked a pair of strings. Bootchie studied the instrument. Then, looking at Pippa the whole time, he reached out and played the same two strings. The men applauded his skill.

"Well, we'll see who gets proficient sooner, Pippa or Bootchie," said Cassius.

"I'm exhausted," he added, "and I'm going to bed. Somebody wake me in time for dinner."

"Bootchie," said Pippa, "we had better put this away for now, so we don't bother the General."

The cat reached out, quickly plucked two strings, then followed Cassius into his room. The twins disappeared into theirs.

"What was so exhausting?" Pippa asked Brian Magnus. "What did you do today?"

"We talked," he said. "A lot. We negotiated. We don't say that the King likes to argue. We say he likes to negotiate. Every little detail has to be wrestled over."

"Negotiate what? Details of what? Tell me!" she demanded.

Brian Magnus was wearing his messenger bag. He reached in and took out some documents. He sorted through them and pulled one out. He handed it to her, saying, "This is the agenda. It all has to be worked out before anything goes into effect." It read:

Topics-

New southern continental trade partners in the wake of Rome's dissolution. Hispania? Greece?

Two new seaworthy ships.

The bridge to the mainland.

Fall harvest festivities.

Pen Avalen brothers and the future timeline of the Angove transition.
Master of Trades as a separate office from Angove.
The wedding of the Angove Arghan and Philippa Agrippa.
Will Auryn Pen Avalen marry Merryn Pol Gwynne?
Double wedding at Harvest time?
Marianis Brothers installed as King Arthek's advisors.

Arghan had already mentioned these things to her, except for the last item.
"The King wants Bruno and Brutus for his own?" she asked in surprise.
"Yes," said Brian Magnus, "he likes and trusts them. He wants to have them prominently placed. Kussulyer Bretonek is leaving soon, going back to Brittany. The King will make them his top advisors. He may even proclaim that they will rule as twin Regents in the event of his death. He's stalling. He hasn't given up on the Queen having another child."

"I think he's ready to let the Princess marry Auryn," he continued. "Auryn will eventually be the next Angove. He won't be eligible to rule. The Princess doesn't want to rule, especially if it means not marrying Auryn. The King will not force the Princess to marry someone more suitable, or to take responsibility for the crown. She's his baby girl. He really has a blind spot there! Anyway, the succession is unclear, but the King is more concerned with stability and loyalty than bloodline. He's not even related to the previous ruler. That line died out. He's actually descended from a much earlier king. The people chose him to rule. And now he's chosen our two friends to help him."

Pippa was speechless. Brian Magnus smiled, saying, "We were surprised too."

Nearly three weeks later, in mid-July, the details had finally been worked out, agreed to, and the appropriate documents were being signed and sealed.

Meanwhile, Philippa had gotten pretty good with the telyn. She had played it for the ladies while they stitched. They seemed enchanted. She'd visited the musicians and played with them. The art supplies had been delivered as promised. Pippa's four musician friends came and played for the ladies while they posed for their portraits. There was a party atmosphere, with trays of food, and jugs of peach wine and lemon water. The ladies were intrigued by the musicians, and vice versa. The white boards made for quick work. The women were delighted with their portraits. She even made one of Bootchie and Hobba with the Princess. Pippa also made likenesses of the Pol Pri siblings and their instruments, as a thank you.

She had been introduced to the kitchen staff, invited to use anything she found in the well-stocked pantry, and had been shown how to fire up one of the large ovens. She had unpacked her oversized cooking supplies and gear, and moved it all into the kitchen. The first cake she made she had offered to the cooks. Then she'd made one for Auryn to share with the other craftspeople.

She would make cakes most days, for the ladies, and for her comrades. The men would come back to the rooms after the meetings, often with Arghan, and devour them, with cups of chamomile tea. They seemed agitated, and would often sit and talk, long into the night. She had ordered more white boards. She made likenesses of her friends sitting together, conversing, and one of the General stretched out on the floor, with Bootchie curled up on his chest.

On the day that the meetings concluded, she had finally unpacked both of her trunks. Her clothes were all arranged in the wardrobe, and her cuirass hung from a hook on its side. Little Jupiter was sitting on the mantel in her room, on the tin tray, with her collection of flowers, feathers and stones. Under it all was the pocket cloth that had been Arghan's. She had rinsed it out, but it still had Cassius's blood stain on it. So she kept it.

Her gear trunk hadn't been fully unpacked since her departure from Ares Mons. She took everything out: sword, bow, quiver, dagger, belt, helmet, plumes, pteruges, arm guards, greaves, the centurion cape, scarves, and the little old leather bag that contained her signaculum tag and enlistment coin. There was her Army cup and shovel, and a vellum folder with the Ares Mons sigil, which held her study materials and certificates of training. There were also two folded tarpaulins, and some empty sacks. And there was her hammer and knife from Mount Temple, and the coin box. The box was empty, but it still smelled like cinnamon. She put those three items on the sill with the statue. All the things from Mount Temple, together. No more scrolls. They belonged to Trevena now. It felt a little strange to be without them, but she had learned everything that they had to teach. It was good to let go, she thought. That's what a Stoic would do.

There was dirt and debris at the bottom of the trunk. She decided to clean it before repacking it. She started to sweep the trunk out with a broom and dust pan. She could see that the broom was not doing a thorough job. She unfolded one of the tarps, and wrestled the open trunk until it was upside down. Then she beat on it, up and down, with the broom handle. She flipped it back over.
The tarp was covered with debris. She took it to the common room and went onto the balcony to shake it out. She came back to the room, and refolded the tarp. She used the empty sacks to repack all her gear. Then she picked up a full

sack, and went to the trunk. There was a sheet of vellum in the bottom. She put down the sack and stared. *Why hadn't it fallen out?* she wondered. She picked it up, and read-
'In gracious acknowledgment to the All Mighty Father God, who proclaims his son, the Messenger of God, as leader and commander of all in these verses... '

It was the document! Somehow it was in her gear trunk. She set it aside, on top of the folder, smiling at the mysterious ways of Brian Magnus. She put the rest of the gear in the trunk.
She took the folder and the document and put them on her bed. She climbed onto the bed and looked through the folder at her old study materials.
'The Roman Soldier is always prepared.'
There was one thing that we couldn't really prepare for, she thought. *The end of the Empire. The dissolution of the Service. The fall of Rome.*

She picked up her picture of the Jupiter Optimus Maximus Temple in Rome, which was sitting on her nightstand. She looked at the rendering of the perfectly constructed temple. There was Jupiter, in his prime, flanked by Juno and Minerva.

She mused: all the scholarship, the devotions, all the stories, the art, the temples, cities, villas, baths, mosaics, all those accomplishments, weapons, battles, victories, the plumbing and bridge building and roads and all the other Herculean feats of logistics and engineering. Would it all be forgotten? She thought about the forges and workshops at Ares Mons, and her hard-working comrades and teachers, and she wept. What would happen to all that knowledge? Would it be lost?

She looked at the temple through a blur of tears. What would become of the Old Gods? She drew a deep breath, and dashed the tears from her face, trying to remember that she was a Stoic. She put her finger on the image of Jupiter, and recited-
"All-nourishing Creator, who in all
Sweet breath implanted, and made God the guide of all."
She put the card back on her nightstand, and the documents in the folder. She put the folder in the trunk, and closed it.

When the men came back she was on the balcony, playing the telyn, and looking out over the western sea. She came in to meet them.
"It's finally over!" cried the twins.
Cassius scooped her up in a big bear hug. "Now we can have some fun before the summer ends."

Brian Magnus announced, "The date is set. There's to be a double wedding. In September. Gwynngala. The month of the pale wheat. On the Equinox. At the peak of the harvest festival."

Arghan said, "I hope you don't mind that Auryn and Merryn are to be wed at the same time."
"I'm so delighted," she replied. "For them, and also because that will take a lot of the attention off of us." She kissed him.
"I'm relieved that you feel that way too," he said.
"And," Cassius said, "Bruno and Brutus are going to be made officers of the court."
She hugged them. "That's amazing. But not really surprising. I've always known that you boys were special."

Cassius said, "I'm sorry that I've been so irritable lately. I've never cared for the sparring that takes place at the diplomatic table. It's so tedious, going over the same things, again and again. I have to hold my tongue."
"I'm with you," said Arghan heatedly. "It was maddening. I've gone to bed with a headache every night these past few weeks."
"Really?" said Brian Magnus. "I rather enjoyed it."
"So did we," said the twins.
They all looked at each other and burst out laughing.

The next day Cassius, Pippa, Bruno, Brutus, Piran and Santo went swimming in the ocean. Arghan had excused himself after breakfast, saying that he had some work to do in the shop.
The six of them had put on their swimming clothes, grabbed their towels, and descended the steps. The tide was in, and the beach was narrow. They took off their shoes, set down their towels, and walked in. They were up to their knees.
"Watch out, it gets deep very quickly," warned Piran.
"Doesn't the salt water burn?" Pippa asked. "The eyes and nose, I mean."
"You get used to it," said Cassius.
"I don't," said Santo. "I try to keep my head above the water."
"I think I will too," she said. She took a cautious step. Then another.
Then the ground disappeared, and she was in water over her head. Her feet found the floor again. She was standing, chest-deep, coughing and sputtering. *It burned!* She could hardly bear to open her eyes.
She felt something against her leg. *There was some kind of creature in the water!* Then she realized that Cassius had dived under, and was coming up below her. She remembered this move. She clambered onto his shoulders, and he stood up, grabbing her legs to hold her securely in place.

"Oh, we know this routine," said Bruno. "Santo!" In a moment Santo was riding on Bruno's shoulders. "Wait for us!" cried Brutus. He came up under Piran. It was understood without anyone saying anything that there would be a battle. Hollering loudly, the riders pulled and wrestled with each other, while their mounts tried to keep their footing. In the end, Bruno and Santo were left standing. But not for long. The others attacked them and pulled them over. Gasping, laughing and coughing, they staggered to the shore and collapsed onto their towels.

The trip back up wasn't quite as exhausting as before. Just sticky and sandy. Pippa was chafing by the time they reached the top. A bath was most welcome. She still wasn't convinced that ocean swimming was for her, but it had sure been fun. They had acted like wild children. Like soldiers on leave. She smiled at the recollection. After so much time spent behaving properly, it had been just the thing.

She went to the beach often that summer. Her legs got strong from climbing the stairs.
They usually went with the group, but sometimes it was just Cassius and her. With the group, it always ended in a melee. With the two of them, they mostly just floated in the shallow warm water by the shore and sunbathed on their towels. The General was enjoying his retirement. Pippa was enjoying it with him. The Army seemed very far away.

In August, Pippa, Arghan, Cassius and Brian Magnus made a journey to the village of Trevena. They started at dawn. It took nearly four hours to get there in a lurching cart, switchbacking all the way down, and then up. Some sections of the trail were so terrifyingly vertiginous that Pippa closed her eyes. The persistent howling wind didn't help matters.

The tiny village was set back from the cliff, and somewhat sheltered on one side. The villagers welcomed them, addressing them as 'Arlydhi Dhintagel', Noble Lords of Tintagel, which is what they called this headland of Trevena. The people here benefited from trade with the castle. There was only one road in the settlement, dotted with shops and houses. Even though the village was small, there was a thriving market, a windmill for grain, an armorer, and a blacksmith shop which sold farm implements.
They got lunch from a vendor: crab cakes and pickled cabbage on soft fresh bread. There was a bee-man selling creamed honey. Pippa bought four jars. They went into the armorer's, and admired the intricate detail of the finely crafted helmets, breastplates, shields, buckles and collars. Arghan bought Pippa a set of inlaid bronze buckles.

The ride back was just as harrowing. As they began to descend, Pippa stared across the gap to their destination on the far cliff, and said, "I can see why they would like to have a bridge."
Brian Magnus said, "And you can see why building one presents a challenge."
Pippa thought of her father, Phillip Agrippa, who died while working on a bridge.
"Yes," she said. "It's deadly."

The next day, Arghan finally invited her to come to the workshop. It was clean, and had been re-organized. He gave her a place at the bench to work, and taught her to use a hammer and small tools to create forms on a piece of silver that was stuck into a bowl of pitch. Then the metal was turned over, and different tools were used to decorate the front. She made a cat, although it looked more like a couple of blobs until Arghan worked on it too. By the time it had been flipped over and covered with facial details, fur and whiskers, it actually resembled Bootchie.
She came to the shop most days in August. The door to the room that was off limits stayed shut. She didn't ask about it.

September had arrived, bringing a cool change to the weather, and a new sense of urgency to the castle.
Preparations were under way for what looked to be the biggest harvest festival they had ever seen. News of the wedding of the current Angove to the Roman soldier, and of the future Angove to the royal Princess, had spread up and down the coast. Everyone who was invited to the harvest celebration was now invited to the wedding festivities. The planners were hard at work, trying to arrange accommodations for all the important guests. Tents were set up along the terraced gardens and on the lawns. The ships were squeezed together to make room for more, and the nicer ones were fixed up to be used as floating guesthouses. Any spot that could be used for accommodation or entertainment was taken over.

It had been decided that the weddings would not happen simultaneously, but two days apart. Pippa and Arghan would be married first, in a simple ceremony, the day before the equinox celebration. They chose to be married in the vineyard, with the great hall as an option if the weather was bad. Then the Princess and Auryn would wed the day after the equinox in the great hall. There would be four days in total, of celebration, feasting and entertainment.

Branok and Costentyn had left for home soon after their arrival in Trevena. Now they returned with Wenna, Branok's wife and Costentyn's mother, who was the sister of Sten Pen Avalen.

Arghan and Auryn's parents, Awel Glor and Sten, arrived two days before the first wedding, from Pen Avalen, which was located three days east and slightly south of Trevena. Pippa could see that Arghan resembled his father, slender and pale, and Auryn resembled his mother, round faced and golden-haired. They were younger than she had expected. They were polite, and the mother was friendly, but the father seemed a bit detached from everyone. They stayed in the Angove's rooms with Arghan and Auryn.

After their wedding, Auryn and Merryn would be moving into apartments in the royal quarters, although it was assumed that if and when Auryn became Angove, they would take over those quarters. Pippa would be moving in with Arghan after his family departed. She had mixed feelings about the move. She wanted to make a home with her husband, but she also didn't want to leave her comrades. She had shared her thoughts with Arghan.

"I'm happy that we'll be living together. But, I may also want to stay with Cassius and Brian Magnus sometimes. We've been together almost ten years. They're my family. I'm hoping that you and I have our whole lives ahead of us. But I know that my time with them is limited. They are going to leave, and I'm afraid it will be sooner than we realize. I hope you understand."
He said he did. Then he confided in her.
"I'm glad that you like it here. I hope you won't get too attached though. If all goes to plan, I'm only going to be Angove for seven more years. I signed up for twenty, and I've done thirteen. Then, it's back to the apple orchards. I should have mentioned it sooner." He hesitated. "Do you think you could be happy married to an apple farmer?"

"That sounds perfect," she said. "After seven years, I'm sure I'll be ready for a break. This life here is pretty intense. And I love orchards. It sounds idyllic. But, how did a family of apple farmers become Angoves in the first place?"

"It started with my grandsire, Desin. He was clever with his hands. He was a skilled smith at a young age. And he had ambitions. When the last Angove had died without a replacement, he had decided that he should go to Trevena and get the job. He was the youngest of five sons. They didn't really need him on the farm. So he went, and he got the position. He was very successful. He married a relative of the royal family, and traveled the world, establishing trade relations. He was always scheming."

"He was the Angove for forty-three years, until his death. My father was trained at the castle to be the royal smith, but he also spent time on the farm. Same with me, going back and forth."

"When his father died, Sten became Angove. No more going back and forth. He never really liked it. He'd been Angove for fourteen years when he got injured in the forge. He lost his left little finger. In truth, he could have kept working, but he used it as an excuse to quit. So suddenly he was out and I was in. I was the youngest Angove ever at sixteen. I told the King that I would do this for twenty years, and then I wanted to go back to the orchards. He agreed, on the condition that my brother would then take my place."

"The thing about the Pen Avalen family is... we're lazy. Clearly my grandsire wasn't. He had ambition. Personal, social, and political ambition. None of us have had any since. It's one of the reasons that the king likes us, and trusts us close to him. But it's also a source of frustration for him. He can't understand why anyone would want to live on a farm when they could be at Trevena."

The day before her wedding, Pippa was with her comrades in their quarters. Cassius said, "We have something for you, Agrippa. For your marriage."
"If it's a wedding present," she said, "we should wait for Arghan."
"No," said Cassius, "this is just for you."

Brutus and Bruno carried in a small chest. It was made out of wood, and covered with hammered tin panels. She opened it. It was full of gold and silver coins. Roman coins.
"The King didn't get it all," said Cassius. "We saved some for you. We know that you're marrying a good man, who will take care of you. All the same, we want you to have your own fortune."

"Thank you," she said. "The real fortune is knowing that you care about me."
She hugged them all, then came back to Cassius and hugged him again.

The night before her wedding, Pippa was with the women, and Arghan was with the men somewhere. Apparently it was tradition. From this point on, she and Arghan were not allowed to see each other until the wedding. Pippa sat in the common room with Bootchie. The women were gathered around her. Some had brought gifts. There were baskets of lemons and oranges, trays of dainty sweetmeats, bolts of fine new fabric, flowers, scented oils, trinkets, and dozens of embroidered cushions. The ladies sat around examining the gifts, sipping rose water, and talking quietly amongst themselves about fashion, hairstyles, food and children. Philippa couldn't help wondering what the men were up to. Certainly something more exciting than this. Thinking that made her feel guilty. She smiled at her visitors and ate a sticky sweetmeat, washing it down with flowery water.

The next morning, she was standing on the balcony, trying to dry her hair into curly ringlets, without much success. Over the past half hour, ships had been arriving by the dozens. The horns were sounding constantly, a high note for the southeast, and a lower tone for the west harbor. Cassius came out on the balcony, bleary-eyed, still in his nightgown. He spent some time cursing the horns for giving him a headache. Pippa smiled. She knew that it wasn't the fault of the horns. The men had come back in the small hours of the morning, singing, joking, giggling like children, shushing each other, then giggling some more. Then the snoring had begun. She suspected there had been some wine involved. She hoped that Arghan would be in better shape than Cassius.

Bruno and Brutus appeared on the balcony, fully dressed, but not quite as perky as usual.
"Did you have a good time last night?" she asked innocently. The twins just replied, "Yes."
Cassius grunted. Then he stretched, yawned, and looked at her.

"Here," he said, "let me help with that." They stood in the morning sun, watching the ships, as he twisted and re-twisted locks of her long hair.

Bruno and Brutus put breakfast on the table: a pitcher of lemon-mint water, melons, cheese, and bread. Pippa dug in, as did the twins. Cassius picked at his food. Bootchie sat nearby, eating a bowl of little fish. He would put a whole one in his mouth, the tail sticking out, and happily crunch its little head, sucking the whole thing down his throat and then licking his lips. Cassius looked at him, shook his head, and reached for a cup of water.

The ceremony was scheduled for late afternoon. Pippa had been instructed to stay in her quarters until she was called for. She lay on the couch for awhile. She played the telyn on the balcony. Mostly she just paced around nervously, twisting her ringlets.

At mid-day, a servant arrived with her lunch. She smiled. A boiled egg, a golden saffron griddle cake, sea cress, nasturtiums, candied walnuts, cold stewed apricots with honey, and a pitcher of water with mint. "Thank you, Brian Magnus," she said out loud, certain that somehow he could hear her. "This is as good a wedding present as I could hope for."

In the early afternoon the ladies arrived to help her prepare. Her clothes were all arranged on the bed in one of the spare rooms. Cassius and Brian had put together her ensemble. The day before, she had modeled it for them. There was a long white kirtled gown, threaded with silver. Like her blue one, it was a bit

shorter in front. Underneath, she wore slate grey leggings. She had cream colored shoes, decorated with grey trim and her new Tintagel buckles. Over the gown was a long sleeveless vestment, made of a purple, blue and grey fabric.
She had planned on wearing the neckpiece Arghan had made for her, but he had insisted that she wear her armor, saying,
"Everyone around here has seen ladies adorned with my neckwear, but they've never seen anything like you when you're wearing your cuirass."

The Queen and Princess were there, as well as Awel Glor, and some other female relatives. The royals had brought their maids. Two of the maids carried in a large mirror and set it onto the log holder in front of the fireplace. They were all standing around Pippa, who was now only wearing her small clothes, covered with the brown cloak. The maids brought out the clothing piece by piece, setting them on the couches and chairs. Each piece received a murmur of approval. The cuirass came out last. There was a bit of a shocked silence. Then Awel Glor said, "Well, now, isn't that beautiful? I can't wait to see it on." Pippa smiled gratefully at her soon to be mother-in-law.

The maids took off her robe and helped her get dressed, piece by piece. It was strange and awkward, especially the leggings, and it took way longer than it would have taken on her own. *Is this how noblewoman get dressed every day?* she wondered. *How very tedious.*

When she was dressed, the Princess brought her headpiece, which she and the Queen had designed for Pippa. It was a harvest wreath, made with preserved golden oak leaves and marigolds, and fresh silver willow buds. The botanicals were bound to a tin coronet with a silver thread, strung with tin and gold rosettes. The maids put it on her head.

Awel Glor presented her with a bracelet. It was a gold chain, and on each link was a little silver apple. "This was mine when I was young," she said. "Would you like it, Philippa?"
"Oh, yes, thank you. It's beautiful. And I love apples." The older woman fastened the bracelet on Pippa's wrist. The maids turned her to look in the mirror. Pippa smiled. She looked pretty, and impressive, like a sweet lady with the heart of a warrior.

They all went to the vineyard. The vines were heavy with autumn grapes, just beginning to turn from green to purple. The Pol Pri siblings were already there, warming up their instruments. They cheered when they saw Pippa in her wedding outfit, and played a little fanfare as she approached.

The ceremony would take place under an arched trellis at one end of the yard. Roses, cedar, and silver willow had been artfully woven into the grape vines covering the trellis. Pippa went up to the arch. In the center, she saw something that looked strange, yet familiar.
"What's this?" she asked.
"It's your wedding shield," said the Princess with delight. "Arghan made it for you. Auryn helped. He made the zodiac pendants."

It was the boss they had found, with the entwined couple. It had been shined up, just on the surface so that the dark recesses made the mysterious branching figures easier to see. The roundel was set in the center of a large bronze hammered disc, which was enclosed by a copper border. There was a ring of dark wood inlaid not far from the edge of the disc. In it, her twelve nails had been driven at regular intervals. Very thin gold and silver wire had been strung from nail to nail, creating a repeating pattern that resembled a twinkling star, or a flower. The nails held gold pendants, showing the signs of the zodiac. At the top was Virgo.

So this was the secret of the off limits room. *Poor Arghan,* she thought, *trying to get this beautiful piece done in the midst of all the meetings and drama.* Her heart filled with tenderness for him.

The ladies then ushered her to a gate at the far end of the vineyard.

"When we come back out, we'll return to the entrance through here," said the Queen, pointing to a narrow screened passageway along the edge of the yard. They went through the gate. The ground dropped down into a sort of grotto, surrounded by cedar trees. On one side was a small mossy pool, and a stone bench. On the other was a tiny but elegant pavilion, festooned with garlands of rose and marigold.
The front entryway curtains of the pavilion were drawn open. Inside, there was a bed, covered with linens and sheepskins, a small stove, a table, two chairs, and a supply of food and drink. There were two small dressers. One of them held soft new ladies' garments. In the other were fine new men's garments. Then Pippa realized, they were meant to spend their wedding night in here. She had been wondering how that was going to work out.

They walked around the side of the pavilion. There was a small stove under a water tank, and behind a decorative screen, under a sailcloth awning, there was a bathtub. A table held bath scents, soaps and cloths. Towels and bathrobes had been hung whimsically from tree branches. The wedding planners seemed to have thought of everything. It was absolutely wonderful.

Now she just had to wait. She and the women stood at the entrance to the pavilion and listened.

The musicians were playing. Soon a servant came running up and said, "It's time, good ladies."

The women all went to the gate. The attendants stood by, as the wedding party went in. First the flower-children, then the Princess, then the Queen. Pippa went last, through the gate, down the shadowy corridor, and out at the other end. She blinked in the bright light. She was behind the guests. An attendant escorted her to the center aisle. The Queen and Princess were still waiting. The children were throwing rose petals as they walked.

The Princess gave her a hug and then proceeded. A few moments later, the attendant signaled the Queen. She too gave Pippa a hug, and then went out.

After what seemed like a long time, it was her turn. The music changed. Pippa's first impulse was to march quickly down the aisle. But Cassius had advised her to take her time entering, walk slowly, look at everyone, and to savor the moment. It was good advice. As she stepped into the aisle, she remembered how she and the Princess had asked for Hobba and Bootchie to be in both ceremonies. The Queen wouldn't even consider it. She said, "Having animals in a wedding ceremony has been tried. We will not try it again." So poor Bootchie was home alone, missing the party.

She walked slowly down the aisle, looking at the guests as they looked at her. There were oohs and ahhs as she came into view. The sun was warming her breastplate. She could feel her curls gently bouncing as she walked. She smiled at everyone. They smiled and nodded at her. She passed the King and his entourage on one side, and the Pen Avalen family on the other. She reached the trellis and took her place next to Arghan, who was looking splendid in a steely blue tunic over grey trousers and a silver collar. Bruno and Brutus were dressed in matching russet tunics with cream colored trousers and vestments. They too wore silver collars.

Brian Magnus and Cassius Ambrosius stood in the center facing the crowd. There were both dressed in white robes, with vestments of blue and silver. They were radiant looking. *Even prettier than me,* thought Pippa, smiling.

The ceremony began. A crier standing off to the side translated into Kernowek after each speech.

Cassius recited,

"Love is a kind of military service, and no assignment for cowards.
Where those banners fly, heroes are always on guard.
Soft, those barracks? They know long marches, terrible weather.
Night and winter and storm, grief and excessive fatigue.
Often the rain pelts down from the drenching cloudbursts of heaven.
Often you lie on the ground, wrapped in a mantle of cold.
Be patient and tough; someday this pain will be useful to you. Ovid."

Brian Magnus recited,
"I sing the truth: but some will say I lied,
Believing no deity was ever seen by mortal.
There is a god in us: when he stirs we kindle:
That impulse sows the seeds of inspiration.
I've a special right to see the faces of the gods,
Being a bard, or by singing of sacred things. Ovid"

Bruno and Brutus recited,
"The happiness of your life depends upon the quality of your thoughts. When you arise in the morning think of what a privilege it is to be alive, to think, to enjoy, and to love. Marcus Aurelius."

Pippa was delighted with the selections. She hoped that Arghan liked them too. Cassius and Brian had wanted to consult with them about the readings and vows, but Pippa and Arghan had said that they'd rather be surprised.

"Arghan and Philippa," said Cassius. "They are both courageous, kind, artistic, energetic, thoughtful, self-sacrificing, humorous and dutiful. They are two of the best people you could ever meet, and we are thankful that they have each other, and that they have you all."

Brian Magnus said, "We went halfway around the world to find a husband for our Pippa, and when we did, to our delight, he was from back here in Trevena." After translation, that got a round of cheers and laughter.

"And now," said Cassius, "here is an original composition from the great King Arthek's own court musicians, the Pol Pri family."
There were two telyns and a drum. They all four sang. The song was slow and rich. The sound was compelling, and a little haunting. They repeated the line five times.

"Karer ha karores, kesvewa, tre yn an dy'gol deys."
Lover and lover, live together, home in the harvest home.

Cassius said, "Arghan, do you vow your love and loyalty to Philippa?"
"I do."
"Philippa, do you vow your love and loyalty to Arghan?"
"I do."
"Both of you together," continued Cassius, "repeat after me, this quote by Virgil." He smiled at them. "Love conquers all things, so we too shall yield to love."
"Love conquers all things, so we too shall yield to love," they replied.

Bruno and Brutus brought forth the shield. Brian Magnus said,
"On the day of their betrothal, Pippa and Arghan found this bronze artifact. It shows a couple entwined, growing roots and branches. Arghan created this wedding shield to hold it, incorporating twelve nails that Philippa forged during her Army training. They are intricately connected by strands of gold and silver. The nails display the signs of the Zodiac, thanks to the worthy contribution of Auryn Pen Avalen. There are two handles on the back. It's a two person shield. May this couple be blessed and protected through the coming years."

Arghan and Philippa held the shield.

"I present to you," said Cassius, "Arghan Pen Avalen and Philippa Agrippa, husband and wife."

The wedding of the Princess and Auryn had been completely different. It went on for hours. A group of clerics had come over from Brittany to perform the service. Pippa and Arghan were on a front bench. They were sitting with Cassius, Brian Magnus, the twins, and Arghan's family. First Pippa had walked down the aisle as one of Merryn's attending women, and Arghan had accompanied his brother. Everyone wore white and silver.

On the other front bench was the royal family and their special guests. One of the priests talked for so long that the King started snoring. Auryn and Merryn were obliviously happy in their matching silk and linen ensembles, smiling at each other and blushing throughout the ceremony. The reception was grand. Afterwards, the couple were sequestered in their new royal chambers, and the festivities continued.

Pippa and Arghan's reception had also been grand. They had all gone to the dining hall after the ceremony. The couple was applauded, toasts were made, and then the feasting had begun. Pippa and Arghan had stayed for a while, then taken their leave. Everyone cheered as they exited the hall. They went back to the vineyard and began their married life.

They had stayed in bed until late in the morning. Then they heated the water and had baths. They'd put on the soft clothing from the dressers, and had a lunch of fruit and cheese. Then they sat by the pond watching the bright orange and yellow fish dart about.

"I wish Bootchie was here," said Pippa. "He's never seen a fishpond."
"There's no reason why we can't have visitors," said Arghan. "Especially since we're meant to camp out here until my parents leave."

Pippa had found a servant stationed at the gate, and sent a message to Cassius and Brian Magnus:
'Bring Bootchie and come see us.'

They arrived half an hour later. Pippa hugged them both.
"Do you want us to leave Bootchie with you?" Cassius asked.
"No, stay with us a while," said Pippa. "Some of the grapes are ripe. They're so good! It's nice here." She hugged Cassius again. "And we've missed you."

"Pippa missed you," Arghan had said. "I just missed Bootchie. I still haven't forgiven you for making me drink so much the night before my wedding."
The men laughed. "Sorry, son," said Cassius. "It's tradition."

That night had been the harvest festival. There was a tremendous feast, and the local farmers received honors and accolades. Then there were bonfires on the beach, music and merrymaking. They had spent some time with Arghan's parents. His mother had made easy conversation. His father didn't say much.

After the festivities, Pippa and Arghan spent another night in the vineyard. The next day they decided to leave, both admitting that they missed their own beds, and agreeing that they could always come back to the vineyard if they wanted to.

Sten and Awel Glor had departed the morning after the royal wedding. Pippa brought some of her gear to Arghan's place. Her new place. It felt strange, although she had to admit that the huge bed in the master room was amazingly comfortable, rivaling even the General's bed back in Vindavia Nova.

They got into a routine. They would spend time every day in the workshop, and in the afternoon with Cassius and Brian Magnus. Occasionally they spent time with the twins too, but Bruno and Brutus were often kept busy by the King. They were delighted with their new noble positions.
They're never so happy as when they are in service, Pippa thought.

She alternated her nights between her new home and her old home. Each time she went to her new one, she would bring something she owned and find a place for it. Some things she just got two of. She had purchased a slightly better telyn, and she kept that one in the Angove suite. Cassius and Brian began coming over for meals, and for late night visits. They would bring Bootchie. Sometimes he stayed after they left. He now had a litter pan and food dishes there too. He seemed happy enough.

Their view from the terrace was one of the best in the castle. While the weather was good, Pippa stayed out there a lot, playing her telyn. After the weather grew chilly, the terraces were closed off with translucent sail cloth. She still went out on them, just not as often.

The north wind blew fiercely. The sheep were gone from the distant hills. All the animals were boarded for the season. The stairs to the beach were closed. The once full trees were bare, except for the hardy evergreens. Most of the ships and boats had been raised and dry-docked, the sails and ropes stored in cedar chests. The fleet looked skeletal and bare. Only the toughest, chunkiest little ice breakers were kept in action. The fierce wind tried to turn them over, but could not.
Once it began freezing, the terraces were covered with wooden shutters, all throughout the castle. The bright places that had been flooded with light were now dark, lit dimly with lamps, and with fires that never quite seemed to pierce the gloom. The days were spent in quiet activity or sleep.

Most evenings, everyone gathered in the dining hall, in front of the massive fireplace. Stories were told and songs were sung. Dances were danced. Jugglers and acrobats practiced their skills. Children ran around and played ball, made forts out of tables, and spent hours feeding the fire with little sticks. Women sat close to the hearth and did intricate needlework in the semi-darkness.

Pippa played music with the Pol Pri family almost every night. Her husband and friends came to listen, and drink spiced wine, while outside the wind howled, the sky pelted the castle with freezing rain, and lightning lit up the sea.

Bootchie had become very social. With the castle all closed up securely, his carrier had been mostly abandoned. He traveled on Cassius's shoulders, holding onto his hair like reins. He came to the dining room with them most evenings. He had his own chair, a high stool with a curved back. It was his throne. He enjoyed being the center of attention. Other cats prowled the dining room, hunting for mice, and occasionally stopping to get petted. Bootchie was oblivious to them.

In December the weather changed. The wind stopped, and the temperature grew slightly warmer. Some of the shutters were opened a little to let in the light. Then it began to snow. It snowed for three days straight, and then it snowed a little every day. In between snow showers, the sun shone brightly on the wintry landscape. People bundled up and went outside. Men went out hunting and ice fishing. The children burst out of the castle, happy to be outdoors in this frozen wonderland.

The snow was dry. Everything was covered in soft mounds of fluffy powder. The castle was glazed with a sheen of ice crystals. Pippa had never seen anything like it. It had never snowed much back east, and when it did it was a wet snow, which led to a lot of mud. This snow was like sand, only lighter.

They explored the grounds, finding interesting ice formations. Water had been poured on the upper lawn to make a skating pond. Arghan was really good at it. Cassius and Brian Magnus were too. Pippa was hopeless, even with their help, but she liked to watch them.

After a week, the snow began to pack. A sled run was made on a long and steep area of pastureland. The sleds were large stiff pieces of heavily waxed sailcloth with curled up ends. Hay bales were set along the wall at the bottom. You either had to run into the wall, or fall out of the sled before it hit. Either way, it was brutal. Pippa loved it, especially after she realized that if she sat behind Cassius and held on, all the stinging snow spray hit him and not her. The exhilarating sled rides were over quickly, and it was a long trudge back up the hill. The next day they would be bruised and sore, but by afternoon they would be out there again.

Midwinter came. Evergreens and holly wreaths were hung throughout the castle. The King held a series of long winter courts. Gifts were given, jokes were delivered, poems were composed, accolades were made, and stories were told. There was a big dance. There was plenty of spiced wine, and the music went on almost until dawn. People slept on the tables. After a week of these festivities, the dried evergreens and holly were put into the fires. The castle smelled good for a long time after that.

The weather became fierce again. Everything was shuttered tight. There were no more outdoor activities. January and February brought ferocious winds, bearing sleet and ice. Pippa could hear it hitting the west wall, sideways in the wind. She was still alternating her sleeping quarters, even though her room in the old quarters wasn't very warm. The fireplace didn't draw well. Some nights she would crawl in beside Cassius. He radiated heat. Bootchie would be there too, curled up in a ball, his tail covering his pink nose to keep it warm.

In early March, the weather warmed up a little, but the rains continued.
One day the King sent for Pippa, Cassius, Brian and Arghan. The King wanted to talk. Arghan translated. King Arthek had finally read all of the Military History of General Cassius Ambrosius. He told them that he had tried to learn Latin, but he had given up on that. He'd had Arghan translate the book into Kernowek. He also had his scribes copy the maps and drawings. He hoped that they didn't mind. They assured him that they were honored.

King Arthek had a lot of detailed questions about the battles. How many men, how far was the distance, how long did it take, were there trenches dug, that sort of thing. Cassius said that he really didn't recall anymore, but Brian Magnus filled in the details.

They sat beside a roaring fire. Orrys and Ulna were stretched out on the stones. Philippa perched on the edge of the hearth, petting their warm fur while the King spoke. He praised Cassius for his skill as a general, and for all his achievements. He told them how shocked and saddened he was to hear of the betrayal of the Auxiliaries and the slaughter of the men. And how astonished he was to learn that it was Philippa Agrippa who finally killed the hated enemy. He asked her about the details. She told him the whole story of Vela's arrow, and how they had unexpectedly discovered Pruntus Dax. King Arthek called for them every night for over a week, until they had finally exhausted the topic.

In April it was announced that the Princess was pregnant. So, in fact, was the Queen. The Royal Family had been nervously keeping the news to themselves. Now they proudly proclaimed it. The King was beaming and fussing over his wife and daughter. Physicians and midwives had already been consulted. Special meals were prepared for the expectant mothers.

The air warmed up, the ice melted and the green world began life again.

They were in the dining hall one morning in late spring. Pippa and Arghan were sitting with Bruno, Brutus, Cassius and Brian Magnus. Cassius wasn't eating, she noticed. He was very still. Pippa was about to speak to him, when suddenly a drop of blood trickled from his eye. She gasped. Brian Magnus quickly wiped it away. Arghan had seen it too. He looked alarmed.

Pippa touched Cassius on his shoulder. He smiled sadly at her, then looked at Brian Magnus. Brian nodded at him. Cassius hung his head, but he nodded back. Pippa was getting a knot in her stomach.

The horn of the western harbor watch sounded. Everyone was surprised. No one expected a boat this time of year, especially from the west. The word spread. It was a single coracle. A large coracle, but still only a small and lightweight craft. It had just appeared out of the mist.

Brian Magnus motioned to Pippa. She got up, and he pulled her to the side. He said,
"They see a boat. You act as if you see it too. Understand?"
She didn't understand at all, but that didn't seem to matter.

The stairs down to the beach had been opened the week before. People were going down there to see this strange boat in the western harbor.

Cassius said, "Come on. It's time."

Their little group went outside and began descending the stairs. Pippa moved as if in a dream.
"What's that boat doing here?" asked Arghan. He sounded apprehensive. She looked at the harbor, but she didn't see the boat.

"It's for us," said Brian, as they wound their way down the stone steps. "We'll miss you, friends."
The companions reached the bottom and headed towards the western pier. Then Cassius and Brian stopped.

"Thank you for this life, Pippa Agrippa," said Cassius. He kissed her, then he kissed Arghan, Bruno and Brutus. The twins were crying. Arghan looked shocked and dismayed.

Cassius and Brian Magnus stood directly in front of her. Everyone else seemed to be staring at a spot on the shore. She heard people exclaiming,

"Where could they be going?"
"Come back!"
"Why are they getting into that little boat?"
"Don't leave us, good sirs!"

Still they stood in front of her.

Most everyone was moving closer to the shore, including Arghan and the twins. Cassius and Brian Magnus escorted her there too. Then Cassius said, "Say goodbye to Bootchie for me."

He began to grow. Almost imperceptibly at first. Then at an accelerated pace. He was a giant. He took a step out into the water. Still he grew bigger. He took another step. He was standing up to his knees in the ocean, well beyond the sea wall. He kept receding, yet growing bigger. He smiled and waved at her. A huge wind was blowing his long hair in all directions. Pippa had the sudden memory of seeing him underwater, his hair flying, grinning and waving.

Then, he was so big that it engulfed everything. He was moving away at lightning speed, but he was expanding just as quickly. A great grey wall with a flash of silver appeared in front of her. She fell over backwards, and she blacked out for a moment.

When she opened her eyes, she saw Brian Magnus hanging in the sky above her. He was Brian, and yet he was not. He was also that other one, the emaciated one with the strange eyes and head.

He smiled at her with that wide bird mouth, as a great gust took him up into the air like a kite. Pippa could see thousands of nearly invisible filaments of light attached to him, pulling him through the air and up into space.

Arghan came into view, crying, "Pippa! Are you alright?"
"MOVE!" she shouted, pushing him out of the way. There was nothing. Not a trace of anything left in the sky or on the horizon.

She heard Bruno and Brutus simultaneously say, "They're gone."

She sat up and turned to Arghan. He looked miserable and bewildered. She threw her arms around him saying, "I'm so sorry, my love. I'm in shock. Please forgive me." He held her close, then helped her to her feet and held her tight again. He was weeping.

"I don't understand," he said. "Are they really gone?" She nodded, her face pressed into his chest.

After a while, she came up for air, wiping her eyes on her sleeve. The rest of the people had gone back up the stairs after they had seen the little boat disappear from view.

The four of them stood together on the strand, staring into the mist. They stayed there for a long time. Then Brutus said,

"Gain is loss and loss is gain. People come and go."

Bruno, Pippa and Arghan joined in: "That's the Army, that's life."

"Like the Big Man said, let's enjoy it while it lasts."

They turned away and began the climb back up to the top.

Annotations, Maps and Illustrations

Chapter One - Apple Cake

Philippa Agrippa - Soldier of Roman Britain.
Britannia Prima Sud Est- The Romanized lower southeastern eastern region of Britain.
Ares Mons Training Camp - A training fort in Southern England.
Centurion - Leader of a century, roughly equivalent to a Captain.
Vindavia Nova Fort - A fort in Southern England.
Dar and Murti - Two oxen.
Malus - A donkey.
Decani - Plural of decanus.
Decanus - Leader of ten, roughly equivalent to a corporal or platoon sergeant.
Brutus Marianis - Scout, Men of Ares Mons.
Bruno Marianis - Scout, Men of Ares Mons.
Emperor - Leader of the Roman Empire. At the time the story begins, the co-Emperors were Flavius and Honorius.
Aries Erasmus - Centurion at Ares Mons Training Camp.
Mercury - Roman God of speech, travel, boundaries, and transitions.
Augur - A diviner who watches flocks of birds.
Erastus Minor - Men of Ares Mons, soldier.
Terranes Julius - Men of Ares Mons, aide and Quaestor.
Albion - Celtic name for Britain. Albus, white, referring to white cliffs on the east coast.
Etruscan - From Etruria, an influential civilization close to Rome. Modern day Tuscany.
Socrates - Greek philosopher from ancient Athens.
Gaul - Modern day France, and parts of Belgium, Germany and Italy.
Eternal City - The city of Rome.
Belgic - Originally from modern day Belgium.
Catuvellauni - A powerful Celtic tribe in southeast England.
Celts - A loose affiliation of tribal groups that once covered most of Europe.
Kohl - Charcoal eyeliner.
Trisantonis - The Arum River in southern England.
Bognor Regis - A town in southern Britain.
Mount Temple - A temple shrine near the Trisantonis, devoted to the Roman Gods.
Popina - A restaurant.
Ceres - Goddess of grain and harvest.
Mars - God of martial activities, valor and order.

Venus - Goddess of love and beauty.
Jupiter - The All-Father, sky god, god of justice, strength, joy and prosperity.
Father Florian the Red - Priest, scholar and philosopher.
Hestia and Hygieia - Goddesses of the hearth, cleanliness, and chastity.
Tomasen - An acolyte to Father Florian.
Hibernian - Irish.
Tyronius Danu - Archer, Men of Ares Mons.
Virgin Warriors - Fourth century B.C. Roman/Etrurian female warriors.
Republic - Before it was an empire, Rome was a republic.
Samnites - The Sabines, a rival tribe of early Rome.
Cuirass - Breastplate.
Hector Magnus - Archer, Men of Ares Mons, standard bearer.
Julius Phaedonis - Men of Ares Mons, decanus.

Chapter Two - Mount Temple

Davines West - Men of Ares Mons, soldier.
Apollo - God of the sun.
Father Maximus - A priest of the Temple.
Jenisec - Acolyte to Father Maximus.
Justinian Justinius - A conscribit.
Atticus - Servant to Justinian Justinius.
Amazons - Greek warrior women.
Scrolls - Rolled vellum or parchment sheets.
Vellum - A thin sheepskin for scribing, heavier than parchment.
Deuspater - Jupiter, the deus-pater or god-father.
Conscribit - Recruitment officer.
Denarius - Early Roman coin. Plural Denarii.

Chapter Three - Precedence!

Signaculum - I.D. tag; an engraved seal in a leather pouch worn around the neck.
Phillip Agrippa - Immune/engineer, father of Philippa Agrippa, deceased.
Altheia Ilithia - Etrurian priestess, mother of Philippa Agrippa, deceased.
Greaves - Shin guards.
Pteruges - Soldier's segmented skirt.
Focale - Red neck scarf.
Gladius - Sword.
Tiro - A recruit.
Immune - Technical specialists such as engineers and physicians, exempt from combat.
Anselenus Markus - Quartermaster at Ares Mons.

Salve, Salvete - Greetings, single and plural.
Septimius Gallus - Aide to Aries Erasmus.
Senovara Domini - Training officer at Ares Mons.
Tristanus Albia - Marshal Officer at Ares Mons
Jacamus Sands - Supply clerk at Ares Mons.
Marcus Aurelius - Roman Emperor and philosopher.
Zino of Citium - Founder of Stoicism.
Tungrian - Originating in Belgium, the Tungrian was a large Roman Army cohort in Britain that was frequently reformed.
Comitatenses - Field Army units.
Sixth Legion - Legio Sexta Victrix - a Roman legion based in northern Britain.
Thin-striped Tribune - A bureaucrat.
Anchor of Christ - The anchor was the original symbol of the Christian faith.
Bull of Mithras - The bull was the symbol of the cult of Mithras.
Staff of Asclepius - A staff entwined with one snake.
Asclepius - The first physician, a Greek.

Chapter Four - Ares Mons

Contubernium - A squad of eight men, led by a decanus.
Century - A group of 8-10 contuberni, led by a centurion.
Cohort - A group of six century, roughly 480 men.
Legion - A legion of 10 cohorts, roughly 5,000 men.
Horse Legion - The cavalry unit of a legion consisting of 120 men.
Hestius Attacroni - Master smith at Ares Mons Training Camp.

Chapter Five - Apollo Row

Miletes - A basic soldier, equivalent of private/PFC.
Dubris - Dover, England.
Durnovia - Dorchester, England.
Durovernum Cantiacorum - Canterbury, England.
Legatus - Army commander, roughly equivalent to a general.
Cassius Ambrosius - Legatus of Vindavia Nova.
QuattroVentis Potens - Mighty Four Winds.
Signifier - Standard bearer who wore the head of a bear.
Auxiliary soldiers - Non-Roman citizens granted citizenship once they retired.

Chapter Six - Quattro Ventis Potens

Aquilo, Favonius, Auster, and Eurus - Winds of the north, south, west and east.
Paulinus Valinus - Beneficiari, a retired soldier working as a clerk.

Augustus Ionias - Thin striped tribune at Vindavia Nova.
Broad belted Tribune - The broad belted tribune commanded auxiliaries.
Philemones Calla - Adiuncto (adjunct) to the General.

Chapter Seven - Payday

Quaestor - Accountant in charge of the treasury.
Vulcan - God of the forge.

Chapter Eight - A Late Afternoon Bath

Dimocletus - A cart driver.
Julia - Daughter of Dimocletus.
Artemis - A servant of General Ambrosius.
Beni - A servant of General Ambrosius.
Caduceus - A messenger's staff, entwined with two winged snakes.

Chapter Nine - A Bit of Drama

Optios - Officer aides to Centurions.
Dumnonioram, Britannia Occidens - Kernow, Cornwall, in Western England.
Londinium - London, England.
Bosses - Round metal cloak ornaments.
Brian Magnus - Intelligence officer of Vindavia Nova.

Chapter Eleven - Pushing and Pulling

Pillars of Hercules - The Straits of Gibraltar.
Maia - May.
Juno - June.
Kalends - The first day of the new month.
Hades - God of the underworld.

Chapter Twelve - A Friend or Two

Temesis - The Thames River, the river god Tems.

Chapter Thirteen- The Realm of the Gods

Keli - Kitchen worker at Vindavia Nova.
Marcella Dinas - Engineer's daughter at Vindavia Nova.
Vela the Wise - Celtic chief of the Belgic Catuvellauni.

Chapter Fourteen - Water and a Prayer

Darius Po - A Roman citizen.
Pruntus Dax - Outlaw commander of a rogue auxiliary.

Chapter Fifteen- Meet Bootchie

Bootchie - A fluffy orange and white cat.
Battle of Tameris Bridge, the Battle of the Red Mere, and the Battle of the Gaulish Sevens - Places of continental victories for General Ambrosius.
King Magnar the Valorous - a Belgic/Celtic King.
Borrum - Celtic wind spirit.
Stribog - Godfather of the winds.
Dogoda - Goddess of the west wind, goddess of love.
Consul - Governor.
Corinium - Cirencester, England.

Chapter Sixteen - The Virgin Warrior and the General

Ban - A pony.
Mika - A pony.
Mount Olympus - Mountain sky home of the Gods

Chapter Seventeen - Justice Served

Outliers - Soldiers and other agents who patrol the borders.
Portus Adurni - Portsmouth, England.

Chapter Eighteen - The Secret Plan

Cornouia - The land of the Cornovii tribe, Kernow, Cornwall.

Chapter Nineteen - Fulcrum

Codex - A bound book.
Regulus, Xerxes and Dod - Artists at Vindavia Nova
Jupiter Optus Maximus, the Capitolium- The Jupiter temple in Rome.

Chapter Twenty - A Draggable Man

Novio Magus - Chichester, England.
Lusoria - Small Roman Army troop transport ship.

Iberia - Peninsula comprising parts of Spain, Portugal and France.
Brigantium - Coruña, a coastal city in Galicia.
Gaddes - Cadiz, Spain.
Portus - A large port in the city of Rome.
Ostia - A smaller port outside the city of Rome.
Palatine Hill - Home of the Emperor
Camelodunum - The Roman British capital, Colchester, England.
Dumnonia - Roman name for Cornwall, England.
Trevena - A settlement on the Tintagel headland.
Branok a'n Ros Dowr - Navigator of Trevena. Crow from the Wetlands.
Costentyn a'n Ros Dowr - Sailor of Trevena. Constantine from the Wetlands
Auryn a'n Ben Avalen (Auryn Pen Avalen) - Goldsmith at Trevena. Gold from
the Apple Hill.
Merryn a'n Bol Gwynne (Merryn Pol Gwynne) Pennsevigis - Sea Born from the
White Pool, Princess
Arghan a'n Ben Avalen - (Arghan Pen Avalen) Royal Smith at Trevena. Silver
from the Apple Hill.
Arthek Gallósek- Great Bear.
Elowen Glas Lagas - Blue Eyed Willow.
Princeps - First, greatest.
Santo a'n Bol Sten (Santo Pol Sten) - Sailor of Trevena. Little Alexander from
the Tin Pool.
Edern Pinbren - Sailor of Trevena. Eternal pine.
Piran Glowbrenn - Sailor of Trevena. Little Dark Coal Man.
Awel Glor a'n Ben Avalen (Pen Avalen) - Mother of Arghan and Auryn. Breeze
from the Apple Hill.
Sten a'n Ben Avalen (Pen Avalen) - Father of Arghan and Auryn. Tin from the
Apple Hill.
Angove - Royal Smith.

Chapter Twenty-One - Domini Domini

Diodorus Siculus - A Greek historian.
Pythias of Massalia - A 4th century B.C. Greek explorer and author, the first to
visit and map Britain. He named it Pretani, which evolved into the Welsh name
Prydain, which is what likely led to Pretannia/Britannia. The name is usually
translated as the 'painted folk'.
Belerion - Land's End, in Cornwall.
Astralgi - Knuckle bones, slang for processed tin.
Ictis - Mount Saint Michael, Cornwall, England.
Baya Ronda/The Rounded Bay - Mount's Bay, Cornwall, England.
Karrek Loos y'n Koos - Grey Rock in the Woods, Ictis

Vectis/ the Bar - Isle of Wight, England.
Durnovaria - Dorchester, England.
Klog Eythin- The Furze Cliff, Dorset, England.
Sea-Door - The Durdle Door, Dorset, England.
Wheel of Taranis - Symbol of the Celtic Sky-god.
Horse of Epona - Symbol of the Celtic horse goddess.
Triple Leg of Manannán - Symbol of the Isle of Man.
Crane of the sea-father Lir - Symbol of the Celtic sea god.
Neptune - God of the sea; Poseidon.
Domini - Plural of Lord, Dominus.
Magnus Maximus - Rogue Emperor of Britain and Gaul, also known as Macsen
Wledig, the legendary hero of the Kombrogian (Cymric) Wealas (Welsh).
Hispania - Spain.
Ratha Pol - Scratchy Pool. Lake Radipole, Dorset England.

Chapter Twenty-Two - The Lost Wind

Cibus Orientalis - Asian food.
Diadonis Garhus - Soldier from Ares Mons.
'In Gracious Acknowledgment to the All Mighty Father God' - Quote from the
Cymbeline Prophesies, a mysterious ancient text.
Vindeles - The isle of Portland.
Isca - The city of Exeter, England.
Lys Ardh, the High Court - The Lizard peninsula, Cornwall, England.
Portha Kernow - The Port of the Horn, Porthcurno, Cornwall, England.
Kernowek - Cornish language.
En Noer, Enys Meur, Ennor - The Island that became the Scillies, before it was
submerged.
Stoic - A follower of the philosophy of stoicism.
Constantine - Roman Emperor who institutionalized Christianity.
Coptic - Late Egyptian.
Osiris - Egyptian God of death and rebirth.
Krshn - Krishna, the Hindu/Sindhu incarnation of Vishnu, the sustainer god.
Hermes - Greek name for Mercury.

Chapter Twenty Three - My A'th Kar

Coracle - Traditional British boat made of timber and skins.
Tintagel - Village in Cornwall, England.
Orrys and Ulna - The King's hounds.
Kussulyer - Advisor
Arcadia - Idyllic home of the Greek Gods.

Chapter Twenty Three - Walking with Giants

Telyn - A Welsh/Cornish harp with three sets of strings.
Govenek, Gorwel, Growen, & Gras a'n Bol Pri (Pol Pri) - Hope, Horizon, Granite and Grace, of the Clay Pool, royal musicians at Trevena.
Desin a'n Ben Avalen (Design Pen Avalen) - Grandsire of Arghan and Auryn.
Ovid - Publius Ovidius Naso, an early Roman Poet, author of Metamorphoses.

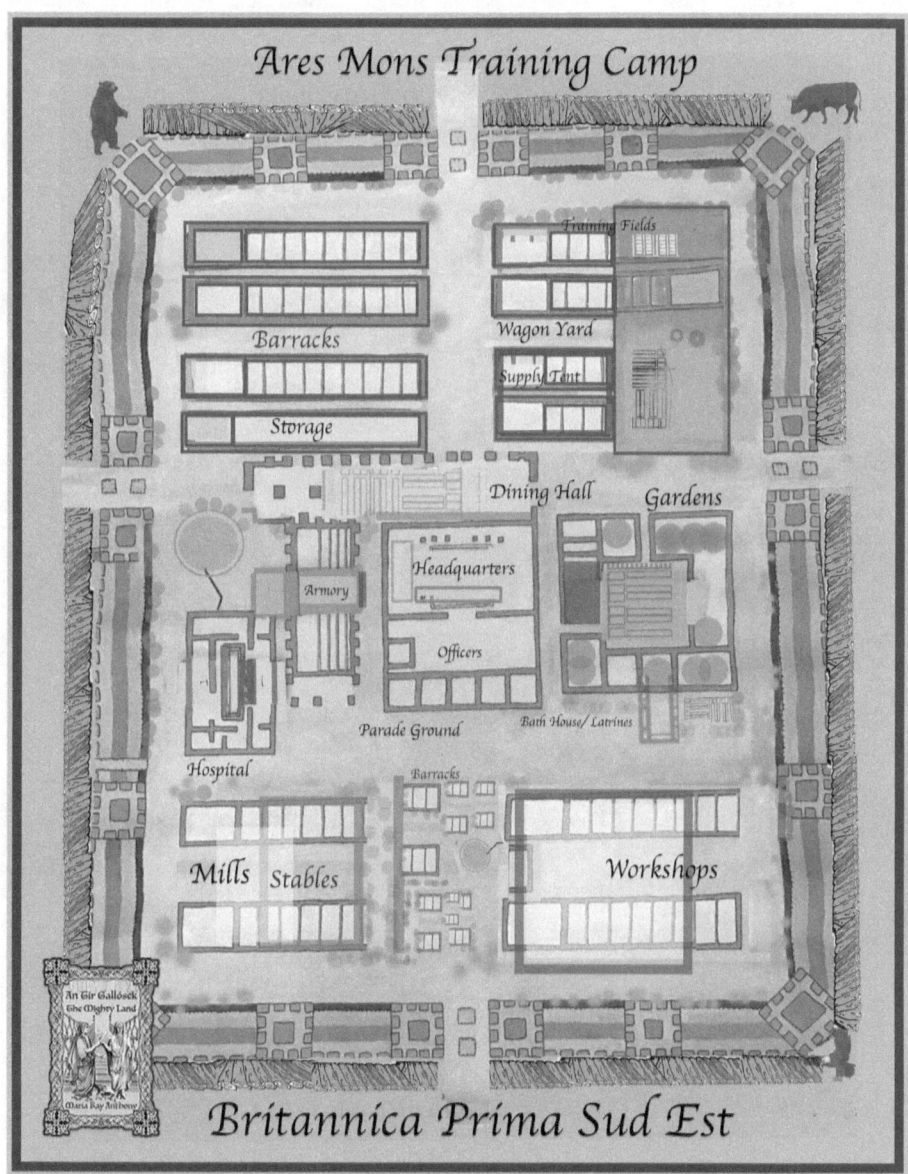

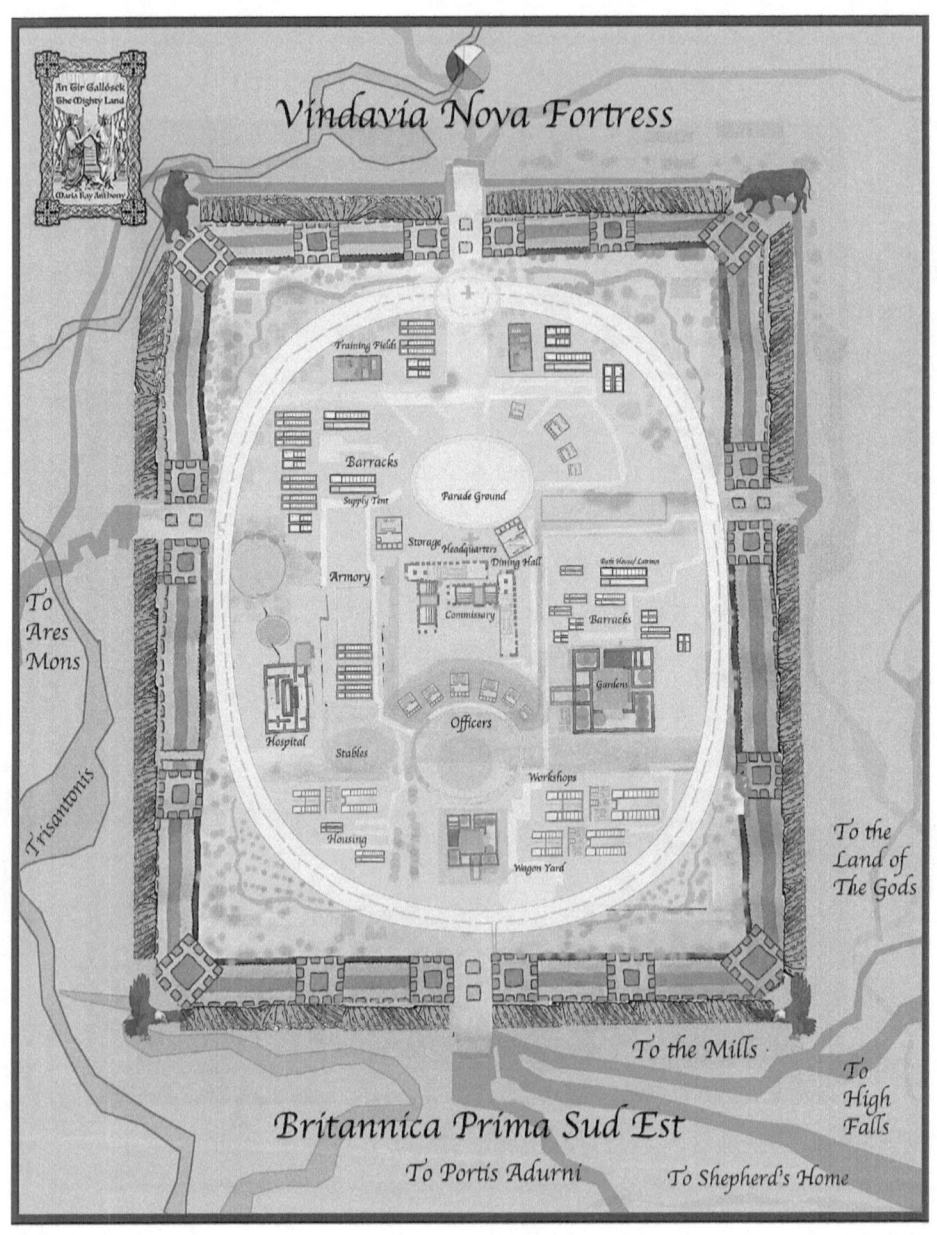

Vindavia Nova Fortress

Training Fields

Barracks

Supply Tent

Parade Ground

Storage Headquarters

Dining Hall

Bath House/ Latrines

Armory

Commissary

Barracks

Gardens

Officers

Hospital

Stables

Workshops

Housing

Wagon Yard

To Ares Mons

Trisantonis

To the Land of The Gods

To the Mills

To High Falls

Britannica Prima Sud Est

To Portis Adurni

To Shepherd's Home

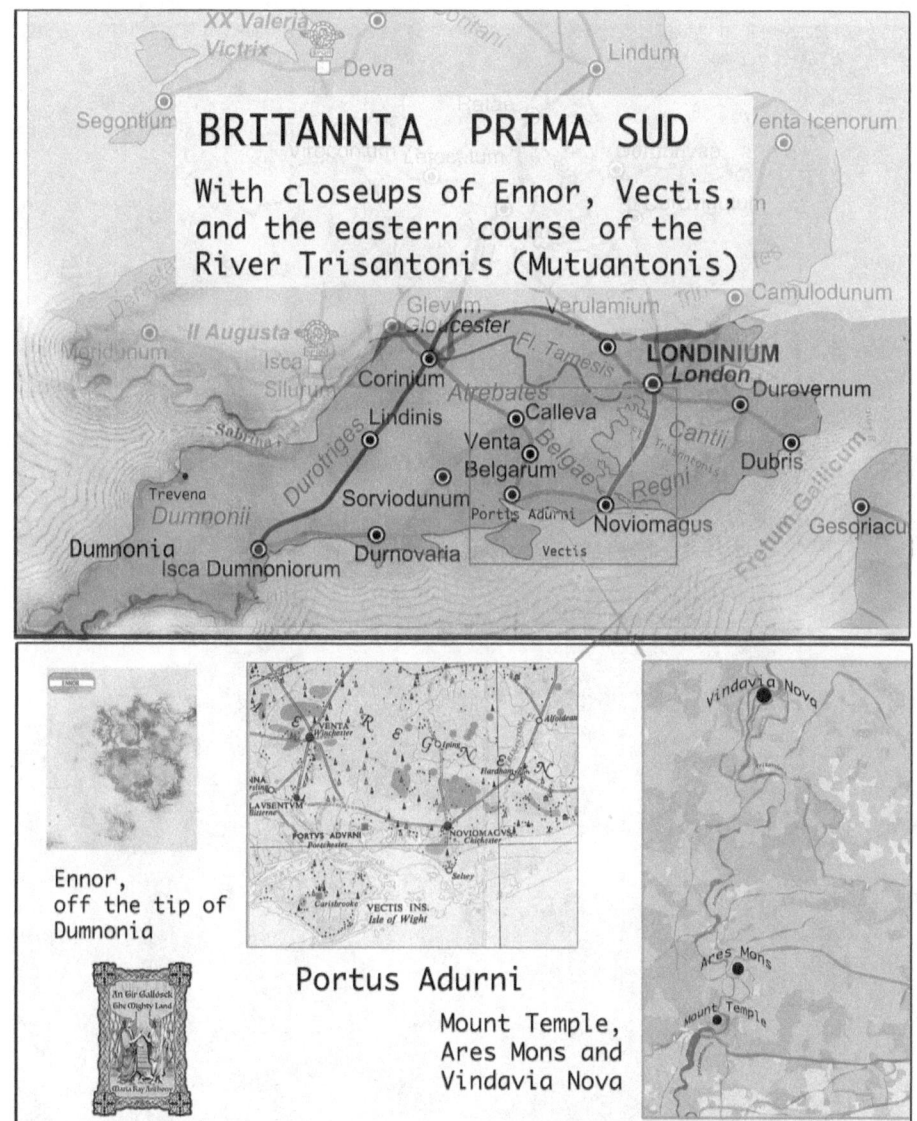

Ennor,
off the tip of
Dumnonia

Portus Adurni

Mount Temple,
Ares Mons and
Vindavia Nova

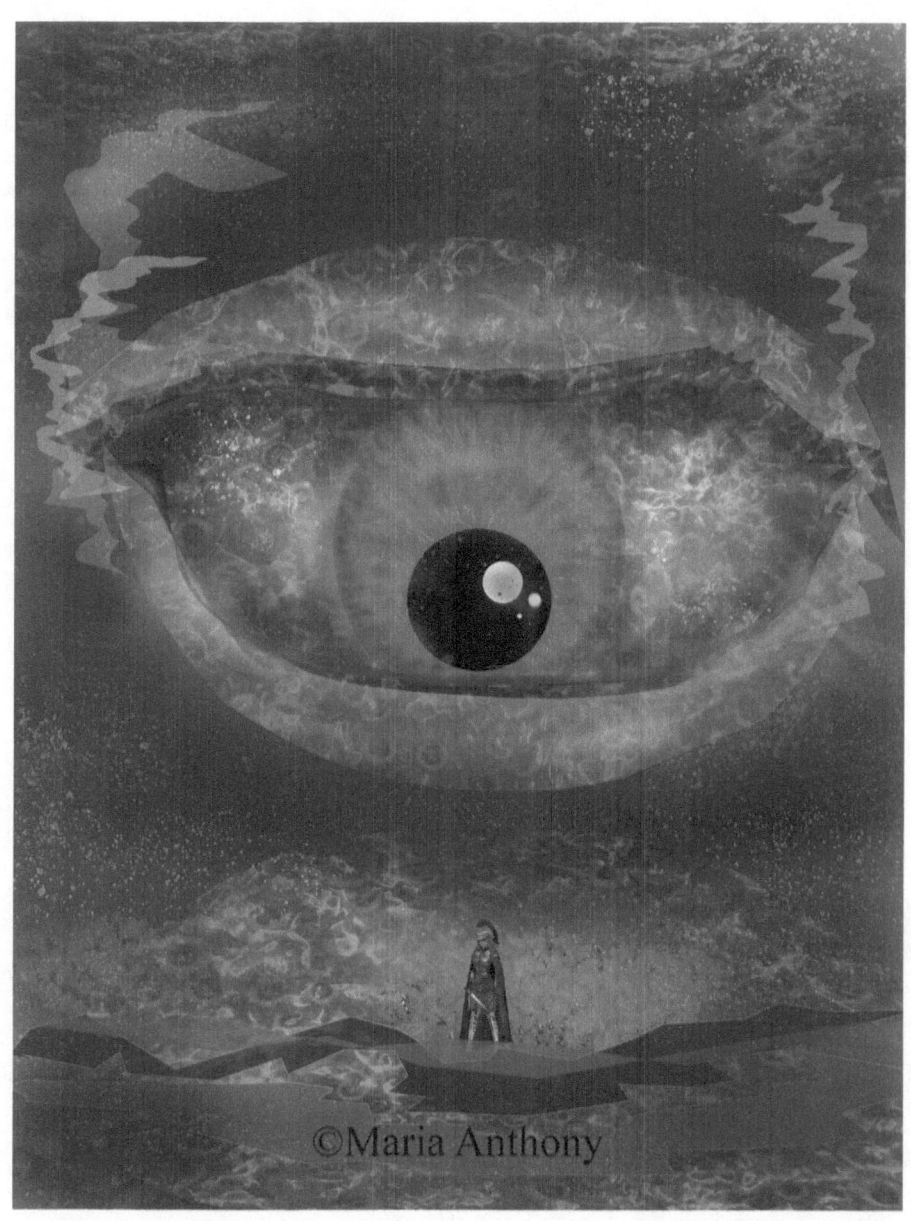

Maria Kay Anthony is a musician with a lifelong love of history, myths, and legends, especially those originating from the British Isles. She has worked in a variety of professions. She has been a metalsmith, visual artist, touring musician, veterinary assistant, music teacher, science teacher, filmmaker, and farmer. She is also a US Army veteran, having served in her youth with the 26th Signal Corps in Germany, where she built towers and installed microwave equipment. The Mighty Land series reflects her interest in these topics and others, such as astronomy, horticulture, boats, adventure, travel, technology, engineering, medicine, spirituality, philosophy, psychology, and languages. Maria currently lives in the green rolling hills of eastern Kansas with her husband Monty, but they hope to relocate ere long, with Cornwall being the preferred destination.

POB 1554 Lawrence Kansas 66044 USA
Borlowanbooks@gmail.com